Four Seasons of Winter

Lela Markham

Published by Breakwater Harbor Books

ISBN # 978-8-9875018-3-2 E-Book edition
ISBN # 979-8-9875018-4-9 Print edition

For permission requests, write to the author/publisher, addressed "Attention: Permissions Coordinator" at the address below:

Lauri Sliney
Aurorawatcher Publications
500 Ketchikan Avenue
Fairbanks, Alaska 99701
lelamarkham@gmail.com

License Notes

This is Book 4 in What If Wasn't series. It references events from in *Red Kryptonite Curve, Dumpster Fire, and Pocketful of Rocks*, and so cannot be read enjoyably as a standalone.

Thanks!

This book is dedicated to Bernard Sliney, who recently taught me that not all alcoholics recover and sometimes those of us who love them must stop caring. I'll prayer for you always. Goodbye.

No book is the work of a single individual. The author gets all the glory but standing behind every published writer is a host of support personnel. Peter, Ben and the rest of their friends are borrowed from many struggling young teens I knew over decades as an unchurched teenager, a church youth leader, and a mom. I worked in a community mental health for 15 years and many of my observations on mental illness, including gender issues, are informed by those experiences and the many conversations I've had with staff psychiatrists and social workers (who don't necessarily all agree). All the counselors in this book are based upon former coworkers and friends.

The title of this book comes from the song *Reason* by the Christian group Unspoken

"This year's felt like four seasons of winter, and you'd do anything to feel the sun…but God has a plan."

The overarching theme of this novel is "He who began a good work in you will bring it to completion at the day of Jesus Christ." **Philippians 1:6**

DISCLAIMER

This is a book written by a Christian who doesn't write Christian genre literature. It's a book for both Christians who don't wish to candy-coat humanity and non-Christians who don't mind if some of the characters hold beliefs they don't. It deals with themes of a dark nature. Non-Christians and even some Christians swear, have sex with people they're not married to, and men who aren't gay have sex with other men in prison because that's the society we live in. Sorry, Christians. I'm not writing the Mitford Saga. If any of the themes in this book cause you angst I don't apologize, but I recommend you count the cost of reading this book. It may not be a "sweet" novel, but it's an honest novel, dealing with themes real people, including Christians, deal with. You might enjoy reading it, but you must do what's right for you.

For non-Christian readers, I think I've proven I can write a book with Christian characters in it who are real without devolving into a Hallmark movie. I hope you'll agree. Enjoy!

Table of Contents

"You can't stop the future. You can't rewind the past.
The only way to learn the secret is to press play."
Jay Asher, *Thirteen Reasons Why*

Four Seasons of Winter

Harsh Reality

Peter
November

As I work down the corridor, my push broom gathers a small pile of fuzz and hair. It's my second day doing this stupid monkey-could-do-it job and I don't have a partner today because I'm not stupid and I can do this job asleep. I glance right into a cell where two men make something that smells like rotten fruit and makes every cell in my body scream to find out what it is. This can stop anytime as far as I'm concerned, so I swing left to catch the other side of the corridor, swallowing bile as the illusionary taste of bourbon with a back of vomit washes over my tongue.

"Hey, pretty boy. You want to take a break with me?"

I'm *not* a homophobe, but I feel my heart rate increase and fear-sweat joins the alcoholic fever on my skin. The dark-skinned man on the other side of the bars reaches for me and I step away. He laughs cruelly. I'm getting to know that laugh as my roommate Dorff has the same one. Excuse me. Not roommate. *Cellmate.* I shouldn't forget where I am. Not that I could. I'm in hell and I utterly deserve to be here, even though I hate it. It's been a week in the fire and the nature of an indeterminate sentence means I can't calculate how far it is to the other side.

Is that part of the punishment? If hope is a moving target dodging in the fog, it's hard to set your sights on a goal.

My pile isn't impressive. Sing Sing's floors get cleaned often enough that the burden of the broom man is light indeed. It's make-work. I know it and I hate it, but it's all the staff deemed me capable of doing after assessing my skills. They're probably right. I've never done a lick of real labor in my life and my attention span is about 15 seconds.

Fortunately, sweeping doesn't require a lot of attention to detail. Just pull everything into a pile and dump it in the dustbin. It gives me a lot of time to think about my life – currently and in the past. I'm getting good at refusing to think about Alyse, which is absolutely necessary if I'd not going to break into tears at random intervals.

I pause to let two prisoners pass before continuing across the corridor. I can still smell whatever those guys are fermenting. It smells rotten, but every cell of my body insists I would enjoy poisoning myself. Thankfully, the memory of how close my last drunk came to being my last anything helps to remind me that I may want that poison, but I don't need it and I *can* ignore it.

I leave my pile to the side of the stairs and pass down this side hallway that leads to some sort of mechanical room. The stairs run up one side of the wall and it's clear that whoever did this job before me wasn't coming in here daily because there's scraps of paper and actual dust bunnies. Did we come in here yesterday?

Suddenly, I feel a shift in the fabric of time and space. The weight of all the concrete and steel above and around me presses down, threatening to suffocate me. I've been here at Sing Sing for a week now and this feeling of being buried alive still comes in waves. It plunges me into the depths of this place, threatening to overwhelm the low-level sameness of every day. You get up at the same time every day and the whole prison is plunged into semi-darkness at the same time every night. Between getting up and going to sleep, there's unremitting boredom. My cellmate spends an inordinate amount of time staring at the wall. Frighteningly, I find myself doing the same, though I've read a lot more of the *Big Book* in the last week than I read in rehab because sunset colors start painting the walls if I stare at them too long.

I'm overwhelmed by disgust of my personal hygiene. I haven't showered in days. I rinsed my face and hands up to my elbows this morning, but I feel filthy. It might help if I had some soap to wash up with, but I can't get commissary (what they call the store) for another few days. The bar of soap in my starter kit disappeared the first day and there's no way I'm arguing with Dorph about taking it. At least they issued a toothbrush and tiny tube of toothpaste to me, but they haven't given my retainer back yet.

A shadow forms in the depths under the stairs. Alyse holds out a bottle of scotch and I know a place to get something similar. I've got no money or prison currency, but surely there's a way to get what you need. I smell vomit the more I think about it. Can I suppress my gag reflex long enough to get the benefits of the alcohol?

A shadow flickers across the wall under the stairs and I turn to see what it is, but before I can, arms wrap around my waist from behind, pinning my arms to my sides and lifting my feet free of the concrete floor. I drop the broom as whoever has me yanks down my pants and underwear around my knees. I flail, try to bellow, and get clocked in the side of the head for my efforts. Everything goes black for a second, then white, and then I find myself dizzily staring at the wall. I fight the hands that hold me, but I can't get my feet on the ground, and I know what's about to happen. I might be the newest of newbies, but I'm not stupid. I've seen *The Shot Caller*. And then I realize he has no idea how close to the wall we are.

In dance, we call it an *eleve*. You start out with flat feet and then you *pop* to your toes. I pike, bending my knees to clear the wall, slap my feet on the sheet metal, and pop my legs straight. This gives me leverage to elongate my body and propel us backward across the hallway. Stars obliterate my vision as the back of my head connects with some part of his face. Black, red, and white. His arm lets go as we flop to the ground. It takes me a moment to realize I'm free, but then I'm up and running – well, staggering, with my pants around my knees.

Guards must have heard my interrupted yell because they're converging on the end of the hallway, and I crash into one, knocking him on his ass. A billy club swung by his coworker smashes across my shoulder blades, and I go to the floor on my face, wondering how avoiding a sexual assault breaks their rules.

May

Ben

Morning peeks through the muslin curtains and spreads pearly sunlight across the ceiling. I roll onto my back and watch its slow creep across the engaging blue expanse. A single beam sparkles off the glittering blue chime set hanging at the end of the bed. Prisms of light bounce off the walls.

Previous mornings I would have rolled over and buried my head under the pillow, waiting for my alarm. I don't have to get up. It's Saturday and for the first time in nearly a year, I have it off. I stretch, gripping the iron headboard with my hands and sliding my toes against the footboard. My back pops, my spine flexing. I sit up and look around the room. It's a routine my counselor and I established early on so I could function.

I'm not used to sleeping in, though I'm pretty surprised that I want to get up and do things. I didn't for a long time. Most of these last nine months I've put one numb foot before the other, headed to two jobs, barely stopping to rest, but today, I have time and it doesn't feel like I'm moving through a viscous liquid thick as honey.

I roll off the bed and pad into the bathroom to take care of urgent needs before going into the main room to open my laptop where it sits on the coffee table. While it goes through its morning wakeup routine, I turn on the kettle and spoon coffee into the filter. The east-facing kitchen window glows golden with morning sunlight as I toast a bagel.

I find it in my email and my gut turns over ominously. I could just ignore it, but it's time. My counselor says I'm ready to move on. Maybe. Or maybe I'm just going through the motions like I was back in March when I dutifully replied to the letter of intent email. Do I want to go back to school? Am I ready?

I open the email, scan it, and sit back with a sigh. At least now I know my immediate future. It's not horrible news, but I am so ambivalent. I close the laptop and enjoy the sunlight while I eat my breakfast. Then I shamble into the bathroom to take a shower because the folks get worried when I show up looking like I just rolled out of bed. I did that a lot this winter until I realized I was freaking them out. The depression still wrapped me in its suffocating blanket long after I started showering again.

I'm driving toward the house when my phone dings. I keep both hands on the wheel because the road is narrow and tree-lined, and I don't want to have an accident. It would be unfortunate timing and I have too much going on today.

The neighborhood is aboil with Saturday morning activity. It's the last few weeks of school and everybody is trying to squeeze the early summer into the weekend. I creep past children who shouldn't be playing in the streets and drive toward the dead end.

I park and look at my phone. It's my monthly check-in with Tilly Matrim…er, Wyngate. I need to tell her I'm moving home sometime this summer, but I haven't quite worked out the details, so…yeah, that can wait.

BEN- Cottage is good. How are you?

Tilly acted like wallpaper for most of my childhood – someone who always hung in the background in Pete's home life, but nobody who mattered to me. Yet, after everything fell apart last year, she'd texted me and asked if I'd housesit. I needed to get away from the pain for a while, so I said yes. I think the decision saved my sanity. Hard to believe that someone who had never seemed important before had such a pivotal effect on my life.

TILLY- Doing okay. Spending time with my in-laws in Greece.

A memory of the white villa against the turquoise blue of the Aegean Sea flashes into my mind. They're not really Tilly's in-laws, but Pete's mother's family…and I extinguish the thought before it can take root. I'm having a good day. I don't want to derail myself. I like Tilly, but her connection with Pete makes her risky for me right now.

My dad's next door in the Wexler' yard helping Lyle build something. Pretending I don't hear their greeting, I duck down the walkway to the backdoor of our house. Mom looks up from whatever she's kneading in a bowl.

"Why, is that Ben Anderson? On a Saturday? I thought you'd sworn off Saturdays."

"I'm not working at the athletic club anymore. I start back at Russell's this afternoon." I give her a sideways hug. When did we start doing that again? I hadn't since junior high, but sometimes since Alyse's death…. I'm not thinking about that today.

"That's great." She's dressed for the warmer weather in a short-sleeved top and shorts with her brown hair caught up in a ponytail. "We were going to Pirate's Cove this afternoon. Any chance you can join?

"I've got to be to Russell's by one, so probably not. Thought I'd share the good news with you."

"Good news? We could use some of that."

"Dartmouth will reinstate my scholarship this fall. I've paid off my student loans and I've got enough saved for a year-and-a-half."

She wipes off her hands and starts greasing the muffin tins before she replies to me.

"That's wonderful, sweety. So, are you going back to school?" I kind of deserve that. My attitude has been all over the map these last months.

"Yes, absolutely. There was only a moment's hesitation this morning when I read the email. I think the depression's clearing."

"I know it's been a tough year, honey. How are things out there in the woods?"

"Things are fine."

"And at work?"

I'm nervous about *the Mimi* this afternoon and I'm pretty sure my new partner on the Temple loading dock plans to hurt me someday when he's in a bad mood – and he's always in a bad mood – but other than that….

"It's good. If I were staying through the fall, they'd probably offer me the dock supervisor's position, but I do want to be an engineer."

"That's great." Her voice is overwhelmed by a clattering down the stairs that resolves itself into my little brother Wes, who isn't so little anymore. Wow, he's shooting up.

"Hey – who are you?" he comments and heads toward the backdoor.

"Your brother Ben."

"Haven't seen you in so long I don't recognize you." He's 12 and starting to sprout up. His voice hasn't changed yet, but any day now.

"Yeah, I know, but working two jobs has kept me really busy. Maybe mountain biking next Saturday morning?"

"Morning?" He shudders. It's pretty early for a Saturday now, but I'd want to start out much earlier so we could get a full ride in before I had to go to work.

"It's when I'm available." Mom slides the baked goods into the oven. I already ate but they smell good even raw.

"Yeah, that would be fun. Let me know what time." Wes turns toward the backdoor.

"Where are you going?" Mom's got that worry crease between her brows.

"Going to hang out with Bram."

Mom catches my gaze. I don't know what she wants, but I do know I'm supposed to do something.

"How's he doing?" At least the question delays him for a second.

"Good. He's getting around the house pretty good now. He can say single words. He beats me a lot at backgammon. He still needs a lot of help with chess, but we play every Saturday morning I don't have homework."

"Which you do."

"I have to finish some math, Mom. Maybe two hours' worth of work and it's not even due Monday."

Mom gives me hook-eye again.

"Do you need help?"

"No. She's just panicking."

I remember driving my parents to distraction around age 13. So, he's starting early. They say second children do. I don't try to pull him back and the door is closed in a heartbeat.

"There is something up with him."

"You mean, besides puberty?" I can't remember the last time I had a conversation with Wes, but I'm pretty sure it was before…Before. Everything in life is now divided into Before and After. I'm trying to embrace After.

"Something. I don't know."

She worries a lot about Wes since last summer and I can understand why. We've both had them worried since that night out on the bay, but I'm mostly healed and Wes – I'm not sure why he'd be traumatized that someone he didn't particularly like died, but I know he is.

"Maybe I was easy and he's going to be your challenge." Neither of us mention that my sister Carrie never got to be a teenager.

"Maybe. Can you stick around for the muffins?"

"I can. I came to get some boat-appropriate clothes."

"Could you get the mail too? Wes was supposed to bring it in last night and he 'forgot'. Do you mind?"

"I don't. Is it okay with you and Dad if I move back here later this summer?"

"Of course. Our children are always welcome."

"Thanks."

I moved out in a huff of mental anguish in January when my parents took Pete's side in things. Well, not really. They were trying to be fair, and I wasn't feeling fair-minded.

Pete's stepmother Tilly had just asked me if I could house-sit while she traveled, so it was perfect timing. The original month-long gig stretched through the winter and now into spring and now it looks like she won't be back for some time. I need to email her to let her know I'll be gone in September. Surely, Alan Wyngate has *people* who can check the cottage from time to time. I assume he and Tilly are still married. Maybe they're not and I'm expecting something that won't happen. It's not my problem, however, as I saunter to the mailbox. Tilly and I bonded over shared horror and tragedy, but truthfully, I need to move on from the Wyngates. It might be best for my mental health if I never see them again.

Lily

Facebook is a great place to meet up with people from school.

> **JENAE - I'm going to the Barns Courtney concert next month. My dad said I can bring a friend. You want to come?**

> **LILY – I like Barns Courtney. Sure. Are you sure? Those are some pricey tickets.**

> **JENAE – I'm sure. I always wanted to be closer than we were, but Alyse was so jealous.)**

Jenae's the only friend I have who deals with Alyse and I find that oddly comforting. I've worked out a lot more with her than with the counselor my parents made me see for a while. Well, that's not really true, but I'd like to believe it is.

Mom's voice wavers up the stairway. I sigh. Time for Bram duty.

"Coming."

I turn to my laptop before I close it.

LILY – I got to go.

JENAE – Bram?

LILY – Yeah. Talk with you later.

Mom's already pulling out of the driveway by the time I get to the kitchen. She trusts me. Bram turns his wheelchair and puts a hand on his stomach.

"Hungry?"

He nods.

"Okay, let's see what's for breakfast."

Mom started breakfast – eggs laced with small bits of bacon – before she headed to the grocery store. It's almost ready so I turn off the oven to give it a few minutes to finish. The refrigerator looks pretty dismal.

"Do you want orange juice?" To help Bram understand what I'm saying, I point to the jug.

"No." Bram's sharp pronunciation could be taken as anger, but I know my brother's method of communication. He's sometimes too loud and sometimes too soft. He's still learning to control his mouth and vocal cords. He doesn't hate orange juice. He's just trying to get the word out. I offer him milk. "No." Those are the two options until Mom gets back from the store.

"Water?" He stares at me blankly. He knows the word "water", but sometimes he gets overwhelmed by background noise. He uses the gesture for "again." I repeat the word. He shakes his head, drops his good hand down to fondle the wrist of his paralyzed arm, then points to the icebox. "There's no other juice." I open it to show him there's some ground beef packages and a box of frozen waffles. I doubt he knows there's a freezer in the basement, but it doesn't have juice anyway. The parents filled it with frozen meat.

I set the milk jug and orange juice pitcher on the counter and turn on the faucet. Bram gives me a loopy half-smile and points to the milk jug. I pour it. Maybe it's not his first choice, but it's better than the other two options. Wes comes clattering in the door from the garage, not bothering to knock. He knows where we keep the spare key.

"Hey, what's for breakfast?" He's not asking *me*. He's really genius at getting my aphasic brother to say words. Bram considers the stove for a moment.

"Eggs."

"What kind of eggs?"

Oh-boy! Sometimes Bram can say it and sometimes he can't. Sometimes can cause upsets. Not usually with Wes though.

"Ssss—amble."

"Scrambled." Wes says it carefully. It's unlikely Bram will ever be able to say a word with combined sounds like that, but Wes never stops trying. Bram does attempt the combined scr sound, shaking his head and giving up after three tries. To show my appreciation of Wes's tenacious friendship, I fix a plate for him too. While I'm putting it on the table, I see Ben's Jeep in the Andersons' driveway and watch as Ben stops by it a moment. I haven't seen him since he moved out before Christmas. I stayed home with Bram on Christmas Eve when our two families got together and Ben begged off New Year's Eve, so we really haven't crossed paths since the world's most-awkward Thanksgiving dinner when we weren't speaking to one another or anyone else.

"I'll be back in a bit. Are you two okay here?"

"Sure." Wes probably has it covered. Saturday morning has become a tradition for them. He's seen Bram when he could barely function. These days, he's pretty self-sufficient in the house.

Ben's pulling mail out of the mailbox, so I walk up to our box less than four feet from his expecting to find nothing, but there's a white envelope in there with my name on it. I pull it out without looking at it because Ben looks at me. His eyes widen, his gaze takes a quick tour of my body, and then comes right back up to my face. Yeah, none of my clothes from last year still fit, something I didn't realize until it got warm. At least I didn't get fat. I resist the temptation to cross my arms across my breasts. I am so enjoying shopping this afternoon.

"Hey." Male grunts. Melissa says you can get more out of them if you try.

"Hey. How are you?" I figure that's a pleasant way to say hello to a former friend who you wish wasn't former. Something flickers in his gaze. He looks older than he did last year…more than a year older. It's been a tough year.

"Good. Better. And you?"

"Okay."

We nod at each other. We never dated, but this reminds me of that. I've seen lots of friends go through the awkward phase of post-dating when you have no idea how to speak to one another. Ben and I stare in opposite directions, shuffling our feet.

"School lets out in a couple of weeks?" It's a question, but it causes more questions for me.

"Does it?" I guess it does, now that I think about it. "I'm homeschooling, so I'm already finished. I have testing next week."

"Oh. Cool. How does homeschooling work?"

I guess it's kind of a new and rare thing in New York. It was common enough in New Hampshire that people usually didn't ask questions.

"Well, you work at home, and you can work at your own pace."

"What happened to real school?" *Real* school? I arch an eyebrow at him, and he faintly blushes.

"You have to take all the same requirements. Someone needed to stay with Bram on days when Mom goes into the bookstore, and I wasn't ready for the memories."

He nods, shifts from one foot to another. He takes a deep breath and speaks in a rush.

"Me either. That's why I went away and stayed away. I'm sorry I've been such a jerk."

"Me too." That didn't come out right. "We were both hurting, and we needed time to heal on our own."

Whenever I'd see him after Alyse's death, I'd see Alyse dying. I'm not seeing it now, though I'm thinking it. My counselor would call that progress.

"Maybe…." He stares off across the lawns for a moment. "Maybe we could have lunch sometime. Catch up."

"Yeah." I don't want to gush. Play it cool, high school. He's a college man, after all, and he looks like he's regretting the offer already. "That would be…nice."

He sighs heavily.

"Okay. I'll text you."

"Sounds good." Does he even have my number? I don't expect to hear from him until we meet at the mailbox again, but at least we're talking. I start toward the house, looking at the envelope in my hand.

What the heck?

Ben

I'm sorting through the mail as I head up the walk and I stop, frozen in time, when I see the white envelope with my name on it. I recognize the handwriting immediately. Pete and I were desk mates in elementary school, critiquing each other's cursive. Ours was the last class in our school to study cursive.

Pete-fucking Wyngate is insinuating himself back into my life.

I leave the rest of the mail on the coffee table so I can head upstairs. I stare at the envelope, wishing it weren't here but it is, and I need to decide what to do with it. My former best friend and now convicted murderer is writing to me as if he thinks he has any right to do that and I…. Yeah, I have no idea what the hell to do about this envelope, so I stuff it in the pencil drawer of my desk and close it firmly out of my sight before I turn toward my dresser for shorts, t-shirts, and tank tops.

Damn Pete for harshing my mellow. I guess I'd assumed I'd never hear from him again. He hasn't tried to communicate with me since that night out on the bay and I figured he'd learned his lesson and would leave me alone from now on.

Besides, aren't I one of his victims? He's not allowed to contact his victims, right? Which means I could get time added to his sentence for this stupid. Has he completely lost his mind? Why would he do something that would cost him more time in prison? I guess he hasn't changed a bit.

My mind swirls with these thoughts as I drive to the marina. Yesterday, I'd had a moment, wondering if working on *the Mimi* this summer might not be good for my mental health, but when I see the fishing boat turned pleasure cruiser, I feel like I'm greeting an old friend and not the site of girl slaughter it is. Because he had to have the starboard plating replaced because Pete punched a hole in it, and Captain Russell had the whole boat repainted. Instead of blue and white, it's now a darker blue and orange. That alone sets my fears at ease, although I admit I'm glad to board from the port side.

"Permission to come aboard?"

Cap looks up from a lantern he's working on. The deck's been repainted as well. The verticals are gel-coated, and the decks have a nice friction surface. In fact, it looks to me as if there's not much to do to get ready for the season.

"Hey. Come aboard. What do you think?"

Jeff Russell is a giant, really tall with enormous hands that have been pulling ropes all his life.

"Looks great. Like new." I guess my question carries.

"Alan Wyngate generously offered a complete remodel if I wouldn't sue Pete."

Of course. I remember the letter from the lawyer. Suing Pete never entered my mind, but of course, Cap had lost something – damaged hull-plating, blood-stained deck, water taken into the hull, losing half a cruising season. He deserved recompense. I just deserve peace.

"I figured it would help if we spruced it up a bit."

I nod. I don't want to discuss the last time I walked this deck. I force myself to glance toward the place where Alyse died.

"If you're not ready, son, I understand."

Do *I*? I love the ocean and Pete's taken that from me. I tried to go sailing on *the Clotilde* last summer after the wreck and I never got out of the slip. I couldn't afford to replace the sailboat for what I could sell her for, but I need to give it a try soon or put her on the market.

"I'm not letting him win."

I plan to stride toward that irksome memory, but I falter.

"Pete?"

Russell's hazel eyes bleed compassion.

"Yeah. He doesn't get to stay in my head."

Russell nods, rubs his unshaven jaw, and stares off toward where Alyse died in Pete's arms.

"You get a letter from him?"

I snap a surprised look at him. He grins briefly, pleased at his mind-reading skills, before he sobers.

"It's some sort of waiver program that allows him to write his victims and offer to make amends. He's not allowed to write again if we don't respond." He's got that probing look on his broad face.

"I take it you read yours?"

"Yeah."

"And?"

Russell considers his response.

"Remarkably mature. He didn't ask for forgiveness. He offered to make direct amends when he's able or if I'd rather never see him again, he said he can find service work to do right where he's at or I can select something, and he'll do it."

"So, he's sorry for real now that it's too late." My pulse pounds in my ears.

"I told you what he said at his sentencing, Ben. He doesn't believe there's any redemption for him."

"He say that in his letter?"

"He admits he doesn't deserve forgiveness."

"You wrote him back, didn't you?"

He nods slowly. I bite my tongue from the retort that pushes against my restraint.

"We're not the only ones he wrote. I know Dr. Lundquist got a much less personal letter that said more or less the same thing. Most people are going to ignore him, so I felt someone should reply. I told him if he still feels the same way when he gets out of jail, he can look me up. Since that might be a quarter century from now, I might not feel so conflicted. And maybe by then, he'll have stopped feeling so guilty." Pete used to apologize all the time, but I'm not sure he *feels* guilt. "I take it you haven't read yours yet."

"Not sure I'm going to. I don't need any more of his bull shit."

"There were options. probably to limit any manipulation. I chose for him not to be able to write me back while he's in jail, but once he's on parole, he can reach out, so…." He turns toward the bow. "Want to help rig these lanterns the way they're supposed to be?"

"Yes, of course."

I lean in so I can see what he's doing. Whoever installed these didn't understand about wind and rain, guaranteeing failure of the fixtures. We move toward the stern to secure a pair that are either side of the galley door.

"Ben?" I knew he wouldn't be able to leave it alone.

"Yeah?"

"Hating your best friend…." I open my mouth to ask him to leave it alone, but he speaks before I can gather my breath. "It's hurting you more than it's hurting him. Unless you're planning to write him back and tell him how you really feel, he's just got his own guilt and your angry thoughts just corrode *your* character."

Write him back? Tell him how I really feel? That sounds….

"I don't want to be cruel. I know he's being punished. He doesn't need me kicking him when he's down. But I never want to see or hear from him again."

"There's an option for that. It'll work until he's off parole."

"And, like you said, in a quarter century he might be done apologizing."

He nods and shrugs.

"Maybe he'll be a better man by the time he can make choices like that."

"Or maybe he'll grow up and realize he can't fix it—ever—so why bother trying."

He starts to say something else, but I intercept him this time.

"How's Melody doing?"

She's pregnant with their third child and having a difficult pregnancy. We get on to that topic and then move onto others. The mood lightens and as the sunset nears, the ocean off the bow turns an amazing turquoise with azure above. The clouds turn purple on the undersides. Cap shakes my hand and thanks me for coming. I say I'll be back next Saturday. I'm sure I'll be able to face the foredeck by then.

Lily

It's raining, like it was for a few days after Alyse died. I wonder. I think I might be the only one who remembers that. I sit on the window seat in my room, staring out at the estate across the street. It's somewhat obscured by the rain. I wonder if anyone else in the world is still thinking about Alyse.

I look at the envelope in my hand. Peter writes in cursive. That's amazing. I know how to write in cursive too, but I had to teach it to myself in junior high school. Do guys do that? I don't know and I'm not sure I should care, but it is pretty impressive.

Peter's talent and charm opened a lot of doors for him, but he wasn't able to make good choices and now it all comes down to an envelope that I don't want to open. Or do I? There's a part of me that's curious. What does Peter have to say for himself? But then there's another part of me that is terrified to open this envelope and see what Peter has to say for himself.

My memory reminds me of Alyse breathing blood on that cold boat deck. I don't feel compassion for my ex-boyfriend. He's a killer and I can't find it in my heart to forgive him. Or can I?

Inmate 80831

Peter
November

Why am I being punished for defending myself from sexual assault?

I thought the cell I share with Dorph is small, but this cell is just about as long as I am. Literally. I can touch both end walls with my fingertips and put my hands flat on the two side walls. There's a concrete pier with a thin mattress along one wall and about as much floorspace, partially taken up with the toilet that doesn't slide into the wall like the ones in the regular cells do. I've got a pretty good lump on the back of my head where I connected with the guy's face and a bruise that's really starting to hurt across my shoulder blades. It's impossible to keep time in this windowless cell, but I think it's been a few year-long hours since they put me in here. I heard them bring food around to the other cells and the aromas made me almost hungry, though I'm too scared to actually have an appetite. There's no way to tell time here, but I calculate about an hour has passed, considering that they just picked up the trays. That they didn't attempt to feed me is kind of concerning. They can't starve us as punishment, can they?

I stare at the wall for a while longer, thoughts circling the drain in depression, before a guard comes to the little opening in the door.

"Prisoner 80831?"

I look at the Tyvek bracelet wrapped around my left wrist and nod. His eyes twinkle coldly, and I feel shame. I do that a lot lately.

"Yeah, that's me."

"You're – uh, Wyn—oh, got it. Probably best to be known by your DOC number for now."

I get the warning. My father is a liability to me here. T and Joel told me that too. I get none of the advantages of our destroyed relationship. I need to stay on track but it's oh-so-hard.

"Turn around to the bars so I can cuff you up. You're due in the Disciplinary Office."

I've never been cuffed before and I want to argue that I don't need to be, but I know I'm in trouble and I don't want to make the soup thicker, so I do as I'm told, even though it makes the bruise across my shoulder blades burn, especially when he uses my arms to steer me. I'll walk on my own. Why's he doing this? Joel's warning to not argue comes to mind, but it's hard not to protest.

The windowless office is small and bisected by a desk that a black man in a crisp uniform sits behind. Two heavy metal chairs sit in front of the desk. There's a large black lateral file cabinet against the adjacent wall.

"I'm Disciplinary Officer Rockland. Inmate 80831?"

I nod as the first guard forces me to sit in the chair and then chains me to it with my hands behind my back. Rockland scans a thin file on the desk and makes a notation.

"Been here a week and you're already fighting. You want to tell me what happened?"

His voice is crisp and impenetrable. No compromise. A City accent. I stopped shaking some time ago, but now a shiver runs through me again.

"I was sweeping the floor and this guy grabbed me." He looks down at his file.

"Your pants were down around your knees?"

"Yeah." I've never been comfortable with nudity, but I wasn't going to stick around for the would-be rapist to recover. The guards zip-tied my hands behind me while they sorted the situation. My pants were still around my knees until one of the guards pulled them up while I told him what had happened in the stairwell.

"How'd you get the drop on him?"

God, I don't want to remember what happened in the stairwell. I'm shaking hard again. I didn't *get the drop* on anyone. I reacted.

"I – he picked me up off the floor. From behind. I— the wall was right there, so I pushed off it. I didn't mean --. I don't know the guy. I didn't want to hurt him. I just didn't want *him* to hurt *me*."

Rockland makes a note on the file.

"You know fighting is a punishable offense?"

I didn't, but it figures. Until today, I've never been in a real fight. I got into a couple of shoving matches with guys when I was drunk, but not where anyone got hurt. I knew what my assailant wanted the minute my pants came down. I'm still shaking hard.

"There's a range of discipline I can impose. I could add time to your sentence." *What?* "I could give you 30 days in the cell you just came from." *But, I was defending myself! How is that fair?* "Violence is not tolerated in this facility. This isn't a good start to your period of incarceration. Given that you're in here for a violent crime, you could expect more time added to your sentence."

No, no, please no! I was defending myself. What was I supposed to do? Let him rape me? I don't argue. I doubt it will do any good. I'm shaking so hard, my teeth start to chatter. The more I try to stop it, the harder I shake.

"Good you're scared. 'I didn't mean to hurt anyone", is probably what you said when you woke up after killing that girl." He might as well have punched me in the gut, saying that. Tears immediately flood my eyes. I stare at my knees, blinking, just managing to contain them. He lets the silence hang just long enough to become painful. I'm already in prison and I'm never forgiving myself for Alyse. What could be worse? I hear him lick his lips and swallow before clearing his throat.

"You do have a right to defend yourself from physical assault. Even in here, against other inmates' aggression. Nobody thinks you were the aggressor here. You can't help the way you look." He pauses and I think about how Andy Harmon bird-dogged me all throughout high school. I couldn't help how I looked then either, but Andy never tried to rape me.

Rockland lets the silence hang for a moment too long, like he expects me to do something condemning. I keep my mouth shut and stare at the front of his desk, trying to control my shivering.

"Tyler has a history. He's not an unknown quality. Lots of raped kids in his wake."

I'm still shaking. If this is the daily reality of this place, I have zero chance of ever getting out of here.

"The head injury you inflicted appears accidental. You were defending yourself and his head accidentally encountered the stair support."

Until this moment, I didn't know how I knocked out Tyler. All I did was push off from the wall and as soon as he let go, I ran.

"But you injured a Black Lion, so you are going to have to spend 30 days in Administrative Segregation. It's not the SHU. It won't count against your sentence. It's mostly protective, to give a chance for this to blow over. You really did a number on his head and that's really not your fault. My advice is when you get out, don't tell people it was an accident. Let them think you have mad self-defense skills and then serve your own time and don't accept the offers that will come your way."

"Offers?" My voice sounds like a chirp. He pauses a long moment before answering.

"Gangs like inmates who can defend themselves. Given who your father is, you've got a chance to put this place behind you when you get out. Don't accept the offers."

Given who my father is? The one that's not talking to me?

My arms are going numb. I squeeze my eyes shut, trying to calm my shaking. Rockland shuffles papers for several moments before I feel someone come up behind me, so I snap my eyes open. The escort guard unchains me and jerks me to my feet by my right arm. I dislocated that shoulder about a year ago and the pressure makes it pop.

"I'll walk. Stop!"

"Inmate 80831, don't argue!"

Rockland doesn't say anything while the escort guard, whose name tag says "Pool" steers me by my spasming arm back to the cell. At least there he uncuffs me so I can settle on the pier to rub my shoulder and accept I'm not getting out of this space for a month. Feeling mostly safe for the first time in a week, I keep my eyes closed for a long time, trying to calm my quivering insides like I learned in rehab. Serenity is elusive, but I silently roll the Serenity Prayer around and around in my head. I can't change that I'm in this cell, in this prison, for a crime I committed. I don't know what strength I have or what I can change in here—not today anyway—but I can accept my circumstances. I meditate on that until I doze off sitting up with my back against the metal wall. I've slept only a few hours a night for the past several days. Closing my eyes risks sleep. In my dream, there are red sails against neon sunset colors and Alyse hits the railing and dies in my arms. I jerk awake to see the sunset painted on the plain walls of a windowless cell and feel her growing cold in my arms. Tears wet my cheeks in the darkness of this cold cell. It's going to be a long 30 days.

May

Ben

I fumble for my cell, finding the vibrating brick on the end table.

"'ello."

"Hey, Ben. Whatcha doing?"

It's Trevor at 2:00 am and his languid voice suggests he's been enjoying the evening.

"Trev. It's…uh—2:30 in the morning."

"Is it that late?"

"Having trouble sleeping?" He has nightmares sometimes. More than I do. Another thing to feel guilt over.

"I haven't been to bed yet. Making up for lost time."

"Lost time?"

"Folks put me in Briarcliff."

Silence falls. I push up against the headboard, rubbing sleep out of my eye.

"How was it?"

"Horrible. Puked for a week."

"Sorry. But you know that stuff isn't good for you?"

"Neither's being in pain all the time."

I suspect the pain he's feeling is less physical and more mental. He had a rough time after that night on the bay—broken bones and all. I've had two best friends in my life and both of them are addicts. Trevor doesn't drive these days, so I don't think he'll kill anyone but himself. My heart breaks for him.

"You're home already?" I talked to him a week and a half ago…maybe two weeks. I kick myself for being that bad of a friend, but talking to him kind of depresses me these days.

"Naw! Cheyenne came and got me."

"Theriault?"

"Yeah."

"How's she doing?"

"Okay, I think." There's an edge to his voice that I can't read. Of Pete's two surviving victims, Cheyenne and Trevor were hurt the worst. Interesting that they'd end up growing close. Dancers who can't dance.

"So, your parents let you back in the house?"

"I didn't try. I'm staying with Hil."

My gut twists. Trevor's stepbrother Hillary is a great party mate, but Trevor needs care that Hil can't give.

"You safe?"

"Fuck, no!" Trevor laughs. "Of course not. I'm having too much fun for that." Then he takes a quavering breath. "It just wears off too damn fast." He chokes on tears. "You ever wonder about that night?"

I do. There are a thousand what-ifs about that night, but I can't go there with Trevor. Could Pete answer those questions? I'd have to read his letter to get started with that and then – do I really want to risk reaching out to him?

"I got work in the morning, Trev."

Silence from the other end. I can hear rain on my roof.

"Right – a life. I should get one of those someday." He sniffles. "Hey, could you come get me in a few days? I'm going to need some things Hil can't provide."

"You shouldn't be at Hil's. Call your dad."

"They'll put me back in Briarcliff. I ain't doing that again."

"Even if it kills you?"

"I'm not dying. I'm going to live forever, whether I want to or not."

"You can want to, Trevor. Just choose it."

"It's not that easy. It hurts so much. More when I stop."

"That's what all the addicts say."

"Screw you, Ben! You've no idea. *You* didn't get hurt. Neither did *he*. And, *she* died. So, you shut your mouth!"

"I'm not listening to this, Trev. You need to go back to Briarcliff and stay. You're going to end up sick or dead. You may want that now, but in the future, you'll look back on this as something you had to get through, but survived."

I'm sounding like my dad. I'm not even 20 and I'm sounding like my dad.

"Screw you! I don't need to listen to this." He clicks off the phone and I'm left listening to dead air. I set my phone on the nightstand and stare into the darkness, listening to the rain. There's a part of me that wants to go to Hil's boat and get Trevor right now. He doesn't have a choice but to go where I take him. My counselor has been working on this need I have to rescue the people I care about. I did it with Pete, now I'm doing it with Trevor. Truthfully, Trevor doesn't need me. Hil might be a neglectful guardian, but he won't let Trevor die. He's probably got Naloxone in his medicine cabinet.

I make plans to soothe myself. I work in the morning, but Temple is closing the line at noon to do some retooling, so I'll have the afternoon off. I could take *the Clotilde* out for a sail. My stomach clenches with anxiety as I see Pete sitting in the stern, his hand on the tiller, his other hand pulling rope. Not ready for that yet, I guess.

Maybe mountain biking. Not Laurel Ridge because Pete's ghost will be riding right behind me the whole way. How can a guy be alive and yet haunt the living? I guess it's back to the dunes. At least they're convenient.

I sit up a while longer, but finally slide down under the sheet and fall asleep, soothed by the pitter-patter of rain on the roof

Lily

Melissa comes out of the dressing room rocking a basic black dress that's at least one size too small for her buxomness. I don't know what to say when she asks me how it looks. Her breasts spill out the top like a bowl of overripe fruit. I'm not a fan, but if she likes it….

She looks at herself in the mirror and sighs.

"Too much, huh?"

"Would your parents let you out of the house wearing it?" She makes *uh-uh* face and turns around.

"Go get me the next size." She goes back into the dressing room, and I head to find the same dress *two* sizes bigger. She really wants to be thin, but you look fatter if you wear tight clothes.

She does like the larger dress, and it highlights her streaked blond hair. It's still a sexy dress, but she doesn't look like a prostitute anymore. After paying for it, we head into the mall to get some lunch. I'm starving, but while this mall still has a great department store, the food selections aren't great. It's kind of Subway or nothing.

"Did you finish that painting?"

I started a painting taken from a photo of the Long Sands lighthouse when we were in a painting class last winter, but I didn't finish it before the class was over. I've been dabbling with it a bit since.

"I still have some foreground to do, but it's looking pretty good. I'll send you a photo when I get home. Has Natalie got back yet?"

"No. Another couple of days. She sent me photos from Cape Hatteras."

"She sent me some too."

"We should all go to the beach when she gets back."

I don't say anything. Melissa and Natalie don't know about Alyse because I haven't told them. It's not that I'm opposed to beaches because of her death. It's just that the ocean reminds me of it. My counselor says I need to get past it. I wonder if Ben is yet. I only ever talk with Jenae about it.

I'm finished with my sandwich, so we head back to the department store to find some clothes for me. Melissa goes right for the sundresses and suddenly I'm rushing back a year to Alyse leading me to the same rack, pulling out the one with the hydrangeas on it and declaring it the One for Me.

Tears well up in my eyes and I need to turn away for a moment to mourn my dead friend and wonder if her brother ever is overwhelmed by the enormity of the harm he's caused.

"What's your favorite color?" Melissa asks.

I take a breath to banish the unfallen tears and force myself to sound bright.

"Blue."

She looks sideways at me. and her hand goes to a section of blue dresses. She pulls an aqua one out and holds it to me.

"Ever wear green?"

"Um, sometimes. I'm not opposed."

She moves to a section with that color and finds another dress.

"And you need other summer things, right?"

"Yes. Pants and tops. Especially tops."

She looks around the area and leads me over to a junior section display.

"Don't worry. You're in safe hands."

She sounds so much like Alyse that I almost burst into tears, but of course, we probably all sound alike when we're dressing our friends. At least, that's what I tell myself so I can get through this day.

Ben

Kevin sits quietly in his wheelchair, his gaze on the park-like backyard of his office building. Sometimes I struggle to get started and today is one of those times. He gives me a while, but eventually, he sighs and speaks.

"What's got you so far away?"

I sigh in response. He waits.

"I started back at *the Mimi* this past weekend."

"You seeing it all the time again?"

"No. I'm kind of surprised. Captain repainted as part of the repairs so it's not obvious. I kind of relived it once, but then it stopped."

"But something is still bothering you."

It's not a question. We've been at this since October, and he knows me pretty well now.

"I've been thinking a lot about that day." Now he looks at me sideways. I'm not reliving Alyse's death, but I'm thinking about that day – about the stuff I can't tell anyone – not even the guy with the LCSW behind his name.

"Yeah."

"Will that ever stop?"

"Depends on whether you let it stop."

"I want to. Why can't I?"

He plays with the seam of his pants. He rubs his hands together. I know that means he's warming up to fight with me.

"You apparently aren't ready to. Guilt's a tough thing to let go of."

What do I have to feel guilty about? I wasn't on Pete's boat when it hit *the Mimi*. I'm his victim, not his enabler. Except….

"You know survivor's guilt is kind of a normal thing after a wreck like that. You survived, Alyse died, Trevor was injured, and Pete went to jail. What in there do you feel so guilty about that you can't tell me?"

He's never got that aggressive before. I shake my head. I don't know. Except….

"A lot of missed opportunities with Pete."

"Yes, but his addiction was not your fault. He's the only one who could choose to fix it. If you tell me that's it,

I'm seriously going to kick your butt." He rolls his eyes when I glance at him nervously. Of course, we both know he can't execute that threat. We've discussed the years I spent trying to prevent Pete from going off the deep end. I was a good friend who helped him delay getting treatment for years. Except…. "I don't know what you're holding back, Ben, but as long as you hug that bomb like it's precious, it's building power to hurt you."

I remember the hours and days I spent playing *The Walking Dead* just so I could club zombies with a barbed-wire-wrapped baseball bat. It helped me not tear the faces off my coworkers, but eventually led to me needing to run away from my family. Would that be my reaction if Pete walked back into my life?

"Trevor called the other night."

He straightens in his chair.

"What time?"

"Two…three."

"He has sucky timing. How do you feel about that?"

"He's way worse than Pete ever was. *He* at least didn't call when he was drunk." He cocks his head the way he does when I've said something that deserves consideration. "What?"

"I just find it interesting. He drank at parties and to have gotten that addicted at such a young age, he must have been drinking at home when he was alone, but he didn't burden you with it. That speaks to something deep and dark, something he either couldn't express, or he felt you would reject him for it."

I'd like to think I wouldn't reject Pete if he'd shared something deep and dark, but when he asked for my help, I chose to stay at work, so….

"Did he share something deep and dark? Is that what you're sitting on?"

I think about Laren's hand on Pete's arm poolside in Greece, but I reject the memory and shake my head. We sit in silence for a moment before Kevin glances at the clock.

"Time's almost up. So, this week, I want you to do something I know you don't want to do." I stop breathing, fearing he's going to tell me to drive to Sing Sing Prison and confront Pete. "Take your sailboat out. If Pete's mental specter is a passenger, so be it. Confront it. We'll talk about it next week. And, Ben, you're at a point where you need to start being honest with me and yourself or you're just wasting both of our times. Right?"

I nod. I know I need to talk about it, but if I do…Pete's the bad guy now, but do I want to admit my part in it?

Lily

Mina waits for me to answer her question. I don't want to.

"I'm scared of what's in there, I guess."

We're discussing Peter's letter which is now tucked into the front cover of my Bible. Maybe I'll use the unopened envelope as a bookmark for the next decade.

"Do you think he'll be abusive?"

"No!" Really, no! Peter, sober, was always a nice guy—polite, so unlike the maniac who drove his boat into the side of *the Mimi*. "I think he's probably going to be sad and say he's sorry."

"What is there to be afraid of there?"

I don't know. I just know that it fills me with dread to open that letter. I squirm, trying to find a reasonable explanation.

"Maybe I don't want to feel his sadness."

"His sadness…over?" I sigh because I have so many conflicting emotions on this. "Do you think he regrets his sister's death more than you do?"

"No." That's not true. "I mean, yes, of course. She was his sister. I think…." What do I think? My parents are paying good money for me to work this out. What am I thinking? "He never tried to reach out between her death and going to jail. I think he probably grieved his sister. He *loved* her, as much or more than I loved her."

"But?"

But? Yeah, there's more I don't want to acknowledge.

"He didn't mean to kill her." Mina waits, not nodding, not agreeing, just listening. "I—okay, I didn't *know* that guy who aimed the boat at *the Mimi*. That guy was a stranger."

"He was very drunk and on other drugs. Maybe not in control of himself."

"Yeah, but…. He'd been drunk before and not…. And…and…. " My eyes swim with tears. "What was different was I was standing on the deck next to Ben. What if…what if he did what he did because of that?"

She pushes the tissue box closer to me and I blot my eyes.

"Now we're getting somewhere."

"Are we?" I croak with tears.

"You finally admitted you blame yourself for what Peter did. And that's a great start."

"But I *know* I'm not responsible for what Peter did."

"That's not how you feel. You believe he hit the boat because you were there with Ben."

That's true, but it's also true that I'm not responsible for Peter's actions. A girl could go crazy trying to sort out her feelings about this.

"What if he did?"

Mina smiles at me.

"Then he's still 100% responsible for what *he* did. You need to recognize that. You living your life didn't make him decide to destroy his. He screwed up and you broke up with him. That wasn't an excuse for what he did days later. He had a choice not to do that." She pauses to let this reasonable observation set in. "So that brings us back to the letter and why you're afraid to read it."

I try to select my primary fear among the stew of anxieties.

"What if he feels that way?"

"What he feels doesn't matter. Whatever he wrote in that letter shouldn't determine how you feel about that night on the bay. But…what if he does blame you? Why should he determine how you feel about what happened that night?"

Why? Aren't we all subject to what others think?

"Because…because…." I pause and Mina gives me time to think. "He never tried to reach out and now he does. He's in this horrible place and if he feels like I put him there…."

She waits to see if I'll say more but I can't figure out what I want to say.

"You think the letter will be accusatory and make you feel even more guilty?"

I nod. She's pretty much said what I'm thinking and can't articulate.

"Lily, you don't have to read that letter if you think it'll be a guilt trip. You don't owe that to Peter or anyone else. And if you choose not to read the letter, that's fine. But I think you'd be missing an opportunity to teach yourself something here."

"What?"

"That you're stronger than you think you are. But I can understand not wanting to subject yourself to abuse by a violent ex-boyfriend. It's ultimately your choice what you do with it."

I sigh. I think maybe I want people to make some choices for me, but clearly that's not what will happen with Mina. Whatever happens next is up to me.

Grief

Peter
November

The blue of my vein stands up from my wrist when I make a fist. If I had something sharp, it would be easy to slice it. Would she be satisfied then?

My sister who I killed is standing beside this cold concrete bunk, her long dark hair spread across her light-colored gown. I wonder hysterically if she cut her hair before the pixie cut as she holds a bottle of scotch out to me. It was always past her waist, though usually in a braid. I don't remember it skimming silkily at her shoulders.

The smell and then taste of the liquor flood my senses. Scotch has peaty notes I've always liked, except drinking scotch makes my stomach hurt. I tried to kill myself washing down pills with scotch. Was it a choice of convenience that ended up saving my worthless life? It guaranteed I'd come to this place where all I want to do is die, but I've got no way to accomplish it. Seeking any solace,

I savor the illusionary taste of scotch. Following on that momentary pleasure comes a burning taste of vomit. My stomach convulses, and I rush to the toilet to hurl.

There's a sound behind me and I instinctively turn, having learned that lesson quickly and brutally.

"You okay?"

I don't know this guy. He's middle aged, a lot of peppered dark hair cut short, wearing a white jumpsuit. I think that means he's a trustee, which means he must have been in here a while – like longer than I've been alive.

There's a sink that pops out of the wall above the toilet and I shovel water into my mouth to banish the taste of bile. The one thing good about this cell is they gave me a new kit of personal hygiene items and there's nobody else here to steal it.

"I'm in here." I sit back down on the ledge. "What's to complain about, right?"

"Aside from the uncomfortable mattress, the loneliness, not being able to go outside? It's living the Beverly Hills 90210 experience."

"The what?"

His eyes crinkle with good humor. I just want to go to sleep, except it's not safe inside my head.

"It's a classic TV show. 1990s, boys and girls doing boy-and-girl thangs. You don't watch cable?"

Some, but this isn't ringing a bell. He shrugs.

"Guess maybe it wasn't as popular as I thought it would be. So, really, how you doing?"

He's Puerto Rican with the sounds of Spanish Harlem dripping from every word. While I give serious thought to his question, he watches me through that little hatch in the door. It's a testament to how much taller Americans have gotten that he has to bend a bit to do this.

"I don't know. I feel…." I mull it over in my mind for a moment. "Encased in concrete."

He nods, looking appropriately somber.

"Kind of accurate. This place numbs a lot of people, even in gen pop. In here, it's a lot harder to find the light. But you ain't the first one to end up in here for defending yourself. If you ever want to talk, man…they'll let me…." His voice trails off to nothing as I lay down and turn my face to the wall. I feel Alyse's hair trail across my arm, and I swear I feel her breath on my earlobe. I know it isn't her. It's my guilty conscience. She died drowning in her own blood because of my actions, so I know I must be dreaming. I try to wake up, but now an ambulance driver is shining a bright light into my eyes and demanding something of me in dragged-out speech that makes no sense. Searing pain burns its way down my throat, and I jerk awake, hearing her name echoing in the cell. I hear someone bellow "Shut up" but I don't know him, and he doesn't know me, so really, it doesn't matter. Except I don't sleep again that night.

May

Ben

It's warm for May, which makes the sand lovely for a good workout. Sweat drips off my nose as I churn up a dune and then traverse the top of it. I'm panting and paying close attention to the terrain, but it's still not enough to distract me from my thoughts. I keep feeling Pete behind me. He didn't like the dunes and usually didn't go with me, but for some reason, his spirit is bird-dogging me instead of Trevor's. Maybe I'm getting used to Trevor's changed circumstances. Nothing's changing there. If only he'd decide to live again, but I'm starting to lose hope that will be Trevor's future. Maybe some people just can't overcome things like that.

Why aren't I getting used to *Pete's* changed circumstances? Why is *his* spirit following me all over the dunes? I don't know. Is it a sign that he's thinking of me? Maybe all Trevor thinks about these days is the next hit he can score. What does someone in prison think about? The world outside or what's right in front of them? How would I know? I just know I can feel Pete back there and hear some of his stock phrases. He didn't like the dunes. He preferred green trees and occasional shade. He'd do the dunes with me, though, and make funny comments about camels and sand crabs. Why is he bothering me today?

Maybe it's because I need to read the letter. It's still in my desk drawer at the folks' house and I don't intend to ever retrieve it, though I suppose I should do something about it before I go back to Dartmouth…or when I graduate…get married…have kids…retire.

I'm so conflicted.

I top the dune behind the Hole and stare down the slope. What the heck? Is school out of session? It's not Saturday. I took today off because we were going to get the afternoon off anyway. They're retooling the Distribution line, so there's nothing for us grunts to do. Might as well celebrate that I paid off my last student loan yesterday. I thought mountain biking in the middle of the week would be a fun thing. It is, but why is the Hole packed out with kids?

While my gaze scans the crowd, I see a willowy figure gathering up a blanket. I scan past her and then I rewind. I know her, don't I?

Lily

It's a weekday, so there shouldn't be so many cars parked along the road to Pirate's Cove. I'm glad I'm planning this rather than actually doing it. It would be a horrible mess if I'd had Bram with me.

I park the car, pull as far off the road as I can, grab my beach bag from the back seat, and walk next to the other cars towards the beach. What might attract so many people on a weekday? I pass a school bus. Well, I suppose it might be a school outing.

I see a gathering at one of the pavilions. I remember Tilly telling me Pirate's Cove was deliberately built with limited parking to prevent too much overuse. It's why I've never been here before. I stop to take off my sandals to walk barefoot in the sand.

In New Hampshire where I'm from, there's a series of beaches called the Hamptons. Yes, just like here in Long Island, but they don't jut out into the ocean. We used to go there for weekends and even some holidays. I walked in the sand a lot, loving the feel of the shifting grains beneath my feet. So, when Bram's physical therapist suggested walking in the sand to improve his balance, I thought it a great idea. Nothing is simple with Bram though. You have to find ways to convince him to do some things and I'm pretty sure this is one of them.

I spread my blanket and sit cross-legged on top to stare out at the blue water of the cove. I'd read somewhere this was a dredged body. It was pretty, but clearly artificial – a C of sand backed by scrub-covered dunes. Children play in the water and run across the sand. I pull off my shirt and shorts and reapply sunscreen to my shoulders. Will I bring Bram here? I need to decide. I decide to walk to the far-right point of the cove and then back.

Sand constantly moves so that my calves feel exercised by the time I get back to the blanket. I try to imagine bringing Bram here. Complications are likely. Can I handle an outing like this by myself?

I take a sip of water and watch as a mountain biker works his way along the top of the dunes. He's powerful and solitary. I love bicycling, but I'm not sure I would find something like the dunes fun as a solitary activity.

Maybe I can get Wes to come with us. He's strong enough to move Bram if my brother gets spastic when he touches the sand. I shake off my blanket and pick up my bag to retrace my steps to the car. I hear bike tires behind me and glance over my shoulder to see Ben slowing beside me.

"I thought that was you." He grins at me from beneath his bright orange bike helmet. "What brings you to the end of the road?"

"I've never been, and I thought I'd check it out. You?"

"Tilly's cottage is right down the road." He gestures vaguely. "I try to do a workout here at least once a week even in the winter."

"I've heard about the trails."

"You should try them sometime."

"Maybe a little out of my league. But I did think I'd bring Bram here. The PT says walking in sand is good for his balance. Is there always a backup of cars here?"

"Often, yeah." He glances back toward the beach. "Bram would have trouble with that, wouldn't he?"

One of the things I like about Ben is he's insightful. Or was. It's been nearly a week since we met at the mailbox, and he's not called. I still have his number in my phone, but I didn't call either.

"I thought it was a great idea until I did it myself and now, I think I shouldn't do it alone. Do you think Wes--?"

"Isn't strong enough if Bram were to fall. I can do it with you on Saturday morning or Sunday."

I'm stunned at first. I feel slightly defensive on Wes' behalf. He may not be as strong as Ben, but he does know how to get Bram off the floor, probably better than Ben, who has hardly spoken to me for a year, and now he's offering to help me with Bram. I'm inexplicably delighted and completely suspicious.

"Are you sure?"

"Yes, of course. I wouldn't have offered if it was a problem."

"Sure, you wouldn't. You *never* do anything you don't want to do."

"Never." He laughs. "I guess my reputation precedes me."

"It does. And it's not a bad reputation to have."

His eyes narrow.

"We share that, I guess, the two most duped by Pete."

"He was good-looking and charming."

"And my parents keep insisting he was a good kid at the start. He just took a turn somewhere and I didn't see it. Didn't want to believe it."

"He was kind to me – thoughtful. And, he said he wasn't drinking. I saw evidence that he wasn't drinking."

"Except when he was."

Peter screaming in Ben's face at Trevor's party fills my mind. We nod. After an uncomfortable silence, we change the subject.

"What are your plans for the summer?"

"Hanging out with Bram…mostly. You?"

"I'm working at Temple Manufacturing and crewing for Captain Russell."

"Sounds like more fun than I'll be having."

"I think you're a very loving sister. I also think you need to find some time for yourself. Us wiser pushovers need to guide you younger ones. Don't let it consume your life. Leave a bit for yourself."

"I know. I won't let it happen again." Mina has said much the same things.

He cocks his head.

"So, you're not here with the school group?"

"No. I homeschooled, remember?"

"Home-schooling? Made a lot of friends?"

I took an art class over the winter and made two friends. We meet sometimes. They're not bosom friends, but I wasn't sure I wanted any friends after Alyse died.

"I have one or two. What about you?"

He sighs.

"Trevor and I still talk, but…."

"He's been through a lot."

"And he didn't come out the other side of it a better person."

"That's too bad. And everyone else? Finn and Andy and …." I try to remember other names, but Peter didn't really introduce me to his friends – almost as if he thought they might blow his cover. It's awful that I don't know what was true with him and what was pure fantasy—gossamer illusions spun by a master liar.

"Andy was definitely more Pete's friend than mine and Finn is in Africa. I wasn't very good company for most of the winter." He shrugs.

"Ten?" He blinks at the change of subject. "Next Saturday?"

"Eight would be better."

"Right. You have work in the afternoon. Where will we meet?"

"I can pick you up."

"That won't work for Bram. You said you're staying near here?"

"Yeah. Follow me and I'll show you."

The cottage isn't far, less than a mile down a tree-lined road, then a short curving driveway. He bikes ahead of me, but he never leaves my sight, slowing almost to a standstill at some times. The cottage, painted peach and green, sits among lilacs that still bloom. Instead of a lawn, a wildflower meadow surrounds a brick patio.

"It's lovely here."

"Peaceful and someplace I needed to be this winter."

I nod because I didn't need to avoid as many memories as he did. We're both healing, but I think my healing is further along.

"We'll be here at 8:00 am Saturday."

"I can have breakfast for you."

"Okay. Thanks. This is a really pretty spot."

We suddenly feel awkward with each other in this space wreathed in romance. I can't reconcile Tilly with such a place. She seemed so practical. She also seemed single, so maybe she wasn't who she seemed. Maybe none of the Wyngates were.

I smile and get back into the car. He removes his bike helmet and waves me out the driveway. We're getting better. I hope.

Ben

I never realized what a hassle getting Bram in and out of cars must be. Last year at this time, he couldn't walk, but my parents say he's been walking at home for months. His right side is still spastic, clearly paralyzed. His leg drags and his arm is useless.

My first experience with Bram and cars is when they arrive at my place for breakfast. I don't know what I thought, and Lily clearly knows what she's doing, helping him stand and guarding him from stumbling as he leans on one of those old-folk canes with the four-pronged base. I realize it's a victory to reach the table without falling down. Since it is patio furniture, the chairs are light, and I provide the weight behind the one Bram sits in.

He doesn't really talk. He has a lot of single words, but you have to kind of guess what's going on around them. I have to admit, Pete would be better at this than I am. When we took Spanish in high school, he got As and I got Cs with his tutorial. He also managed pretty well in Greek. I don't want to think about him, but everything seems to come back to him.

We don't talk about him. We talk about the trees and the flower beds Lily is nurturing at home. I hate that my mind remembers how much Pete hated the roses at his house.

"I love there are different kinds of lilacs, so some bloom early and they're just evolving."

"Yeah. I wish our yard had lilacs."

"Plant some."

"I might suggest that to Mom. Still, it'll take decades for them to be like this. Do you know the history of the house?"

"I never asked." I look at the cottage, trying to see its history. "I don't know."

"House." Bram shows that he understands what we're saying. He holds up the half of the bagel he hasn't eaten. "Word."

"Bagel." Lily must be used to it.

"Bbbagel." Bram says it like a magic spell. Then he points at the butter on the saucer in the middle of the table. "Butter." He points to the coffee pot. "Coffee." He points to his glass. "Millllk."

"He's doing pretty good…talking."

"He's exceeded expectations. And the speech therapist thinks he'll continue to improve."

"That's great. I know you guys didn't think he'd ever be able to talk."

"Well, he really still can't, but he understands a lot of what we're saying now, and the words are coming."

"I know Wes and he became good friends."

"They're silly together."

Bram swallows the bite of bagel in his mouth and speaks.

"Wes."

"Right."

Bram points at me.

"Name."

"Ben."

"Bbben. Wes. Sissser. No. Brudder. House."

"I'm house-sitting." Bram's expression says he doesn't know the concept. I glance at Lily, who just smiles back. Bram stares at me expectantly. "This house belongs to a friend. I'm staying here while she's away."

Bram shifts his gaze to Lily.

"He's watching the house."

Bram grins.

"Run." With his good hand, he pantomimes the house running away. Lily and I laugh.

"I mow the lawn." I point to the tiny bit of grass and pantomime pushing a lawnmower. He nods. "I keep the doors locked." I pantomime closing the door and locking it. Again, he nods. "I flush the toilet." I realize that's going to be a problematic pantomime in mixed company, but he pantomimes flipping the handle and makes a whooshing noise. "Exactly."

"Silent."

It's my turn to stare at him in confusion before looking to Lily for translation.

"I'm not sure. Bram, can you think of another word?"

He frowns at her, then shakes his head. He points around at the trees and then brushes his ear, settles back in his chair with his eyes closed, then opens them to see if I understand what he's trying to communicate.

"Is it quiet?"

"Yeah."

"Yes. Very restful." He frowns. I pantomime taking a nap and he grins. We're communicating.

"Sss-leep."

"Yes." For a while when I first moved here, I thought the silence would drive me crazy, but it gave me time to think. I thought I didn't want to do that, but then I did.

Bram's running a finger under his eyes and then pointing to me. I look at Lily for interpretation.

"He thinks you look tired, I think." He gives her a thumb's up.

I don't want to explain that my sleep is interrupted by dreams of that night. I'm not sure I could put that into the simple language Bram needs.

"Two jobs." I hold up two fingers and then get stuck on how to pantomime job.

"Job." Bram blurts and it's a little loud. He pantomimes hammering.

"Yeah." Not exactly, but close enough, kid. "He's really improved."

Lily smiles. Bram laughs. He pantomimes talking and then indicates we're talking back and forth while he's watching.

"A friend of your grandfather has a deaf son. He's been coming for visits. Wes has been learning sign too."

"Is it easier?"

"It's more understandable than pantomime, but he doesn't always get the signs right."

Bram sticks his tongue out at her, and we laugh at him. We've finished eating breakfast and the road will soon start filling up with Saturday beachgoers. She gets him back into the car while I clean up the table and lock up the house.

Lily drives us to the beach and we're pretty close – there's only one car ahead of us. She releases Bram from the extra secure belts in the backseat and helps him to his feet. I don't really know what to do to help, but I'm relieved to see the wheelchair folded up in the cargo area of the Subaru. I suspect this is going to be hard.

Lily stays close by his right side as we slowly make our way through the entrance and onto the beach path. While it's asphalt, it's sprinkled with sand and I worry he's going to slip, but Lily's good at redirecting him when he puts his affected foot down wrong. It's when we turn into the sand that Bram's entire right side tenses up and becomes balky.

He wavers in his cane control. It's like his left side is thrown off by his right.

"So, this is when you lend an arm to help stabilize him."

I grab the cane in my left hand while Bram leans heavily on my right. Lily is actually moving his right leg now and hanging onto the belt he wears wrapped around his torso. Bram's breathing heavily and grunting like this is the hardest thing he's done in a while.

When we lower him to the sand just above the waterline, I know it's going to take a lot of work to get him to his feet again.

Lily pulls a pail of children's sand toys out of her bag and with pantomime and a few words convinces Bram he should try to build a sandcastle.

"Will he want to go swimming?"

"I--."

Bram shakes his head violently, pantomiming that he wants to stay where he is. Lily fills the pail with water and then shucks her coverup. Wow, she's matured. Down, boy! This isn't about *tha*t. That part of my anatomy thinks everything is about *that.*

"It's a little cold to swim, but I'll stay with him if you want to try."

She laughs and Bram gives me a dismissive handwave.

"He's fine right where he is. Want to go for a walk?"

The waves are pretty little here at the Hole and it's fun to walk in the surf. As the sun shifts westward, the beach gradually populates with families and groups of young people. And Gull Island springs up out of the mist. I stop walking and stare out at it, remembering Pete and I hanging out there.

"Hey. What are you thinking?"

"Did he ever take you to the Island?"

She glances toward it.

"Is that the one with the Roaring 20s house?" I nod. "He said he would, but then things fell apart."

"Yeah." It's an opportunity. It wasn't something they shared. "You ought to see it."

"You think so?"

"Yes. We could go there – maybe next Saturday morning."

"Yeah? Yeah! Okay." She looks up at the beach where Bram has laid down on the blanket. "What time is it?"

I glance at the sky.

"About 11:00. I guess it's time to be headed back so I can get ready for work."

"He's getting tired too. By the time we get him back to the car, he'll be exhausted."

"How about we get him to a bench along the path and then I go get that wheelchair, so we make it a little easier on him?"

"Maybe. He gets frustrated when we make decisions for him."

"Oh." I hadn't really thought of that. The guy who can't talk has opinions? Well, maybe he'll see reason.

Bram's actually napping, but he wakes up pretty easily and, after drinking some water, he allows me to get him to his feet. Strangely, walking back to the path is easier than getting here. He doesn't spaz out. He doesn't walk as good as he does on a flat solid surface, but he walks a lot better than he did coming in.

"He didn't know what to do the first time. Now he's adapting."

He's also drooling with the effort of dragging his right side along. Still, he refuses to sit down on the bench and walks all the way to the car. He's breathing pretty hard by the time we get there, but it's an earned winded. From the passenger seat on the way back to the cottage, I see he's dozed off.

"Wow. He's a lot tougher than I thought."

"He's really been trying hard lately. Thank you for coming with us. We never could have done that just the two of us, but I bet we can do it by ourselves next time."

"Sure."

I get out of the car and head into the cottage as she drives away. Pete is now everywhere in my memory, and I regret stirring the pot. Maybe next Saturday is not a good idea. Maybe having anything to do with Lily is not good for my mental health. So why am I doing this?

Lily

I scan through my phone history, but it hasn't changed. Ben hasn't called or texted or even reached out via Facebook or Insta. There's no chance I missed him. I sigh and reach for another bedding plant. Mom lays a flat down beside me.

"It's the last one."

Well, that's good because my lower legs are going numb. I crawl over a bit and plunge my trowel into the soil.

"Something up?"

My mother is psychic. I'd swear to that contention. She can *always* tell when I'm struggling with something. I plant a cucumber before I respond. By then, her silence is forcing me to do what I don't want to.

"Ben hasn't called?"

She doesn't respond for a moment, loosening a plant from one of the cells.

"Did you really expect him to?"

I glance sideways at her. Yeah, I did expect him to. I thought we were getting along.

"I did." I sound uncertain now.

"He's older than you, Lily. Older than even Peter who was too old for you."

"You think Ben is too old for me?"

"I didn't say that. After what you've both been through, I don't think that's the problem. What you've both been through has matured you. But it also scarred you – scarred him. Maybe it would be best if you just accepted him as a friend."

I sigh and settle back onto my butt, letting blood flow back into my feet. She settles back on her own butt. Apparently, we're having a serious conversation.

"Is it a mistake for me to kind of want more?"

"At your age? Absolutely. Of course, Dad and I met when I was 16 almost 17. So young love can work out, but Ben's still healing. The longest relationship in his life was with his best friend and his friend did a horrible thing that hurt both of you deeply. Ben needs to heal from that before he should consider romance with you or anyone."

"So, I'm the 'let's-just-be-friends' girl?"

"For now. But don't wait around, honey. Go on with your life because Ben may opt never to confront those memories that are associated with you."

I sigh, watching a hummingbird float by.

"I'm so wishing I'd had a clearer view last year."

"Life is a series of things we survive, sweetie, so don't regret your missteps. Just accept that you don't always get what you want and sometimes that's for the best."

I shift back to my knees and continue setting bedding plants. It's not the advice I want, but truthfully, it's the best advice I'm going to get. I can't *make* Ben like me the way I like him, so.... Yeah, it's time to just plant vegetables and not whine about my life because things could be so much worse. I see Alyse dying in Peter's arms and know the stark truth of that. I could have been on the smaller boat with Peter. I could have died. So, the memories I have are better than the other fate I might have had. That truth stands stark against what is, and I shiver.

The Weight of Concrete

Peter
November

I drag open my eyes at the sound of a clatter at the door. It's the Hispanic guy again. He's some sort of mental health tech but an inmate. He tries to talk with me every day. Yesterday, I pled exhaustion and put my face to the wall. Today I don't even want to talk.

"Leave me alone!"

"You sure, kid? I'm bringing you mail." He offers a large envelope and a smaller card envelope through the slot. I've been here two or three weeks and beginning to think the world is working hard to forget me. Yeah, mail is intriguing enough to get me to roll up onto my butt and reach for the envelopes.

"Guards say you're sleeping rough. You want to talk about it?"

The large envelope looks official, and I recognize the address as one of my dad's attorneys. I swallow loudly and set the envelopes at the bottom of the bed.

"This place gets to people. The whole place, but especially when they put you in here. It's not as bad as the SHU, but it's isolating and depressing and if you've got any issues, they get magnified."

I lie down and turn my face to the wall.

"Kid, really, you can talk to me."

I ignore him and he goes away eventually. I hear a group going to yard-out. I don't get to go. The feel of snow on my nose didn't feel so fresh behind concertina wire anyway. I roll over and sit up to drag the envelopes into my lap. The card is addressed from my dad's house, but the postal stamp says Florida. I can't figure out what that means, so I look at the legal envelope. It's been opened. They've both been opened. I don't get privacy here in Sing Sing. I work the paperwork out of the envelope.

There's a lot of legalese so I read it three times and it says the same thing in triplicate. I've been disowned. The trust fund has been liquidated and I am no longer my father's heir. There's warnings about using our connection for my benefit.

For a moment, tears threaten. and then I hear the judge's voice saying I deserved this punishment, and the tears dry before they even fall. I don't think about what disownment means for my future. I already can't see a time when I get out of this place. There's just years and years of staring at concrete walls and my sister's body growing cold in my arms. I sit with the back of my head against the wall for a long time before I stir. I want to just sit there for the rest of my life, but eventually I reach for the card.

It's a nice-looking card – a Florida beach at sunrise, which puts me right back on that boat for a moment. I attempt to break the spell by opening the card.

Be grateful for every day. Alyse.

I let the card fall out of my hand as I wrap my arms around my knees and silently mourn my sister who haunts me from beyond. When there's a clattering at the door, I ignore it. I've never been less hungry in my life. I don't know how long I sit there before the lights go out, but I lie down and feel the world slip away into infinite darkness.

May

Ben

My sailboat *Clotilde* belonged to Pete before he sold her to me when he got his speedboat. He said there wasn't room for both boats and his father's yacht in the mooring space. He practically gave her to me. At the time, it felt like a gift. Was it? Maybe. Pete could be really generous, and he never welched on a debt. Maybe that's why Cap Russell and my parents think he's serious about making amends.

Anyway, buying *Clotilde* necessitated me working for my moorage fees. That was how I ended up working for Bennett. When I first started doing odd jobs for him, I didn't get paid in money, but once I moved up to crew, he started paying me. It was my first job when I was 15 and I'm still doing it. I've been pretty lucky with my employers so far.

Pete got *Clotilde* the summer he was 12. I'm pretty sure his father thought he needed to be rewarded for holding it together while his parents divorced. But it was weird how controlled Pete was during that time. Now I know why. Well, I think I know why. He was self-medicating.

Clotilde is Tilly's full name. I didn't know that until last fall when Pete was in the news every few days. I always wondered why he registered the sailboat under that weird name, but I figured he got it from a book he didn't share with me. I love to read technical manuals and my grandfather introduced me to Westerns years ago, but Pete liked a much wider range of reading – fantasies, science fiction, mystery. It was entirely possible that he read the name in a book and decided it was a cool name for a boat. But he really named it after his stepmother. It's hard to believe he kept that secret from me for so long. Maybe he kept it for some dark Freudian reason. Maybe nothing I thought I knew about Pete was real. Maybe it was all lies.

I came here last week after my shift on *the Mimi* and rigged her for sailing and checked her sails. She's ready to go. I just need to decide to launch.

I pull off the cover and fold it neatly, putting it on the floor of the boat so I can use it as insulation. I put the mast up and set up the ropes. It's time. Maybe Pete won't accompany me today.

I push out from the slip, into the harbor, and I feel the breeze tug at my hair. Where will I go? Does it matter? I'll just go inside the bay and maybe confront the memories from 10 months ago.

I don't see Pete in the stern with his hand on the tiller. *I'm* in the stern and in control of the boat. I trim the sail and it catches the wind, moving me across the small waves toward the headlands. I leave behind the other boats, and I feel freedom catch me up in its powerful hand and drag me along toward my future.

The ocean is still cold, and the air can't be more than 60 degrees, but at the end of a long winter, it isn't unpleasant, and I love the feeling of sun on my face, the scent of salt in the air, the tug of the wind on the rope, and the sound of buoy bells flowing across the waves.

And in a matter of minutes, I'm smiling and wondering why I haven't done this in so long.

Lily

A song runs through my head . *Saturday in the park* – I don't remember the next line. Maybe something about the 4th of July? The park is full of people enjoying their day off. A man jogs by with his dog. Two women push baby carriages on the other side of the asphalt path. A group of young men play frisbee. Farther away, another group practice parkour on a special course. A three-piece band of buskers have a guitar case open. They're okay – nothing great – so I toss in a dollar, but I know I won't give more.

Natalie shrieks when she sees me and then comes running at me with her jazz hands flailing above her head. Some old guy walking a bulldog casts us a bemused look as Natalie acts like she hasn't seen me in years. It's been two months, I think. She just got back from visiting her grandparents, which involved beaches.

"Wow, you look great in that top, girl! It's new, right?"

"Growing a cup size means you get a new wardrobe."

I roll my eyes and she chuckles heartily. She's always on and can be a little exhausting, but her sarcastic comments about painting got me through a class I wasn't sure I liked until it was over. I'm taking the intermediate course next semester.

"You aren't huge. You're just right. Come on. Let's head toward Hot Licks. I haven't had a good ice cream in an age."

"In an age?"

"Hanging out with old people will do that."

"Tell me about it."

Her grandfather is apparently as entertaining as she is. She launches into three stories in a row about her grandfather.

"And then Grandma took me to buy this."

She shows off the top of her lacy bra. I feel my cheeks flash hot. I love Natalie, but she sometimes shocks me, and she absolutely thinks it's hilarious.

"Such a schoolmarm!"

A scene from cable TV, I think from *Little House on the Prairie*, flashes through my mind.

"Maybe I should get a poke bonnet."

Now I've stumped her. I google it and show her a picture.

"I don't get it."

"It's just a really old term. Anyway, I could get one of those dresses and that hat, get a job at a historical reenactment museum."

"That's taking the joke too far. So, what have *you* been up to?"

"Mostly just staying with Bram all summer."

"Always?" She looks worried.

"Well, no, but – I thought this one guy liked me, but then he sort of drifted away and—well, I don't know. False hope, I guess."

"Boys are fickle, Grandma says. Where'd you meet?"

"We've known each other for over a year. He's our neighbor."

"Your neighbor? I don't remember you talking about a neighbor our age."

"He's a little older. I think he'd be a sophomore in college if he'd gone back last fall."

"College dropout?"

"No. He's going back this fall.

"Maybe he thinks he's too old for you."

"Maybe." I don't want to get into Peter and Alyse with Natalie because—she's light and they're darkness and I so want the light. We're reaching the Hot Licks hut, so it's an easy distraction. Such great ice cream! But Peter lingers in my mind like an old friend. For a moment, I taste his lips on mine – last year on Fire Island. If things had been different, would we still be dating? I can't help but wonder. Was I just a summer dalliance for him? Or did he really care for me? And, if he did, should I be thinking about Ben now?

Ben

I pause before entering the foredeck, letting the memory wash over me. I've managed to avoid the foredeck with Captain Russell's help until tonight, but Justin, one of the other deckhands, missed the sailing and so I need to get my crap together to do my job. No cockpit for me tonight.

There are three tables here and they need a waiter. I breathe out and take my first step onto the foredeck in a year. I see Pete crouched near the far railing, Alyse crumpled in his arms, the unearthly wail he gave when he realized she had died. I pause, swallow tightly, and pick up the pitcher of water I'm supposed to be using to fill water glasses. I don't have to deal with the wine and cocktails because I'm legally not old enough yet. I step forward to the first table.

"Ben, nice to see you tonight." Dr. Lundquist has been a close friend and client of my father's accounting company for as long as I can remember. He was aboard *the Mimi* that night.

"Hi, Dr. L." I fill his wife's water glass, then his, then the glasses of the couple they're with. Behind them, an amazing sunset starts to build above the land. This is going to be harder than I expected.

"You doing okay?"

"Just remembering."

"Us too," Mrs. L says. "But it's a beautiful night and Jeff needs the business."

I nod and swallow. I move to the other tables to fill water glasses and then step down the other side of the boat, pausing to wipe my face with the back of my hand. I can't believe I'm crying. I slip into the side door by the galley and Ludmila, the chef, glances at me.

"Is it too much?" She was here that night too.

"No, I'll get over it. It just hit me for a moment."

"Yeah." She nods for a moment as if experiencing her own memories, then shakes herself and points at the rack beside me. "Grab the tray of antipasto and bread and serve it."

There's no time to indulge in grief. We have a cruise to accomplish. I deliver the first course and then the salads. The diners have big goblets of red wine and I almost wish I could gulp one down, except I know it'll make me sick and clumsy and the last thing a waiter on a sunset dinner cruise needs to be is clumsy.

After serving the entrees – chicken with rice pilaf and braised carrots, steak smothered in mushrooms with a pasta side, or shrimp alfredo with the braised carrots – I have a bit of time to pause on the side deck and think about that night. I stopped experiencing Alyse's death sometime between the salad and the entrée, but I feel the illusion of Lily standing beside me.

I feel guilty that I've been ditching her. I know I should get over it. She didn't cause what happened and I shouldn't blame her for what Pete did. And maybe now that I've met the foredeck squarely, I can stop thinking she's the source of bad dreams.

I see Shatarah clearing the entrée tables, so I head into the galley for the coffee pot. After I fill the customers' cups, I bring out their desserts.

That night, it was just hors d'oeuvres and wine. Dinner's somehow different. I've survived the night and I'll handle more. Pete's self-destructive behavior doesn't get to destroy my life.

Lily

I just passed "the spot." I met Peter there last spring. I biked on the left side of the bike path, he walked in the middle, and we both overreacted. I ended up in the bushes, bruised and shaken, and Peter seemed so kind and reasonable, made sure I got home, and took Ben's verbal assault without complaint.

Is that just how I want to remember him? I can accept that he went to a dark place afterward, but I can't find the shadows in that day more than a year ago. Am I in denial or is that the truth?

My phone buzzes in my pocket just as I near the edge of town.

JENAE– Did you get a dress for the concert?

My parents would strangle me if I spent money on a dress for a single occasion, but I did get one dress I think will look great for the concert.

LILY– I got one. It's red…so unlike me. It's about mid-thigh, off the shoulder.

JENAE– It sounds lovely. Send a picture.

My chest suddenly feels funny. It's weird. I feel almost like a guy asked me for a naked photo.

LILY– I will if you will.

"Hey, what are you doing?"

I shift my attention from my phone to Ben, who is standing near the entrance to Hot Licks, a fancy ice cream place. It seems odd that he's here. It's midweek. Shouldn't he be at work?

"I was having a conversation with a friend. What are you doing?"

"Got off a little early from work. Thought I'd get a late lunch, then I changed my mind because I didn't want to be alone. So, I decided to do ice cream instead. Want to join me?"

Jenae hasn't responded to me yet, which is weird. I stuff my phone in my back pocket. I'm not sure how I feel about Ben. He seems to have forgotten all about taking me sailing.

"I don't have a lot of money on me."

"I'm inviting you."

He runs hot and cold and I try to understand that he's still healing from our joint trauma. Maybe I'd be better off if I avoided him.

"Sure. Thanks."

I lock my bike to a nearby lamppost and he waits for me so we can walk along the pathway to the ice cream cottage. Spring is just underway, but the bedding plants already have flowers. The line is short because ice cream season just started.

"Um, I should apologize for Saturday. I should have called, but it turns out I don't have your cell and…."

It's not like he doesn't know where I live.

"Something come up?"

The guy getting ice cream in front of us casts us a friendly smile as he steps away from the Order window. Ben indicates I should order first. I get a single scoop of strawberry and Ben gets a double of something called aggregated bliss. The description sounds like rocky road.

We sit down on the bench opposite the Pick Up window. I figure he's forgotten my question.

"So, no, nothing came up…except the usual. I wanted to get together with you and then I started thinking about the bay and I couldn't sleep and then I overslept, and it just got worse from there."

"I see."

I want to understand, really, I do, but he's driving me crazy. *Make up your mind!*

"Likely excuse, right?"

"Let's just say I'm not as naïve as I was last summer."

The *creamista* calls our number, and we retrieve our ice cream. He leads the way to an out-of-the-way table surrounded by planting beds.

"Pete pull that crap on you last summer?"

"No. I told you. He tried to be a gentleman. It was Alyse, actually. I was like a fish on the line, and she controlled the reel."

"Not to speak ill of the dead or anything."

"Not to speak ill of someone who can't fight back."

He shifts, eats some ice cream, mutters under his breath.

"Not ready to forgive and forget."

"And you think *I* am?" We stare at one another over our cones.

"Alyse could be manipulative sometimes, but the more I think about it, so could Pete."

Maybe because I don't have so many episodes to think about, I think I see them more rationally. Peter could definitely be manipulative, but Alyse manipulated him way more than he manipulated others.

"I think he and I got together because she thought I'd be a compliant girlfriend who wouldn't challenge her, and he wanted to get close to you through me."

He pauses with his ice cream part way to his mouth. His lips tighten.

"So somehow it was my fault?"

"I didn't say that. They made decisions without our permission. But, for him, it was all about reconciling with you. Even not drinking – it was more about what you thought of him rather than what was good for him."

He sits there a moment, jaw tight.

"Don't you think I know that and feel guilty every day for failing him?"

He stands up and walks away, barely pausing as he drops his half-eaten cone in the garbage as he passes the bin. I don't follow because I suspect I'll just make it worse. My ice cream is melting, so I do eventually get up and throw it away, using my napkin to wipe my streaming eyes and blow my nose.

I'm unlocking my bike when a text comes into my phone. I pull it out of my pocket and see a brown-haired smiling girl about my age. I still don't recognize her, but she said we weren't close because of Alyse's jealousy. I said I'd send her a photo if she sent me one, so I go to snap a selfie, but my eyes look like I've been crying.

LILY– out and about right now. I'll send a photo when I get home.

I mount my bike and head toward home – forgetting what I came to town for and ignoring the vibration of my phone as I peddle. I don't know how I fix what just happened between Ben and me and I care about that.

When I get home, I take a photo of the red dress on its hanger, thus solving my dilemma of feeling somehow coerced into sending photos of myself over the Internet.

Peaches

Peter
December

I open one eye a crack because the smell of food invades my nose. Breakfast consists of pancakes with canned peaches. *Yummo!* Except, I'm not hungry. I don't remember the last time I ate, but I've never been less hungry in my life. I close my eye and try to go back to sleep. It's not hard.

"Hey, no, you don't." It's the Hispanic guy from Ad Seg again. His face swims into my vision because every proximity alert I have goes off. "Stay awake. You eat this breakfast, or they'll make an orderly put a tube down your throat to get some food into you."

I suspect that's going to feel a lot like having my stomach pumped. I feel like hurling at just the memory. Maybe it was hepatitis, but I wasn't hungry for days after the pumping. I open my eyes and push myself further up in the bed. I've been here in the infirmary for…a while…but I've been unable to respond to much, barely aware of what was going on around me. I didn't care. I felt wrapped in cotton wool and trapped, and it was only mildly interesting that I couldn't respond. I still don't care.

The tech pulls up a chair.

"Sorry, but I gotta watch you."

It feels like I'm trying to move through molasses. My hand shakes while I make the supreme effort to slice off a piece of pancake and put it in my mouth where it has all the flavor of sawdust. There's water, so I wash the bite down and then concentrate on cutting another bit and chewing it. When I've eaten four pieces, I'm all out of water and I put down the plasticware and push the bedside table away.

"Nope. You eat the peaches at least."

He pushes the table back toward me. The peaches take less effort to get down even though I hate the mushy quality of canned. After I've finished them, I honestly feel slightly better, but I'm also stuffed. How long has it been since I've eaten?

"Can I be done now?"

"Yeah." He pushes the table to the side. "So, I'm Luis Alba, mental health tech."

I think I'm supposed to say something at this point, but I don't remember what.

"Hi, my name's Peter Wyngate." Alba's adopted a Long Island accent. "I'm the dumb-assed burbite who rang Jamal Tyler's bell and ended his unbroken streak of successful rapes."

I'm not proud of that. It's something else to feel guilty about.

"Leave me alone."

I close my eyes and try to go back to sleep. Luis uses the bed control to bring me all the way to sitting. I blink at him.

"What the hell?"

"You've been here a week. They tasked me with getting you up and functioning before they evaluate you and send you to Kirby."

I have no idea what he's talking about, and he can see that.

"You really are a fish. Kirby is a correctional facility for the criminally insane. If they decide we can't treat your depression here, they'll transfer you there. And it's looking like we can't treat your depression here."

The words "criminally insane" have gotten my attention. I'm a criminal now. I don't feel insane, but my dead sister has been visiting me for weeks now, so maybe I am.

"What difference does it make?" *A prison is a prison, after all.*

"Ah, yes. Difference. Do you really want to spend the next 25 years in a loony bin without much chance of parole or would you rather stay here and get out in five?"

Okay, that's math and I can do that even if I do feel like I'm drowning in molasses. I doubt there's any chance I'm getting out of here in five years, regardless of where I'm housed, but I visited my mother in a mental hospital a few times. I'm pretty sure the crazy people in the resort-like facility were better controlled than the crazy people in the state hospital for the criminally insane will be. I've watched *One Flew Over the Cuckoo's Nest.* But there is still the issue of being so damned depressed I can barely function.

"Look, I know you feel exhausted right now, but the meds should be kicking in soon and your 30 days are almost up. So, you need to start moving again."

My sponsor Rick used to say that being honest helped. I think T and Janice echoed that sentiment. So I decide to try it here.

"I don't want to."

Alba rubs his full lips together, then shrugs.

"Well, then they'll transfer you to Kirby, and with your family history of bipolar, they'll probably give you ECT as the first line of treatment. That's Electric Convulsive Therapy. It might realign your neural pathways enough to break you out of the depression, but … I suspect you don't want to remember your recent past, but you might want a short term memory someday. Kirby turns a lot of patients into goldfish."

I'm still wrapped in a wet wool blanket, but he's hitting me where I live. I don't want to be my mother. I've tested what ECT has done to her and she's mostly still there, but she also doesn't seem to remember much of Alyse's infancy. No, I can't think about Alyse. I grasp for the only other topic in my brain. I don't really want to live right now. I'd plunge the breakfast fork into my wrists and bleed out in front of Alba but it's plastic, so I'm pretty sure I will just break the fork.

"I want to die."

He hesitates a moment, letting the words sink in the space between us.

"Yeah." When I only stare at the table for a moment, he sighs. "Can't really blame you there."

"But you won't let me."

"You'll agree on the other side of this depression." I shake my head. "Seriously, kid. You'll change your mind. Maybe this depression is your first rodeo, but it ain't mine. I've seen lots of guys change their minds."

I can't even begin to imagine that. I don't want to be my mother, but it's so hard. The Serenity Prayer trickles into my slowed-down brain. God grant me the serenity to accept the things I cannot change, the strength to change the things I can….

"How do I change it?"

Alba has a white smile framed by dark skin.

"Well, now you're asking the right questions. We're just going to sit here for half an hour and talk and this afternoon when I get back from my rounds, you're going to walk the length of the ward with me. If you seem to be trying, they'll give you some time before the evaluation. So just do as I say, and I'll get you through this."

I don't want to, but the alternative seems a whole lot crappier, so I answer his questions. My brain barely works.

"You grieving your sister and it must suck to do it alone."

I blink at him, slowly turning it over in my head. Yeah, it sucks that I have nobody to grieve with.

"You missed Thanksgiving, but it's the holidays. If you pull yourself together, you could have visitors by Christmas."

My eyes start to close. I'm so tired.

"Keep awake. Who might come visit? Anyone?"

It won't be Dad. Pretty sure it won't be Ben. I didn't even bother to put the Andersons on my visiting list. There's Joel, Tilly and….

"My grandparents."

"That's good. So, they're still talking to you?"

"Yeah. They know I can't take it back." Tears well up in my scratchy eyes.

"Pull that together. I know it hurts, but nobody here cares."

I swallow hard and scrub my eyes. My counselor T in rehab did years here and he said tears were a weakness. You have to suck it up or you'll make yourself a target.

"Nobody else is going to say this, but I will. I'm sorry you have to grieve your sister alone. You can't change that. You can't hope for that to be different. You can only accept it." I swallow again and nod. "So, what happened in Ad Seg?"

I blink at him, not knowing the slang. He sees that.

"Administrative segregation – where you were before. Things went bad for you, so what happened?"

I try to remember the days I spent there, but it's mostly a void.

"Nothing."

"But something took you from a little depressed to catatonic."

"What?" I know what *catatonic* means. I grew up watching my mother locked in it between her manic phases where she'd redecorate the house and have sex with Sam in the guest room. Was I that bad?

"Kid, they pulled you out when you hadn't moved or talked in two days, and you wet yourself. The only reason you're talking to me now is that the antidepressants are working. So, you spiraled. What happened?"

I shrug. Like, I want to talk about any of this with strangers. Then he puts the card on my lap. After my exhausted brain takes a moment to catch up, I start shaking very hard.

"Who lives in Florida and is using your former home address in New York?"

What?

"I don't…."

"Your sister obviously didn't send this card three weeks ago. She's been dead for five months." That pronouncement feels like a knife to my solar plexus. I literally stop breathing. "So, who lives in Florida and would do this to you?"

There's a huge lump in my throat and there's no way I can talk.

"So, I don't have access to the Internet, but the chaplain does, and I asked him to do some searching. He tells me your mother lives in Florida with her husband and that her family also owns properties there. You talk to her since the wreck?" I shake my head. "You *know* this didn't come from your sister, don't you?"

I want to say "of course", but I know that's a lie and I promised myself I wouldn't lie anymore.

"Ah, kid, you've got the guilts bad, don't you?"

I sigh, nod, swallowing tears I'm barely keeping from falling. Alba picks up the card and runs it by my face.

"This is designed to put you right where you are. Don't give the bitch that kind of power over you."

"I k-killed her daughter."

"You killed your sister. Your mother didn't lose more than you lost and if *you* tried to send something like this to *her* the *jefes* would stop it from being mailed out and you'd end up in the real hole. But they ain't gonna protect you, so you gotta protect yourself."

"How?" I sound terrified. Of a woman who is thousands of miles away and a card that's not wider than my hand is long.

"I ain't you, but I'd not read the card. I'd tear it up and throw it in the trash. But you're going to get out of here someday, so maybe you're going to want the guards to keep it in your personal items so you can get a restraining order against her."

I'm not so numb now. I feel kind of raw. But before I can say I need a break, he sets the larger envelope on top of the card.

"You drew the hard hand on family, I see."

I shrug because to talk about it might make me cry again. His gaze flicks over me.

"We'll talk about this some other time. Go ahead and take a nap and I'll be back to make sure you eat lunch and go for a stroll.

I yawn and close my eyes. I really think I won't fall asleep, but I wake up hours later without any awareness of time passing.

May

Ben

The dream sweeps me before I can protest and I'm rushing toward destruction before I know I'm dreaming.

*The blue speed boat heads straight for us as the sunset blooms across the sky, Pete's hair ruffling in the breeze…*and I sit up in the dark room, breathing hard.

The air conditioning washes cold air across my overheated skin. I throw off the blankets and swing my legs off the mattress.

It's been a while since I dreamt about that night, but I guess it was inevitable after arguing with Lily. I shouldn't interact with her at all. It's not good for my mental health.

I don't hear anyone getting up to check on me, so I assume I didn't scream. I pull on a pair of shorts and ease out into the hall. It's quiet, so I head toward the stairs, stepping over the place where the floor creaks. The third step down groans too, so I step over that. The kitchen is lightly illuminated with a night light, which is new since I left home. I guess the parents decided if they were buying one for Wes' room, they might want to place them throughout the house.

I pull a jug of milk out of the fridge and as the door closes, I hear a thumping noise and look in that direction.

"Hey." Grandpa Jack limps all the way into the kitchen. "Can I get a glass of that?"

"Sure."

I reach down two jelly jars.

"I was going to warm mine. Do you…."

"Sounds good." He lowers himself into a chair by the table. "Trouble sleeping?"

I put the two jars in the microwave before I answer.

"I probably shouldn't have slept here tonight."

"Aren't you planning to move back?"

"Yeah…maybe."

"Your room's right above my bed. I wasn't asleep or I might not have heard your bedsprings. You have a lot of nightmares?"

"Not lately."

"What set you off?"

"Not sure. Maybe no reason."

"Yeah. I have nightmares when I eat pickles and chocolate before bed."

Who does that? The microwave dings. I stir the milk and give it another minute.

"You think you're onto something?"

"I think you're still healing. That goes in waves."

He's not lying, but I'm tired of going under the big waves.

"I saw you and the neighbor girl at Hot Licks earlier in the week. She's a sweet kid. She what's triggering you."

Probably, but I'm not about to admit that. I don't want it to be true.

"Pete sent me a letter."

We watch the timer tick off the seconds.

"What does he have to say for himself?"

"I don't know." We can't really see each other's eyes in this light, but I suspect he's staring at me.

"Chickened out opening it?"

The microwave dings and I take the jelly jars out and sit down in the chair across from him.

"I guess that's true. I'm not sure I'm ready to read his excuses."

My grandfather has counseled a lot of people in his thirty-some years of sobriety. He knows how to take his time. He's been helpful for me this winter.

"How do you know he'll make excuses?"

"I was friends with him for 15 years. It's what he does."

He sips some milk.

"Then why do you feel conflicted about not reading the letter?"

I'm not touching that with a 10-foot pole. I sip some milk. He finally buys a clue that I'm not going to answer.

"I'm worried about you."

"I'm good. I'm getting better. It's just – I don't want to revisit it with Pete."

He sips some milk before answering me.

"And that's a choice you're allowed to make. He's painted himself into the corner he's in and he can't expect forgiveness from you or anyone else."

"So why is he writing me?"

He crosses his arms and rubs his chin.

"I had to go apologize and make amends to a bunch of people when I got sober. Some people told me to get bent before I ever opened my mouth. And I made living amends and let it go. I see them occasionally and I just avoid them because I know it won't do anything good."

"That sucks."

"Yeah, but there've been a few people who have come to me and say they should have listened to me years ago and *they* apologized to *me*. We aren't friends, but we're not enemies and I feel good about that."

"I don't care if he feels good."

Grandpa Jack nods, reaches for his milk, takes a sip.

"Then why are you conflicted about not reading the letter?"

I swallow a gulp of milk. Warm milk is meant to be sipped and I must hold my breath a second to keep from coughing.

"He made me watch her die. He doesn't deserve my forgiveness."

"No, he doesn't. But you deserve to let that rage go so you can sleep nights."

He finishes his milk before I can think of anything to say.

"Reading his letter won't give me that."

"You sure? Because I've lived a lot longer than you, kid, and I've learned that closure comes from confronting what bothers me."

"I—don't know. Can we stop now?"

"Sure. You can't unhear it."

I sigh. I need to change the subject.

"How's your foot."

"It aches and this dang soft-cast itches. Foolish old man, stepping in a hole."

He was mowing his lawn this morning – er, or yesterday morning and he thought he'd broken it, but it's just a stress-fracture. He can't drive for 72 hours, so Dad brought him here for the weekend.

"I was headed here to swap ice bags."

He acknowledges the cooler pack sitting on the table. I pick it up and swap it for one of the three in the freezer.

"Thanks. So, I'm headed back to bed. Seems to me, kiddo, you should do the same."

I nod.

"I'm going to finish my milk, but yeah, then I will."

"Good night."

He rises slowly from his chair, secures his ice pack under one arm, and starts toward the den.

"Oh, can you--?"

"I'll get your glass."

"Thanks."

He leaves me in the quiet of the late night and I just sit there listening to the house and contemplating a letter I don't want to read.

Lily

Genesis must hear my footsteps on the gravel driveway because she looks over her shoulder and sits back on her heels to wait for me to get to her. I step off the gravel onto the softer parking area and then up onto the patio slate at the arbor.

"Hey, Lily. How you doing, honey?"

"I'm good. Mom wanted me to bring you some muffins." I hold out the bag. Genesis stands up, wiping the dirt off her hands.

"Your mother is great." She smells the contents of the bag. "Cinnamon! Have coffee with me!"

She leads the way to the table in the midst of her spring garden, where an insulated press awaits.

"Tim got called into the office, so half my pot of coffee was going to be wasted."

I'm not really a coffee drinker, but there's milk in a thermos, so it's not so bad. She offers me sugar and cocoa. I take the cocoa. It tastes like a mocha.

"How's school?"

"I did my testing this week. Pretty sure I passed them. Everybody else goes to school for another few weeks. What are you doing here?"

"Prepping the soil for my bedding plants. You said you wanted some tulip and lily bulbs last year. I'll drop some over later in the day."

"Thank you so much."

"No problem." We both look toward a noise on the other side of the privacy fence where the main driveway is. A tall man is getting into a Mercedes. He backs up to the garages by the cottage he's living in and then pulls out of the driveway. The driveway needs more gravel, I think. I can't believe Alan Wyngate hasn't noticed his property is deteriorating.

"What's it like having Alan Wyngate as your neighbor?"

"You mean, what's it like for my landlord to be my neighbor? He's quiet, doesn't really bug us, and that's not all that bad. Poor man is working his way through hell."

"Yeah." I don't know what to do with the big hole in my chest, so I try to fill it with a little coffee.

"Did I tell you? Tim found the property we want to build on. This will be our last summer here."

"Oh, that's – good and sad at the same time. We'll miss you."

"We'll miss you too, but it's time. We've enjoyed this house, but we always planned to have a place of our own before we start a family and I'm pregnant."

"Oh, that's great. When?"

"December. We won't be in the house until next spring, but there's a great space outside the bedroom for a nursery here. Governor Wyngate was a great landlord, but his management company's been slow to respond and…well, I love the house and the garden, but he's never going to sell, so it's time to move on."

I hadn't really thought about that. This is family property. Peter didn't seem to know who would inherit it and now…who do you leave it to when you have no kids? Would Peter come back? Would he be welcome to come back? His situation must be so complicated. Genesis sees I'm struggling with something.

"How do you forgive someone who killed your daughter, even when it's your son?"

I nod. Genesis places her hand on her belly. She doesn't look pregnant.

"I hope and pray I'll never face such a dilemma. I'll pray for you as well."

"Thank you. I'm going to miss you."

"We won't be moving until next spring. Lots of people have come and gone since we moved here."

"That's right. You rented rooms."

"We did. And Matthew lived in the caretaker's cottage. The three little houses used to be rented too."

"Why are they empty now?"

"I don't think Governor Wyngate had the time for it while he was in office, and I think he doesn't care now. Who is he giving it to? Tim said he thought Alan might sell him this house when he first made the offer, but then he came back and said 'no'. It's family property. He owns it, but his parents still have a say."

Again, are Peter's grandparents looking out for him? I'm so conflicted. Will I ever break free of his orbit? He's like a black hole, sucking us all toward him. Or was Alyse the black hole and Peter was trapped in the event horizon too? I just don't know.

"I hope whoever follows us takes care of the garden. There are some wonderful perennials here that might have been started two centuries ago."

"And the fountain. I always love that thing." It's not going right now.

"Tim will fire it up this weekend. Pretty sure it wasn't here when this was a carriage house, but I think it might have been in front of the mansion."

The only thing I remember about the mansion is Alyse's scoffing at it. She'd called it "the old house." Peter had been non-committal. He loved old architecture, but he didn't know much about the old house except that his mother hated it. These days it's a bed-and-breakfast, a white behemoth of a house across the creek.

"I'm doing a landscaping design this summer where the clients want something like this. Way bigger though. Blue stone instead of slate, a river of perennials, the arbor. I always wanted to do a pergola here, but there really wasn't room, but this project will let me do that. Are you looking for a parttime job this summer?"

"Maybe. I'd have to talk to Mom because of Bram."

"If she says 'yes', I'd love to hire you as an assistant. I'll have a crew, but I really need someone who can do some of the running for me."

"I think that would be a fun way to spend the summer."

"I just don't want to lose contact with you and your family. You are amazing people."

I flush with embarrassment and Genesis laughs and moves onto another subject. It seems strange to have a friend in her 30s, but our mutual interest in gardening brought us together after Ben suggested I introduce myself. She let me come cry on her shoulder through this difficult winter and I know I wouldn't be feeling nearly so stable without Genesis. If there are any amazing people living on this street, it's her and Tim.

Ben

Although I technically work for Captain Russell only on weekends, this Tuesday night is a special thing because Melody went into labor this morning. They did a midwife delivery, so he's needed at home. I'm not in charge. He's got a 1st mate – Jack, who has been around almost as long as I can remember – but Captain Russell's departure left him down a hand, so Jack called me.

Melody Russell's plan is to provide various types of cruises, often around the sunset, but sometimes during the day or later in the evening. I hardly even thought about it when Jack rang me at work to ask if I could cover tonight. The sun was still fully up when I got here. Tonight, it's just snacks and beer and a handful of tourists. I'm doing what I did that night – counting heads. There are 12 people. Twelve people came aboard, and I haven't lost any so far. I don't have to worry about taking trays around, although I do clear the beer bottles from time to time.

I'm having a good night, hardly any memories of that night. The sunset is still a porcelain blue with layers of pink and purple just developing. For a moment, I pause to suck in the beauty. And then Merrick Winters comes into view, his red-and-white sail against the sunset just like it had been that night.

I hear the roar of the speedboat as I pull Lily back from the railing. A shudder runs through the old fishing boat as Alyse cartwheels over the railing and slides across the decking. I feel the metallic taste of rage fill my mouth as I'm watching Pete mourn Alyse.

Then I'm playing *The Walking Dead* and every zombie bears Pete's face.

I step into the companionway above the galley, suck in a deep breath, and scream it silently into the emptiness.

I do this several times, not holding in, but keeping it silent, until the pressure building within me releases and I lean against the bulkhead, wiping tears from my cheeks. Lily comes to my mind. She seems be better equipped to handle the tragedy that Alyse became in all our lives. And maybe healing comes from facing what hurts so much.

Lily

I take the shore road as a shortcut, not wanting to be biking after dark. The sun slants across the macadam, dappled here and there as it filters through trees. The warm air isn't yet cooling and sweat clings to my skin as I peddle.

There's water to my left. The air feels heavy with humidity as the sky turns beautifully blue with streaks of pink and purple. I pause to look over the bay and marvel at the beauty of the Long Island Sound wrapped in amazing color. I want to paint this. I stop my bike to pull out my phone to snap a photo of this inspiring image. The shutter barely opens before an image wavers into the viewfinder.

I stare at the red-and-white sail, suddenly transported back to that night almost a year ago -- Alyse broken and dying in Peter's arms, him helpless to bring her back. I wipe tears from my cheeks, but they're wet again in a moment. Alyse will always be dead. There's nothing I can do about that.

My mind fills with something I read last night, and I grow still as I consider the message God has to give me.

"In the same way, the Spirit helps us in our weakness, for we do not know how we should pray, but the Spirit himself intercedes for us with inexpressible groanings. And he who searches our hearts knows the mind of the Spirit, because the Spirit intercedes on behalf of the saints according to God's will. And we know that all things work together for good for those who love God, who are called according to his purpose, because those whom he foreknew he also predestined to be conformed to the image of his Son, that his Son would be the firstborn among many brothers and sisters. And those he predestined, he also called; and those he called, he also justified; and those he justified, he also glorified." Romans 8:26-30

My tears dry as I consider not why that verse came to my mind, but why my mind pulled up the entire passage. Yes, the Spirit speaks for us when we don't even know what we should be praying. And, yes, I believe God can turn all things – even things as bad as Alyse dying – to the good of those who love God because He has called us to His purpose.

It's the predestined part that puzzles me. Who am I supposed to be thinking of? And how do I know?

I'll have to spend some time in focused prayer about it. For now, I stare at the blue and scarlet colors of the sky mixing together like good and bad weaving life's story together into a beautiful but imperfect mosaic.

My phone buzzes in my back pocket and I pull it out to read Ben's text.

BEN – Would you like to go sailing Saturday morning?

Thank you, Jesus. It's You, right?

Post-Traumatic Stress

Peter
January

All cells look alike, but Luis' cell has been personalized. He's a trustee. He doesn't have to have a cellmate, but he takes in kids like me. I'm a little scared I might have to pay for this privilege. I so far haven't gotten a gaydar vibe from him, but he's rescuing me from being treated like a mental patient and I keep having nightmares, so he has to want something…doesn't he?

I scored right below the line for going to Kirby. I'm going to stay in Sing Sing, but the original plan was to send me to ICP – the in-house mental ward. Luis, not wishing to see me warehoused for a long sentence, volunteered to direct my reentry into the general population. Some of the other mental health techs had said this is something Luis has done for dozens of younger inmates over the last decade or so.

Dorph's cell had been pretty utilitarian, but Alba has a television on the desk and books on the shelf above the desk.

I learned from Dorph that seniority determines who gets the top bunk, so I'm back to sleeping curled up so my feet don't go through the bars. I put my mattress on the lower metal shelf and set the laundry bag on top to deal with later.

"Make your bed." Luis speaks as soon as I straighten.

I'm already tired from walking from the infirmary. Near as I can tell, I didn't eat for two weeks. I arrived here thin from withdrawal and now I'm downright skinny from not eating. I can see that's an argument that won't work with Luis, but I start to open my mouth to plead my case anyway. He shakes his head.

"Rules, man. You follow the rules of my house like I'm your daddy. You followed your daddy's rules, right?"

I sigh. Does he really want an answer? He's waiting, so….

"Did *you* follow *your* father's rules?"

"*Mi padre* was a drunk and drug dealer who ordered me to go to Clinton where we killed two people, so…yeah."

Wow, that's dark! I sigh again and rub a hand through my frowsy hair.

"*I* might not be here if I'd followed *his* rules."

Luis's laughter surprises me.

"Good insight."

I've spent the last month sick and depressed. The first antidepressant helped but messed with my liver. I turned yellow again. The second antidepressant didn't seem to do anything, and I retreated into catatonia again. The antidepressant I'm on now seems to work, but I don't feel right and sometimes my body feels really weird – almost electrified and I need a laxative to counteract its drying effects.

"Make your bed. I ain't your maid."

He climbs onto the upper bunk and sits tailor-fashion so I have room to move. I suck at bedmaking, a fact I see written on his face when he climbs down to inspect my work.

"Lessons tomorrow. You get the bottom part of the locker." It's next to the toilet. The bottom half is empty. Fortunately, this toilet slides into the wall. Alba's got the coveralls he's not wearing hanging on a hook, next to his winter coat. The shelf has neatly folded underwear. He grabs the handle of the bin under my bunk. There's a stock of commissary items and some personal clothing in neat piles. There's some space if I want to store anything…if I have anything to store. He pushes it back into place because he knows I don't have anything else.

"Ask permission before you take. Got it?" I nod. "Don't burn my eyes. You gotta pee, say so and I'll look the other way. Same with taking a dump. I ain't gay and I don't want to see your dick. Same with me. Don't look."

"I'm not gay either."

"I kind of got that when you bashed Tyler's head in."

I remember Disciplinary Officer Rockland warning me to keep it to myself, so I don't say it was an accident.

"Put your clothes away and I'll show you around."

I know he won't let me lie down so I do what I'm told. I've got two green coveralls and two sets of laundry-stained underwear that I'd throw away in the real world. I'm wearing one set, so I hang up the other. When I pull my Big Book and the Bible out of my bag, he looks at his shelf of books.

"Last guy wasn't much of a reader. I'll make some room."

I didn't expect that, but I don't argue. Frankly, I'm too tired to do more than what I'm told. This prison block is pretty old and vast. It's the largest building I've ever been in. I say that to Luis as he puts some books in the bin.

"A Block is a little bigger, but yeah, it's big." He shrugs. He's used to it. A Block totally awed me, but I can't go there for a while because that's Tyler's territory. Luis hasn't told me how he's doing, but a couple of prisoners in the infirmary told me Tyler's still in the real hospital. That doesn't sound good, and I do feel bad about it.

Luis shows me the prisoner laundry and a little kitchen used by the trustees. I'm not allowed to use it, he explains, but I can ask trustees like him to make me snacks and some of them will do it just because they like you. I also can't use the laundry, but I can arrange with some prisoners to do my personal laundry.

"They're called porters. There's this guy, Tran. He will do your personal laundry for free."

"For free?" Not that I have anything personal to launder, but it's weird behavior for this place, I think. "Why?"

"Don't know. He won't say. He's got outside money and 30 years, so he's found something to do. If you want to spend some money, I suggest underwear. It's surprising how human you feel when you've got clean underwear every day that ain't been worn by anyone else."

It's the simple things, I guess, that get you through. I don't have any money, so it'll be a while before I can take his advice. We continue the tour.

There's a small workout area with free weights chained to the wall and a bench so repaired with duct tape that it's upholstered in the silver material. Again, it's a trustee area, so I can't use it and don't feel like it now.

We move into the general population area. He points out the cameras and where they aren't. I know I'll never go where there are no cameras again. I suspect they're here to keep the guards from abusing prisoners, but they also capture inmates attacking one another.

We return to the cell and Luis pulls out an envelope. I feel a gut punch.

"It ain't that woman." I spent Christmas in the infirmary, but Luis didn't lie to me. A card came from "Alyse", but he had the guards put it unread in my personal effects. Because Joel is my attorney, he visited me in the infirmary, and I asked him if he'd just hang onto them. I'm not sure how to deal with it, but for now, I'm protecting myself. All similar correspondence will go to him. Luis promises he'll tell me, so I won't be surprised by dozens of hate letters when…if…I ever get out of here.

"You know Jack Anderson?" It takes me a moment to work through Anderson being Ben's last name and Jack being Ben's grandfather. He said he'd write, but I figured he was just trying to be kind to the kid headed to prison.

"Yeah. He's kind of a friend."

"So, you can…."

He pauses as the overhead booms through the block.

"That's your number, isn't it?"

They repeat the announcement and I look at my bracelet.

"Yeah. What do I do?"

"Well, leave the envelope on the desk because you can't take it into the visiting area. It's Contact, so you must have put whoever it is on the list. Any idea who it is?"

"There's only four people on my list. One just wrote me a letter."

"You okay with this?"

"I guess. It's humiliating, but…." I sigh.

"I'll show you."

Dorph didn't give me any help, but Luis seems like a nicer guy. We walk to the guards station, which is a weird collection of cells that are closed off from the rest of the block. A guard at the desk behind the bars looks up and asks me who I am. I guess they know Luis. Remembering what Rockland said about my last name, I read my number off my wristband.

"Prisoner 80831, you got visitors. Come with me."

"I got work, so don't sleep until after dinner." Luis reverses directions as the cell door opens. When I freeze, uncertain of my next allowable move, the guard gestures impatiently for me to move forward, so I do. I'm still separated from him by a wall of bars. The first gate closes behind me and a split second later the second set opens. Then I come to a line of other prisoners waiting before a serious steel door. When it finally opens a few minutes later, we set out in a line down a long corridor. The guy behind me touches my rear and I glance over my shoulder and try to look mean. He's a fat guy in the same green jumpsuit I'm wearing.

"Hey there, beautiful."

I studied acting for dance, but I doubt I can look scary without looking ridiculous, so instead, I turn back to see where I'm going. I'll deal with it if he touches me again. I have to, don't I? How do I take care of it? I have no idea.

We're getting closer to a gate, and I feel this curious emotion – like there might be freedom on the other side, but I know that's not true…and then he touches my butt again. I turn to say he might remember I gave someone brain damage and find the guy behind him nudging him on the shoulder.

"Cut it out. You know who he is, right?"

"The fish?" The fat guy frowns.

"Connected. He also bashed in Tyler's head, so cut it out."

The fat guy squints at me.

"Too bad. You sure are beautiful."

"I'm not gay."

Fat guy and my rescuer laugh.

"What difference does *that* make?" My confusion over Fat Guy's question must show on my face.

"If you can't be with the one you love, kid, you love the one you're with." The tall one shrugs. "But Alba's got morals, so you ain't gonna have a house spouse. But, ya know, if you ever need anything…."

He winks. It's not the first man ever to hit on me. I strongly favor my mother's side of the family and they're beautiful Greeks. But I get absolutely no gay vibe from the tall one. The fat one, sure, but the tall one…. How long does a man have to be in here before he no longer cares if his sex partner suits his orientation?

The gate slides open, and I follow the guy ahead of me. This is new territory for me, and I suddenly feel out of sync and overwhelmed. I've been propositioned by gay men before, but I already know there are men in here who don't care if I'm not gay. I can barely function through the process of going into Visiting. There's rules that I agree to without actually hearing what's said. Most rules here seem to be posted on the walls, so I probably didn't need to hear what the female corrections officer said.

They're waiting at a table that has three chairs. Mike and Lucy are already seated, so I aim for the seat on the opposite side of the table. Before I get there, they stand.

"Hey." Mike envelopes me in a hug. I try to return it, but my arms feel heavy. Same when Lucy hugs me. As I take my seat, the walls of the room become painted in sunset colors.

"You lost weight." That'll happen when you don't have an appetite.

"I'm okay." That sounds like a lie, so now I have to explain myself. "My liver enzymes were up for a bit so I wasn't hungry, but that's under control again." It's not the whole truth, but I don't want to worry them about something they can't control.

"You need anything?" Mike looks concerned.

Freedom? But that's not on offer, so I shrug. Alyse materializes behind them, and I look away to try and banish the hallucination.

"How are you guys doing?"

"Good." Mike frowns as if something disturbs him. Does he sense her behind him? "Holidays without you were a little weird."

I lower my head in shame. Alyse wasn't there either. She glares at me from behind them.

"I'm sorry."

"We know you are." Lucy holds out a hand and I take it. Her eyes glimmer for a second, but she doesn't allow herself to cry.

"Um…the house sold." Mike looks like he wishes he hadn't said it.

"Dad and Tilly move to Albany, then?"

They exchange glances and then Lucy sighs.

"Well, your dad's in Albany, but probably not for much longer. He's decided to resign."

I hadn't heard that. The latest news I heard was at least a month old. In my depression, I haven't really cared.

"I guess I trashed his approval ratings. Something else to be sorry for."

"Those were recovering." Mike nods to himself like he believes it. "He's having a hard time with it all. Grieving—well, grieving you both."

I'm sure the disownment helped him cope. I don't say that. I don't want to put them in the middle. I know I earned it. It still hurts. I stuff my free hand between my knees and pinch the flesh of my inner thigh. The pain helps.

"I don't know what to do about that."

"Nobody expects you to do anything about it, Peter. You should just be aware."

"Prisoner 80831, hands in view at all times."

I'm starting to know my number and I let go of Lucy's hand to bring both of mine to the edge of the table.

"They said we could hold hands." Lucy's confused.

"I think we can, but mine have to be visible at all times and this one wasn't." I barely lift my right hand. "How's Tilly?"

"She hasn't been to visit?"

"I'm told she tried when I was in the infirmary. I didn't really feel up to seeing her and they weren't going to force me when I was sick." Crushed by depression that day I barely registered that I was missing a visit from someone I'd want to see if I could.

"You haven't tried to call her?"

"The admin had her listed as one of my victims at first, so removed her number from my call sheet." I found that out when I tried to call her. I haven't put it back yet. Not sure if I'm ready to talk with her. I shrug. Alyse dances *pas de chat* by the next table over. I clench my fist so tight I feel my nails pierce my palm.

"She wouldn't be able to come right now. She and I took a European river cruise in November and your father gave her a world cruise for Christmas. She'll be gone nine months or so."

"Avoiding a legal separation, right?"

They both look anywhere except at me, but eventually Mike makes eye contact.

"What's going on with them is not your fault. Your actions might have revealed the cracks in their foundation, but the problems already existed."

I sigh. I'm going to feel guilty anyway. Right now, *everything* is my fault. Luis and the staff psychologist both told me that's normal right now and I'll have to get over it eventually so I can function.

"World cruise sounds interesting. She didn't get to do much traveling, taking care of us."

Damn, I'm about to cry. I blink hard to prevent it. Lucy takes my hand again.

"This place is pretty depressing, isn't it?"

I look around the Visiting room. It's at least got light streaming in from the high windows.

"Yeah, but I'd be depressed anyway, so…."

We sit in silence for too long for my comfort.

"Anything they can do to help you?" Mike's eyes glint with appraisal.

"They put me on antidepressants. It's a process, but I think I'm less depressed than I was in the beginning."

"Is there anything we can do to help?"

I shrug because I've got nothing to say.

"Let us know." Lucy's tone is firm. I nod, far less firmly.

The silence that follows is painful. The sun comes in the high windows and bounces off the walls, brightening the blue of Lucy's eyes like a beacon. That I don't feel hope is a clinical curiosity to me.

"What's going on with everybody else?"

Mike tells a funny Bosco story. He's a dog, but yellow Labs are such goofballs. I'm not really feeling like smiling, but they get a few obligatory grins out of me as Alyse dances behind them. I don't want them to worry. I've caused them enough pain.

Finally, my hour is up, and they're escorted out while I line up to go back to the block. Only there's more involved going the other way and some of it is horrible. It's not just the inmates who want to get in your backside. It's the guards too and I suspect fighting back against them will end up in a deep dark hole for years. Because it's my first time, the guard explains they have to check me for contraband and if I don't fight it will all go quicker. My body is no longer my own and I want to scream.

Luis went to work while I was gone, but he left the letter on the desk. It's a single page of stationery covered in the curvy loops that come so naturally to Jack Anderson's generation. Fortunately, I can read cursive, which a lot of people my age can't.

> Peter –
>
> I kind of expected you to give me a call sooner than this, so I figured I'd write and see how you're doing. I hope you're dwelling on the Serenity Prayer and going to 12 Step groups. I don't know that sobriety will make it ALL worth it, but hopefully it'll make some of it worth it.
>
> I filled out a contact visiting form and got a card back. I'm thinking I'll come up sometime in March. Your birthday's on the 17th, right? If your folks are coming, let me know and I'll pick another day. I just don't want you to think nobody cares, because there are people out here pulling for you. **Jack**

Wow, he addressed me like I was a friend. Jack. Can I get used to that? I don't know, so I fold the letter into the envelope. He's not who I want to see, but he's better than no one, I guess. I'm tired and want to lie down, but dinner will be soon, and I promised Luis I'd eat. I stand to reach down the Big Book but then someone looms on the other side of the bars that form the front of the cells. I don't know this guy and that concerns me, but he stops at the threshold.

"Those your parents in Visiting?" That's a weird question. Maybe he was in the Visiting room. There

were so many people I didn't know there."The guy didn't look like your Pops." Right, they've seen my father on television because he's the governor.

"They're my grandparents."

He nods, his dreds bouncing up and down.

"So, here's the thing – you owe us for Tyler. We expect payment. Not a lot of us have access to cash, but I bet you have outside resources."

I stare at him. I'm alone and I have no money in my commissary account. I don't even have belongings.

"You hear what I'm saying, man? Your grandmother wears nice shoes and that was a cashmere sweater, right?"

Maybe. I wasn't evaluating their clothing. I was too busy trying not to respond to the Alyse hallucination.

"You hear me, man?"

"Yeah, but…I don't have any money. My father disowned me."

"Oh, boo-hoo. Ask your grandparents."

I hear someone down the hall say something and he moves along. A moment later a Corrections Officer appears at the door of the cell.

"He trying to shake you down?" He's Hispanic and you can hear an underlying flavor of Puerto Rico in his Spanish Harlem accent.

I want to say 'yes', but a dozen prison movies flicker through my mind. *Snitches get stitches.*

"Yeah, you're not going to answer that. Good instincts." He smiles at me. "But here's the thing – if they get money out of you this time, it'll never end. Since you gotta ask outside people for that money, sooner or later they'll stop supplying it or you'll have to tell someone to wait and then you end up shanked in the shower. So, talk to Alba. Listen to what he has to say."

Perez (so his name tag says) nods in a friendly fashion and wanders away. I lower myself into the desk chair and sit there shaking until the dinner bell rings.

May

Ben

It's still dark outside when I pick Lily up. At least it's not raining as we head down the pier to the tiny slip I rent from Russell. *The Clotilde* awaits.

"I've never been sailing before." She's huddled in a ski jacket which is going to be a problem if we capsize, but the bay is dead level so I'm not too worried about that.

"Never?"

"We weren't part of the boat set up north."

"Trust me. You're in good hands. I've never drowned anyone." I almost want to tell the story of the time Peter and I capsized *the Clotilde*, but I don't want to invoke his spirit, so I don't tell the story. I'm pretty sure it was his fault anyway. He owned it, after all. Truthfully, though, I was older, so should have been a bit more responsible than I was.

"Want a donut?"

Her mother made us a half-dozen. My stomach growls in anticipation, but I want to get on the water before I have one. The sky is lightening, so it's time to head out. I install her in the bow and push off of the dock. *The Clotilde* is small enough you can treat it like a canoe or rowboat, so I paddle out to the breakwater, raising the mast only where the wind won't carry us into another boat. The morning wind catches the sail just as the sun hooves above the horizon. I set the sail so I can now eat a donut. Oh, my! Homemade. *So good!*

"You okay?" I have to speak loudly since the wind that carries us forward also causes the boat to flee my voice. She's sitting there in the bow with her mouth hanging open. "Not seasick?"

"I'm amazed. It's…wow."

I take it that she loves sailing. I've only had one girlfriend and she hated it. The deepness of the ocean under us scared Pam. Lily's hair has grown since last summer, so she's pulled it back in a braid that reminds me of how Alyse always wore her hair. I'm not invoking that spirit either. Lily wears hers straight down her back, not over her left shoulder. And she really doesn't look anything like Alyse, who was absolutely beautiful. Lily is something different – real, lovely but not perfect. Her teeth aren't perfectly straight and her mouth isn't completely symmetrical. Her hazel eyes twinkle with joy as she scans around the quiet bay. The morning ferry will be here soon, but for now, it feels like we're the only two people on the water. I twitch the rudder slightly to correct our course.

"Where are we going?"

"The Roaring 20s House. Gull Island was built by an industrialist in 1922. It was quite the place for a while. I looked it up. There's a speakeasy under the house. He lost his money in the Crash and the bank took the property. It became a hotel and then it was bought by another family. It was their Hyannis Port. Their grandchildren sold the property about 15 years ago, but whoever the buyer was lost his shirt in 2008. And so it stood empty for nearly a decade.

It was bought by someone a couple of years ago. They rebuilt the dock last fall, but that's all the activity I've seen."

"Who bought it?"

"The library records didn't say. It's a trust."

"So, part of someone's inheritance?"

"What do you know about that?"

She looks like she might not answer…or maybe rethinking her answer. She probably got the same letter I got about Alan Wyngate liquidating Pete's trust fund and offering a payout in return for not suing Pete into permanent pauperhood. I didn't want any of Pete's money, but Lily's family has some expenses that might make it tempting.

"I wrote a paper about it this winter. If a rich family gives a lot of assets to a descendant, they owe taxes on it immediately, which means they might have to sell off family property to pay them. If the rich person puts the money or property in a trust, the recipient cannot pay as many taxes – at least not all at once. The trust has to pay capital gains on the earnings and then you pay regular taxes on the annual or monthly distributions."

"Wait, does that mean they pay *more* in taxes?"

"Overall? I think so. Capital gains is like 20% and then it's ordinary income tax on the distribution."

"Wow. I've been reading through this book – *Economics in One Lesson* – and I'm starting to understand that taxation isn't a healthy thing."

"Healthy thing?"

"Yeah. I mean, the tax man takes a quarter of my income before I even get my check. I could pay off my student loans a lot faster."

"Mom says taxes make it harder to stay in business."

"There you go."

The breeze has taken us close to the island shore. My boat is too small to make effective use of the dock, so I put into the little bay Pete always used to beach the Malibu. I drop the sail and glide into the shingle.

"So, we wade…."

"No, I'll lift you across. Just give me a second."

She's more solid than I thought. It's not fat. She's medium height and athletic. It's muscle. I set her on the sand and turn back for the backpack lunch I packed. She's putting on her shoes, so I don my hiking sandals.

"Do you want to check out the house or hang out on the beach?"

"I want to see this cool house."

"Come on then." We wander our way through the clumps of sea grass and other plants Pete knew the name of, but I never bothered to learn. I guess I thought I could always ask him. There's a path that leads up to the headland where the house and some other buildings reside. The climb is a bit steep. I'm impressed that she doesn't ask for a break on the way up. Near the top, I see signs of brush clearing. Whoever rebuilt the dock has plans, it seems. It's good we're coming so early in the year because we might not be welcome later.

We get to the top and I stop because I'm breathing a little hard and so is she. I pull out both water bottles and hand her one. Where we're standing, you can see the ridge of the house roof, but we're mostly surrounded by brush that needs to be cut back.

"I think this used to be an arbor." She points out a wood spar that might have been an upright at one time.

"That makes sense. This would be a great view if the brush were cleared."

She nods. With the basic brush clearing whoever did since the last time I was here, you can see the ocean so long as you're standing. We cap the bottles and continue forward.

The three-story Victorian with a wraparound porch looks to still be in good shape, though a few of the fret boards are peeling white paint and the blue body paint is growing dull and checked. I learned about Victorian style from Pete. He seemed really excited about architecture. Could he become an architect now? Weird that I hope he can have a life after he's done with his sentence.

"Wow! It's beautiful. How'd you find it?"

"You're kidding, right? You can see it from the main shore. We just set out for it and then it was just a matter of figuring out where we could land."

She opens her mouth as if to ask who is "we", but then she thinks better of it. She knows the answer. Trevor doesn't sail or boat. Well, I guess he does now that he's living with his step-brother Hill. I think he might have gone out a few times with Pete, but—yeah, she knows we shouldn't talk about Pete.

"I can imagine what it must have been like when this was Speakeasy Island. You know, my grandfather owned a chicken farm on the St. Lawrence River during Prohibition. He had a boat and he'd ferry people across to Canada."

"Wow. That's daring."

"Is it any more daring than people who smuggle drugs into the country now?"

"Probably not, although we're rapidly becoming a country where drugs aren't even illegal."

"Do we think that's a good thing?"

"I think it's a mixed bag. Seems cannabis is pretty harmless, but there's a lot more dangerous drugs out there that people want to legalize."

"And, yet, we kind of proved prohibition doesn't work."

"Exactly. Classic conundrum."

She nods, presses her face to the dusty glass.

"Great architecture in there."

I nod because I've pressed my face to the glass a few times. It's worth preserving. I hope the new owners keep the old buildings and don't tear them down for something new.

"Ready for 2nd breakfast? Pre-lunch?"

I made breakfast burritos and brought cups of cut-up fruit.

"You bring a lot of girls here?"

"No." I'm pretty sure Pete brought Cheyenne here, but we're not talking about him. "I know it's hard to believe, but I'm not much of a player." Her giggle makes me smile. "I dated a girl named Pam and I invited her a few times, but she wasn't really very outdoorsy."

"I like the outdoors." She realizes what she's just intimated, and her giggle becomes a little hysterical.

"Maybe you should come mountain biking with me sometime."

Her hazel eyes twinkle as she spoons a mandarin orange section.

"Hmm, might be a little scared of embarrassing myself trying to keep up."

How candid! I think I like that in a girl.

"I promise, I'll go easy on you."

She smiles at me, and I find myself gazing at her pink lips and thinking something I shouldn't be thinking. Breakfast. We should definitely eat breakfast. And then hike the island. Anything but what I'm thinking.

Lily

Jenae and I have been keeping up a banter all day as I "watch" Bram. Except for making lunch, he doesn't really need me. It takes him forever to dress himself and do his ADLs, but he doesn't want help. He's trying to be independent nearly two years after the stroke that changed his life forever. He's adapting.

So, I'm bored. I was reading a book – and enjoying it – when Jenae texted me with "How's it?"

Who speaks like that? But I reply and soon we're laughing and joking back and forth. She's at school and I'm done, but we're both bored. Meanwhile, Bram's taking a nap because living exhausts him. I have to be here *just in case.* Outside, Wes is practicing skateboard tricks in the cul de sac. It's fun to watch him, but it makes me sad because Bram will never be able to do that.

JENAE- Remember Ms. Jakes?

It takes me a moment to remember the English teacher who always had a smile on her face.

LILY- Fake Jakes? Sure. What's she up to?

JENAE- BORING! We're watching a movie. 1984

I've watched that movie. My parents made me watch it a couple of years ago. And I read the book a few months ago. It's a scary vision of the world. I wouldn't call the movie boring. Sobering.

LILY- How far in?

JENAE- Class will be over in 20 long minutes.

LILY-It gets better. You need to pay attention though. There's a deep meaning.

She doesn't shoot back at me immediately.

JENAE- How bored are you?

LILY- I wish I were outdoors.

JENAE- Not possible with your brother?

LILY- Technically, I can go out to the yard, but I did gardening yesterday so there's not much to do out there.

JENAE- This movie is just something to fill out the last few days of school. Why can't they just send us home?

Bram shuffles out of his room leaning on his walker. He doesn't see me because he's blind to the right, but he's clearly headed to the kitchen. I follow him. He's just getting a glass of water and using a plastic cup because – well, it might have been in the drain rack, or it could be he's starting to understand some of what we've been trying to teach him. If he falls with a real glass in his hand, he could seriously hurt himself. He sets the cup on the counter and turns his walker, takes a tentative step toward the table. Setting himself firmly, he reaches for the cup and lifts it across to the table. It's way too close to the edge, but I stay silent. It's only water, the cup won't break, and I want to see what he's doing. He shuffles around the table, breathing heavily until he gets to his wheelchair and lowers himself into it. He gets himself appropriately settled and then rolls over to the cup and puts it in the drink carrier, then rolls toward me.

"I do." He grins and then I move out of his way, and he rolls into the living room without any help at all. I wonder if he'll remember where he left the walker.

JENAE- You there?

LILY- Yeah. Bram sitting.

The garage door is open to let the breeze cool the house and I think I hear Ben's voice.

LILY- I think Ben is here.

JENAE- Ben? The neighbor? Bram's friend?

LILY- Wes's older brother. What do you think? Do I have a shot?

JENAE- Shot?

LILY- You know. He's a college guy.

JENAE- You like him?

LILY- Yeah.

JENAE- How long have you known him?

LILY- About 18 months. They're neighbors. And he was Peter's friend.

JENAE- Oh.

She doesn't text more for a long time. I pick up a few items and help Bram find a nature show. He doesn't like speech-heavy programs, though it is about time to sit him down with his aphasia program. I'll let him watch the nature show to the end of the episode.

JENAE- If he was friends with Peter, he's probably a creep.

I stare at the screen, surprised by the reaction. Ben is *not* a creep. I set up the laptop. Bram ignores me, laughing at meerkats. When the episode ends, he surprises me and turns off the television, then rolls to the table and settles himself in for the next lesson. He's pretty good at repeat-after-me. It's remembering the words tomorrow that has him struggling.

I sit down by the front window and scan through today's texts with Jenae. I hadn't expected that response. She's been so supportive about Peter. Why would she react negatively to Ben? The obvious answer is that Peter is history and not likely to show up anytime soon. Meanwhile, Ben is here, right next door.

I try to think of what I'd say to Jenae if she were standing in front of me and I can't really bring up her face, which causes an uncomfortable feeling in my chest that I can't analyze.

Ben

The thing about working the early shift is I get off work at 3:00 pm, so I pick Wes up at school and then I decide to join him at his simple skateboarding setup. I grab my board on my way through the garage. Wes smiles at me. It's late afternoon and already getting hot, but I create my own breeze as I take the jump.

We try to one-up each other, and I try not to dominate him. I've been skating since I was 9 and so has he, so I've had almost eight years more experience. Trevor and Pete were always better than me, but neither of them is a factor now. I am enjoying this comfortable time with my little brother. Wes is a good kid and I want him to stay that way. Eventually, though, a car approaches our location.

Alan Wyngate pulls over to the side of the street and gets out of his Mercedes, pulling out several grocery bags from the back seat. He smooths over his frown to smile at me as he locks the doors and heads toward the property across from ours.

"How are you, Ben?"

"I'm good. Do you need us to move?"

"No, it's fine. I'll move it later – or wait until tomorrow."

"You're living here now?"

"Temporarily." He shrugs and chuckles. "I sold my house, and I don't want to live with my parents. My property management team has been worth the money I pay them, so there were no other vacancies in my catalog."

He made his money in real estate. If Pete wasn't exaggerating, that's hundreds of properties. I guess that's kind of impressive.

"I was planning to move home from Tilly's cottage. I could do it earlier."

He blinks at me. It's been a long time since I've seen him in jeans and a T-shirt. He's in good shape for a man about my father's age. Something sad moves in his eyes.

"Yeah, it doesn't belong to me. This is good. It's quiet. I'll see you sometime."

He walks around our course and disappears through the boxwood hedge with the frontline of Rose of Sharon bushes. I guess my suspicions that he and Tilly are getting a divorce are correct. Wes bumps my arm.

"Who was that?"

I sigh.

"Pete's father."

A line appears between his eyes.

"He's slumming?" His tone implies a negative attitude.

"He's no longer governor, so…maybe."

He stares at the opening in the hedge for a moment, then picks up his skateboard and heads toward our house.

"You're done?"

"Yeah, I'm hanging out with Bram this evening. Can you put this stuff away?"

"Oh, sure. I've got nothing better to do."

It's getting dark anyway, so I use the remaining light to drag the ramps up on the edge of our lawn, and then I go into dinner because Mom's a good cook and I'm not seeing Pete sitting across the table from me so much anymore.

Lily

I lean back, sighing, feeling the ending of a novel that I'm sure my parents would object if they knew I was reading it.

Five years on and happily married and Silas still struggles to forgive himself for his sins.

This story about a girl falling for a felon is fiction and probably speculative, but I wonder if Pete hates himself. Will he by the time his sentence is up? He'll have a long time to think about it, to brood on it. He still felt guilty about ending his parents' marriage, so he's certainly capable of holding himself accountable for years on end.

I should read his letter. After all, he must have considered it important.

But should I really care about what Peter considers important? For a moment, I see the blue speedboat heading toward the exact spot where Ben and I stood, and I feel a white-hot poker of rage for my former boyfriend.

I close Kindle and open my Bible app. I'm reading through Ephesians. I'm not sure why. Because that's the book God directed me to? I am God's workmanship, created in Christ for His good work, saved through faith and not of my works so I have no reason to boast.

I'm not better than Peter. I was with Ben that night in part because I wanted to show Peter he didn't matter to me. Maybe…maybe….

Mina's counsel must be working. I don't think Peter rammed *the Mimi* because I caused it. He might have been jealous of me and Ben, but he was the one who chose to ram a larger boat. He didn't have to do that. I've successfully interrupted a thought that has plagued me for months.

I should read Peter's letter, get it over with. But there's a part of me that hangs back, that lets it remain a bookmark in my Bible. He shouldn't have the power to disrupt my life. I am not responsible for his actions.

The letter remains in Numbers where I'm unlikely to seek it out for however long I need to decide to either read it or destroy it.

There! Decision made! Not!

Necessary Sacrifices

Peter
February

I nearly chicken out a few times while I stand in line for the phones. There's nothing spontaneous in prison. Everything takes planning, even when I don't want to have the conversation.

Luis surprisingly agreed with CO Perez that I shouldn't pay blackmail to the Black Lions. Tyler tried to rape me. I had every right to defend myself. The fact that I caused permanent damage isn't really my fault either. And I have no money of my own. Yeah, I suspect Lucy and Mike would give me money if I asked, but there is enormous risk in that. First, it makes me dependent on them when they're struggling to forgive me for my sins. That's how Luis expressed it and I guess he's right. Killing your sister has got to be a sin. Every time they cut a check to the sinner, they're going to remember the sin and so I can't be dependent upon them. Anything I get from them must be freely offered, not coerced, and entirely their own idea.

The second risk is that the Black Lions will never be satisfied. Give them the first payment and they'll expect more and then more. The payments will grow and the time between will shorten. Sooner or later the amount or the interval will run over the unstated limit, and I'll be ripe for the picking.

There's only one way to deal with this and I hope Lucy understands. It will help with other things too, things more terrifying than the Black Lions.

I can only call people on my pre-authorized 15-person phone list. Yes, Lucy is on my phone list, but I also have to schedule when I want to stand in line for my 15 minutes on the phone. I get in line. If everyone takes their full 15 minutes, it's going to take an hour. But if you're late for the line, you don't get to make your phone call, so I'm there ahead of time.

Finally, after an hour, I get to the phone. The problem with calling their landline is that I have no idea if they'll answer it. Who calls landlines anymore? Who even has them? My grandparents. Joel said the prison would require the landline first. They want to make sure I'm calling my grandparents and not someone else. Who is left in my life to call?

The phone rings and rings and I am about to hang up when it picks up.

"Hello? Wyngate Enterprises." Lucy sounds uncertain. How long has it been since someone has called this number? Why do they even have a landline?

The automated phone system announces that it's a call from Sing Sing Prison. She can press 1 to accept the call and 2 to deny it. There's also a third option where she can deny the call permanently. My heart is in my mouth waiting for her decision.

"This call is monitored and can be used in a court of law." Beep.

"Hey, it's Peter."

"Hey." She sounds pleased to hear my voice. A middle-class woman sucked into the life of one of the richest families in New York, she's a great actress, pretending she fits in…or pretending she doesn't wish I wouldn't call. "How are you?"

"Okay." I'm not sleeping because when I doze off, I have nightmares. But Luis recommended I don't manipulate them with that information. I so want to, but I'll try not to. "Sundays work for you?"

"Yes, of course. We called about visiting on your birthday, but…."

"I didn't—I can't—not this year." Knowing I might flinch on this phone call, I've already removed them from my visiting list. It would take a while to put them back on and that might cool the Black Lions in the meantime. Luis' idea.

"You okay?"

"No. I'm just…. Um, I have a problem." I lean into the phone. It's not going to help if people overhear what I say to her. There's a black guy with dreds speaking sweet nothings to his girlfriend at the phone to my right and a giant of a white guy with some scary-assed tattoos talking serious business in code to my left. Neither of them seems to be a threat, but what the hell do I know? The white guy's tattoos seem threatening. The be-dredded black guy who tried to shake me down was noticeably shorter than this be-dredded black guy, but for all I know they could be best friends.

"Some people saw, um, wealth when you visited. They want money."

"How much?" Yeah, I knew she'd accept that I need her help. For a moment, I want to start begging and then I opt to tell the truth.

"It'll never be enough. You can't visit for a while. It's putting me in danger."

There's a long painful silence.

"Peter…."

"I can call…and we can write. I can email limited numbers of people too. There's a process, but…."

"And you don't want to see us?"

"I don't want to die." Well, that's not exactly true, but….

"You were seeing whatever it is you see…during the visit."

She *knows* me. I grunt as the wall behind the phone paints with the sunset.

"I'm telling you the truth." There's another painful silence, so I repeat. "I'm telling the truth."

"I know." I hear her swallow. Surely, she's not crying. Who is disappointed that they can't visit their murderer in Sing Sing Prison? Her voice quavers as she continues. "Maybe writing will make it easier for us to say the things we need to say."

"Maybe." I don't know if it will make anything easier. I'm not sure I *want* to know. She's right about the things they need to say to me, but will distance make it easier? I just don't know.

"Visiting endangers me, but it also endangers *you*. They have people outside and you guys aren't unknown." I'm pretty sure I hear a sniffle. "I'm sorry. I don't want to do this, but I'm going to tell them you guys turned me down, threatened to disown me. It's the only way I can protect myself and you."

"Peter, you know we love you, right?" Her voice quavers with tears.

Do I know that? I *want* to believe it, but there's a hole in my heart where Alyse used to live and I'm not certain of what I know right now.

"Sure. It's the reason I'm doing this. I'll write. I promise."

I'm going to start crying so I hang up instead. Neither of the two guys next to me seems to be paying any attention, but as I walk away from the phones, I see two guys I'm pretty sure are Black Lions, so I let my distress at what I've just done show. I'll soothe myself later with the knowledge that Lucy wouldn't lie to me. She'll write. I'll call. It's *not* the end of the world. It just *feels* like it.

Late-May

Ben

I worked through Memorial Day weekend and slept in on Monday, but by afternoon, I think Trevor's probably awake, so I ring his phone. It's not unusual for him not to answer the phone on the first go. He's got challenges. So, I ring once, wait a couple of minutes, and then ring again.

"Hello." I hesitate because I'm pretty sure the voice on the phone is Grey, Trevor's dad. This is Trevor's number, but Trevor doesn't speak in what Pete used to call a Transatlantic accent. He said Alan Wyngate would sometimes mock Grey for retaining the accent taught to them in their adolescent boarding school. "Ben?"

"Yeah. Is he okay?"

"He's alive. He almost wasn't, but fortunately someone had Naloxone on them. I checked him into Briarcliff. I made sure Cheyenne Therriault knows he's got no money to buy drugs. Hil had the shit scared out of him, so he's not going to help either. I think he's not got a choice to stay there this time."

"Good." I'd been expecting it for a while.

"Weird that you're the only friend who has called in the two weeks he's been there."

"Yeah – I guess it's been about three weeks since he and I talked. I let it go to voicemail a couple of weeks ago. Got an interesting rambling speech about the universe and God and…sheep."

Grey chuckles and then sighs.

"You've been through enough with Peter. I get why Trevor has alienated you."

Grey is a singularly interesting man. Maybe it's the journalism training. Maybe it's the libertarianism. He absolutely loves his son, but wouldn't say if Trevor was not guilty until the cops pretty much proved that Pete drove the boat. I didn't agree with it, but I admire that fair-mindedness. Dad says he's pretty sure Grey Grey (I forget his real first name) and Alan Wyngate are still best friends.

"Trevor isn't endangering others. If he wants to kill himself, I'm not sure I want a front-row seat, but I do still care about him. Let me know when he can have visitors and I'll show up."

"Sure. It'll be a couple more weeks, I think. How you doing?"

"Okay. Working full-time at Temple and then weekends for Russell. So, I'm pretty busy."

"Busy's not bad. I wish I could find something to keep Trevor busy."

"The drugs were keeping him pretty busy. I haven't had a sober conversation with him in months."

"Yeah." He sounds sad.

"It's not your fault, you know?"

"Yeah? He was doing some of those drugs a long time before Peter crashed that boat, so I can't really blame it on him. That's what the counselors say."

"Counselors have limitations." I'm quoting Kevin, so maybe it's a professional analysis.

Grey chuckles again.

"So, have you gotten a letter from Peter?"

How does he know that?"

"Um, yeah."

"What does he have to say for himself?"

"I'd have to read it to know, but I'm scared he'll suck me back in if I do."

Wow, that was honesty I hadn't planned to deliver.

Grey takes a long pause before he replies.

"You're going to force me to open this thing, invade his privacy. I see how you are."

"Sorry. I'm just not there."

"I get it." He smacks his lips softly. "I should probably read it anyway and it's not like the prison system didn't read it before they allowed him to send it out. According to his lawyer, who I called after it showed up in the mail when Trevor was in Briarcliff the first time, says the envelopes are so thick because there's a letter from the Department of Corrections explaining why he's been allowed to reach out to his victims and a card where you can designate your future interactions with him. And then, the letter he wrote."

I sigh.

"I get it. Trevor and you were his best friends and you both got hurt by his actions. But I still don't think he meant to hurt you. He was out of control."

"Yeah, I'm starting to accept that. Still doesn't mean I want to get back on the merry-go-round."

"I hope you never have family that gets on the merry-go-round. But I'm going to keep loving my son and trying to do whatever gets him healthy."

"Of course. So, call me when he can have visitors?

"Do you want to know what the letter to Trevor says?"

I freeze. Is he asking for support in a tough situation? Yeah. That's what that sounds like.

"Now?"

"I just opened it. Scanning through it…he writes the right words."

The last thing I want to hear is anything Pete wrote, but my parents would say "support the hurting" and Grey has to be hurting.

"Sure."

Grey clears his throat and I hear paper shuffle softly before he speaks.

> Trevor – Wow, this one's a hard one. How do you apologize for what I did to you? I can't. I'm not even going to try. I regret it to the very core of my being and there's nothing I can say that apologizes for it. I wish I'd listened to you when you tried to take the keys away from me. I didn't and I have nobody to blame but myself for where I am right now. If it helps any – and I doubt it does or should – this place SUCKS and the bitch of it is that I know it'll never be enough. I totally deserve to be here, and it totally doesn't pay my debts. I'm not looking for any sympathy. Please don't mistake this for that.
>
> In Alcoholics Anonymous, I'm learning that I need to be willing to make amends to the people I hurt. It's supposed

to help me stay sober and – I don't know – maybe it's working. 246 days...and yes, it's available in here. Only I know I can't make amends to some people and – yeah. I don't know what to do with that guilt – not yet anyway. Alyse – yeah, can't even deal with that yet. Just writing her name hurts.

So, my sentence is 5-25 years, which means I've got at least another four before I can make any sort of direct amends. And – I don't know – well, it doesn't matter. I need to make amends as I can and most people, I know, I won't be able to until I'm out – four or 24 years from now, or somewhere in between. And, I hope you'll let me when the time comes.

But for now, with you, I know I've got to be honest with you even though I'm scared I'm going to insult you. This in no way absolves me of my debt to you. It's just that in taking my own inventory, I noticed that we enabled one another a lot. I provided a lot of booze to you, and I don't think you're any less of an alcoholic than I am. As much as the boat wreck, I'm sorry for helping you get hooked on that witch. I don't have an excuse for that either except that misery loves company – or, well, my misery used to love company, and now – well, alone is a really good place to get to know myself. I mean, it SUCKS and I HATE it, but I've got a lot of time to work on what got me in here. And, I don't know what condition this will find you in – I hope it's better than my imagination. I'm praying you'll get some help if you haven't already. I just really hope you'll decide to live because I don't want to be responsible for any more deaths. PLEASE.

Peter

Neither of us says anything for a moment.

"He's got eerie timing." How did he time that?

"Kind of prescient."

"Surprisingly."

"Is it? I always found Peter more thoughtful than many of Trevor's friends. He got a DWI and *quit drinking*. Tried to, anyway. Meanwhile, Trevor keeps going back to the trough as soon as he has the means."

"You think Pete's better than Trevor?" Oops, I said that aloud.

"No. No! Peter is deeply flawed. So is Trevor. And maybe Peter's a little further along on the healing path because some hard things happened to him. 'This place SUCKS!' He's not asking for sympathy. He's stating a fact."

"What happened to Trevor sucks too?"

"Don't I know it? And so does Peter. 'Nothing I say can apologize for that.' It's not the 'I'm sorry, I won't do it again" BS. I'm exhausted of hearing it from Trevor. I think I'd lose my composure if I heard it from Peter." We take a second to absorb that thought. I want to say 'I gotta go" but I feel I should wait until he's done talking. I think I'm probably being a pushover again, but I was raised to be nice. "Do you know the story of my uncle?"

I turn over that non sequitur, but as far as I know Grey Grey has no relatives. After several heartbeats, he answers his own question.

"This happened in the 1960s. He was a college student, driving drunk and high. Something happened. He crashed his car up in the White Mountains. His girlfriend and one of his passengers were killed, another seriously injured. According to the skid marks, he might have been trying to avoid something. He never really could remember. Being who the Greys are, he never did a day in jail. The press not owned by the Greys vilified him. Dartmouth kicked him out of school. He got death threats. His parents were barely speaking with him. His girlfriend's family, who had been happy for their engagement only a month before, sued him."

Grey pauses to let me consider how dark it must have felt. He's right. Wow, his uncle had a rough time of it, and not unlike what Pete's gone through.

"Charlie stepped off a tension bridge a year later. They never found his body, but the suicide note he left was pretty clear – he felt abandoned, and he couldn't live with the guilt. I don't want Alan to know what my grandparents or

Dad felt about that. He's already lost his daughter. He doesn't need to lose his son too. Ideally, Peter will go through this horrible time, and he'll get out and be a better person."

"In the bosom of his family?"

"That's not certain. Alan isn't ready to forgive. Apparently, Peter isn't either. He pushed his grandparents away, won't let them visit."

"Why?" Pete without an audience. That seems…unlikely.

"Grief and guilt, I'm guessing. Powerful combination." There's a long pause and I hear him grunt. "How's the young lady who was with you that night?"

"Lily? She's good." I'm smiling because I think I want to reach out to her and invite her out this week.

"Oh? You got a little something-something?"

I feel my cheeks grow hot.

"Maybe. We're moving in that direction."

"Good for you. One of the things that might help Peter is if he gets out and sees everyone moved on with their lives."

"You don't think that'll just depress him?" For the first time, I wonder what Pete would think of my being friends with Lily.

"Yeah, it will. And if he learns the lessons he needs to learn, he'll move on and grow from it."

It's weird that the guy who raised Trevor, who has been married five times that I know of, has such insight into my screwed-up best friend. Maybe he needs to be that wise to save Trevor. But it sounds a lot like Grandpa Jack, so….

"You should go. Still a nice afternoon out there. I should go see what Carol's up to."

"Carol?"

"My wife."

Okay, married *six* times. Well, that might have a little something to do with why Trevor's been an addict since high school. His *mother's* been married at least four times. There's something deeply Oedipal about that, I think.

Grey wishes me a lovely afternoon and closes the call. I look at the front window where the light spills across the bare hardwood floor and wonder if I should call Lily.

Lily

This is a great evening. There's a gentle cool breeze that makes the warm evening tolerable. John Anderson's delicious burgers scent the air. Best of all, Ben is paying attention to me. He acts like I'm the only one here in the Andersons' backyard. He's leaning against the back wall of the house and I'm leaning against the porch railing and we're talking about absolutely nothing important and it's the best conversation I've ever had.

"Lily. Lily."

Bram hardly ever calls me by my name because the double "l" sounds are difficult for him, but it has the desired effect. I look his way. He and Wes are sitting at the picnic table. Well, Bram is sitting in his wheelchair at the end of the picnic table and Wes is sitting on the bench.

"Taste."

He points to a bowl of the dip.

"Yes, it does taste good. I made it."

He giggles.

"What's special about it?" Ben gives me a quizzical look.

"Artichoke hearts, olives, cream cheese, and sour cream."

"Sounds delicious. You want some?"

I don't know. Eating in front of guys – risky. He takes my lifted eyebrows as a positive answer, and we get chips, dips, and lemonade. John announces burgers will be ready soon.

"This is the first time he's been to one of our cookouts, right?" Ben nods his head toward where our brothers are sitting.

I run back through my memory of the last year. Bram tried last summer—once—but all the background noise and people to keep track of were just too much for him. He begged off after a half-hour. He's getting better or adapting. He's an hour in and not showing annoyance or exhaustion yet. It's a lovely thing. Improvement takes so long. The doctors say he'll never be normal and that's probably true, but he's already exceeded their original prognosis. I shouldn't be pessimistic.

"You went somewhere."

"Just thinking about Bram and how much he's improved this year."

Ben looks thoughtful.

"Pete was the first one to treat him like he was still in there, right?"

"He was. Bram's speech therapist says some people have a special sense and they make really good speech therapists. Of course, Peter's not going to be a speech therapist now." I shrug. "Two roads divide in a yellow wood…and he took the one less traveled."

A lot of philosophy can be found in Robert Frost's poetry.

"Yeah, and that's too bad. Pete is a talented guy. It's too bad he screwed up his life."

It *is* too bad. And this dip is delicious. It's gotten even better in the afternoon it spent in the fridge. And I absolutely don't want to talk about Peter. He's my past and Ben—well, he feels like he might be the future.

Ben

Kevin does a seat lift before answering me. Not for the first time, I wonder if he can feel his legs. I'm never asking that question but I wonder.

"We're back to Pete. Okay. He screwed up his life. What's that got to do with you?"

"I feel like I helped him do it."

"How did you do that?"

Admitting the crux of the matter is terrifying. If I *know* what I did will I feel the guilt more?

"I was the designated driver at a lot of his parties. I enjoyed them too. At the end, I wanted him to go to rehab, but I refused to give him a ride."

There! I've said it! Kevin doesn't seem surprised. He's staring at his knees. I wonder if he can feel them. I'm trying to distract myself.

"Yeah, it would have been nice if someone had responded appropriately when he asked, but ultimately, he needed to get *himself* to rehab. There's no guarantee that if you'd driven him there, he would have actually benefited. You don't know that he wouldn't do what your friend Trevor's doing—going in and out, gaming the system. You decide – which is worse?"

I'm fed up with Trevor and not answering his calls. I guess I got to that point with Pete too, but I softened when he seemed repentant. That makes me wonder if I'll forgive Trevor if he gets sober for real. I don't know what I'll feel in a few months. I'm going to have to decide how to explain it to Trevor.

"No comment?"

Kevin knows me. I'll figure out a way not to confront myself directly.

"Can I feel conflicted?"

"You can. *That* is the honest answer. I'm proud of you."

That feels good, but it doesn't solve my basic dilemma.

"Pete sent me an amends letter I can't bring myself to read. What am I supposed to do with it if he says I hurt him?"

Kevin rolls his wheelchair back to a bookcase. I never noticed before that all the books are on the lower shelves and there's decorations on the higher ones. It makes total sense. I think his pretty wife, who I've seen at church and in a photo on his desk, probably helped him with that. He spends a moment scanning the books and then returns with one in his lap. He hands it to me.

Don't Give the Enemy a Seat at Your Table by Louie Giglio.

"Give forgiveness a chance. It doesn't mean you're going to forget what Pete did, but maybe you won't hang on so tight to your anger."

My dad has quoted Giglio a few times. I suspect our pastor would consider him a progressive. Heck, our pastor might consider me a non-Christian at this point.

"Yeah, I'll read it." I open the Internet on my phone, navigate to Amazon, find the book, and buy it. Kevin laughs and sets the book on an end table.

"You kids and your gadgets. So, now, let's talk about when you'll read it."

"I'll start this evening." He gives me a skeptical look. "No, seriously. I'm tired of being angry. I know it's not good for me. I *will* read it starting tonight."

Kevin nods. I guess I've passed a test…or will when I come back next week to discuss what I've learned.

Lily

Mina pours me a cup of tea from a pretty china pot. I'm beginning to really enjoy tea. It makes me feel like I'm talking to a friend rather than a mental health professional.

"Any major developments this week?"

"I think Ben and I are moving toward dating."

"Good. He sounds like a nice guy. Have you put Peter to bed yet?"

I sigh. She isn't a friend. If I want to talk to a friend, I can call Natalie.

"I still have his letter in my Bible."

"Good bookmark. Why haven't you read it yet?"

I change my mind on that subject every day, sometimes multiple times a day. I think Peter will be angry with me. I'll be so mad at him if he's not repentant. I'm going to blame myself if he's in a lot of pain. I try to tell her what I'm thinking.

"But none of that is real. You're making that all up in your head until you read the letter. Wouldn't you rather know what he's really thinking rather than what you imagine?"

Put that way....

"What if it changes how I feel about him?"

"Your mind changes on him weekly. I submit that he can't change your feelings about him. You control that. He is just a passerby. Always was."

I sip the tea. It's still a little too hot, but that gives me a moment to consider her words.

"Okay, so he gets whiny and asks you to wait for him? Just as an example. What would be your response to it?"

"Go away! I don't feel warm fuzzies for him."

"You've moved on?"

"Yeah. I've stopped talking to him in my head."

"Improvement. So, he begs you for forgiveness?"

"I'm trying to forgive him. He's going to have to be patient and show repentance."

"And, if he was angry?"

I pause, thinking about Peter screaming in Ben's face the last time we were all three together.

"I don't know. You think that's what I'm afraid of?"

"What do *you* think?"

I kind of wish she'd tell me what to think. I taste the tea. Tasty. I think I like turmeric.

"I'm afraid he'll be angry."

"That's a reasonable fear."

"Is it?"

"Yes. You've struggled not to feel guilty, and he has reason to be angry about you being on the boat. He could justify it anyway, even though you were there because of his behavior. And, his letter might be angry, but let's consider that he had to go through a formal program to be allowed to write you, which means someone read this letter before he sent it out. They officially have your back. The letter probably won't hurt you. And if it does – you can come vent to me, and I'll tell you he's wrong."

It sounds so easy, but I know it won't be. Falling for Peter came easily, recovering took much longer and is taking a lot more effort. Maybe that's why I fear his letter. It feels like a step toward him rather than continuing to walk away.

Fish

Peter March

I pry my eyes open when Seth speaks. It's dangerous to doze off in the yard where there's a lot of unstructured activity, but my eyelids are so heavy.

"You sleep last night?"

Seth leans against the wall near the weight stacks where Luis is proving he isn't old. The guy's muscles have muscles. I stare at the wan March sun just beyond the guard tower and concertina wire. It's hard to relax knowing there are rifles trained on all of the inmates. The rifle holders don't care about me. One wrong move and my life is forfeit. I shiver.

"I have a choice. I sleep or everybody else does."

"And we thank you for that – letting us get some sleep occasionally, but you can't keep that up forever."

"Yeah." I know that. I *do*. I've cycled in and out of the infirmary a few times because the hallucinations get worse if

I don't sleep. The doctors drug me to let me get some sleep, but I don't want to get hooked, so I'm trying not to go back to the infirmary this time around.

"What's triggering you?"

"You're kidding, right?" I indicate the world we live in.

"You're nice and safe in your house at night with a cellie who ain't gonna hurt you. Don't lie to yourself, kid."

At present, I seem to have three 12-Step sponsors. I don't know—maybe I need them. I haven't slept a whole lot since I last got out of the infirmary. The nightmares are brutal. Even when I dream of pleasant memories, they turn dark.

"Your sister died in your arms. You dreaming about that?"

"Yeah." There's another dream I can never remember. She's in it, but it's weird, too weird to describe to anyone. "Kind of normal, right?"

"Sure, but – kid, you need sleep. *I* need sleep. *Luis* needs sleep. People who are on the verge of hurting you need sleep."

"Sleep's overrated." Luis has traded places with one of the other guys, so now he leans against the wall on the other side of me. I don't have a coat like they do, but the facility issued me a hoodie, which I have my hands pulled up into the sleeves.

"I'm sorry."

"I know you don't mean it, kid. That's why you're working out today. Something's got to make a change before your goodwill runs out."

"I didn't wake up screaming last night."

"You didn't sleep. You're going to end up back in the infirmary. That's not a solution."

"They got meds." Joey's a weedy looking guy who can lift more than I think he weighs.

"That I can get addicted to?"

Joey frowns and then laughs, showing bad teeth. My tongue goes to a place where one of my top teeth appears to be moving forward of the others. That was bound to happen without a retainer.

"I'm fighting the smell of that hooch every day. I'm not adding another addiction to the party."

"Yeah, I get it, kid. Hey, hey, hey! Don't start that without a spotter!"

Seth moves in to where Juarez is settling in to lift. Luis bumps my elbow with his.

"We'll figure it out." The man is an optimist. I'd be screwed without him. "Come on. Get into line. Exercise might help you."

I move to the outside of the stacks. There's a lot of people out here in the chill March air, working on their fitness. There's no way I can lift what these guys lift. Dancers are strong, but it's all body work. Still, I'll try not to embarrass myself.

"Hey, killer!" We all of us look in the guy's direction. He can't be much older than I am. He's been here about a week and already fallen into bad company. Luis says he'll be all tatted up in no time.

"I'm talking to you."

He's looking right at me. I've never spoken to him before, so I don't know what his beef is with me.

"I'm coming for you."

"I don't even know you."

"Doesn't matter. The Black Lions got a beef with you."

"Tyler tried to rape him. There's nothing owed." Luis frowns at the kid, then chatters something in some language that I only recognize as Spanish when the kid replies. Then the kid scurries away.

"What's supposed to happen there?"

"Good question, kid. You're one of the tallest guys around and some of the fish think it's a way to make their bones. It's got less to do with you than you think."

I trust these guys—more or less – and I need some advice.

"I got lucky with Tyler. I have no real fighting skills."

Luis and Seth exchange glances.

"Okay. So that can be remedied." Seth grimaces. "Tomorrow. Today, it's weights. You need to learn to sleep."

Luis hands over his gloves because the bar is cold. I lay down on the bench and watch as Luis and Seth decide which plates to put on the bar.

"Say 'stop' if you think we're going to break you." Luis is a thoughtful guy.

"That's good. Right about there."

"Really?" Seth looks skeptical, then shrugs. "Okay. We can always add plates."

I think a hundred pounds is plenty. I'm not Superman and I haven't slept through the night in weeks. But maybe tonight. I can still hope.

"You know…maybe it's time to write some amends letters." Seth speaks to Luis, who is spotting for me. I'll do what they tell me, so they don't need my contribution. I breathe deeply and lift the bar clear. It's heavy. I lower it to my chest and then lift it up. I doubt I can make an eight count, but I'm going to give it a try. It's a struggle and I'm not weak. It's just been a long time since I lifted a ballerina over my head. On the fourth lift, though, I know I won't get another.

"Good start," Luis says. "Stretch and then let's do the shoulder lift, then biceps." He's a very determined guy. He reads my expression. "One, it might help you sleep. Two, look like you could put a kid like that through a wall and he'll be less likely to threaten you in the future."

Well, put that way….

June

Ben

Saturday morning at my parents house feels normal for the first time in a long time. I didn't have a nightmare before the sun peeked through the window a half-hour ago. I'm reading while I wait for Lily to wake up so I can invite her to breakfast. Louis Giglio has a message just for me.

"This is how God delivered His people from bondage in Egypt. He didn't build a bridge over the Red Sea. He parted the sea so they could walk through it. Oftentimes, God's plan is not to build a bridge over troubled waters. Instead, His miraculous plan is to give you the grace and power to go *through* the troubled waters. 'Your road leads to the sea, your pathway through the mighty waters—a pathway no one knew was there." **Psalm 77:19**

My cell's buzzing breaks my attention and a warm glow flushes through my body as Lily's name flashes across my screen.

"Is Wes okay?"

"Far as I know. I've only been awake a short while. What's up?"

"It's Saturday. He usually comes over, has breakfast with Bram and they play board games. It's weird for him to be late."

I have sleeping shorts on, so it's not weird when I cross the hall and knock on Wes' door. There's a grunt, so I push it open.

"I'm sick. That Lily?" He looks positively green.

"Yeah. You don't look like you should interact with humans."

He grunts.

"How to explain that to Bram?"

"Don't worry about it. Drink some water. I'll scrounge up some ginger ale and take care of Bram on your behalf."

"Yeah? Thanks."

"Sure. So, Lily, it'll be 20 minutes, but if you have bacon I can make it in ten." I pull Wes' door closed.

"I have bacon."

"Great. Headed your way now."

I've never dressed so fast in my life. Who needs to shower? On my way through the kitchen, I explain matters to Mom, who says she'll take care of Wes, and then I'm headed next door.

Lily and I are having breakfast together on her dime. It's not what I had planned, but maybe I'm not that good at making plans. I'd kind of forgotten that she's Bram-sitting on Saturday while her mom works the bookstore.

The smell coming from the kitchen as I cross the garage is heavenly. There is something about bacon and maple syrup. What an incredible aroma!

Lily stands at the stove wielding a spatula while Bram makes his slow way, leaning on this weird triangular walker, from the living room to the kitchen table. He lowers himself carefully into his waiting wheelchair.

"He's getting good at that."

"The harder he works, the more he progresses. Bram, juice, milk or water?"

He screws up his face.

"Yes."

"Nope. There's three choices there." She holds up her index finger. "Juice." She holds up her middle finger beside her index finger. "Milk." She holds up her ring finger beside the other two. "Water."

He holds up the two fingers.

"Say it."

"Milk" comes out as mmmmeek, but he's close enough for Lily, so she pours him a glass.

"Ben?"

"I smell coffee."

"Yeah, the 'rents left at least a cup."

They use an old potter's rack as a coffee and mug station, so I grab a mug and pour myself a cup. There might be two left in the pot. After tasting it I add a touch of powdered milk from a café sugar dispenser and then take my place at the table.

During breakfast, Lily and I talk about this concert she's going to in a week. I love Barns Courtney, but the tickets are pricey. I wonder how her parents got talked into that.

"So, Bram, which game do you want to play." I like Lily's method, so I try the finger designation. "Backgammon, checkers, or chess?"

He chooses chess.

"That seems a little ambitious." I look at Lily.

"No, he and Wes have been playing a lot. He's gotten pretty good at it. You sometimes have to remind him of the possible moves, but he's getting better even at that."

Bram smiles.

"Me smart," he announces.

"I know you are. You wouldn't have come back so far if you weren't."

He glances at Lily. I've overwhelmed him, I think.

"You're smart." She repeats the gist and I guess that's all he needs. He smiles. She brings the chess set over to the table.

"Do I help him set up the pieces?"

"No, he can do it. He sometimes gets the king and queen swapped because he's using your set up as an example, but he's remembering that more now too."

Bram sets up his pieces correctly. He's having a good morning. I carry plates over to the sink where she's loading the dishwasher and whisper to her.

"Do I try to win?"

"That's backgammon. In chess, you're still helping him not to lose."

"Seems fair." I go back to the table. Bram grins at me. His smile is still a little crooked, but when I first met him a year ago, he had no movement on his affected side. Now I can almost not tell until I look at his fisted right hand.

I'm a pretty decent chess player, so I'm trying to go easy on the guy, but halfway through the game, he suddenly crows and moves a bishop into position.

"Um, check."

No way! But it's not only check, it's essentially checkmate. I've got one move I can make, but he's got me on the next move. He's brain-damaged though, so I go ahead and make the next move. He touches his knight.

"Um, goes?"

He points to the square where I'll be mated. He's not sure and there is one other spot it could go, but he's got me.

I got complacent with the brain-damaged kid, and he got me.

"Yes."

He makes his move.

"Mmmmate." He smiles at Lily and then surprises me by lifting his palsied hand out of his lap in a rough imitation of a fist bump.

"Wow! Wes has been doing that every time he wins a backgammon game, having him use his good hand to lift that one for a fist bump. When did you learn that, Bram?"

"He managed it the other day in occupational therapy."

We both start at Lyle Wexler's approach.

"Sorry to startle you. I need water for what I'm doing." He displays the plastic bucket in his hand and approaches the sink. "I meant to tell you, Lily. I just forgot."

"It's great! We're going to have to find all kinds of reasons for him to do it now."

"We are. So, good to see you, Ben. You move home yet?"

"Another couple of weeks."

"Good. What are your plans after this summer?"

Oh, boy! He knows I like Lily.

"Going back to Dartmouth, actually."

"Still tackling engineering?"

"Yup!"

"Good course. Hey, Bram, you want to come out to the backyard?"

Bram frowns and glances at Lily. She pantomimes.

"Go with Dad. Backyard. Sun."

He nods and maneuvers his chair back from the table so he can stand and make his slow way after Lyle.

"That game took an hour."

"Yeah. Thank you for being patient."

"No problem. I've never enjoyed being beaten more than just now. Is that his first win?"

"I think first legitimate win in chess, yeah. Wes always manages to do something accidentally on purpose that will throw one in about five games Bram's way, but this time, he really beat you?"

"He did. I got careless."

"Wes has been saying he was getting harder to discount. The knights and castling are the two things he needs to be reminded of."

"He remembered castling – asked for verification, but he knew what he was doing."

"He's just come so far. It's amazing."

I glance at the old-fashioned tea kettle clock over the door.

"I need to head to work, but.... Could we go to dinner tonight?"

"Why, Mr. Anderson, are you asking me on a date?"

"Um, maybe. Do you need to ask your parents?"

"No, they've already given permission and I know Dad's home this evening to be with Bram. So, yeah."

"You got their permission? When?"

"It's been a while." She's giving me this weird smile that I don't know how to interpret, but I'm not sure I really want to analyze it too much because...well, if you stare at something too long, sometimes it disappears and that's the last thing I want to happen with Lily.

"I get off at six. Pick you up at seven?"

"Sounds good. McDonald's casual or...."

"Whatever's appropriate for the Golden Shanghai."

"Okay, I'll see you then."

Lily

The low light twinkles off the golden accents of the restaurant's ornaments – Chinese masks and laughing Buddhas. The red tones of other items add interest to the bright colors. Our table is positioned in front of a carved depiction of a sinuous dragon in gold and red against jewel-toned blue.

I ate out with Peter on Fire Island and once at a diner out on the Hamptons, but this is my first real dinner out with a boy and really Ben isn't a boy. Peter still had a boyish quality. Ben seems like he's about to be a man.

"Have you been here before?"

Might as well tell the truth.

"We don't get out much as a family."

"Right. Bram makes it complicated, right?"

"Background sounds make it so he can't understand anything."

"Wow. That's – I mean he's getting better. I can see that."

"His brain is damaged. He'll get better, but he'll never be normal."

Ben frowns. He looks like he'd like to argue. I don't know what to say. Peter would have argued, suggested doctors don't know about the human will. Ben is more rational, calm, and willing.

"He's already improved more than the doctors expected. Maybe he'll surprise them even more."

"Maybe. I pray that's true. I just – sometimes I get tired of hoping for better."

"But you pray?"

"I do. I started going back to church with my parents after Alyse's death."

"Right. Did it help?"

"It did. I know your folks attend. Do you?"

He pauses, then shrugs and shakes his head.

"I kind of faded at college and then—kind of feel like if there's a god, Pete would have at least been hurt that night."

Do I be honest?

"That was the subject of my first prayers." His eyes widen. "Early, after denial, I wanted him hurt. But every time I opened the Bible, I found God chiding me for that thought. Peter's in a bad place going through a tough time and I'm just hurting myself. My rage doesn't make his life worse."

"You read his letter yet?"

"No, but I know I should."

The waitress comes to our table. Her accent is pretty thick, and her blue-and-gold gown fits her stick-thin frame like a glove. We haven't even tried to select food, so we order drinks and read our menus. We agree on some dishes that we think we'll both like and order when she returns with our colas.

"I'm sorry about earlier." His shoulders hunch. He's not wearing a suit, but he did wear a nice dress shirt and casual slacks.

"Earlier?"

"This spring. I spent most of the winter just trying not to think about it and that meant keeping you at arm's length."

"Yeah. I was avoiding you too."

"But I kept doing it after we met earlier and that was wrong. I'm surprised you came with me tonight after that."

"We can agree to disagree on Peter. We don't have to talk about him."

"We don't, but he's with us even when he's in Sing Sing." We nod in agreement, but then he switches topics. "I had fun with you and Bram this morning."

"It's a fine and pleasant misery."

"Not like that. He's actually a smart kid. I can see why'd you give up school to give him a chance to recover."

"I didn't give up school for that. He was my excuse. I wasn't ready to go back to school and see Alyse everywhere. I needed time to heal."

"So, will you go back next year?"

"I don't know. Homeschool has advantages. It takes me about three hours a day to get all my work done and I finished a month early."

"But, what about the quality of the teaching?"

"I used the public school curriculum and I just took my testing and I scored above-average. I did a lot of extra reading. I did some intense research on historical topics. I made use of a gym membership for gym. I took an online science class and also Spanish online. I got the same instruction as the kids that went to public school, but then I had so much more time to spend learning other stuff."

His eyes twinkle. The waitress brings a pot of tea and two small round cups without handles.

"So, what did you do all winter?"

"Not much. Worked at Temple, kept Tilly's cottage, worked out a lot."

"Sounds boring."

"We had an exciting summer. Maybe I needed to rest."

It's a joke, but there's also truth there. I slept for months after Alyse's death.

"You didn't do anything fun?"

"I tried. I spent a lot of time mountain biking the dunes."

"It always looks like fun when other people do it, but I don't know if I could."

"That Gary Fischer of yours is more than up to it."

That what?

"Oh, my bike?"

"It's worth every dime you spent on it."

I frown. Alyse gave it to me as a gift. I knew the blue and silver bike weighed little and had incredible gearing. She assured me she'd outgrown it and I didn't know how to say 'no', but I also loved the bike, fun to ride all last summer, and a great source of solace even during this winter's rare dry spells.

"If you want, we could go to a low-level course some Saturday morning and get you started."

"Maybe. I don't know. I might disappoint you."

"You couldn't. Besides, I need a biking partner. It used to be just us guys, but Pete – well, and Trevor – yeah. Finn's in Tanzania. I think I just—it doesn't feel the same when I'm alone. Wes went with me a few weeks ago, but…. I think he's too young. Or something. There's like this barrier…." He waits while the waitress sets out our platters of food. It smells delicious! "Sorry, hardly first-date material."

"Hmmm. How would I know? Peter and I never really dated." I feel my cheeks go hot.

"Time to eat." He takes the bowl off the rice and I uncover the almond chicken. There's broccoli beef and sweet and sour shrimp. Of course, the egg rolls and barbecue pork.

"You're not going to use a fork. That's sacrilege. There are chopsticks. Use them."

"I don't know how."

"Really?" He pulls his chopsticks out of their wrap, snaps them apart, scrapes them together. "Let me show you. Get yours ready."

It's hard work, eating with chopsticks and we end up laughing for a good quarter-hour while I struggle to get the knack. My hand starts to cramp. He finally relents and lets me use a fork.

"Next time, no mercy, though."

He's planning a next time?

"Since I failed at this task, I suppose I owe you a mountain bike ride."

"You sure? I get that you might still be thinking about him."

I shake my head. He's staring at my face, and then he sighs.

"My counselor--."

We both stop and laugh because of the synchronicity.

"You first."

What had I meant to say?

"My counselor says I have to face memories squarely. Now you."

He chuckles nervously.

"My counselor says the same thing and that's about what I was going to say. I generally tell my counselor to get stuffed at that point."

I'm not sure how to respond to that. His hazel gaze flickers across my face.

"He was my best friend since kindergarten and I don't know where or when he took a turn, but you say he was a good guy with you and…I'm confused."

He pauses so I suppose I need to answer with something. It's not like I haven't thought of Peter over the last year.

"Maybe he wasn't completely gone round the bend. Maybe…maybe…well, I don't know. He didn't want to be the way he was…the way he ended up. Maybe we're missing something…his perspective. We know *our* viewpoint. We don't know *his*."

"You said you hadn't read the letter?"

"I haven't. I'm scared to…alone. But maybe we need to, to finally put an end to the questions. He's been working on what's wrong and maybe he can finally explain it so we can stop focusing on it."

Ben pinschers a shrimp between his chopsticks and stares at it fondly. He chews thoughtfully.

"I hear you, but don't expect an answer tonight."

"I don't. I'm still trying to break free of his orbit…or hers…so I'm willing to listen to your solutions too."

"Mine? You mean, just ignoring it until I develop an ulcer? Not sure that's the healthiest solution. No, I know it isn't. But I'm not sure I really want to know his side of things. Sometimes it feels like it's a magic spell—that somehow Pete can reach out to me and suck me back in against my will. I don't want to feel compassion for him. I don't want his POV to calculate into things."

I do the same thing he did with a shrimp and manage to actually get it in my mouth.

"Mountain-biking? When?"

"Do you have an afternoon – like 4:00 pm free?"

Ben

I hear my desktop ding as I clean the kitchen in Tilly's cottage, but I wait until I've swept the floor before checking my email. Two junks and one from Finn who is still on. I navigate to Facetime, and he pulls up in a misty background.

"Hey, bro! How you be?"

Finn is a little nuts, but he's about the last of my high school friends that I'm talking to.

"I be good. And how's the monk's life?"

"I'm Protestant. We're not actually monks."

Finn not having sex seems unlikely. Of course, Finn not drinking seems unlikely, but he's over a year sober now.

"So how's the chicks?"

"Virginal. But I'm trying to be good. Safe sex is not a substitute for an IPA. We go into the big village once a month and an ice-cold Coke is heaven."

"I'm taking your word for it. So besides thumping the Bible, what are you up to?"

"Training baby missionaries. Guess who showed up this week?"

I draw a blank. Seriously, Pete is the only friend I can think of who ever came close to Jesus – for a brief moment at camp between 7th and 8th grades. Since there's no way Pete is in Africa, I admit I've got no guess.

"Pamela Torneau."

I'm slightly surprised. She was one of those people who *talked* a lot about God, but who never seemed to really know Him. I think how mean she was to Pete after the wreck with Cheyenne. Yeah, he deserved condemnation, but she seemed to enjoy that he didn't get the words of his apology right. Pete explained to me later that he never considered his word choice – accident versus wreck. Nobody ever called him on it, so Pam just seemed mean to him. Could we have gotten real repentance from him if we hadn't played guessing games with him?

"Her dad is a pastor, so I guess that makes sense."

"You think so? She was such a stuck-up bitch in high school. But – well, I guess we all reevaluated our lives last year. She's back on the righteous track."

"How do you figure?"

"She came to the Third World, man. Bugs, dung, women who don't wear tops. It's been fun watching her adapt."

"Do you think she'll make it?"

"I don't know. I bet if I asked my trainer if he thought I'd make it when I got here, he'd not be complimenting my natural man. But this place – it's amazing and I'm doing good works. More than just praying for people. I just finished building a water catchment for a village. They were so grateful for what we think of as just normal. I'm hoping Pam catches that bug. So, how's Trevor doing?"

"In rehab, I think. Or not. He's revolved a few times."

"It's got to be hard to go through what he's going through, especially with opioids. I'm so grateful I never tried them. I'd cycle in and out too, I think."

I try to imagine Finn's surroundings, but all I can imagine is his bedroom from his mom's house.

"I've got no real experience in addiction. I tried pot and I'm not sure I liked being numbed out and not dreaming."

"Good for you. I still dream about smoking a bowl, but it doesn't compare to when I worship God. What are you doing these days?"

"Still working at the cabinet factory and for Captain Russell."

"You went back? How was that?"

"It bothered me at first, but now I don't really think about it. I went sailing and he wasn't with me. He haunts mountain biking though."

"Well, that sucks. His letter help any?"

Whoa, how does he know?

"Letter?"

"What, he didn't write you?"

"How do you know he's writing letters?"

"Well, he writes me."

"How does he even know your address?"

"I gave it to him when I visited him in rehab."

"You never mentioned."

"I don't have to run my relationships by you and Peter needs the few outside friends he's managed to keep. So, I take it he hasn't written you yet."

"He wrote me. I haven't read it yet. Maybe I won't."

There's a long pause.

"I'll pray for you, that you will read it. I don't know what he wrote, but he's using a rough time to come to a better place. It's not easy to get a waiver to write your victims, even amends letters. Just give him a chance. You don't have to forgive him. He won't argue that he deserves it."

"And if he does?"

There's another pause. I guess I asked a tough question.

"Then you can burn his letter and refuse to interact with him. But you know, I wouldn't let him get away with not admitting his culpability."

Finn spent a year apologizing to everybody before he moved to Tanzania to be a missionary. I distrusted his sobriety at first, but he'd never really hurt me, so I accepted his apology without a fight and I'm glad when he messages me. I *believe* he wouldn't let Pete whine or blame others for his mistakes. But I don't trust Pete to write the truth to anyone. Or maybe I don't trust myself not to fall for his crap again.

"I'll think about it."

"Good. I'll pray for you. I'm coming back to the States for Thanksgiving and Christmas. Maybe we can get together."

"Yeah. I'll be back from Dartmouth for Christmas. Give me a call."

My cell lights up, so I check it. Dad's wondering if Wes is with me. I glance at the clock. It's past 9 pm.

"I think I need to go. I've got a call coming in."

"No problem. I was just taking a break from the heat. Ta-ta for now."

He signs off and I call Dad.

"He's not with me. How long has he been out?"

"All day. It's summer. We weren't worried about it until he didn't show up for dinner and now it's dark." My parents resisted being helicopter parents with me and it turned out okay, so they're doing it with Wes.

"He's not with Bram?"

"No, we checked that before we bothered you."

"I could drive around, try to find him, but that's a needle in a haystack."

"We were hoping you'd know where he might be hanging out."

"I know where my friends and I hung out, but that was kind of a long time ago. I'll swing by the beach and get back with you."

"Thank you."

The beach Pete and I drank our first beers at is deserted. Maybe it wasn't Pete's first beer. And what would I think if my 12-year-old brother was here drinking beer? Pete was 13, I think. I was 14. Too young for sure. I'm glad I haven't found my brother.

I drive by a couple of parks and try to remember where any of his friends live, but it seems like Bram is his best friend, which is a little weird for a 12-year-old to be best friends with a guy who can't talk. But I don't pursue that. I drive by a pocket park near Van Valkenburg High School and there are a bunch of teenagers hanging out on the picnic tables, but they're older than Wes and I don't see him among them.

It's 11:30 when my phone dings.

> **HELEN- He's home. Claims he was playing video games and lost track of time. I think he was smoking pot.**

Ah! Well, that's not horribly surprising. Trevor was smoking pot when we were 11. But my parents raised me before they raised Wes, so….

> **BEN- Don't kill him. Everybody does it at some point. I got work in the morning, so.... Glad he's home safe. A couple of weeks of being grounded in the middle of summer will be painful.**

I pause at the corner of Main and Old Post and enjoy the night for a moment before I turn toward Tilly's cottage. Wes just became a teenager, for all that he won't be 13 for a few months yet.

Driving around looking for Wes gave me time to think about what Finn said about Pete and the letter I don't want to read. I haven't come to any conclusions other than to admit I'm a coward. I'm afraid of the power Pete has always wielded on me and so I hesitate to read the letter and I'm not sure I'm ever going to get over that.

Lily

It's busy at Nails today. I guess it's Home Improvement Saturday. Dad tells me to stand in the line while he gets what he needs. The line is a good place to people-watch from and as I gaze around at the mostly male customers, I see the clerk. She's shorter than me and her hair is cut in one of those crazy bed-head styles. I know her from somewhere. She's chatting with the customer in front of her, smiling and laughing.

It comes to me. Macaria. Trevor's ex, Finn's friend. They rescued Alyse and me at a Hamptons party we had no business being at. Peter and Ben came when Finn called them, but Macaria was also there. She came to Trevor's birthday party too. She's nice, but I watch her slide some currency into her pocket as she's chatting up that customer. I don't know what to think about that. She's stealing from her employer. I remember a different person.

I remember Peter saying things about her. He liked her before Trevor did, but he didn't like that she smoked and did drugs. He found her unpredictable…unreliable. It's sort of like what Ben says about Peter and Trevor now. Trevor does a lot of drugs, possibly dealing with the pain from the boat crash. Peter – well, ultimately, I must admit that Peter is a drunk. Nice when sober, but the devil when he drank. Is Macaria showing the other side of her personality? The nice girl who wouldn't let two younger girls be exploited steals from her boss. I don't know what I'm going to say to her when I get to the cash register. Maybe she won't remember me. A girl can hope, right?

I'm hoping Dad will come back so I can bow out before I reach the counter, but the guy in front of me is speedy. I'm turning to tell the guy behind me he can go ahead when I hear Macaria say, "Hey, Lily! It's so nice to see you."

I see Dad working his way toward me. I can't ignore her, so I hope my smile is genuine as I turn.

"Hey. Um, Macaria, right?"

"Yes! How are you doing? That was a horrible thing, wasn't it?"

"It was, but I think I've healed from it.

"Good." She's thinner than I remember and the lines on her face have deepened. She's Peter's age – 18, but I swear she looks older. "At least you weren't hurt like Trevor. Or Alyse." She looks sad for a moment. "That was always the risk with hanging out with Trevor. I was surprised to hear it was Peter driving the boat."

Dad sets the basket on the counter.

"Hi, Dad."

"Oh, you're Mister…Wessex…that's not it."

"Wexler." Dad grunts. He starts taking the items out of the basket and she begins ringing up our order. I watch her run his card and as far as I can tell, she doesn't do anything weird with it. Maybe she's only pocketing the cash. It occurs to me that it would be easier to cheat with cash. Just don't ring it up and whoever does the books will never know. I feel so guilty even just standing here.

"Well, it was great to see you. I don't have time to talk, but I hope we run into each other when I'm not at work."

"Yeah, that would be great." I follow Dad toward the door.

"How do you know her?"

Dad asks this as we approach the car.

"She was friends with Peter, Trevor, and Ben."

"You smell the pot on her?"

Okay, I'm not really familiar with that scent, but now that I think about it….

"She's a cigarette smoker."

"Naw – I know the difference." He laughs nervously. I suspect he has smoked cannabis. "That might have been there too, but she's been toking sometime in the last couple of hours."

"I feel sorry for her." I stare at my dad across the roof of the car. "Who turns to drugs to cope with life?"

"There's a lot of reason people want to, Lily. But it never solves anything."

"I know. I saw that with Peter, Trevor, and Alyse."

"Alcohol is a drug." The newspaper said Peter had a lot more than alcohol on board that night. Dad sighs. "We need to get home so I can fix that door today."

We slide into our respective sides of the car.

"I wouldn't wish what happened to you on anyone, but I'm glad you learned to stay away from drugs because of it.

I nod. "Me too."

"What about Ben?"

I tilt my head, looking at the road ahead of us.

"I think he's not the type of person to get addicted to things, but I'll think about it if you want."

"I want. I like Ben, but you don't want to make a similar mistake with him."

I nod. He's right. I should think about my decisions and make sure I'm making wise ones. Parents are useful, even when I sometimes chafe against them.

Flesh & Bone

Peter
March

I'm nervous, so I write slowly, copying the letter I'm sending today. Luis agreed with me that I nailed the message. Well, no, *I* agree with *him*. I judge myself too harshly and I'm terrified I'll make my situation worse. I trust Luis to have a good analysis of my production. He often won't let me send a letter when I think I've gotten it as good as I can. He makes me read it again and then rewrite it.

> Dear Captain Russell – Wow, how do I say this without sounding whiny?
>
> I should have listened to you and not just once but dozens of times. And I don't know why because I don't remember why I endangered your boat. It seems really deliberate and I don't know how to

sincerely apologize for that. Which is kind of the point, I think. I'm not supposed to apologize because that's manipulative. I've apologized a lot and didn't change. Now I have to show you that I've changed.

Only I can't because I'm in here and you're my victim and I can't interact with you. If you choose, I can when I get out. Maybe you'll have some hulls to scrape. Or maybe you're just going to say 'Never come around again' and I totally understand if you say that, but I hope you don't. It won't erase any of the things I've done, but

Yeah, it won't fix it, but I still hope you'll let me do it. If it doesn't upset you, I mean. I really don't want to cause anymore pain to anyone, so thank you for reading my letter. If you never want to see me again, you can suggest something that's lifestyle amends – and I'll do it here if I can or when I get out.

I really do regret what I did, and I don't know a better way to say that and not sound whiny.

Peter

I wanted to finish that sentence with the trailing "but", but Luis said to move it along. I've written a good letter. I can't do better and that should be enough. The 'but' shows I'm struggling and that's not wrong. I hand the copy to Luis, who is perched on his bunk like some sort of gargoyle.

"Address the envelope and we'll mail it tomorrow."

My fingers tremble as I take the letter back. If I could finish that sentence....

"No, you're done." Luis reads my mind. I sigh. "Stop stressing yourself out."

I fold the letter, address the envelope and slide the letter in. I still want to lick the flap, but the COs will just tear it open and cost me my stamp. It takes two-days' pay to buy a stamp, though I still have a supply from when I started and had no money. I think the AA group pays for those. I'm scared to ask and discover I owe someone. I'm going to need to buy stamps pretty soon because I have an income now – 10 cents an hour, 60 cents a day. It takes two days for me to buy a stamp, so I'm not inclined to waste them.

"It will be fine. Chill out, *chico*."

I cock my head. I did well in Spanish in high school. *Chico* is like calling someone "kid", but I've never heard Luis use any endearment other than "boss" or "jefe" for the COs and "man" for other people. I shrug and move on.

I've managed to sleep for a week. I keep jerking awake about every two hours, but I've also managed not to scream. My natural inclination, as in everything, is to judge myself harshly, but Seth complimented me this morning for not waking up the tier. Am I making progress?

I read the Big Book this morning and so I reach down the Bible. It's still not my thing. I'm in this book called *Numbers*. It starts off pretty damned boring. When I wanted to give up one page in, Luis said there were some good parts mixed into the math and to just work my way through it. It's not really called *Numbers*, for starters. The Hebrew title is "In the Wilderness." At first, it just smacked of math nerdiness to me, kind of like I imagine reading a telephone book would feel, but there's a travel story filled with life and death survival stories woven in. There's food falling from heaven, people following a pillar of fire, a water-gushing rock in a desert, and an intriguing spy story. More than anything it's about trying to find a place of rest.

God, I resonate with that! Maybe that's why I get this meaning from it. Am I still so homesick and lonely, desiring to get back to a place where I can feel safe? And can I even get there?

God set Israel a table in the wilderness where they easily could have starved or died of thirst. They didn't trust him with direction or provision. Time and time again, over a 40-year period, God provided for them, and they refused to pass the test. They became embittered and wanted to go back to Egypt where they'd been slaves because they thought it was safer. Most of that generation never entered the Promised Land because their hearts were hard.

Is my heart hard? I don't know, but Luis doesn't seem to think so. Would he assign this reading if he thought I couldn't be saved? But can I be? Alyse's blood makes my fingers sticky even as I turn the pages. I pause, feeling her breath on my neck. Her eyes looked so desperate as I gathered her in my arms on the deck of Captain Russell's boat. Her gaze begged me to reverse what I'd just done. I begged her to breathe as the light died in her eyes and….

The hand on my shoulder pulls me out of the memory.

"You ready to talk about it, *chico*?"

"This is my 40 years, isn't it?"

"Something like that." He takes a deep breath. I wait. "It doesn't have to be that long, and you don't have to die without crossing the Jordan."

I'm cold as Alyse's body grew that night.

"I killed her."

"And you're going to live with that for the rest of your life. The question is do you want Him to help you with that or are you just going to let the guilt crush you."

It's too much. I pull away, hunching my shoulders and he pulls his hand back, never forcing me, letting me make my own decisions.

"I'm sorry," I mutter as he returns to his bunk.

"You don't owe me an apology, *chico*. You're the only one you're hurting here."

I put the bookmark in the Bible and settle back on my bunk to consider what I've read and how it intersects with that dead body in my arms.

June

Ben

She keeps up with my slowed pace and I'm so proud of her as we stop at the highest point of the Blue Only for water. She grew her hair out this winter and she's got it pulled back in a high ponytail, a purple bike helmet making her look like a pretty alien. Mud covers her shins and she's glowing with good health. I can't resist but grab a pic of her as she lowers her water bottle.

"Ugh, I am not photo-worthy."

"Nonsense!" I show her my phone. "I like this one the best."

"Seriously?" I lift the phone to catch a photo of us together.

"I've never had this much fun with a girl before."

"You don't mind that I can't go as fast as you?"

"You just need some practice. Wes can't keep up either. Heck, Pete and Trevor, hungover, needed me to slow down."

"Don't invoke him."

She's right, of course. I mount my bike again and set off down the trail. The sun's out against a hard blue sky and it feels like a hot summer's weekend just starting.

"I'm off at 6. You want to meet up?"

I'm loading her bike on the Jeep.

"Um, no, I'm going to the Barns Courtney with a friend. It's done at like 10."

"That's the girl you told me about, the one from school?"

"Yeah. The one I don't remember."

"That's weird."

"It is. But you know, if you want to pick me up it would keep my dad from having to do it."

"It's in Huntington, right?" I think the Paramount is east of here along the coast. I do a quick look on my phone. "Yeah, I could do that. We can let him know when we get back to the house."

We laugh and joke all the way to Port Mallory. I'm really enjoying time spent with her, even when the topic eventually turns toward Pete once again.

"I guess it's time to read our letters." I want to be free of his power over me and maybe it is just like the monster in the nightmare. If you face it squarely, you find out it's only about 15 pounds and can fit under your arm. "Let me finish unloading these, then I'll run inside and get mine and meet you at your house."

From my window, I can see my parents, the Wexlers and Wes gathered in the backyard trying to teach the paralyzed kid corn-hole. I grab the letter from my desk and head back to Lily's house.

"They're so amazing." She's standing in their back sunroom watching the gathering in our backyard.

"I'm always excited to see Wes's commitment to your brother. Anyway."

She sighs and sits down at the table here, staring at the white rectangle in her hand. Then she uses a butterknife to slit it open and pull out the contents. There's a letter from the Department of Corrections explaining everything and a card with various choices on it that we can return to DOC if we like. Then there's Pete's very legible script on lined notebook paper. With a sigh, Lily starts reading it aloud.

> Dear Lily, I've been trying to sort out that night – why I aimed my boat toward you and Ben – and I don't remember my motivation. Drunk doesn't need a motivation. I regret that behavior and all the other things I did to manipulate you. It wasn't that you weren't important to me, but that my addiction was more important to me and—
>
> I'd take it back if I could and I can't, so that leaves me with nothing to say. The thing is – you don't stop being a liar when you say you're sorry you lied. To stop being a liar I have to learn to always tell the truth and that's really hard when the truth is I did some horrible things I can't take back. There's a part of me that never wants to go near anyone who reminds me of that, esp. Alyse, but I know I can't make amends that way. And I don't know if I can make amends to you. If I can, let me know what you want. Obviously, there's things I can't do right now, but I will when I can. If you'd prefer never to see me again, you can

> *choose some lifestyle amends you'd like me to make or…well, I'll do something if you don't respond. I have changed and I plan to go on getting better, but you don't have any reason to believe that, so…. I don't really have anything else to say. Thank you for even reading my letter.* **Peter**

She's crying and wipes tears off her cheeks, dropping the letter on the table. I pick it up. Like Grey pointed out, Pete doesn't say he's sorry. He says he regrets it. That's a step up from the banal "I'm sorry". Pete maybe gets it now, but far too late. A lot of lives were destroyed because Pete didn't understand regret until it was too late. I now regret picking up the letter as my gaze falls on the word "liar". A million and one examples swell in my mind and I want to shred the letter, but it isn't mine to assault.

"I can't do this. I'll see you tonight at 10."

I leave my letter in her capable hands and flee the scene because I'm not ready to face the monster my guilt has turned Pete into.

Lily

Jenae meets me at the will-call window, having already picked up my tickets. She looks exactly like her picture, though she's a little taller than I thought she'd be. Her hair is cut short, buzzed on the sides and wavy on top and she's wearing skinny fit jeans and a Barns Courtney t-shirt.

We hug, which feels awkward. There's something about this…I can't quite put my finger on it, but something feels…wrong. Still, this is Jenae and I do think I remember her from freshman year at school. I just can't put my finger squarely on my memory.

I pause to text my dad, to let him know that I'm safely inside and have connected with Jenae.

"Do you mind if we send a photo to him?"

"No, that's fine."

We go almost cheek to cheek, and I send the double-selfie to my dad. Then we turn toward the auditorium and make our way to the seats. This is open stadium, standing room, so not the greatest "seats", but we're not behind a concrete pillar, so I have nothing to complain about as my favorite band takes the stage.

The opening act is decent as Jenae works us to the railing, so we don't have to fight to see. Then Barns and his band take the stage with *Glitter and Gold*, which was famous for some British series starring the guy who played Dexter, which my parents didn't allow me to watch, but I saw at friends' houses. Not the British series. I watched that with my older brother. I mean Dexter. My parents banned it from their house.

Jenae and I beating our hands against the railing, rocking to the beat. A brief memory of dancing with Peter at a diner out on the Hamptons drifts through my memory. It's probably because Barns' voice is deep like Peter's. His hands were really long too, I remember as I watch Jenae's wide hand beat the tempo next to mine.

My phone dings, so I glance at it in case there's something I need to know.

LYLE- Jenae is a guy?

What? Oh, my goodness. Now, I *remember* Jerry, a skinny boy who took a liking to me, who Alyse treated like crap. And then I met Peter and forgot all about the frosh.

He…she…seems to be really enjoying the music…which I can no longer hear because all I can think is "this is a date?"

Barns is well into *Fire*, which is one of my favorite songs, but I have completely lost the beat. How could Dad see in one selfie what I didn't see in months of texting and even meeting him…her…in person?

I've been through a lot in the last year, so I eventually find the music during the song *99* and when Jenae smiles at me, I manage to smile back. There's still so much to deal with and I've never had to confront this topic before. What am I supposed to do.

During the intermission, *she* puts *her* arm around me and I put a hand against *her* shoulder, which is too muscular to be a girl's.

"We need to talk."

His eyes shift and then come back. He knows what's coming.

"We're friends, but we can't date."

"Why not?"

"I'm not gay."

Something flashes in his eyes.

"You sure about that? You and Alyse were sure pretty cozy."

I could be angry at that accusation, but I've worn grooves in the self-reproachment tracks, so I immediately ask myself what I did wrong. Did I have a hand in confusing Jerry who now wants to be Jenae? I don't know. Alyse could be cruel, and I didn't yet know that about her. Does that make me responsible for her behavior now? I don't know. I just know I can't do *this*.

"I will reimburse you for my ticket. Ben and I are getting closer and…I just don't like you like that."

"You're a transphobic bitch!"

His voice has deepened and I'm suddenly acutely aware that he's bigger and stronger than I am and we're way closer to a sudden drop than I want to be for this.

I open my mouth to argue my viewpoint, but suddenly the venue lights come on full and a man's voice comes over the loudspeakers.

"Ladies and gentlemen, as many of you know, there was a police shooting in Long Island City earlier today. Given the distance we are from that, we didn't anticipate any difficulties, but there are riots forming in nearby towns and the authorities have asked us to close the venue. Contact our corporate offices in the morning for a partial refund and we really apologize for the inconvenience. We suggest you get out of the area as quickly as possible. Go home and stay safe. Barns and his band's going to rock us out the door."

Barnes and his band are taking their positions in the bright light and strumming out *I've Got That Good Thing.* They look a little freaked, but they're professionals, so they don't meet a beat of the song. When I turn back, Jenae has disappeared into the crowd. I'm on my own. It's only 8:30 pm. What am I going to do?

Ben

News of a police shooting made me antsy. Some psycho guy was strangled to death by an assaulted bystander on the subway earlier this week and there have been protests in the City. Then a cop had to draw down on someone this morning. You'd think it wouldn't make me wonder about Pete's life in jail, but for some reason I've got *Shawshank* featuring Pete Wyngate playing in my head all evening while crewing the sunset cruise.

"Folks, we're headed into the harbor early tonight because there's riots reported in Patchoque and Long Island City."

The mostly tourist group gasps and starts to gather their belongings – the wives reminding their husbands they need to avoid the larger towns on the way back to the inn. They still get to see the sunset as we're pulling past the breakwater.

"You said you were supposed to pick up Lily at 10:00 pm?" Cap is letting his brother Carter count heads and guide people down the steps to the pier while I'm collecting drink containers from the stern.

"Yeah. Kind of nervous about that."

"According to my phone, there's a group gathering at Bethel AME Church. That's about a mile from the Paramount, so it might be okay, but I think that little girl has been traumatized enough. Go on and be there when the concert lets out."

"You sure?"

"I'm the one offering, aren't I?"

Within minutes I'm on the Smithtown Bypass headed east. There's a lot of police presence, especially after I get on Veteran's Memorial Highway. As I near Huntington I smell smoke. There's a roadblock where Broadway meets New York Avenue.

"I'm trying to pick up m-my sister at the Paramount."

The young cop flinches at the sound of fireworks as an older man argues with another cop about the same thing.

"I get it, man, but it's not safe."

"It's safer for her *with* me than by herself."

A crease deepens between his eyes.

"There's a parking lot just south of here. We're not supposed to stop people on foot."

That sounds a lot like encouraging rioting, but I'm not going to argue. It's already 9:00 pm. Will they let the concert out early? Maybe it would be safer to let the band keep playing. Not that I'm in charge of that.

I lock my car and get my bearings. The Paramount is about a mile. I can run that in ten minutes. Nobody tries to stop me as I take off north as fast as I can run toward the sky glow of what I fear is a burning building.

Lily

People push and jostle as I make my way toward the exit. Nobody's panicking, but they're stressed and a lot of them are too young to be here by themselves. I finally feel the soothing cool of fresh air only to see the smoke drifting in the air. To the east, I hear people roaring as if they're at a football game, only I suspect they're not cheering for basketball or soccer.

I stare around, hoping to see Ben just magically waiting for me in a war zone, but that so isn't my life. I have no idea what to do. Can Ben even get here to me?

I try calling him, but all circuits are busy. I remember my brother Jemmy saying that sometimes a text will go through when a voice call won't, so I text Ben.

> **LILY- The concert let out early and I'd normally just wait, but there's a riot a few blocks over. Which way should I head to meet you?**

It seems the message went through, but how do I know? Damn Jenae for abandoning me! And the concert-goers are thinning fast. I don't see anyone I know, and my heart starts jumping in my chest.

"Young lady, are you okay?"

He's an older man in a grey coat and for a moment, I'm thrilled to see anyone who looks normal.

"Hey, sir, do you have a way out of here?"

"Yeah, come with me." He's about my dad's age. Why do I feel like ants are climbing on my skin?

We turn down the sidewalk and for a moment my mind tells me I can trust this man, but then a group of people in black run by me and I'm spun, losing track of which direction I was going. When I sort myself out, the man is being beaten by the black-clothed group and I'm on my own again. I can't help him, so I put distance between us. It's only when I reach the other side of the street that I realize my small purse with my ID, lip gloss and cell phone is no longer over my shoulder. I scan the opposite sidewalk where someone is attempting to build a fire and decide I don't need ID or my phone. But with or without ID, I have to figure out what to do next.

Blood & Clean Socks

Peter
April

I move my mystery meat around in the mash potatoes to satisfy Luis. I just got out of the infirmary this afternoon and I'm more than ready for bed. They upped my antidepressant dose to the maximum, which is killing my appetite. Or maybe it's just a side effect of the depression.

I wrote a bunch of letters. I lifted weights and practiced fighting with Caleb. I even mailed off the letters I'd written to Trevor, Ben, Lily, and Captain Russell. I had a good couple of weeks. Then the nightmares returned full force and my only solution was not sleeping. I don't remember them pulling me out of the cell. Luis said I stopped functioning. I would have died of dehydration if I'd had my way.

The only good news is that I'm probably not bipolar. If I were, this much antidepressant would surely throw me into mania, and I'm still depressed.

"It's not art, kid. It only counts if you put some of it in your mouth, chew and swallow."

"I'm not anorexic. I know that."

"Then do it."

I sigh and bite a piece of ground meat covered in potatoes covered in gravy. I chew. I don't think I can swallow. I gag as I manage to choke it down.

Caleb and Luis are discussing something from the Bible. Something about wanting to avoid sin but the body goes toward sin. I never knew that was in the Bible. I choke down another bite of food. Across the way, some Arian Nation types are making loud comments and threatening one another with violence in a friendly manner. None of it matters to me. I'm so overmedicated, I just don't care.

Across the room, there's a commotion and angry words. Luis's head swivels as he hones in on the activity. I slowly drag my attention off the food I don't want to eat to notice what's going on. Some guy with an inner-city accent is calling someone a vile name and then there's a scuffle, followed by angry words in Puerto Rican Spanish.

Luis grabs my arm and pulls me toward the far wall, his gaze scanning the situation and the guard stations. I don't see a guard. Where the hell are the guards? When we reach the far wall, Luis puts our backs to it.

"It's going to get messy…bloody…and then the guards will hit the alarm and come in. When that happens, put your face to the wall and your hands above your head on the wall. Don't look right, don't look left. If they try to get a rise out of you, ignore it."

I start to turn around and he shakes his head.

"Don't turn your back on this, *chico*. It can turn our way in a heartbeat."

My pulse races and it's hard to focus on what he's saying. The crowd parts as more prisoners head our way and I see a man slumped against the cafeteria counter, blood flowing down his front from at least three places.

And just that quickly, my sister is dying in my arms again. I can feel blood gluing my fingers together and blood bubbles rise and fall between her pink lips that slowly turn grey as the light dies in her eyes.

I wake up much later in the semi-darkness of the tier. I can hear Luis's light breathing above me and a guard pauses on the far side of the bars that separate the cell from the tier. I close my eyes so he can't see that I'm awake and I sense his flashlight beam pass over me and then move on. I wonder how bad I was that I don't remember getting back here.

Well, wait! The surreal fragments of memory come back out of order. A guard prodding me in the kidneys. Luis talking. Puking in the toilet after we get here. Sitting on my bunk, feeling the blood on my hands while Luis asks me questions. Is this where I go when my mind flees reality?

I hear Luis shift his weight and then he appears over the edge of his bunk.

"You okay?"

"Don't know."

I wish I could adjust the pillow on this stupid mattress, but it's built-in, hard, and lumpy. I straighten up against the wall behind the bunk. I'm not going to sleep for a while and me sleeping when I'm not tired is me having nightmares that drive the people around me crazy. Luis drops off the top bunk and drops his separate pillow onto the floor. As a trustee, he gets some perks he doesn't share.

"What happened?"

"Colveccio earned it. They went after him. Now he's out of everyone's hair." He senses my horrified stare. "I'm not as cold as all that. I've been praying he'd learn to keep his mouth shut. He didn't. That'll get you shanked. He was warned. He didn't listen."

After swirling around my horror a few times, I sum up my thoughts.

"I hate this place."

"It's a tough place." He sounds flat. I don't know if it upsets him or not.

"Where were the guards?"

"Yeah, sometimes they look the other way. It makes for a better time for them, and it gets rid of troublemakers."

"But it's their job to keep the peace."

"Getting rid of Colveccio keeps the peace."

A shudder shivers through me.

"You did good though. Until you got here. I mean, you definitely needed someone to lead you back, but you didn't argue with the guards. So what happened to you?"

I'm not sure I can safely say what happened. I take a couple of deep breaths and let them out slowly, following the advice of the psychologist who saw me in the infirmary.

"The blood it—uh—yeah, my—my s-sister…."

He waits for me to say more, but I'm fighting tears that can't fall here.

"So you were back there on that boat?" He says it softly. I hear myself swallow as I nod. "Okay, so that's good to know. That happen when you don't see blood?"

Luis said he took me as a cellmate when he didn't have to have one because he didn't want to see me sucked into the mental health system from which there is no escape and, if I'm a little overmedicated at the moment, it's not nearly as bad as Kirby would be. A part of my contract with him is honesty, even when I don't like it.

"Yeah, especially in my dreams."

A guard pauses at the bars again, but he doesn't say anything, just continues like he doesn't see Luis breaking the rules.

"Hanson, he's a cool dude for a CO. So these dreams – they always about the boat, your sister, that night?"

"I don't know. There's some—I don't understand some of them." They're too overwhelming to describe – Alyse with her hair loose about her shoulders disappearing into the room where I found Mom and Sam…. It's not real. It's a product of my fevered imagination.

"Stay with me, Peter." How does he know? "You know they're letting me read your file?"

I didn't, though I vaguely remember telling Dr. Sherwin that I didn't object. Now my pulse quickens with fear.

"Sam—your stepfather?" I grunt in assent. "You ever think of writing to him, saying "make her stop writing me?" I haven't. He takes my silence for what it is. I've got nothing to say. "I know you feel like you deserve it, *chico*, but you don't." The soft light from the tier falls across his face, emphasizing its leanness, filling in the lines to give me a hint of what he must have looked like when he walked into Sing Sing a quarter-century ago. "Something happen with him and her?"

"They had an affair. I caught them. I told my dad. He kicked her out. It probably wouldn't have mattered though. She was already pregnant with my little brother. Dad would have found out anyway."

"That's not what I mean. There's things you and I can't discuss here because somebody might overhear." Oh, that! I remember the eerie feeling of her fingers against my chest.

"Did I dream that tonight?" He grunts. I guess I did. I don't remember waking up. Do I talk in my sleep?

"So I got you on Boudreaux's schedule for Wednesday – day after tomorrow. Once a month is not enough, but there's stuff you're sitting on that you've got to admit to someone and he's the safest. And if you want me to hear it, you can request I be in the session. Then we don't have to discuss it, but we know it's there. Yeah?"

I kind of liked counselor Boudreaux the handful of times I talked to him in the infirmary. There's another guy, I forget his name, who isn't bad, but out in the real world, I'd find another counselor. Boudreaux is from New Orleans and I suspect he comes from money. We sort of understand one another.

"Yeah. I'm sorry for being--."

"Bury 'I'm sorry' in a deep grave, *chico.* We're going to lick the depression, knock your monsters down to manageable size. But you need to stop being sorry for the things you don't control."

"Don't I control waking everybody up every night?"

"What's your alternative? Not sleeping leads to bad places." A distant gate buzzes, opens and closes. "That's a shift change. You got another few hours to sleep. I think you got five hours with interruptions, so hit the rack, try to get a couple of more."

"And if I wake everybody up?"

"I think I got a plan for that."

"What?"

He grins crazily.

"You got any clean socks?"

June

Ben

I'm running along trying to stay away from the knots of sullen individuals dressed in black. I clearly didn't come dressed for a riot, but my legs are holding up as I run north, trying to keep a steady pace while paying attention to my breath control. I don't want to be so out of breath I can't respond to trouble if it comes my way.

To my left, someone has managed to set a car on fire. Looks like it had been a nice car before they broke the windows and ignited the upholstery. I need to keep this in mind so I'm not bringing Lily through danger…if I find her. I'm starting to doubt this plan as I see younger kids running past me dressed in Barns Courtney t-shirts. *Shit!* My phone vibrates and I pull it out while still running.

LYLE– You're picking up Lily? Everything okay there?

What do I tell him? Do I tell him anything? I don't want him to decide to put himself in danger. Enough of us are doing that as it is.

BEN– I'm here. Haven't found her yet. Will text you when I do.

I put my phone back in my pocket and squat to tie a shoelace. As I straighten, I hear a roar, and then large white-and-black figure races toward me screaming "White motherfu—" as he hits me in a full tackle. I never played football, but I've played rough-and-tumble with my dad my whole life. Even startled, I manage to turn us, so we don't land with me on my back under this tub of lard. That leaves one arm free to punch him in his flabby gut, which gives me a moment to scramble free. I grab the aluminum softball bat he dropped.

"Stay down, man! I've got no beef with you, but I *will* hurt you if you come at me again."

My elbow is bruised, and I'm way hyped on adrenaline now. Ignoring the chubby guy in black, I turn toward the Paramount and run. If Lily is out in this, she's in big trouble and I need to find her before someone hurts her. And then I see a girl in a red sundress with her shoulder-length brown hair loose about her shoulders, looking like she's trying to find someone on the other side of the street.

"Lily." I'm gasping, starting to feel the assault I ran away from. "Lily."

Lily

Ben's out of breath, but I've never been so glad to see anyone in my life. He's covered in sweat, but his left hand grips an aluminum baseball bat.

"Are you okay?" he asks.

"Now that you're here. I didn't know what to do."

"We get out of here." He tugs on my hand, but I need a second. "Come on. We need to get out of here."

I don't see my purse or phone. I need to concentrate on staying alive, not worry about my stuff. Ben leads me with his left hand to keep his right free for the bat.

"Have you had to use that?" I'm nervous and I tend to babble when I'm stressed. He glances at me before returning to scanning the crowd.

"A guy tried to hit me with it, and I took it away from him."

I throw him an impressed look and then he hustles me away from a group of squabbling crows in black. If this riot is about race – a white man killing a black man – why are all the rioters white?

"My car's about a mile away. That way -- if we get separated. It's a public parking lot. Go there and wait if I'm not with you. Do *not* try to find me."

I nod. I'm wearing a sundress and sandals. I'm useless in this situation. As if my thought triggers something, he pulls off his light jacket and hands it to me.

"You stick out like a sore thumb. Cover up."

I guess I do look like I didn't come for a riot. He's wearing shorts and deck shoes. Does he blend better? I doubt it. But he's a tall athletic guy with a baseball bat. I zip the jacket up and roll up the sleeves.

As we leave downtown Huntington behind, the groups of black-clad rioters are replaced with teenagers looting stores. Some of them are black. I hope that girl with the waist-length dreds doesn't get arrested for those three boxes of Jimmy Choos she's carrying. How does looting a store make up for the subway guy being dead? Ben must look scary because none of the looters come close to us. A few exchange glares with him and decide to bother someone else. My calves start to burn with the pace, but I don't complain. A Charlie horse won't kill me. Some of the people Ben is scaring might. I remember the kind man who offered to help me getting viciously beaten by the mob of white kids.

Maybe something more has happened since I heard the latest news.

"What's this all about? The subway thing?" I need to keep my mind off how much my legs hurt.

"There was a police shooting tied to it this afternoon." A kid with a stack of Nintendo boxes nearly stumbles into us. Ben raises the baseball bat, and the kid decides to go around us.

"So white kids show up to burn the town down?" That is so confusing.

"It's a thing, I guess." Neither of us thinks this is a good idea.

We've got to be close to his car by now and fortunately we're leaving the mobs behind. Or maybe they're all making smores around the building they've caught fire.

He swerves over into the shadows when we near the cops who are turning away frantic people in cars who are probably trying to pick their kids up at the concert. I think I see Jenae getting into a car, which whips a U-turn and gets out of the area as quickly as possible. The squealing tires pull the cops' attention and Ben uses the distraction to get around them and into the parking lot.

Ben

It feels like we've reached safety as we get into my Jeep, but that's a false hope. My cell is lit up with Nixel reports – don't go here, don't go there. I don't see any notifications for the most direct route home. I hand my phone to her with the message screen open as I unlock the doors.

"My dad's losing his mind."

"Text him. Tell him we're together."

I'm shaking, so I try to calm myself before I start the car. There's a crowd moving our way down the road from Huntington. I start the engine. She's still texting. How long does it take to text "I'm with Ben"? I use the rag I keep for oil changes to wipe the bat clear of my fingerprints and unroll the window just enough to toss it away. I guess I learned a few things from Pete's brush with the law.

"Put your seatbelt on. We need to move."

I pull out of the parking lot headed in a different direction than the crowd. There's still heavy police presence and we get stopped before we get on the expressway. The cop asks us for our ID and Lily explains in a voice shaking with emotion that hers was stolen from her as she was trying to get out of the riot. The cop stares at her for several heartbeats and then hands my license back.

"Go on. Get her home to safety."

"Thank you, sir."

I pull away, praying the cop won't have a bad night.

"Did your friend get home safely?"

"I saw *him* getting into a car. I think he's okay."

"*He*? I thought…."

"Yeah, so did I."

Her laughter sounds a little hysterical. I guess it's been a night for her.

"We live in interesting times."

We chuckle together as a statie cruiser roars past, lights flashing. I'm not pulling over. They can fine me. This is not a night to get caught on the side of the road.

"Is he a guy trying to be a girl or a girl trying to be a guy?"

"Guy trying to be a girl and very upset that I'm not gay."

"I'm glad you're not gay too."

Again, a nervous chuckle.

"Is that why you didn't remember a *girl* named Jenny?"

"Yeah. His name is Jerry."

A second statie cruiser roars past us. I'm a good 10 miles over the speed limit and I've never felt so confident that cops aren't going to pull me over. My cell dings again.

"Now Mom wants to make sure I'm okay. Were your parents so helicopter?"

"I'm a boy. The expectations are different."

She casts me this crazy smile and then returns to texting Madelaine. I turn north into Port Mallory and wonder why there are cars parked along the side of the highway. There's a swarm of police lights swirling around the Temple factory. I keep driving because I know my employers would prefer I get Lily home safe rather than check on their property.

Just shy of the city limits, I catch up to slow-moving traffic.

"What's going on?"

"I don't know. Maybe a lot of people headed home earlier than expected."

I keep a respectful distance from the cargo door of the Range Rover ahead of us, forcing myself to go slow and not panic. My speedometer registers 5 miles per hour. We're going nowhere fast. I reach the corner of Broadway and Post Road and the car in front of me turns right because a barricade has been erected to prevent us going straight. I turn also and then realize my mistake as protesters surround the Range Rover.

"Oh, my god!" Lily's eyes bulge as her voice climbs. "What do we do?"

We've come to a complete stop as protesters begin banging on the Range Rover. I calculate if I can get around them in the left lane, but then I realize there's another car locked in the mob that way. I throw it in reverse and look over my shoulder. The guy behind me had the same idea. But I can't go as fast as him because he's going first.

"That guy's got a gun."

Guns don't scare me. My grandfather and father are both gun guys. I've been to the range several times and I even bagged a deer with Grandpa Jack a few years ago. Which is why I recognize the semi-auto the guy is pointing at the other driver, who apparently was better prepared for this than me because as the barrel of the AK-47 enters his window, two light streaks pulse the other direction and the guy with the rifle falls, clasping his shoulder.

Then I can't see anymore because the mob surrounds my car. Lily screams as someone hits the passenger window, shrieking something about white privilege and racism. The car rocks on its springs and Lily grabs the chicken handle. I can't really pay attention because the window beside me blows out and I feel hands grasp me, grasp the wheel, and try to pull me from my seat. They can't do it because of the seatbelt. Lily reaches across and lays hard on the horn with one hand while scratching one of the hands holding the wheel with her other hand. The hand releases the wheel and I mount the curb to drive the sidewalk, hitting the gas. Protesters fall away a little at a time as I speed up to about 10 miles per hour. My back window shatters as I drop off the curb at the far end of the block and then I hit the gas and speed toward our neighborhood at the speed limit. I want to go faster, but I don't want to take a cop away from the riot to deal with me speeding. I keep creeping over and then slowing down. My heart races and I taste metal in my mouth.

I wipe blood from my nose and glance at Lily. She's crying.

"I'm so sorry about all this." Her voice wavers barely above a whisper.

"I'm glad I came. Just hang in there. We'll be safe at home soon."

There are no lights behind us, which I take as a good sign. We'll be fine. We've lived through worse. But things could have gone very badly and only a mile or two from our houses.

Lily

I'm crying as Ben drives toward home. The sky behind us is red drifting smoke against the black of the sky. Ben keeps wiping his bleeding nose.

"Are you hurt?"

"I think it's just from the punch I took. My nose doesn't feel broken." He wipes his upper lip again. "What about you?"

I inventory my body. I have glass in my hair, but no obvious cuts in my skin.

"I think I'm okay." I wipe tears. "Why is this happening?"

Ben shakes his head, laughing shakily.

"It's the victim mentality, I think, but really it's people so in love with their own misery that they don't take the time to consider they don't have a right to tear up other people's lives."

He's shaking now and his voice takes on a gravelly quality. He's angry and I can't blame him. Now that the danger has passed, I feel a wash of anger wash through me. I've felt this before, back in the winter when I passed from denial to rage at Peter's actions and how'd they affected everyone around him. It was none of our faults and yet—there are similarities to this situation. I'm not crying anymore.

"I'm sorry to involve you."

He glances sideways at me, frowning.

"I told you. I'm glad I came. We'll be safe at home soon."

"Will it be safe?"

"Your dad is a veteran, my dad is a gunowner. We'll be safer there than anywhere else. Think of all the poor people who live closer to town."

I do and I shudder.

"Why would they be so angry about a guy protecting people from a maniac on a subway?"

"I don't know. There's just a lot of people looking for an excuse to be angry about anything."

We're topping the hill that drops into our neighborhood. My adrenaline is still running high, but I already feel as if I can breathe better.

He pulls up to the curb between our two houses. It only takes a moment for my parents to come to meet us.

"Are you okay?" Mom demands as I bend over to shake the glass out of my hair.

John comes out to join us.

"You take a shot to the face?"

"I did. I better get inside and get some ice on it. Lily, get some sleep and don't worry – I wouldn't have wanted to do anything else tonight."

He looks battered and bruised, but he smiles as he turns toward the house.

"I'll toss a tarp over your car," John shouts after him.

He waves, apparently knowing his father would be thinking of that.

"You're okay?" John asks me.

"Yeah, I think so."

"Why didn't you call us?" Mom is examining me carefully.

"My phone was in my purse, and it disappeared from my shoulder."

"That was a couple of years old," Dad notes. "Probably time to replace it anyway."

They gather me between them and lead me into the house while John comes out of his garage with a tarp. It's been a horrible night.

House Rules

Peter
June

We all watch the television where I recognize the images in the background of a riot.

"Port Mallory? That's your town, yeah?" Jamal bumps my knee. Luis lets people hang out in the cell and I don't feel like I can object, although I think five people is too many.

"Yeah. That's Broadway about a block off Main Street. Post Road." I expected to feel homesick at those images, but all I feel is worry for the people I love.

"Jesus, look at them!" Caleb's gasp draws my attention back to the small screen perched on the desk. Is that Ben's white Jeep struggling through the crowd?

"You going to pass out?" Caleb looks concerned.

"What? No! I just…I know someone with a car like that."

"Do tell? Rich guy knows someone who doesn't drive a Mercedes." Jamal chortles. I don't hate Jamal. He's one of the few black guys here who doesn't have a chip the size of Poughkeepsie on his shoulder, but he grates on my nerves sometimes.

"Cut it out!" Luis leans over the edge of his bunk. "House rules!"

Luis has rules about respect that existed before I got here. He didn't really have to teach them to me, but Jamal and some others cross the line with me sometimes.

Declan grunts and Jamal shuffles. Caleb's sitting on the only chair, and I don't have to let anyone on my bunk, so both Declan and Jamal sit on the floor. If Jamal weren't here, I'd probably have let Declan sit on my bunk.

"I just…your daddy's the governor, right?"

Okay, we don't get a lot of new news in here unless a trusty allows us to watch their TV. Maybe Jamal really doesn't know what's going on.

"The father who disowned me used to be governor, yes."

"How come he ain't governor no more? He's got like another year. What happened?"

"*I* happened." How he knows anything about my father is a mystery I choose not to pursue. I give him a "think about it" expression and then Caleb nudges my knee. All these guys attend church services with Luis. Caleb is an OG Christian, which means he was a Christian on the outside. I'm not sure what to think of that. Ben's family attended church and I vaguely remember walking an aisle at a summer camp I went to with him. But I've never gone to church on my own and I'm not sure I want to start, even though they keep inviting me. Do good people like the Andersons go to jail? Caleb seems to be a nice, ordinary guy.

"How far do your friends and family live from this?"

"I don't think there's a riot in Oldfield, which is where my grandparents live."

"You still care about them after they refused to help you?" Jamal's frowning.

"Man, you're an idiot sometimes." Caleb groans. "Just because they're mad at him doesn't mean *he's* mad at *them*." Well, that's insight. I'm not mad at them. I mourn them.

"I'd be mad at them."

"Those the only ones in harm's way?" I guess we're ignoring Jamal now.

"If Ben's the white Jeep, no."

"Ben?"

"He's my best friend – was, anyway?"

"What do you care about some rich dude who isn't talking to you anymore?"

I'm about to slug Jamal and maybe Caleb can see that.

"You ain't like a lot of us, Peter. It ain't even that you grew up rich, because you don't act like Richie Rich. You're like regular people."

I frown at Caleb, uncertain if that's a compliment or not. Maybe it's his accent. He's from somewhere in the Midwest. Kansas? Arkansas? He laughs.

"That's a good thing. Rare in here. Easy to misplace in here. Don't let that happen."

I already feel so disconnected from the world outside these walls that I don't know that I haven't already misplaced whatever Caleb admires in me.

An alarm sounds and everybody stirs. Lockdown starts in 15 minutes. You can hear guys finishing up card games and conversations out on the tier. Seth drops from Luis' bunk and nudges Declan, who isn't much of a talker, and he climbs to his feet.

"Thanks," he says, and disappears out the opening in the bars.

"Hope everybody is okay back home." Seth follows Declan. Caleb gives this weird wave and follows them. Jamal looks at Luis.

"I'm being mouthy again, ain't I?"

"Yup!" Jamal looks at me next.

"Sorry, man. Next time just tell me to step off."

I nod at him. Since he gave me permission.... He leaves the cell and Luis drops lightly from his bunk.

"He's right. You need to set boundaries with these guys. But Caleb's right too. You don't need to get too used to this place."

"How do you keep from doing that?"

"I don't know. Being a lifer is all about acceptance. But you got a future beyond these walls."

"In 24 more years."

"Naw, you're eligible for parole in four. Probably won't get it the first time, but betcha get it the second time – so six years. That ain't bad. But you can't get too used to this place."

"Am I?"

"Naw. You still care when you see a car that could be Ben's. Just – remember what Caleb said. *This* is not your home." He turns off, then unplugs the television and I pull my legs up tailor fashion so he can put the tv in the bin under my bed. Except for the COs, we're the only two people who have keys. "I'm grabbing socks since lights-out is coming."

"Maybe this morning's hard work means I'll sleep tonight." One of the other sweepers had to call out, so I volunteered to do his part. I can feel the extra work in my shoulders and back, tiny little movements building up to a workout. A 10-hour shift means a bit more money in my account.

"Here's hoping that 156 days works the charm."

Luis always approaches topics with humor, and I appreciate him for that, but after so many nights interrupted by nightmares, I've about lost hope of sleeping through the night. He's got to be as exhausted as I am. I keep waiting for him to decide I've outstayed my welcome.

I pick up my notebook and pencil and once more consider my amends letter to my dad. Maybe, if I can finish it and not sound like a whiny child, I'll finally be able to sleep through the night.

That's bargaining and I know I shouldn't do it, but…yeah, it's hard not to play what-if in my situation. Luis bounces a rolled-up sock off my forehead, snagging it on the return.

"Do not get all broody on me! Your friends are fine, and you can't do anything about it even if they aren't." He stretches out a hand to take the notebook. I let him have it because I know he's just going to put it on the desk. "Big Book, Step 8."

I sigh, but do as I'm told because…house rules.

June

Ben

The headache I've had all day is easing so I head downstairs in search of coffee. Dad's unloading the dishwasher and it seems like nobody else is around.

"Sorry." I get some bread and toast it. I can't do much about dirtying a plate and butter knife.

"It's fine. How you feeling?"

"Headache's gone." There's a bruise around my left eye where I assume a fist connected when we were trying to get out of the mob. "Riot still going on?" I nod toward the muted television visible in the living room.

"Not in Port Marion. They tried to set some boats in the harbor on fire and Russell and some of the other marina men opened fire hoses on them. You did make the news, though."

"I did?"

"Sit down while you eat. It'll loop again."

I take my toast into the living room, and sure enough, after a few minutes, there's a clip of my Jeep on the sidewalk, weaving between the buildings and the lampposts. I submitted a police report before I went to bed last night, so I figure if anyone got hurt, a cop would show up at the house by now.

Dad sets a tray with a carafe of coffee and two mugs on the table.

"The guy with the gun is dead and the driver who shot him is in jail for murder."

"My god."

"Yeah. You did get a call earlier today from the police. It was that detective from Peter's case. I told him you were sleeping, and he said to call him back today or tomorrow. They're looking for witnesses."

"Great. I don't seem to be able to get away from being a witness."

"May this be a better experience for you than the last time."

We disagree about Pete, but we don't disagree about this. We silently sip coffee for several minutes, enjoying each other's company.

"Where's Mom and Wes?"

"Next door. We decided not to go to church today, so we had a service with the Wexlers."

"And Grandpa Jack is okay?"

"Yeah. He had a group of idiots come down his street last night, but they just shouted and didn't venture up the driveway."

"That's good." My grandfather is also a gun owner and not afraid to defend himself. It's good for the protesters that they didn't risk their lives and good for Grandpa that they didn't force him to make any life-or-death decisions. "What makes people so angry that they go after innocent people just living their lives?"

"You have to wonder. I don't have an answer. Dad said they were shouting about the white race should give their houses to black and brown people. And, before the riot started here there was some guy – BLM activist – gave a speech at the Whalers statue about how black people are done waiting around to be repaid for their labor on our behalf."

I'm remembering the Carsons who used to be our next-door neighbors and were long-time clients of my dad's accounting company. They were effectively millionaires when they retired and moved away. Incidentally, they were black. Yeah, some black folks in the US are still doing badly. So are most of the white people in Appalachia. I know a lot of my Dartmouth classmates would consider me a racist for these thoughts, but I didn't see any black people trying to kill me last night. And as Pete hopefully knows all too well now, I don't play nice with people who try to kill me. And I saw a sea of white faces last night.

"Was he at least black?"

"Ish." My dad has a subtle sense of humor which I'm well-acquainted with, so I snort. Barack Obama was "ish" back when he was president.

"I guess I should go call Detective Mariskov."

"It's Sunday. You could probably wait for the morning."

"I have work, so I'll do it now and get it out of my hair." I start to reach for my cell in my back pocket. "How's Lily?"

"She seemed fine. I guess the concert was pretty good until it ended, and she has to spend tomorrow getting her ID reissued."

I don't remember her even mentioning she got mugged until the cop asked for her ID. I guess she's tougher than I thought she was. I guess that's a gift Pete gave us…scar tissue that acts as a great shield.

Dad gives me the phone number and I call Detective Mariskov. And I'm surprised when he answers.

"Ben Anderson, at the center of a conflict again."

"Not my choice. Might have helped if the police had been on Broadway to tell us to take a back route home."

"I'm not arguing with you. It was a miscalculation to avoid violence by having the police stand down. Do you have injuries?"

"A black eye and a headache that I'm pretty sure is a minor concussion, but isn't bad enough to go to the hospital. My driver's side and back windows were smashed. I left a message on my insurance company's phone right after I filed my police report."

"Could you pick out the people who assaulted you?"

"I--." I close my eyes and try to sort out faces from my fear for Lily's safety. "Maybe. There was the guy who grabbed me. I think he's got nail gouges on his hands from Lily."

"She's coming tomorrow to look at mug shots."

"Can I get mine via email so I can make it to work?"

"Sure."

"There was some red-haired woman with a blue streak in her hair. She's the one who used the rock to bash my window in."

"Well that stands out, though she might have covered the streak by now."

"I'm pretty sure I won't forget the guy with the AR15 pointed at the driver in front of us."

"He's dead, so we don't need anyone to ID him. You saw the other driver shoot him?"

"Yeah. It was definitely self-defense."

There's a long silence. Of course, he doesn't want to hear that the shooting was righteous, but I won't deny it.

"Well, it's good to have a clear-headed witness. Most of the people caught up in that mess are having trouble with details. You and Ms. Wexler kept your heads."

"I tried. Still a little annoyed there were no warning signs – barricades, something."

"You're not going to let that one go, I guess."

"No. The police have an obligation to protect innocent people and their property."

"*Warren v District of Columbia* – the police only have a legal obligation to protect individuals who are in custody. Like it or not, the general public has to protect itself."

"How's that going to work out for that driver who defended his life against the guy with the AR?"

"Oh, he's already been charged. You would be too if anyone but you had been hurt when you drove away."

"That's so screwed up. So, can I go now?"

"Yes, of course. I'll email those mugs to you. Let me know if you decide to go to the doctor and there is a concussion diagnosis."

"Okay. Thanks."

"Uh – you ever hear from Peter Wyngate?"

That's a weird question.

"A prison-sanctioned amends letter I haven't read yet. Why?"

"It's a thing. He apologized to me for forcing me to investigate him."

"Wh-at?" That sounds so absolutely not like Pete. "He offer amends?"

"Not exactly." Mariskov chuckles. "He's pretty clear that he's never going to feel comfortable with cops again and since it's my job, he's apologizing, not offering amends. He says he just kept seeing my name and it bugged him, so he wrote a letter to me in hopes he'd stop feeling that way. I hope it works for him."

"You do?"

"He's accepting his punishment. There's an advantage to being a cop. I called. He qualified for the program that allows him to write these letters because he's keeping his nose clean. Maybe the spoiled rotten brat returns when he leaves those walls or maybe he's growing up and facing the music. I gotta admire that. Some people do come out of prison as better people. I just figured you were on his list and might want to hear my take on it. I'll let you go. Thanks for being a good witness."

"You know I'll be a defense witness for that guy's murder trial."

"I respect that. Sometimes the application of the law isn't perfect."

Not perfect? Yeah, the application of the law let Pete get away with injuring Cheyenne so he could kill Alyse. Absolutely imperfect.

I hang up and hear Dad moving in the opening to the kitchen.

"Do you need someone to read that letter for you?"

I'm saved from answering by Mom and Wes coming into the kitchen chattering happily. Dad squeezes my shoulder and lets the topic pass.

Lily

I didn't sleep very well last night, seeing Ben fighting for control of the steering wheel, hearing the sound of breaking glass, shouting, smelling the smoke of fires. I finally got up and read until the sun came up, wrapping myself up in a gold sweater the size of a circus tent that my grandmother sent me for Christmas.

There's something so comforting about studying the fruit of the Spirit. I learn something new every time I read Galatians 5. "But the fruit of the Spirit is love, joy, peace, forbearance, kindness, goodness, faithfulness, gentleness and self-control. Against such things there is no law."

Today, I'm reflecting on self-control and how so few people today seem to possess it. They want to live the way they want, no external controls on their behavior, and then without self-control, they hurt people. Ben and I could have been seriously hurt last night by people who lack self-control. Maybe I'm more aware of this than the average 16-year-old because of what I went through with Peter. His lack of self-control meant I had to watch Alyse die. I seriously just want to punch some people, slap some sense into them. What they did last night was unacceptable on every level.

There's a knock on my bedroom door. It's Mom, who really needs to wait for an invitation to enter, but I don't yell at her. I'm grateful for her concern. That should last about three days.

"How are you?"

"Fine. Still strung a little tight. My mind keeps spinning around what happened last night."

"The riot or the gay guy pretending to be a girl?"

Okay, I deserve that.

"I don't think he's gay if he's a biological male trying to get with a biological female. He…or, er…she is trans. Or maybe non-binary. He got angry and stormed off before we could discuss it."

"I'm so glad I didn't grow up in this day and age."

My mother pushes her grey-shot red hair off her face and sits down on the edge of the bed.

"Was it really less complicated?"

"Definitely. Even when your brother was growing up, it was less confusing."

"I'm not confused. I'm not gay and as long as Jerry thinks he's a girl, she is off limits. And probably off limits after that because confusion on that topic makes him delusional."

"You got to wonder what's occurring in his life that he wants to deny who he is."

"I don't have to wonder. We're probably not friends any longer so I don't have to worry about it."

"I'm sorry. I know you want to have a bosom friend."

"Someone like Aunt Larissa—oh, yes."

Larissa is my mother's best friend since 5th grade and they're still long-distance friends today. I'd love to have a friendship like that. I thought maybe I might be developing it with Alyse, but then she got jealous of my relationship with Peter. Maybe I just didn't really know her at all.

"Penny for your thoughts."

"They're not worth that much." Do I tell her? Maybe it would help if I shared. "Peter's letter stirred some stuff up and then last night.... It's just got me spinning around last summer when I thought I'd put it to bed."

She doesn't speak immediately. I didn't really notice it before last year, but she doesn't just jump right in. She thinks before she responds.

"We are the sum total of our pasts, Lily. We can't go back and change it. We can only deal with it. And sometimes that takes a few passes. We think it's done and then something gets it going again. Triggers us."

Normally I reject the concept of triggers. Mina says it's a cheap escape—a way of shifting blame to others. It also gives us an excuse to stay sick and I definitely don't want to be like that. But Mom's not wrong. Last night has me spinning around last year and I don't know how to make it stop.

"What are you reading?"

"Galatians 5. I'm focused on self-control today."

"Or the lack thereof?"

"Something like that."

She laughs nervously.

"They are out of control and that can make you connect to the past and the other undisciplined people from back then."

"How do you know this?"

"I've been a mom for nearly 21 years. You learn a lot. And, I've always loved psychology. So, now the question is...what are you going to do about it?"

"I don't know."

"You do, but you want to avoid it, so.... Let me know when, if, and you can borrow my car to make the drive."

For a moment, I don't know what she means, but then I remember – this all starts with Peter, and I know where to find him.

Ben

Temple is technically in Port Mallory, but its access road is in Tooker Station. Either way, there are no signs of rioters along the road. The parking lot is a little empty-looking as I pull in. People are here, but there are fewer cars than normal.

The side entrance I usually take is locked and there's a sign that instructs me to go to the main entrance. There's security guards in the lobby. Temple has a single security officer who doesn't wear a uniform, but it looks like Brad the owner isn't taking any chances today.

"Hey, Ben." Hank greets me. "Bobby and Chuck are both staying home today because there are still riots near them. Would you be willing to stand-in today."

Hank's the head of distribution which is a major division of the factory.

"Me? Why?"

"Well, you've got the most longevity on the dock and Chuck suggested you could do it."

"Yeah, of course. There are still riots?"

"They've moved away from us, but Terryville and Setauket both had riots last night. We're letting employees stay home if they feel they need to and there's riots within their vicinity. Where'd you get the shiner."

"I got attacked in my car Saturday night during the riot in Port Mallory. I'm okay, but I can certainly understand men with families wanting to stay near right now. So, yeah, I'll supervise the dock until they get back."

"Thanks. I'll try to swing by and check on you."

By mid-morning I want to know what's up with Billy who is, for inexplicable reasons, not threatening the college kid I put with him because his regular partner – an ex-con who intimidates even Billy – apparently was arrested Saturday night.

"Hey, Billy, can I talk to you a minute."

He ambles up to the upper tier of the dock as the college student casts both of us a questioning glance before disappearing into the truck. Billy ends up standing a double-arm's length from me, giving me a truculent stare.

"How's Owens doing?"

You can't go at Billy directly. He's a 6'5" ex-con who always seems on the verge of violence.

"Who?"

"Your partner for the day?" He glances toward the truck, almost seems to smile.

"He's in too much a hurry, but otherwise okay."

"Okay. Good to know."

"Who punched you?"

I'm kind of surprised by the question. Billy never seems to care about other people.

"I was trying to get through one of the riots Saturday night, and somebody punched me."

Actually, I had no luck with the mug shots, but Wes and Bram worked together to give me a pretty good composite sketch of Blue-Streak which Detective Mariskov says they already have a hit on, and then he forwarded a driver's license pic with the ID information blurred out and that's the guy who fought me for the wheel. We're just waiting to see if his DNA matches what Lily scraped from under her fingernails.

"Why's you wanderin' round in riots, man?" He seems genuinely perplexed and maybe slightly worried about me.

"A friend was trapped in one and I went to rescue her."

"Cool." I stare at him. It's like Invasion of the Body-Snatchers. He shrugs. "I better get back to work."

"Me too. Hope the rest of your day is good."

He shrugs and turns away from me. I'm not meant to understand this man, but….

"Um, can I ask you a question?"

He turns back. Maybe he just has that kind of face all the time. It's like that cashier at the grocery store who has quintessential resting-bitch face. Annoyance can etch itself into a face and maybe I shouldn't be intimidated by it.

"Depends."

It's on the tip of my tongue to ask him if he served time in Sing Sing. Maybe he could tell me something about Pete's life situation. But then I think about how touchy Billy can be. Do I really want to turn a pleasant encounter into an unpleasant one?

"Never mind. I just realized it would be rude to ask."

"Maybe so. You gonna ask about the tattoos?"

I glance down at his forearms. I've been curious about those since I met him two years ago.

"Kind of."

He nods.

"They my past, don't gots to be my future."

Whoa, that's kind of deep!

"Where'd you do your sentence…if I can ask that question."

He considers whether I can for a moment.

"I did most of it in Clinton, up north, which sucked. I did my last month in Sing Sing, which is comparatively a decent place—for a maximum security prison filled with murderers and such. You asking coz you had a friend go to prison last year, right?"

"Yeah." He knows that? He's surprising me all over the place today.

"This place gossips like a church quilting bee. Where he?"

"Sing Sing."

"That sucks. All that level…sucks. But it is what it is. Ifn he survives, he'll be diff'rent when he come out. Ain't no gettin' round that."

He shrugs again and walks around me like the conversation is over, which I guess it is since I'm standing by myself.

Lily

Bram's physical therapy doesn't need me watching it, so I go out to a bench on the hospital's green lawn and open the Contacts in my new phone – bought this morning. All my data seems to have rolled over nicely. I also got my temporary license issued. Since Mom and I did that this morning, I brought Bram to PT.

I have a ready excuse for not calling Jenae. Besides, I felt like I needed a few days to calm down. What he said to me was said in anger. So…my thumb hangs over the Phone icon for a moment before I open the Text function.

> **LILY– I got my phone stolen in the riot. Look, I'm sorry if you're upset with me. You startled me. I didn't know and then you surprised me. I hope I didn't ruin our friendship.**

When he doesn't respond for a long time, I open a book on my phone and spend some time reading. I'm about to head up to get Bram when a text comes in.

> **JENAE– It was unrealistic to present myself as one thing and then just announce how I feel about you. Would you give it another chance?**

> **LILY– As friends, yes.**

Again, there's no response for the longest time. I have to pick up Bram, so I start heading back. My phone vibrates in the elevator.

> **JENAE– I'm non-binary.**

> **LILY– I don't date girls.**

> **JENAE– I'm trans. It's different.**

> **LILY– Maybe if we're friends for a while, I'll come to understand, but right now, I don't.**

Again, it takes a while for a reply to come through. Bram is often exhausted after physical therapy, but he wheels himself one-handed all the way to the car and manages the transfer on his own. My phone vibrates while I'm folding his wheelchair into the cargo area.

JENAE– We can try. Did you have trouble getting out of Huntington?

Okay, I'm a little annoyed about him leaving me alone in the middle of a riot.

JENAE– I'm sorry I bugged out before things got going. I tried to get back to you, but I couldn't find you.

I sit down in the driver's seat, trying to decide if I believe her. Bram seems comfortable enough.

JENAE– Then I got outside, and they were beating people up. And my dad was texting me, telling me where to meet him. Then I saw you with the guy in the shorts. You seemed to know each other. I figured you were safe, so I headed to my dad.

He sounds believable.

LILY– That's Ben.

JENAE– He's cute.

A chill slides down my back. I doubt Ben would be pleased to know "Jerry" thinks he's cute. I remember how Peter handled a gay guy on Fire Island. He was comfortable with his masculinity. I wonder if he's a target in prison.

"Lily, we go." Bram's looking at me in the rearview mirror.

"Yeah, sorry. Let's head home."

He smiles at me. Does he understand or has he just guessed the appropriate response?

My phone vibrates while I drive home. When we get there, I get an exhausted Bram into his chair and then into bed before I check my texts.

BEN– you want to go to ice cream tonight, maybe 6. The riots aren't in PM now. If your parents say it's okay, of course.

JENAE– You don't like that I noticed him?

JENAE– Hello?

JENAE– You're proving my point, homophobe. I have a right to be who I am, and you have no right to object.

The doorbell rings and I peek out the sidelight before opening it to a flower delivery. I thank the girl and apologize for not having any cash on me for a tip, then close the door. The card says "for Lily". Wow, Ben moves fast. I tear open the wrapping for the mixed bouquet of chrysanthemums, daisies, and stargazer lilies. Smiling happily, I set them in the center of the dinner table. The card is unsigned, which is intriguing. I glance at my phone.

Bram's asleep for an hour or two, so I text Mom about the ice cream date while choosing a top in case they let me go.

MADELAINE– If you're going with Ben, yes, but keep your wits about you. Can you ask Wes to hang out with Bram until I get home? I promised Jodi she didn't have to close.

I text Wes and he says he can do that. He'll come over with Ben. I decide on another top. I don't really have a favorite because most of my clothes don't fit this year. And that makes it hard to choose.

Jenae keeps sending texts, which I start ignoring while I go through my closet. There will be time enough to deal with his…her…pique after I've enjoyed an evening with Ben.

Confession

Peter
June

I'm trying to stay awake while this guy drones on about how his brother isn't taking his calls for a couple of years now and he wants to fix it, but can't. I'm there, man. I'm not even allowed to call my dad, so how do I even start to make amends? I'm starting with a letter, and I hope he'll open the door a bit. I haven't talked with anyone back home except Lucy and Joel in six months. I'm going nowhere with amends.

"Anyone else?" Seth moderates the meeting tonight. He's like Luis – takes in the vulnerable so they won't be hurt. Will we leave prison as better people? Declan seems to be staying out of trouble. Nobody comes into Luis' house and tries to strong arm me. If I hang out with their weird little cliché of Christians, I get less harassment. So, I like Seth just because he's a good person – far as I can tell.

"I don't want to whine." I said that aloud. Everybody stares at me and now I wish I hadn't opened my mouth.

"I'm writing this letter to someone. Someone I really hurt. And I don't want to whine. I'm trying to explain to him that I'm learning my lesson in here, and it comes out whiny. So I write the letter again. Trying to figure out how I know when I've reached my goal. And then how do I accept that he might not accept my repentance? I worry I'm wasting my time. I know I'm not. When I get it right, it'll be better for me. I hope."

Someone else picks up from a more mature point of view. He's been behind bars a long time and the only amends he's been able to make are lifestyle amends. You do it for yourself and then maybe the ripples waver out into the world. We just have to accept that.

I'm falling asleep again, so I stand and lean against the wall. The CO sees me do it and he doesn't seem concerned. I'm able to stay awake until the meeting ends.

"Keep coming back. It works if you work it."

Does it? Some days I feel it. Tonight, I'm struggling.

Luis is working the infirmary this week, but I've been sleeping pretty well because this latest antidepressant acts as a sedative, especially since I'm on the maximum dose. I lay down, I wake up in the morning stiff from not moving. I don't dream. The doctor says if I can go six months without active suicidal ideation, he'll cut back to a half-dose. That weird rash is better, though it still sometimes feels like my arms are on fire. I'm still pooping bricks. I'm still always thirsty. I still struggle to enjoy food. I'm getting good at not falling asleep during the day. Evenings are harder because I take this stupid pill right after dinner.

There was no one from outside the facility in the meeting tonight, so we get to forego the sexual molestation, but we still get patted down because the meetings are sometimes inter-block exchange venues for small amounts of drugs. CO Carson doesn't apologize for handling my junk, but you can tell by the way he does it, he doesn't enjoy it any more than I do. His partner, however….

"You looking to get engaged, Ramirez?"

"You got something to hide, Chavez?"

"Man, move on. Don't make this worse than it is."

Seth's advice gets a scowl, but Chavez does move on, after casting a hostile gaze at CO Ramirez and me. I'm just cooperating. What the hell?

"You okay?" CO Carson asks as he's patting down my shoulders. "Looked like you were struggling."

He seems like a nice guy, but COs are not your friends.

"I'm good."

I spend my entire walk back to our house thinking about that term "I'm good." I meant he didn't need to be worried about me, but what it really means is a lie. I'm not good. I have blood on my hands. Lack of active suicidal ideation doesn't mean I'm not still depressed and self-loathing. Alyse sits on my bunk, blood on her mouth and hatred in her eyes. I turn the chair so it isn't facing her and try to read the Big Book, but I can't shake the feeling that she's behind me. She's wearing jeans and a saffron yellow swingy kind of dress-shirt, her short black hair riffling in the wind. She's laughing and there's no blood on her lips, but then I see the blue hull of *the Mimi* and stand up to break the spell. By the time I do 30 pushups, she's gone. I finish up with 20 burpees and then try to settle at the desk again.

I've read half-a-page when I feel breath on my neck and I turn to see her as she lay in my arms, dying. I bolt for the doorway and almost bowl Luis over.

"Whoa, *amigo* where's the 9-1-1?"

I blink at him, glancing back at my bunk, a shudder running through me. She's gone, but I know I saw her there. Luis lays a gentle hand on my arm.

"You know Seth and Declan wouldn't mind a visit to their house if you can't stay here?"

I look down at my hands that are covered in blood and wish I were allowed to cry.

"Bad evening, huh?"

I nod. The lights-out alarm sounds. I want to run, but that's not going to happen.

"The wreck?" He never calls it an accident. I know it wasn't. Sometimes I wish I could still lie to myself.

"She was right there." I point to my bunk. He glances that way.

"You know she ain't there, right?"

"I know, but…."

"It doesn't help. I don't know what to tell you, kid. PTSD sucks."

"I suck. What I did sucks!"

Luis grins.

"Yeah. Make it past tense and you're right. You screwed up and you're paying for it. So, some of what you're going through is deserved. But I think you're too hard on yourself. You need to learn to control it."

"How?"

"It takes time. And I know that's not what you want to hear."

I sigh and sit down on the edge of the desk. I'm not ready to sit down in my bunk. Jacobs must be maintaining the pruneau because I'm smelling it and then I think about how bourbon would release the tension in my neck. And then my stomach turns ominously as I smell vomit and scotch mixed together. That's probably PTSD too and I don't really want that to go away.

"That been stinking all night?" It's not in my head? Great!

"I don't think so. I wasn't aware of it until just now."

"So, it's not that."

"I think the topic of amends at the meeting got it started."

"You get any work done?"

I nudge the letter that sits beside the Big Book. I wrote a sentence. He skims it, circles something, puts the book on the shelf and puts the letter in the folder where I'm keeping all the copies. He then reaches my Bible down.

"You're done for the night." He hands me the paperback Bible. "Try reading a Psalm."

I sigh, but I do what I'm told as a buzzer sounds and then the door in the bars closes. We're not going anywhere for nine hours, so I might as well read the Bible.

You who dwell in the Shelter of the Most High, who abide in the shade of the Almighty,

Say to the Lord, "My refuge and fortress, my God in whom I trust."

He will rescue you from the fowler's snare, from the destroying plague,

He will shelter you with His pinions, and under His wings you may take refuge;

His faithfulness is a protecting shield.
You shall not fear the terror of the night nor the arrow that flies by day,
Nor the pestilence that roams in darkness, nor the plague that ravages at noon.

Luis sits at the desk and he's reading his Bible, something in Hebrews, a book that is way over my head. I shift my shoulders against the metal wall behind me.

"A problem?" Luis looks over his shoulder.

"Do you really believe this?"

"Probably. Which are you reading? Is that even English?"

He's teaching me Spanish while I'm improving his English.

"I think it is, technically. I'd say 'which one are you reading', but I don't think 'one' is required."

"So, which one are you reading?"

"Psalm 91." He sticks a slip of paper in his spot and flips to the Psalms.

"Not feeling too sheltered?"

"It's like everything is coming after me right now. So, what this says doesn't seem right."

Luis turns around and puts his bare feet on my bunk, which I don't mind, and he knows.

"First – you aren't a believer, so this doesn't apply to you."

"Then why are you making me read it?"

"Because if anybody needs a higher power, it's you."

We've been discussing this for a while and he knows I don't reject the concept of God, but I can't bring myself to trust the white-bearded guy in the sky.

"He isn't your father. He won't abandon you. That's the message of this psalm."

"But only if you're a believer?"

"Yes. Is that what you learned at camp?"

"I guess. It's been a minute."

Luis grimaces. He hates that term.

"How old were you?"

"Twelve."

"Same year your mother…left?"

We don't talk about what else she did where we can be overheard.

"Yeah."

"So, you went home and everything went bad?"

It was seven years ago, so I tumble it around in my mind. Camp did come before Mom.

"Kind of."

"And you never followed up?"

"Ben tried to talk to me about it a few times, but I started drinking and it just didn't make sense after that."

Luis stares at me over his reading glasses.

"So, reading it…what do you get out of it that you can use?"

"What you said—God, Higher Power, whatever – it's not my dad. I won't get disowned."

"Okay. Go on."

I shake my head. I can't move forward with it. Luis laughs.

"So, I'll tell you what I get out of it. The middle part always bugs me. It's God's word and I believe it, but it doesn't apply to me in a personal way. The only wars I been in are gang wars and that was a long time ago. So, I take the first part and the last part. God's sheltering me, but the last part is God talking, saying if believers cling to Him, He will protect them. And that's my experience."

I stare at him. He hasn't shared his story with me. I wait, sensing it's a big deal. Other people have referenced it before. I know Luis was not *this* man when he came in the gate.

"I was 16 when we killed those people. I didn't do it. I was in the backseat high off my butt and that saved my life. Me and my brother Tomas. He was a year older, but still a minor too. Didn't matter. We were accessories and Jorge killed the wife of someone important. Someone had to pay, so it was Tomas and me. They put me in an adult jail. Stuff happened. Then I came here. I was 17. I was a skinny kid who thought he was tough, and I had a mouth on me. But my cousin was head of the Golden Lions. I thought I was protected. And then they came for me."

It would be inappropriate to ask who *they* were, even though I want to know. He keeps talking after the pause. He's not making eye contact, which I guess might be shame. His voice doesn't betray him like mine does.

"You think you're tough and I fought back. I'd promised myself it wasn't gonna happen again and I shanked one of them to make it clear. I'd have gotten a bit more time for that, maybe turned a 10-year bid into 15, but then I lost my mind. When the guards pushed in, I fought back against them. I cut one of them, so I ended up in the hole."

He makes eye contact now.

"You got a taste of that in Ad Seg, that feeling of isolation, but it's worse in the hole. When you're in there, you got nothing. A mattress and a blanket. You can jog in place, do pushups. You can talk to yourself. They'll let you read the Big Book and the Bible. I read the Big Book like four times before the chaplain came in. I told him I wasn't interested in his cult, but he left the Bible anyway. So, then I finally cracked the Bible because I was losing my mind from boredom. I could quote the Big Book in my sleep. So, I was desperate, and it opened at Romans. Don't ask me why. I just started reading. This was a used Bible. Whoever had used it before made notes in the margins. So, after Romans I read Gospel of John because the note said I should. I just kept reading. I couldn't put it down. I'd get so angry with God sometimes. I was raving out of my head because it's soul-crushing to be in isolation. But it was like I couldn't get enough. It was something to think about, to keep my demons at bay."

He's staring at a fixed point where I'm guessing the past is stored.

"Three years. I turned 18 and 21 in that hell. I'd read the Bible five times and I'd convinced the guards I wouldn't hurt myself or one of them if they let me keep a journal. I went crazy in there, but I also came back from it after I met God. So, *chico*, when I say I met God in there – I don't mean I went looking for Him. I mean He found me exactly where I was. I wasn't looking for redemption, but He redeemed me anyway. I didn't feel guilty about what Jorge did. I was in the backseat.

"But after Jesus brought me to life, I cared. Yeah, I didn't directly kill those women, but I'm guilty of it because I didn't lift a finger to stop Jorge. And once I admitted that, saying 'I'm a sinner' wasn't so hard anymore. I started to see my sin everywhere – heck, I saw a guard three times a day for meals. Sometimes they'd talk to me, make sure I wasn't losing it again. I'm pretty sure a couple of them thought I was." He laughs and the humor makes it to his eyes. "But a couple of others were Christians, and they'd arrange to feed me last so they could talk to me about what I was reading. You know Shillinger?"

He's one of the Type 5 guards who is usually in the mess hall, so I nod.

"He was young back then." Luis smiles to himself again. "He'd sometimes come back after dinner, talk to me—*correct* me. I was coming up on four years in there. They were letting me go to exercise by then. There's this little yard. You're not allowed to interact with other prisoners, so you run around in a circle by yourself. Or just lean against a wall and enjoy the fresh air. You only get 15 minutes. Anyway, one day I'm coming back from the yard and for reasons I'll never understand, there's another prisoner coming out. Shillinger's walking behind him. And suddenly, the guy turns around and shanks him. One good stab, but he was rearing back for more. I'd grown in four years. I'd built my body." He gestures to his toned biceps. "I grabbed the guy's shanking arm and drove his hand and the shiv into the concrete wall instead of Shillinger's throat. Then the guard who was supposed to be bird-dogging me catches up and deals with the guy – who is probably still in the hole. I ain't never seen him since. I stripped off my shirt and staunched Shillinger's wound, talked with him, kept him calm until the other guards got there. About a month later, I got my disposition hearing a year earlier than scheduled. Life without the possibility of parole, but I got to get out of the hole early."

I'm still waiting because I think he has more to say.

"So back in those days there was a process. Someone had figured out that you can't just take someone who hasn't interacted with human beings for years and throw them out here with thousands of prisoners." We exchange 'you think?' looks and he laughs. "I didn't like the first counselor, so they sent me one of the chaplains who is a Catholic priest. I'm Puerto Rican, so I must be Catholic, right?" I shrug because I have no idea what Catholics believe. "Then the Episcopal guy dropped by, and we didn't see eye to eye. You were raised Episcopal, right?"

"That's the church my dad's family belongs to, but I was baptized Orthodox. Never really went to either one much."

"That was us with the Catholic church. We'd go for the holidays, but *mi madre* practiced Santeria. You know what that is?"

I frown. I've seen it depicted in movies. Something to do with zombies. I shrug. He laughs.

"Yeah. I didn't know what it was until years later. So, anyway, the evangelical chaplain was the guy I connected with. Not Pastor Jones. This guy was Fredericks. And he told me a lot of guys get religion in the hole and then it doesn't mean anything when they get back into the population. He was a little surprised when I argued with him. 'This ain't a religion. How would I do religion in here by myself? God made me alive when I was dead before and I intend to keep on talking to Him.' He just stared at me for the longest time and then he laughs and says 'Occasionally guys surprise me and I think you might be one of those exceptions.' So, he was a big help in that transition and after I'd been shoveling walks for a few months, he hired me as his assistant. He's the one who talked me into taking classes, teaching Sunday school. He helped me retire from the Golden Lions and find a way to do it peacefully. It gave me a support system when I really needed one."

"Like what you're doing with me?"

"Kind of. I didn't keep him up at night, though." He points a jokingly accusatory finger at me. The lights out buzzer sounds. We still have 15 minutes. "So that's the story. Any of that familiar to you?"

There's this weird pressure in my chest. I don't know what to think of it, but I feel compelled to tell the truth.

"Yeah. At camp. What they were saying started to make sense. I didn't feel at all pressured to walk that aisle. Not from people anyway. And I wanted to go to church with Ben's family and…well, my life always seems to have roadblocks and side streets."

"Are you saying something changed inside you?"

"I don't know. It's something to think about, I guess."

"Sounds like progress to me. So instead of reading Psalms, you should read Romans."

That feels like a challenge to me. Luis stands up, puts his Bible away and reaches under the bed to pull something out. It's an old battered Bible that looks a lot like one of those you pull out of a drawer in a hotel. He hands it to me.

"This is THE Bible, isn't it?"

"Yeah. The notes are better than anything I can produce, though I've added a few. And maybe if you get things right with God, it'll be a little easier to forgive yourself."

I hold this precious bit of cardboard and paper in my hands. Will I find forgiveness in its pages? Do I deserve to find it?

"I don't know that I want to."

"I know. Just give it a shot. Don't flinch and see where it takes you."

I nod. He unzips his uniform and turns toward the toilet. I look out across the tier to where Jacobs and his cellmate are bedding down. Faith as an alternative to what they'll sell me in exchange for my soul? It shouldn't be a tough choice, but because I am who I am, it is.

June

Ben

I don't know why I want to take Lily back to Hot Licks. It's new – just opened last summer and I know Pete didn't have time to bring her there. It's great ice cream. It's a warm June night and I want to spend it with her, showing her that the world is not a cruel place.

So, I'm thrilled when I pick her up at her house like this is a real date. I'm pleased she doesn't burst from the door to get into the car, but let's me walk up to the door like a gentleman and escort her to the car. Wes pushes past her to join Bram in his room where he has a nice television. Wes is working with him on learning how to play the original Zelda on SuperNES.

"I'm locking the door. Don't open it to anyone. Mom will park in the garage, so she won't need to ring the front door."

Wes grunts, still walking toward Bram's room.

"He knows what he's doing." She rolls her eyes at my assurance, rechecks the lock and closes the door behind her. She pauses halfway down the walkway and stares at the red Mustang.

"What in the world?"

"The insurance covers a rental car while mine is in the shop. I asked for something basic, but they upgraded me. Why not, right?"

"And they rented to you?"

"Sure, with a lot of really expensive rental insurance."

"Is that why you're taking me out tonight?"

"I did kind of want to show off." I hand her into the passenger seat. She's wearing these calf-length dark-blue pants – shorts – I don't know what they're called – and a summery shimmery top of a lighter blue. I showered and changed my clothes. Maybe I'm a little underdressed. But I've got a cool car.

"Thanks for the flowers," she says.

"Flowers?"

She glances sideways at me, a slightly mocking look on her face.

"Really? You didn't send them to me?"

"I sent no flowers."

She frowns, shrugs, and then laughs.

"I guess I have another admirer. But whoever that is, I'd rather be with you."

That makes me smile and I basked in the warmth of her presence.

You can still see the aftermath of Saturday's riot although the Main Street businesses have already been working to erase the graffiti. The Speakeasy has plywood where its front windows used to be. I drove by Hot Licks on my way home, pleased to see it was still open and seemed undamaged. Dad said they were in the newspaper today. Apparently, the owners' family and friends turned out to defend the place. Nobody died but a few broken bones might have occurred.

The patio string lights aren't lit as the sun is still lingering above the horizon. There's a line. A flyer announces that the Hot Licks jazz band will be playing on

Saturday night *weather permitting.* I can smell chocolate and something fruity – blueberries? And the air is soft and warm, the scent of salt drifting in from the harbor. A long way off, I hear a ferry horn.

"It's hard to believe this was bedlam just a few days ago."

"I hear it's still dangerous in Long Island City."

"Yeah. I guess White Plains also had trouble. It's been a bad few days."

"Why?" She looks like she seriously wants an answer. Do I want to give it in such a public setting? There's an Asian man with a black woman two behind us, so probably not right now. But someone has to say the truth…don't they? I keep my voice low.

"A white Marine stepped in to prevent a black mentally-ill homeless man from hurting people on the subway. He's a Good Samaritan, who's now going to need massive legal help not to go to jail."

"What does the color of their skin got to do with it?" She sounds perplexed and mildly touchy.

"It shouldn't have anything to do with it, but these days people are sure that explains *everything.* Notice that when a black man ran through a Christmas parade of white people a few years ago, he eventually got multiple life sentences, but there were no violent riots insisting justice for his victims."

It's our turn at the window and that exchange goes well. We sit down in the pavilion to eat our cones.

"How long will it take to fix your car?"

"I'll get it back before the weekend. Why?"

"Just making small talk." She licks ice cream. "Uh, I talked to Jenae today. *She* thinks you're cute."

"Ugh! I never know what to say to things like that."

The biracial couple walk up to the other side of the big round table from us. Oh, no!

"Do you mind if we sit here?" the woman asked. They're young, but I'd guess closer to 30 than 20.

"Please." Lily gestures and they sit down.

"We heard you." Okay, so now I'm terrified. "And you're right. The riots -- ." She shakes her head. "I'm Karen. This is Garrett."

I swallow the lump in my throat and hold out my hand toward Garrett first. That he shakes my hand is a good sign.

"Ben and she's Lily." Lily shakes hands with Karen.

"There was a time when we were on the verge of it not mattering. You are both too young to remember that, but you have good parents who taught you that it shouldn't matter. So did we." Garrett grins at Karen.

"And the current nonsense makes social situations awkward. We just thought we'd do our part to ease some of the cringe." Karen picks up her ice cream spoon to eat her sundae and moves on.

We talk amongst ourselves for about 20 minutes and then they announce they have to get home to relieve the sitter and we wish them well.

Lily giggles.

"That could so have gone badly."

"Yeah. I thought that too." I glance at my phone. I want to make sure to get her home on time. "Regatta is next week. It's hard to believe it's been a year."

She nods.

"I'm going with my friend Natalie to the anti-regatta, she calls it."

"Good. Cap Russell has decided to do the Regatta Tour, even though I don't think any of us are really feeling it. He told me to take the night off."

"Would you rather spend it with me?"

"I don't think I'll be very good company."

She puts a hand on mine.

"I understand. You can call me if you change your mind."

I nod. I wish I could spend the evening with her doing something not at all related to the regatta, but I think I'd wreck our friendship and whatever else might be budding.

"Time to head home."

She checks her phone, sighs, and gathers her crumbs while I gather mine. Her phone vibrates. She frowns at it.

"Trouble?"

"I hate spammers." She shows me the screen.

LILY– Be home by midnight.

"I didn't know they could do that."

"Clone your number and text you? Sure. Or maybe it's that stolen phone—some creepy Antifa-type who thinks it's funny."

I see goosebumps raise on her arms.

It's dark as we head to the Mustang, but we're nowhere close to midnight.

Lily

The bonfire's already going when we arrive. Music thumps and people gather in various groups. There's a picnic table with food and another with drinks, some of them illegal for the age of the majority of the crowd. Natalie gives Melissa and me a crazy grin and heads forward, arms waving to the music, hips gyrating. Melissa and I exchange glances and join the crowd a little less dramatically.

Pirates Cove looks completely different at night with several dozen teenagers dancing to throbbing music around a couple of big bonfires. Melissa and I scan the crowd for Natalie who invited us to this "quiet beach party with just a few friends." I guess she doesn't know that a few is only three. Natalie sees us before we see her and she comes sashaying our way, waving her arms over her head to the beat of the hip hop music.

"So glad you're here." Then she bellows out, "Everybody, this is Lily and Melissa. Lily and Melissa, this is everyone."

I don't think anybody heard her, but it doesn't matter because she sweeps us over to a beach blanket with food and drinks. There are some sodas in a cooler, but there's beer in another cooler. Natalie's clearly drank at least one and she encourages us to have some. But Melissa looks at me with anxiety in her eyes while I shake my head. I have no interest in what beer tastes like. Peter once described it as fizzy piss water. I can imagine that flavor and imagine is good enough. I grab a cola and so does Melissa. While we stand there trying not to look out of place, a boy with what my dad calls a Jew fro comes toward us.

"Hey, Natalie's friends."

"Lily."

"Melissa."

"Larry. Do you want to dance, Lily?"

I don't want to leave Melissa by herself, but I do want to dance. I glance at her, and she nods. So, I agree. One song leads to another and after about three, Larry suggests we take a break. I grab a water, noting that Melissa is dancing with a circle of girls. Larry grabs a beer. I try to tell myself this is just what teenagers do at beach parties, but memories of Peter come to mind. I'd like to believe it's just something normal, but I don't think I'll ever be able to view drinking alcohol as safe. Larry doesn't push me to drink a beer, so that's a good sign. Then again, neither did Peter.

We drink our beverages and then we dance some more. Larry says he's going for a drink, and I ask him to bring me a water. I'm standing letting the sweat dry when a blond guy I've never seen before asks me if I'd like to dance and I agree. We dance to one song and then we go over to where a group of people have gathered by one of the bonfires. They're making smores and laughing.

The group is talking about school, of which I obviously have nothing to contribute.

"Didn't you used to go to Port Mal?" one of the girls asks.

"Yes. Year before last."

"Where'd you go to school last year?" Larry asks.

"I'm homeschooling."

"Ooo. Are your parents Mormons?" the other guy who danced with me asks. He never asked my name, and I don't know his.

"No, they're not. Homeschooling was my decision."

"Why?" Larry looks honestly curious.

"My brother is homebound, so someone needs to stay with him, and I volunteered. I'm – I just didn't want to go to school."

Suddenly I'm at that house in the Hamptons and I feel so out of place. I just want to go home, but Melissa drove and, come to think of it, I haven't seen her in a while. The second guy sidles up to me.

"Want to make some smores?"

"Um, sure." There are already some roasting switches made. It's been a while since I've roasted a marshmallow, but I remember the process. It turns out a delightful golden brown and the chocolate melts between it and the graham cracker. Mmm, good eats!

"You gotta little," Mike says. He told me his name while we roasted marshmallows. I'm thirsty. I wonder whatever happened to that bottle of water Larry went to get. Mike moves in, his lids hooded and languid, his hands going around my waist. I push back from him.

"You're moving a little fast for me." One of the things Peter taught me was that I don't have to accept the advances of a boy just because he's interested in me. Peter actually gave me permission to tell him to drop dead if he ever violated my boundaries. Then when I did that, he got drunk and killed his sister. Too much of my thoughts revolve around him, but it is what it is.

"You need to let go, baby. You'll have fun if you do it."

He's got hold of me and he puts a hand behind my head to hold me so he can kiss me.

"Stop it!" I say it low, preparing to go louder if I must. But he drops me onto my back in the sand and I can't push free. As his lips close on mine, I turn my face aside.

"Stop it!" I say it louder this time as it occurs to me that this is a drunk young man who might well not care if I want to have sex with him.

And suddenly, he's off me, his grasping hands dragged away from my body.

Ben

I tried watching Netflix to avoid the regatta, but *The Midnight Club* just made me restless. Maybe I shouldn't watch stories involving death. I knew that at Halloween. How did I forget? I know, worse than stupid. Kevin would chide me.

So, I decided to go for a walk. Pete and Alyse fill my mind with a sidecar of Trevor, so I walk without thought. I look up at the sound of hip hop, having no idea where I am. I look around. Pirates Cove. I guess not everybody in town goes to the regatta. Would I have if Pete hadn't encouraged me? I know I wouldn't have taken up sailing—at least not that young. Most middle-class people in Port Mallory don't.

I'm thirsty and there's a water fountain in the Cove. I turn up the walkway and stay in the shadows as I go to the water fountain by the bathrooms. The group of teens by the bonfires are laughing, some dancing, others making smores. They are no more intelligent about alcohol than I was at that age. Eating food with beer is important and smores really don't count. I drink long and deep and consider my responsibility here. A year ago, I would have said not my business, but I've lived a lifetime since and now I don't know. While I'm considering my obligations, I hear the tone from the bonfire change, so I turn to look at them.

I'm standing in the dark and they're standing by a bonfire, so it's like I'm the audience and they're the stage. I clearly see the boy try to kiss the girl, but then he takes her down onto her back in the sand. She's pushing against his chest, screaming for him to stop and I recognize her voice.

I'm down the sand and at the two struggling figures on the sand before I even work out what I'm doing. I grab the kid in the plaid shirt and toss him back, careful not to toss him into the fire. And then I reach down to pull Lily to her feet.

"What the f…." The boy is gagging sand.

"Back off!" I order. Lily stares at me as if confused "You okay?" He's kneeling beside me. "Can you stand?"

"What the heck, Mike? She told you no." Another boy is pushing the would-be rapist away from us. Lily climbs to her feet, pushing against me. She stares after the two boys, then scans around as if she's looking for friends. Most of the kids are looking around as if it's suddenly occurred to them they ought to clean up and get out of here.

"Let's get out of here." Lily pushes against me again. I nod as we move toward the parking lot. "What are you doing here?" she asks when we get to the pathway.

"Same as you. Avoiding the regatta. I went for a long walk and here I am."

Her gaze quits scanning the cove's tiny parking lot looking for my car. I got the Jeep back, but it's still sitting next to the cottage a couple of miles away. I offer my hand to her, and we start walking. I think we're going in the right direction. I've biked this way before. I just wasn't paying attention to get here. It's good Lily trusts me to lead her along a dark road. We've been walking several minutes before the first car passes us on the other side of the road. At first, we don't say much, just enjoying the peace and quiet, but after the first car passes us, she keeps looking over her shoulder.

"You…you're okay?"

"Yeah. I just keep getting myself into these stupid situations. Thank you for rescuing me again."

"I always wanted to be a knight in shining armor." I laugh, but she's serious.

"Well, I never wanted to be the damsel in distress."

She's being far too hard on herself, but I don't know if I should say that. Maybe I just need to listen. She casts me an exasperated glance.

"I shouldn't go stupid places, right?"

True, but….

"I've got no room to talk. When we were sophomores, Pete and I were at a beach party. and I got so drunk Pete had to drive me home. Except he was only 15 and he wasn't supposed to be driving."

"And he'd probably been drinking too, right?"

"He said not, and my car wasn't damaged. It would have been if I'd driven it."

"I am never going to understand him."

"Yeah, me too."

Away from the light, the sky is dark except for glittering stars spread like diamonds across a velvet cloth. She drinks in a lungful of warm air and spreads her arms like she's embracing the night. I grin at her. We have a long way to walk.

When we finally get to Tilly's cottage, the warmth has dropped away and we're both shivering.

"We should go inside, warm up before I take you home."

"Um, I told my parents I was spending the night at Melissa's house."

I unlock the door and we enter the warm cottage before I say anything I might regret.

"Seems you learned a few lessons from Alyse you might want to rethink." I move toward the kitchen in the open-plan main room. "Tea or cocoa? Or I could make a pot of coffee."

"Tea." I move to fill the kettle.

"So, you're right. I shouldn't fib to my parents."

"Fib?"

She rolls her eyes then nods.

"It wasn't exactly a lie. I was going to spend the night."

"So, where'd she go?"

"I don't know. I didn't see her car in the parking lot. I left my jacket in there."

"So, you weren't looking for my car?"

"Um, no. Somehow I knew you were walking." I raise an eyebrow. "It was a beautiful night for a walk."

"It was. Would have been better with a jacket."

Tilly's electric kettle heats up quickly, so I direct Lily to the living room while I pour water over the teabags. I search through my cupboards and fridge and bring a tray to the coffee table with rye crackers, goat cheese, and orange marmalade, all leftover from a visit from Mom after I started feeling better in May and she came by to spend an evening with me.

Lily is flipping through the photo album on the coffee table. I started it sometime in the winter at Kevin's suggestion. It was hard at first, looking at photos of my trashed childhood. The last page I got to has a picture of Pete, Trevor and I at the top of Laurel Ridge's hardest mountain bike route, drinking water and laughing at some joke I don't remember. I think Finn took the picture. It occurs to me that I might have been the only one actually drinking water.

Lily wipes away a tear.

"You really cared about him, didn't you?"

"I hope you understand. He's my first boyfriend. He destroyed himself and that's not on me, but someone should care that he's never going to be that boy again." She sighs deeply. "Neither are you or Trevor. Your childhood ended that night on the bay. So did his."

She closes the album and shifts it to the side so I can put the tray down.

"Ooo, fancy!"

"Entirely my mom's doing."

"Is she a prophetess?"

"Something like that." I hear the rain on the roof. She smiles.

"I love that sound!"

I think about how we'd have to get wet to get to my car. Oh, well. She's supposed to be somewhere else. I wonder when she'll realize she should call her parents.

We eat and talk. I tell her a funny work story. She tells me about a beach in New Hampshire. We talk about songs we like and ones we hate. We each pull up songs on our phones to introduce each of us to new artists. We talk about her take on *The Stranger* and my take on *The Brothers Karamazov.*

We don't kiss and we don't go into the bedroom. We just talk and laugh and nibble food. And then we lay back and listen to the rain on the roof and at some point, I doze off.

Lily

I woke up before dawn and texted Mom, assuring her I'm safe and admitting I'm with Ben, but also making clear that we're just talking and trying to find our way through the Peter issue. Ben woke up a little while later, and suggested I wear some of Tilly's clothes. I can launder and return the jeans and t-shirt and she'll never know the difference. I realize we're similar coloring. I guess I never thought that before. Was Peter attracted to me because I reminded him of her? Wow, a person could go crazy trying to understand this guy. I mention it to Ben, and he offers to drive me to Sing Sing, saying he's already called into work.

"You're ready. I'm not. But maybe taking you there will make me ready."

I'm surprised at Mom's response to my text.

MADELAINE– I'm proud of you, honey. And we're trying to trust you and Ben.

The quickest route to Ossining from Long Island is through Manhattan, where some streets are lined with tents and tarp-structures. The homeless problem seems to be getting worse. I shiver as I contemplate what life must be like for these people. The early morning streets are virtually deserted of ordinary people. Everybody is asleep, I guess.

Now, Ben's pulling into the parking lot of Sing Sing prison. It's interesting how parts of this complex are some of the most beautiful Art Deco buildings I've ever seen.

We introduce ourselves at the visitors' center and the receptionist informs us we'll need to see Peter through the glass because we're neither of us on his contact list. Having never heard these terms before, it is kind of hard to follow, but mostly it makes sense so long as I think about it.

"How old are you?" She's looking at my driver's license.

"Sixteen."

"How old are you?" She looks at Ben.

"I'm not going in."

"Well, it's the only way she can go in. At least one visitor must be over 18."

Ben's jaw bunches. After a significant delay, he reaches for his wallet and hands her his driver's license.

"Why do I think I'm going to regret this?"

I smile my thanks while the receptionist is looking something up in the computer.

"I can't speak for you, but I know I settle this by talking to him."

"And I'm terrified he pulls me back in when we're in the same space."

"He's not Svengali. He's just human."

Ben looks uncertain. The receptionist comes up to the counter and puts both our driver's licenses down.

"I'm sorry, you are both on his victims' list. There are waivers, but you won't be able to visit today."

"What?" I'm left flatfooted by the quick change of direction.

"It's a Department of Corrections rule. He can't interact with his victims without special waivers. That includes visitation. And it's also during his work assignment, so he couldn't come to visitation for several hours."

Work assignment? Peter never had a job when I knew him. Is it something he's doing because he's bored or is he required? Or did his grandparents disown him too and he needs the money?

We don't say anything as we walk back to the car. Then we pause and stare at each other across the roof. I break the silence.

"Why is life so hard?"

"Because we need pancakes. I saw a diner as we were driving here. Let's go. You'll feel even better with bacon."

Choices

Peter
June

I woke up this morning feeling like Alyse died yesterday. It's becoming a familiar feeling and when I've gone through it in the past, I've gone with it, let myself slide into blackness. But today, with Luis' story echoing in my mind, I try to fight against it. He's been through so much worse for longer than I've been alive. I don't need to mope. It's my turn to get up first, but when I fail to get out of my bunk after I sit up, Luis drops off his bunk and starts getting ready for the day. I avert my eyes. Normally, I close my eyes, but today I know I'll fall asleep.

It's usually cold here in the morning before the sun heats up the concrete and metal, but I can feel the temperature already rising. It was warmish yesterday. I bet it'll be hot today.

"You okay?" He looks done, ready for his day.

It takes effort to respond.

"Depression's a choice, right?"

"Mostly. That doesn't mean you're not in pain today. Do I need to delay bar time?"

"I'm going to try to fight it."

He stares at me for a moment, then shrugs and climbs into his bunk. I struggle to barely get up, but I take my time getting cleaned up and dressed. He's right. Washing my face and underarms does marginally push the depression back. I lean against the wall between the desk and the toilet rather than sit back down. My eyes want to close.

"Do you need to go to the infirmary?"

"For what? They can't up the dose. I have to learn to deal with it."

"You need to talk about something?"

"No. Alyse is dead and I'm just really feeling that today."

"Okay. So, we'll go to breakfast. You *will* eat. I'll even let you have a cup of coffee. And then you'll go sweep floors. I'll be at work when you get off, so go hang out with one of the guys. I think Declan and you have the same schedule. Do *not* lay down."

I give him a lazy salute.

"This is good, Peter. I know it's hard, but by the end of the day, you'll see you were right to do it."

I'm not convinced, but I'm doing it. We're not really supposed to talk in the chow line. It avoids trouble when people aren't allowed to interact while *hangry*. I listen to the quiet babble around me and try to imagine wanting to interact, but I can't. This feeling of being wrapped in a wet blanket feels like it has been my life forever.

Declan and Seth join the line and speak softly with Luis.

"You okay?" Declan's not much of a talker. He had a head injury before coming to jail, something to do with his crime, and so he listens more than he talks. I'd prefer he'd talk and let me listen, but the guy has limitations.

"Bad day."

He cocks his head, and a line appears between his eyes. He doesn't do well with people who mumble.

"I'm having a bad day."

He nods slowly and responds a little faster than he normally does.

"Day just started."

I roll over what he says. Message? It started rough, but the rest of it doesn't need to be bad?

"You sleep?"

"Yeah. I had a little nightmare right before I woke up, but I did sleep all night."

"Maybe --." He pauses like he's chasing words around in his mind. "I think…you should…keep busy."

His flat tone and earnest expression actually make me laugh. Well, chuckle. I'm still wrapped in wool, but maybe the blanket is a little less suffocating.

"That's the plan."

Declan scratches above his left ear. He can use his right arm, but it's weak.

"After work…you ever read *Moby Dick*?"

"Yeah. In high school."

"Um, I'm reading. You come by and…and we can talk."

I don't know how Luis does it, but he's somehow provided me with bumpers without saying a word.

"Sure." Now I'm going to have to remember the details of a book I read a half-decade ago. I sure miss the internet. It will give me something to contemplate while I push the broom.

It could be a good day. If I choose it.

June

Ben

It's rare for me to take a day off, but I'm glad I spent the morning with Lily. Her Mom seemed okay with our activities, such as they were, when I dropped her off. Grandpa Jack's truck is in our driveway. The house is quiet when I enter the side door. Grandpa looks up from what he's working on.

"Hey."

"Hey? You the only one here?"

"Yeah. Your dad wants to replace the deck, so I'm here doing measurements. What are you doing here? It's not a holiday, right?"

"I drove Lily up to see Pete."

He stares at me for a long beat. I've surprised him.

"How'd that go?" His eyes say he's worried.

"We weren't able to do it. He can't visit with his victims, even if we're willing."

"Right. He's in prison. I suspect even if he were willing, the visit would be denied." I nod in agreement. I think that's what the woman said. "You were really going to visit him? Did you read his letter?"

"No. I drove her, but then they said she couldn't go in without an adult and I said I would. But then they informed us about the rule."

"Disappointed or relieved?"

"Mixed feelings."

"Maybe they'd be less mixed if you read the letter. Why haven't you?"

I sigh, tell him to wait, and run upstairs to get the letter.

"You read it and decide for me."

"Yeah?"

"Please."

He uses his pocketknife to open the letter and then reads through it. He then sets the pages on the table.

"There's nothing wrong or denigrating in there. You should read it."

I stare at the pages. I recognize Pete's handwriting. And that's all I want to recognize. I fold the pages and stuff them back in the envelope.

"Okay then," Grandpa Jack says. "I'm going to head home now. At least you're a little closer to reading it than you were when you walked in the door."

He lets himself out the side door and I sink into the chair he vacated. I hold the envelope in my hands and contemplate my choices.

Lily

I stare at the blinking cursor on my desktop. I pick up Peter's letter and try to find the first point I want to address. Finding it, I set the letter down and hold my fingers over the keyboard.

"Hello, Peter. Thank you for writing me. I believe you regret what happened and I'm sorry you must go through so much to … pay for your crimes …."

I sigh and delete what I've written. I've done that four or five times since I sat down to write Peter. The truth is

I'm not sure I should write him at all. He has to feel so isolated and reaching out to him might give him ideas I don't want to give him.

> Dear, Peter, please understand that I don't hate you, but I don't want anything to do with you.

God, that's so mean! I delete what I've written. I am about to close my laptop to head down for dinner, but an icon lights up in my taskbar.

LONGISLAND43217- How are you?"

I don't spend a lot of time in open Facebook conversations, so I hesitate to respond.

LONGISLAND43217- Are you there, Lily?)

A herd of geese walk over my grave, and I close my laptop with a firm click. I turn off my bedroom lights and stare out at the dusky evening. Wes is dragging the pieces of his half-pipe into his yard, but I don't see anything else out there. I quit shaking. The Andersons are having dinner with us tonight, but Ben isn't with us.

"Something wrong, Lily?" John Anderson asks when he has to ask me twice to pass the potatoes.

"Sorry. Um, yeah. This message came across Facebook. I didn't recognize the ID, but he knew my name."

"Did you ask him what he wanted?" Dad sets his fork down.

"No. He scared me."

"Good," Mom says, but John is frowning deeply.

"Something?" Dad asks.

"Yeah. That's weird. Maybe it's just one of those guys, but – I don't know. Maybe we should reach out to Joel Barnes, ask him if Peter has access to the internet."

"Why would he reach out to Lily like that?"

"Not sure he would, but we should eliminate him as a possibility. Have you thought about calling the police?"

"Why would they take that seriously?" Mom's frowning. "We know she's not making it up because she's known to us."

John shrugs like he accepts her point. The subject moves on. It's an election year for commissioners. I think politics is boring. I can feel someone watching me through the patio doors and I know I'm paranoid.

Ben

I got there late and then ate too much at dinner, so I suggest a walk with Lily in the moonlight. She seems a little reluctant, but she comes out with me.

The neighborhood smells incredible! I don't know much about flowers, but they're all blooming this evening. The sun isn't completely down yet, and the sky is lighter above the darkening street. She's really quiet compared to usual and I don't mind at first, but after a while I wonder if I've done something to annoy her. Girls can be hard to interpret.

"You okay?"

She looks up at the sky.

"I guess." Her uncertainty worries me. "You know that feeling when you think someone is watching you?"

I stop walking and turn to stare at her as the evening gets darker by the minute.

"Yeah. I've had that feeling."

"I've been having it for days."

"Why?"

"You're going to laugh."

"No, I won't. I promise."

She stares at me and then sighs.

"I'd swear someone followed me when I was doing errands for Genesis."

I'm finding it hard to breathe. She's put her finger on something that's been bothering me for days.

"Did you ever find out who sent those flowers?"

"No. I kind of thought it might be you just being weird, but I know it's not."

"Sorry. I'm paying off student loans."

"Yeah, I get it. I also don't like dying flowers very much. They're great for the first day, but then they make me sad as they fade. Reminds me of funerals."

Neither of us want to be reminded of funerals.

"Duly noted. The flowers have been making me nervous. I couldn't figure out who would be sending them to you. Do you think they're tied to who was following you?"

"Why wouldn't they be?"

"I don't know, but I favor Pete for the flowers. It's his style."

"He never gave me flowers."

"He would have if things had worked out." She looks at me with doubt. I don't care. "He can't do much else these days but obsess about you, and this all started right after his letter."

She's considering it.

"But he's not following me," she finally says.

"Well, that might be true, but it's entirely possible he hired someone to follow you."

"Why?"

"So he feels more in contact with the outside world, maybe."

She takes a deep breath and puts her hands on my shoulders.

"I thought I was paranoid, but you sound very obsessed." I start to protest, but she speaks over me. "If you really believe this, you should reach out to Joel Barnes and see if he has a way to find out, but I don't think it's Peter. I think you're grabbing at straws."

I feel a momentary desire to shake some sense into her, but I don't. I take a deep breath and tell myself to calm down.

"I'll reach out to Joel Barnes."

She has taken her hands off my shoulders and now rubs her upper arms.

"Are you cold?"

"No. I just have that feeling again."

I glance around. We're in front of the Callahan's house and I don't see any cars I don't recognize. But I kind of have that every-step-you-take feeling myself.

"Let me walk you back to the house."

She doesn't argue and because someone might be watching, I don't kiss her. I tell her to keep safe and lock the door on her way in. Then I stare out into the night for a bit, but nothing moves so I head for our back door. I need to talk to Dad.

Lily

I roll over, punch my pillow and close my eyes for the thousandth time. I try to settle out my breathing so I can relax, but it doesn't work, so I flop over onto my back and stare at the moon-washed ceiling.

What is Ben planning to do and how much can he affect Peter's life? Yes, if Peter is sending me flowers and not identifying himself, he's acting inappropriately, and he needs to stop. Still, he's in a situation where he can't fight back. Can Ben cause him trouble he can't handle? Since I've read his letter, I feel sympathy for him even though I suspect he would reject it. He's in a difficult situation and we shouldn't make it harder for him. Should we? But if he's sending me flowers....

I've been cycling through these thoughts for hours and I'm nowhere near sleeping. I growl softly and slide out of bed, snapping on my lamp so I can see to retrieve my sweater. I wrap it around my sleeping t-shirt and turn off the bedside lamp so I can turn on the reading light at the window seat. I grab a book I've been working my way through and settle down to read for a while.

The Young Unicorns by Madelaine L'Engel is deeper than I thought it would be. Mom said it was one of her favorites as a teenager and I didn't think it would make me think, but there's more to it than the typical slightly paranormal story I expected. It's got me thinking about trust and how hard it is to reestablish once it's been violated.

It's four am and I'm starting to yawn. I put a bookmark where I finished and snap off the reading light. Outside the window, the front yard is a study in silver and black, like old photography. I never noticed how striking the view was, probably because I'm never awake at this time. Nothing is moving out there, but I feel like someone is staring at me again. I wrap my sweater around me as I scan the street. Ben stands across the street, in front of the wall that separates Genesis' house from the street. I shiver. Has he been standing there watching me read? I reach for my cellphone and ask him that question before I go to bed. I'm just getting comfortable when the phone dings.

> **BEN– You weren't supposed to see me. I thought you would be asleep. Just checking out the neighborhood. Goodnight.**

Less creeped out now, I fall asleep.

Lies We Tell Ourselves

Peter
July

I stare at Mr. Boudreaux who waits for my answer. Alyse died a year ago today. I managed to pretend it wasn't before he brought it up.

"I heard you were sleeping through the night until last night. What triggered you?"

"Nothing more exciting than the date."

He's got strange eyes – they're kind of hazel, but really a mixture of brown, green and gold, like some kind of art glass kaleidoscope. It's uncomfortable to be under his gaze.

"Come on, Peter. Don't do this to yourself."

"Do what?"

"Spiral. As long as you won't talk about it, it has the power to eat you alive."

I sigh. I'm tired from the nightmare train I lived through last night. That single cup of coffee yesterday morning was probably a bad idea. I managed not to scream and wake everybody else up, but I didn't sleep except in fits while sitting up against the wall. The last time this happened, I ended up back in the infirmary, so Luis recommended an ER meeting with Boudreaux.

"I see her everywhere. How is talking about her going to make it better?"

"What do you mean you *see* her?"

I swallow tightly. I've tried to talk with Luis about this and I can't. This is a private office. If I cry here it doesn't matter. I open my mouth and fail to say anything. He waits. I take a deep breath and let it out really slowly.

"I just see her."

"Dying in your arms?"

Shit! He's just stabbed me where I'm already bleeding.

"Ssssometimes."

"What happens the other times?"

"Sssshe's standing there…behind you."

His office is painted in sunset colors. He doesn't look behind him.

"So, alive?"

I nod reluctantly. *I'm crazy. He's going to tell me I'm crazy.*

"That's consistent with PTSD, Peter." I nod. Luis has told me this. "Is it denial? You want her to be alive, so you see her alive?"

"Nnno. I think…I know she's dead. It's just…I don't believe in ghosts, but that's kind of what it feels like."

"Accusatory?" I nod. "So, this is when you're awake. You do know you can control that to some extent. You may feel like you can't, but if you tell her to go away, she kind of has to." Luis has said it too, but it's not as simple as they think. "And, yes, I know it's not easy. You feel guilty and it feels wrong to not torture yourself, but you do control it if you choose – well, to a certain extent anyway. Can you tell me about your dreams?"

"They don't make a lot of sense."

"No, dreams don't. So, tell me what you remember."

"Last night?"

"Whatever."

"Some of it was…was Alyse. Dying, dancing…." My voice gets really hoarse. Boudreaux nudges a tissue box my direction. "My mom." A light appears in Boudreaux's eyes.

"Tell me about her."

"Like what?"

He smiles like he's trying to keep me from clamming up.

"When did your folks break up?"

"I was 12."

"What was the last straw?"

I want to complain that he should read my file, but I know I need to get something out of this.

"I caught her and my stepfather – he's my stepfather now -- in the guest room and told my dad." My voice wavers. I *know* there's more to it than what I'm saying. I feel her fingers against my chest. But that's not all of it. "She tried…tried to have sex with me."

"When?"

"After I found them but before I called my dad."

"Tried?"

"I pushed her off and—I was not turned on by my mother."

"Of course not." I don't think he's mocking me. "But she's in your dreams?

"Yeah."

"For how far back?"

"Occasionally…since she left. Since I got here—some nights and I don't know why."

"Are those worse than when you dream of Alyse?"

"Last night it was both of them."

He takes a moment to consider this and then leans forward with his hands on his knees.

"So, I did read your file and I know your mother and sister looked a lot alike. You think that's got anything to do with it."

A chill creeps over my body, making my shoulders stiff and my neck sore. He's patient, which means I have to talk. So, I finally do."

"Maybe." My voice comes out breathy and weak. I feel like I've run 20 miles flat out.

"You okay?"

I shake my head.

"Take a deep breath, hold it for a 1-count, and let it out slowly. Think about letting the stress go. In and out, slowly."

I try to obey. I'm not really good at it, but I'm calming down.

"The thing about PTSD is that triggers are a symptom and so is trying to avoid them. The more you try to avoid the triggers, the more you make them worse."

Lovely. I'm breathing hard again. My hands are numb, and I feel my fingers sticking together with blood.

"I can't," I whisper.

Boudreaux's gaze lingers on me.

"Yeah, it's hard to face it. If you're willing, I can help you through it, but I don't promise you'll enjoy the process."

Am I willing?

"Will the nightmares get better?"

"If you work at it, eventually."

I stare at my hands, wishing there were any way easier than this. I know my life isn't meant to be easy after what I've done. Will there ever be a time when things don't hurt anymore? Or at least not hurt so much?

"What do you say?"

"Where would we start?"

Boudreaux considers a moment.

"Your mother."

Sweat breaks out on the back of my neck.

"I'm – why?"

"Because I suspect all your problems go back to her. Dealing with it won't fix everything else, but it will be best if you start where you started."

I feel sick, but I'm so tired of not sleeping until I end up in the infirmary and then they drug me so I can't feel. I want something better, even if it means facing things I've never wanted to face before.

"Okay."

It doesn't feel better when I agree to work on it, but I hope it will in the future.

July

Ben

I stare at the third question on the list, thinking this is the stupidest thing I've ever encountered.

What have you been doing since you last attended Dartmouth?

Wow, they want to know what I did on my summer vacation. What a stupid question that I don't want to answer. But I want to get back into Dartmouth and my feeling is that the school could decide not to let me back in if I answer wrongly. I'm not a legacy or a diversity candidate. Straight, white males are not considered cream of the crop, even if I scored a 1610 on the SAT and graduated with a 4.1.

My cell buzzes and I automatically reach for it, assuming Mom is calling to wonder why I skipped dinner with the Wexlers. It's not that I wanted to skip spending time with Lily, but that I need to get this paperwork done.

"Hey."

"Ben?"

"Yeah." Who is this? Sounds a bit like….

"It's Grey. Have you heard from Trevor today?"

"I haven't heard from Trevor in a while. I thought he was in rehab."

"He disappeared from there a couple of hours ago."

"Oh. Well, I haven't heard from him. What should I do if he does reach out?"

My gaze falls on Pete's letter propped against the lamp on my desk. I guess it's progress that I brought it to Tilly's cottage rather than leaving it at the house.

"I frankly don't know, Ben. He needs to get back to rehab, but if he won't stay, what good will that do? Thank you for caring, Ben. I've got to go."

"Of course."

We hang up and I get back to work on my paperwork. I'm about to e-sign it when my cell rings and I reach for it, still expecting to get a lecture from Mom.

"Thank God! Hey, man, I need some help."

"Hey, Trev. What's up?"

"I need help. My card's not working and I owe this cabbie money. Can you help me out? I'll pay you back. You know I'm good for it."

I try to steady my voice. I want to tell him to quit calling me. But then something better occurs as my gaze once again settles on Pete's letter. This has been a long time coming.

"Sure. Give the phone to the cabbie. I'll settle him up."

"Thank you! You're saying my life." He fumbles with the phone and a moment later I hear someone breathing.

"Hey, man, what's the card number?"

"I'm not giving you my card number. You should call the police and report him for theft."

"What?"

"Yeah. I'm his friend and I'm saying he would be better off going to jail instead of wherever you're dropping him off at. After the police come to arrest him, call me back and I'll pay you twice what he owes you."

He laughs and the phone goes dead. I e-sign my document and send it off and then stare at Pete's letter. I guess it takes a while to go through the arrest process. I also guess I just blew off my second oldest friendship. Trevor sounded sober, so he might well remember this and never forgive me. That makes me sad, while at the same time, I know it was the right thing to do. I text Grey to let him know what I've done. He responds interestingly.

GREY "I think that was the right decision. Not one I could make but thank you. I'll keep you apprised.

More or less of its own accord, my hand reaches for Pete's letter. I trace Pete's writing with my fingertip. And then I flip it over and slip my finger under the flap, pull the pages out and take a deep breath before I start reading.

Lily

Ben showed up for church this morning and seemed to feel good about it. My parents didn't object when he asked me to go for coffee. It's a beautiful afternoon and we go to the Bean, which has a lovely deck that overlooks the water. He keeps the conversation light and I'm enjoying myself when he starts telling me what he did with Trevor last night.

"Grey is spotting me a semester's tuition and room and board because of that stellar idea. He's already talked to a DA who has agreed to a deal that will make Trevor want to stay in rehab."

"Wow. You obviously weren't expecting that."

"No, I wasn't. So, I ...." He pauses and stares behind me. A young man in a red-striped shirt pauses by our table.

"Lily Wexler?"

"Yes." He's holding a vase swathed in shiny paper.

"These are for you." He sets them on the table between Ben and me and departs as abruptly as he appeared.

I smile at Ben across the vase. He looks...constipated. The card says *"With greatest admiration."* Since Ben isn't saying anything, I tear open the paper and stare at the yellow tulips.

"Wow, you really went all out!"

"I didn't." I meet his gaze. "I'd love to take credit, but I didn't do it. And that's kind of weird, right?"

I clasp my hands on my biceps, trying to suppress a shiver. How did the sender know I'd be here?

"Your dad said he was calling Joel Barnes tomorrow, to make sure this isn't Peter."

"Probably a good idea. And they are lovely flowers."

I shake myself off and focus on him. I plan to leave the flowers right where they are.

"You were about to say something."

He blinks at me.

"Oh, yeah. I read Pete's letter last night. You want to read it?" I move the vase to the back of the table and offer my hand to receive the missive.

> Dear Ben,
>
> How do you say goodbye to your best friend? I don't want to, but I know I deserve it – your anger, maybe even your hatred. I made you watch me do the worst

thing I could do, and I can't take it back. That's on me and much as I hate it, I accept that. So, all I can really do is offer to make amends. I know you probably don't want me to, but I hope you'll think about it and let me. Yeah, it'll probably make me feel a little bit better, but I hope it will also be a way to add some value to your life. I can't do anything else and if you'd rather never see me again, then name some lifestyle amends I can do and I promise I'll do it. Because I know I have to be better going forward and I hope you'll let me show you that I am.

And now I'm going to end this letter before I beg for forgiveness and other stuff I haven't earned. I hope you'll give me the opportunity to earn it – to show you that I really regret not just what happened out on the bay, but so many other things. But I know you don't have to, so if I don't hear back from you, I'll try to understand. That's what happens when you fuck up as badly as I did. I get it. So, you might hate me, but I don't hate you. I love you like a brother and I know that's not enough. So, goodbye if this is goodbye, but I'll make sure to keep *my forwarding address available in case you ever change your mind.*

Peter

Ben wipes tears as I fold the letter to put in the envelope.

"You okay?"

"I don't know. And I don't know how to respond to that."

"I know. I can't either."

We sit there at the table while our coffee grows cold and just hold hands and don't talk, because we share a painful past, though I truly hope we have a future worth waiting for. Where does Peter fit into that? That is so impossible to know at this point.

Ben

He wrote to say goodbye. How do I wrap my head around that? Even as I was saying I never wanted to see Pete again, he was working on accepting I never want to see him again. And yet, I can't conceive of Pete never being in my life again.

That's nuts, right? He's always been in it, and he's still got a substantial lease in my head. I really should write him to tell him he's right, we can't ever be friends again. He made me watch Alyse die.

Pete's anguished cry as the light died in her eyes comes to my memory and I sense I'm being unfair, and yet…the bubble of blood rising from Alyse's mouth fills my mind's eye. Damn, Pete, why'd you have to do that?

His letter didn't even attempt to answer that question. Maybe he doesn't know either. I have to wonder how he lives with himself. His letter suggests he's thinking clearly these days. I can't imagine Pete living with the knowledge of Alyse dying because of his stupidity. Nobody ever explained why he wasn't at Alyse's funeral. Of course, it would have been a security nightmare for the governor. The press was all over everything even without Pete being there. It would have been worse if he'd made an appearance. But it seemed cruel that they didn't let him come. Maybe he didn't want to be there…didn't want to stand in shame in front of the rest of us. His letter drips of shame so bone-deep it's never coming out. How does he live with that?

If I could talk to Pete, could he answer my questions? Would he? His letter suggests…maybe. He wants to be better. Why should I sacrifice myself toward helping him survive his own decisions? Okay, maybe it wasn't a decision he made. He was a black-out drunk. Maybe he wasn't in control and didn't make a decision. Maybe he doesn't even remember. He knows he did the worst thing possible, but he doesn't feel it like those of us who experienced it.

And maybe he's sending flowers to my girlfriend. My *girlfriend*? Yea, I think I want Lily to be my girlfriend.

A guy could go crazy trying to sort all of this out. Do I feel compassion for the hurt person who is trying to accept that his life will never be the same or do I speak my primary emotion? Screw you for what you did to Alyse and leave my girlfriend alone! Which letter will I write? Good thing I don't have to decide today.

It's a lovely evening that I'm not paying attention to. Warm, but not muggy. There's a little bit of a breeze and the flowers smell amazing. I pause, watching as a guy passes me on a bike. He puts his bike against the garage and approaches the front door. I've never met him, but I think it's that guy who is pretending to be a girl. I know that's not politically correct, but I kind of resent him for leaving Lily alone in the middle of a riot and then there's the jealousy I feel about any guy wanting to be near Lily. It's impossible to think of him as a her when he's got the hots for my girlfriend.

I could go interrupt them, but that sounds like I don't trust Lily and I do. It'll be fine. If the guy is up to no good, Lily's parents are there to keep things calm. I think I'll go home and…well, maybe prayer will make this whole dilemma more manageable.

Lily

The ranch house stands amid several greenhouses behind a macadam parking lot separated from the multi-lane road by several maple trees. The young assistant pushes the cart out to where I'm parked. This is my last stop and I've still got an hour to drop everything off and get home so Mom can go to the bookstore on time. I kind of wonder if Bram couldn't spend a half-hour alone. It's got to be frustrating for him to be treated like a baby. He can't communicate that, but more and more often, he bristles when we try to help him with something. Yeah, he only has one hand, and he falls a lot when he walks, but at some point, he has to gain independence. Doesn't he?

I set the solar orb in the bed of the truck, its box cushioned by a blanket. I thank the clerk, close the tailgate, and walk around to the driver's side, preparing to get in.

That brown van across the street seems…familiar. Was it at my last location? A weird feeling tiptoes into my stomach and a shiver runs down my back. I start the truck and drive toward the job site in Perryville. The van appears in traffic on the LIE not long after. It hangs back two or three cars. I'm pretty sure it's the same van. The house where Genesis is landscaping the yard is kind of off the beaten track, but I've been there before, and I have a nearly full tank of gas. If this creep is following me, it wouldn't be a good idea to bring him back to the house where I'll soon be alone with Bram.

Then he drops away. I turn a corner and I don't see him follow me. I take a few more random turns before I decide I should go to the project house.

I pull up to the edge of what will be a lawn when Genesis is finished and watch in the rearview as the van continues down the road I just pulled off of. Maybe I'm a little paranoid. I get out of the truck as Genesis and her foreman come walking toward me.

"Great!" Frank says. "We can get going on the rain garden now." He calls to a couple of his guys, and they strip the bed of everything but the moving blanket.

"You got a few minutes? Want to take the tour?"

Genesis is in her element here among the dirt and plants.

I'd like to, but truthfully, that van creeped me out. I don't say that, of course. It would make me seem paranoid.

"I should get home to relieve Mom. Maybe next time. It's coming along great."

I kind of liked the natural look that existed before the piles of dirt appeared and they dug a storm water drainage system, but it's not my yard. I give Genesis a hug and drive toward home, taking the backway out of the neighborhood. I don't see any brown vans in my rearview. I guess I *am* paranoid.

Grandpa Jack

Peter
June

I don't get a lot of visitors. I guess I deserve that. My grandparents won't be coming. It isn't the right weekend for Joel. Ben's grandfather has written before. He tried to come in the spring, but I kept ending up in the infirmary. Strangely, that didn't put him off. I knew he planned to come this weekend, but I kind of thought he'd change his mind. But here he is, and here am I, and I won't be going anywhere for a long while. So, I have to submit to a cavity search after this visit, but that didn't keep me from joining him in the visitation room.

I knew Jack Anderson before prison because he's Ben's grandfather, but we'd also encountered one another at AA during my attempt to stay sober last summer. God, was it just last summer? So much has happened to me since then that it feels like decades. Anyway, besides Joel, he's the only non-family who still seems to care about me. Heck, most of my family is still not speaking to me. I'm whiny, but it's in my head. Finn writes and he told me to see about getting him on my contact list for around Christmas. It's not as awful as I make it out to be. I need to stop whining even just to myself.

After I file through the pat down line and am let into the visiting room, Jack and I shake hands while others hug and some kiss. We don't know each other that well. Hugging, I mean. I don't kiss guys. We sit down on opposite sides of the table, and I put my hands on it so there's no issue with the guards.

"How is it going, kid?" Jack's noticed I didn't start talking right away. I'm nervous and I don't know what I've got to say.

"Just another day in paradise." It's the first thing that pops into my head. I don't want to lie and say I'm doing okay. This place SUCKS and I'm doing well just working my way through it.

He gives me a weighing look.

"You know you earned being here, don't you?"

I nod. It sucks, but I know this is all my fault. Now to explain myself. Being flip avoids the emotions the truth carries with it.

"Just trying to face it with some humor. I'm not very good at that yet."

"It's a sucky situation, to be sure. Depressed?"

"I'm on antidepressants. I'm still depressed, but I feel it less."

"Kid, you're still mourning your sister. That's going to take a long time."

Okay, honesty! Did I expect less from Jack Anderson?

"I think it'll take a lifetime."

Jack nods. I've never before seen him without his iconic ballcap. I guess I thought he was balding like a lot of old people. His hair must have been dark before it went grey and it's still thick, reminding me of Mike's, but not curly. Damn, that's depressing too.

"So, what are you doing these days?"

"Sweeping floors and walkways. I get paid 10 cents an hour."

"Wow! At least when you get out, you'll appreciate the wage increase."

"That's what I'm told."

"They don't have anything where you can use your brain?"

"Sure. I'm on a list. I could work in the library or for the chaplain. I'm not a trustee, so I can't work in administration. And the wait lists are decades long."

Luis helped me with sorting out what I could and couldn't do. I've put in applications to work in the kitchen, the laundry, and maintenance. All have wait lists, and I have no skills in cooking or repair, but there is hope I won't be sweeping and shoveling for the rest of my time here. Twenty-four years. I don't believe Luis that it'll only be four or six years. *They* wanted to try me for First Degree Murder. They're not letting me out early. And maybe I don't deserve to be released for decades.

"You wandered. What's up?"

The temptation to complain is always there. Luis doesn't allow it and even Boudreaux says it's not going to help me so I should stop. But here's someone who doesn't know the rules and seems sympathetic. Surely.... I sigh.

"Just thinking about how my life is going to be very different because of my own stupidity."

"Your sister's life ended, and your friend Trevor broke his back."

"I know. I've got nothing to complain about. I'm alive and healthy. Being miserable doesn't matter."

"I wouldn't go that far." His grey eyes fix me like a pin to a corkboard. "You aren't really paying your debt if it isn't miserable, though I think with time you'll become less depressed."

"How do you know that?"

"A friend of mine is sponsoring an ex-con. I asked him—the ex-con--what he thought. He said you're in the misery phase. The first year feels like four seasons of winter, but you shouldn't be allowed to stay frozen in that season."

I sigh. Yeah, it's been a year of winter for me—a bitter cold winter that feels like it will never warm up.

"My cellmate Luis isn't going to let me."

This gets a twinkle from Ben's grandfather.

"Good for him. Good for you."

"Some days it feels that way. Some days I feel like my face will always be in the mud."

"Hard to feel hopeful if you can't raise your head up now and then to see the future."

"I have a future?"

"You do, but you're in the misery phase. How's amends going?"

"I don't know. You tell me."

"I read your letter to Ben." I'm not surprised. The Andersons are the kind of family where you go to your grandfather for advice when you don't know how to handle something, and I somehow knew my letter would hit Ben like a haymaker.

"How'd he take it?"

"Nope. Remember, you don't get to ask that question."

I sigh. We established that rule when he visited me in rehab. He remembers even if I don't. Ben was my best friend, and it hurts that I can't get him back. I can't even get a little piece of him back through Jack.

"Okay." I swallow unfallen tears. "What did you think?"

He smiles at me as if he's impressed with how well I took his refusal. I'm getting used to "no" as an answer. By the time I get out of here, I'll be an expert in not fighting back.

"It's a good letter. You took responsibility and you can't do better than that. If he rejects it, that's his choice. You tried and you can't do more than that. It's your responsibility to make amends, not to convince him to let you do that."

And that knowledge makes me deeply sad. He watches me struggle with that.

"Peter, I know it's hard to let go, to accept that God's got it, and you don't have to do it all. Your job is to make yourself ready, so that IF he or anyone else gives you a chance, you can actually show that you've changed. So, there's a conversation worth having. Tell me how that's going."

"I'm doing 12 Step almost every day. I'm in the Big Book every day."

"And what are you learning?"

"That I sucked." We exchange glances and shrugs. He gets that I'm accepting that I can't change my past, much as I want to. "That people don't have to forgive me. It's the-not-letting-that-depress-me that's hard." He nods. "Did friends refuse when you got sober?"

"Oh, yeah! But it's been decades, so – there's a few that still make me sad, but for the most part, I've moved on. And, you'll learn how to do that." I shift because we're talking about Ben, and I don't see myself ever moving on from that. "I know. Right now, it feels like you need to do that, but you're not making it better by pushing in that direction."

"So, what do I do?"

"Leave it where it is. You tried. Next step is his. If someone responds, respond in kind. If someone doesn't, leave it alone. You've done your part."

My chest hurts with pent-up tears. He waits while I get that under control.

"It's not just Ben you're thinking about, is it?"

I let my breath out in a long sigh.

"My dad never responded to my amends letter."

"From back in rehab?" I nod, swallowing the threatening tears. "That might be an exception. When you're ready. It's going to be hard because you have to accept full responsibility, even though he probably has some guilt for what happened." I nod because I've been working with Boudreaux about forgiving myself for what my parents did, and they definitely did some things to set me up for my four seasons of winter. "You've already started?"

"Yeah. Luis says he won't let me send it until it's right, and that's great, but I'm scared I won't get it right, ever."

"If you do it right, it's not an attempt to make him forgive you. It's an offer to get to know the new you. I'll be praying that the seed falls in fertile soil *when you're ready to broadcast it.*

He sounds like Luis for a second and I smile.

"Something funny."

"Just that Christians have the same metaphors."

"Someone in here?" I had that same thought when I first got here, but now I smirk.

"Yeah. My cellmate actually." He shifts his gaze. "Something?"

"Just reminding myself not to be judgmental. Of course, there are Christians in here."

"I don't think he was one when he came in." I shrug. Luis never gave me permission to share his story, so I won't. "I'm not, but he's starting to make sense on the days when I have the energy to care."

He nods.

"It might help to realize that if you were out there, you'd probably still be dodging reporters."

"And riots. What's up with that?"

"People pissed off at the wrong people for something that needed to happen. You ever been on the subway?"

I don't get the reference.

"I'm sorry. We don't get a lot of new news in here. The subway?"

"Oh, um, it started when some mentally ill guy was going off in the subway and a citizen stepped in to stop him hurting someone. The crazy guy died. The nuts are blaming the citizen."

"Subway guy black and the guy trying to calm him down was white, right?"

"Yeah. How'd you know that?"

"I live here. I never cared about race. I still don't. But it really matters to some people here."

"Wow." We take a moment to contemplate that. "But you know about the riots?"

"That was big enough news. Saw them on TV even."

"But not the reason?"

"I heard a cop shot someone."

"That too. People get all spun up at the wrong people when something like this happens. Cop got cornered. He shot one of his attackers and they lit up Long Island for it. We're still cleaning up the mess."

Do I care? I've been gone for less than a year and I feel like it's been decades. I care if some of the people – those I still consider to be *my* people – are okay, but do I care about the property damage?

"I don't understand why people get so violent over stuff like the subway." Jack puts his elbows on the table. I just keep my hands where they're visible. "What was the bystander supposed to do? Let the crazy guy kill someone in front of him?"

This feels like a conversation, so I indicate the room around us.

"A lot of really angry people in here, so it kind of seems…ordinary to me now. There are gangs segregated by race and they each have a view of what the other did. And they're never going to let it go because they're certain they're right."

"Are they?"

"Certain? Yes. Right? I don't know. I'm not in any of them so I don't have to agree with them."

"Well, that's good, I guess. Lonely?"

"No. Unaffiliated prisoners are kind of our own gang. You just have to be careful who you associate with and stay cordial with everyone else."

"Cordial? That doesn't sound hard."

"For some of the folks in here, that's a very foreign concept. The world they come from is very violent and this place just intensifies that. But there's also people in here who just did something dumb and had a bad lawyer." I hook a thumb toward my own chest. "Or a good one. Some of them get angry over that and some of them decide to keep their head down and just get through it. I'm hanging with that group."

"Good for you."

I nod. I *know* it's good for me. It's just easier to complain and whine about the circumstances I put myself into as if it were someone else's fault. It's not and I know that. I wonder which of the four seasons of winter I'm in.

"So did you see any of these riots?"

"By the time it got to me, it was a very raucous protest. Or maybe there were protests amidst the riots. I had to repaint my fence, but they didn't come up into the property."

"I saw a Jeep that looked a lot like Ben's in the middle of a riot."

He opens his mouth as if to speak, then closes his lips, shaking his head.

"Everybody you know who I know about is okay. That's all you need to know."

Honesty?

"Now, I feel lonely."

"Sorry, kid. But I answer this and pretty soon I'm scratching your itch to know more and that's not good for you."

He's right. I know it. I need to accept that I will never get my old life back. I might retain a few connections – Jack and Finn, and I got a card from Rick the other day – but the rest of it…. Boudreaux says if I accept my circumstances now and things are better in the future, I'll be pleasantly surprised.

"I know I earned it, Jack. It's just…. I guess if it were easy, it wouldn't be discipline."

"Exactly. You working on lifestyle amends?"

"Yeah. Starting. You got to qualify for formal things. I'm not there yet. But a guy walked up to me at AA and asked if we could talk, so we are."

"Sponsoring? That seems premature."

I laugh.

"It's not sponsoring. More like just someone to talk to. And us normal people – you know, not street criminals – there's not so many of us. You start to think you're crazy because nobody else is like you. It's good when you can talk to someone who has similar experiences."

Now he smiles.

"Yeah, I can see that. For just an instance, I saw a break in the depression."

Well, that's improvement. I don't know how it's going to work out in the future, but if I can start to see some light here, it's got to be better than what I've got now. Right?

"The only thing I control in here is my inner life, but I haven't been able to. Maybe I'm learning how now."

"You had to detox, right?"

"Yeah. My liver wasn't working, so it was hard."

He nods.

"Maybe your biochemistry's been totally messed up and your neurochemicals are moderating now."

I stare at him. Nobody since rehab has mentioned that my body has been through the wringer and my emotions might be all over the place because of it. I'd kind of forgotten that recovery takes about two years.

"I said something you needed to hear?"

"Since my liver started working again, I physically feel better, but maybe there's a lot of things still off-kilter in my head. So, on days when I know I'm not thinking clearly, maybe that's not me so much as chemicals that are out of balance still."

"Maybe. It took…wow, that was so long ago…two to five years for everything to settle out for me. And if I look back on people I know, I'd say two to five years before they start thinking really clearly."

"Great!" I actually chuckle. "And half of us don't make it to five years. No wonder the world is so screwed up."

Jack smiles at me.

"I think this cellmate of yours – he's also your sponsor?"

"I guess. It's not as formal as that in here. There are others who sponsor me too."

"That's good, actually. You still have times when you feel like you *need* a drink?"

"Oh, yeah, but that's environmental. There are guys on the tier who make this disgusting-smelling hooch and I go through withdrawals every time they maintain the crock. But the price for even a sip is higher than I'm willing to pay, so I don't give in, but it's hard."

"That sounds like a good exercise in refusal skills."

I blink at him. His thinking is so outside-these-walls and maybe exactly what I need to correct my thinking. Luis keeps saying I shouldn't get too used to this place.

"Thanks. That's—yeah, still not going to enjoy it, but maybe I should be looking at it as I'm learning how to say 'no' in a setting where the costs are high so it will be easier to say 'no' when I'm in a situation where the costs are lower."

"Glad I could straighten you out with that. If there were no costs, would you be tempted to give in?"

"I'm tempted, but I'm also terrified. I can't go through it again. And I doubt I'd enjoy it. I'd feel Alyse judging me."

I mumble that to my hands. He shifts.

"On the one hand, I'm sorry you have to live with that. On the other…."

I nod, swallowing. My ears pop.

"I'm okay with that." My voice sounds husky. I clear it. "I deserve it."

Silence reigns between us as Kalifornsky and his woman quietly speak in savage tones at the table over. Seems like every time I come to the visiting room someone is splitting with their honey. There are advantages to being single when you come into this place.

"I want to thank you for coming to visit me. How many times did you get here to discover I couldn't see you?"

"This is the third time. And it's fine. The second time Joel Barnes called me, so I didn't even have to drive here."

"I didn't know Joel called you. I didn't know they call Joel when I have an episode."

"You'll have to ask him." He stares up at the far wall. I've got a great view of the high windows that nobody can see out of. I'm betting sunlight is washing the far wall, but turning around might attract guard attention, so I stay where I am. "So, what do you do for fun?"

Fun? Wow. I do things. Are they fun? It takes me a minute to sort through that and he gives me that time, as if he realizes I don't think in those terms right now.

"Weightlifting." I figure that's a good place to start, and it goes from there.

July

Ben

Maybe the secret to honesty is a Bic Stick pen as opposed to a gel one.

> *Hey, Pete! I bet you didn't expect me to write you back. I'm not sure I expected to do it. I'm still angry that you made me watch Alyse die. You may hope you can put that behind you, but we can't. It'll always be there and....*

I pause in my reading and look at Kevin.

"That as far as you got?"

"Yeah – mostly. The next paragraph tells him how I really feel. 'Screw you. Drop dead. I don't care if your life is difficult right now.'"

Kevin winces, then chuckles.

"You don't have to mail what you write, you know? His letter says he doesn't expect you to respond."

"He hopes I do."

"Well, of course he does. He's got nothing but what-ifs. And yet he chose not to burden you with them. That says a lot."

"It says he's learned better ways to manipulate the people who are fed up with him."

"Possibly. I don't know the guy. But I don't think you're making things better for yourself by fighting your inclination to forgive him. He never has to know that you've done it. Do it for yourself. Because the guy that wrote that letter doesn't need your forgiveness. He may still want it, but the fact that he wrote what he wrote speaks volumes about him having moved on from you."

"You really think he's accepted his guilt?"

"That's how I read that letter." He shrugs. "I think that's how you're reading it too." He does a seat lift as I mull over that revelation. "I know it's hard to separate what he did and accept his legitimate repentance." Kevin straightens out one of his feet that shifted on the footrest. "But even if you don't completely buy it, you want to and that refusal to forgive is giving him way too much power over you." He leans back in his wheelchair. "So, are you ready to tell me what you're holding back?"

I scratch the back of my neck. I've admitted it in writing one of the drafts to Pete that I have set on the coffee table.

"That day – earlier in that day – he called me." Kevin's gaze is fully on me now. He doesn't speak, which compels me to continue. "He was a little confused. He wanted to go to rehab, but he couldn't find his car keys and he wanted to know if I'd drive him. But I was at work and Lily was with me, so I said 'no.' He assured me that he could call someone else. I guess that someone else was Trevor, who was probably not a good choice."

"Misery loves company. And from what you've told me, it seems Trevor is feeling guilty about something too."

I glance at him, surprised. It's not an evaluation I'd ever thought of to explain Trevor's behavior of late.

"Maybe. I got a call from him just before I got here."

"And?"

"He wanted a ride from the treatment center. I told him 'no'. I don't know why he can't understand that I'm not going to help him kill himself."

"He's not thinking clearly, Ben. That's unfortunate, but it's a hallmark of most addicts. They all gather people around them who enable their addiction and when their enablers stop enabling them, they can't believe you would be so cruel as to not help them get what they need."

I nod. I've seen that in both Pete and Trevor.

"Now, back to Pete. Are you learning anything about yourself while you're writing these letters?"

Am I? I sigh, stare out at the backyard. It's a scorching hot day out there, but Kevin's office doesn't feel too hot or too cold. Everything beyond those windows speaks of summer and yet…Grandpa said something about four seasons of winter a while back. That's been my life for a year, struggling to unthaw the icy rage that has consumed my heart since that night out on the bay.

"I'm angry. Maybe I'm angrier than the situation deserves and, while I tell myself I'm doing what I'm doing with Trevor out of compassion, I think anger is growing toward him too."

Kevin nods.

"Good insight. So, what do you intend to do about it?"

I shrug. That's part of the problem. I don't know what I intend.

"Okay – first – you are not responsible for Pete's actions. He wasn't ready to quit partying and so he didn't demand Trevor take him to rehab. His letter suggests he's bearing that burden. It's not yours to shoulder." I sigh, nodding slowly. "Second, you have tools available to you. Alanon exists. Check it out." Dad threatened to drag me to a meeting last week, but I don't think he's serious. He's kind of not into forcing people to do things. "And, you have a church family, right?"

I chose Kevin because he goes to my family's church. We didn't really know each other, but I figured I wouldn't get the standard atheist therapist treatment. I might be going through a period where God and I aren't on speaking terms, but I still believe He exists.

"Sort of. I stopped going a couple of years ago."

"Nothing says you can't go back. Or…you own a Bible, right?"

"Yes."

"Nothing says you can't read it." He puts his hands on his knees and leans forward a bit in his chair. "Or, if you've outgrown your parents' church, find another one. You're going back to school, right?"

"Yeah."

"So, find one up there. Everybody who grows up in the churches needs to find a way to make their faith their own."

I nod, but then I sigh, facing my conundrum.

"But if I can't forgive Pete, how do I ever talk to God again?"

"If you never talk to God again, how do you forgive Pete?" I stare at him, surprised to hear my struggle reframed. "Maybe you're starting off on the wrong foot.

Just like you think you're forgiving Pete is for him when it's really for you."

I close my mouth, which has dropped open in shock. He's right, of course. I need to start with my relationship with God before I can do anything else. I know these truths, but I've forgotten them in the chaos of the last couple of years.

"Time's almost up. So, what will you bring me next week?"

I hesitate a moment.

"What if…what if I write a letter to Pete that I have no intention of mailing, where I write out all of it – good, bad, ugly?"

He quirks an eyebrow. I think he might be slightly skeptical.

"If you're ready for that…yeah. And if you're not, we can talk about how you get ready for it." He grins. "I think we just made some progress today. One more thing. Did you let Trevor's dad know he's trying to escape again?"

"No, but I was literally walking in here, so…. I'll text him."

"It's what you can do right now, so…. It might save his life."

I agree.

"Do you think…if I'd said 'yes' to Pete that day…?"

"That's the problem with what-ifs, Ben, it didn't happen. And maybe that's something Pete learned, because he never mentioned it in his letter. You'd think if he held it against you, he'd have brought it up, but he didn't."

I start to open my mouth in protest, but I pause then, shocked. He's right. Pete didn't hold me accountable for any of my failures in his letter. And I wish I knew what that means.

Lily

The tiger lilies are in full bloom and the fragrance is heavenly.

"Wow." It's really all I can say as Genesis puts an empty cup in front of me and reaches for the press of coffee. I can't even smell the coffee over the lilies.

"I know. Can you smell the citrus, jasmine, and rose notes? It's such a warm scent."

I hadn't really analyzed the notes of the fragrance. Genesis's been trying to teach me, but my sense of smell is still unschooled. I get up and lean over the lily bed. I do smell citrus hidden under the sweet fragrance.

"It must have taken years to establish these."

"It must have. They were here when I moved in. I just improved their conditions. I hope whoever lives here after us does the same."

"They'll live for a while without help, right?"

"Yeah. Perennials are tough. They're borderline weeds. Did you plant the ones I gave you?"

"I did. It'll take a long time to fill in that bed, but at least it's started."

"They almost double every year if they've got a good environment. I've relocated tiger lilies that have invaded people's lawns."

"Wow." I move back to my seat. "So, he hasn't gotten a renter yet?"

"No. I don't think he's trying very hard. I think he's kind of depressed."

"Yeah. He loved his kids. I didn't get to know him very well, but the couple of times I saw him with Alyse – oh, he really loved her."

"And his son?"

"Peter thought his dad was always mad at him."

Genesis sighs.

"It's a tough situation. I'm thinking that's Peter's life now. His dad's never going to get over that – not completely."

For a moment, I feel sad for Peter, but then I remember he killed Alyse and the sadness steps back into the shadows.

"You know lilies have a lot of meanings?"

"I'm aware. Purity." I say it in a silly voice because really, it's silly.

"That's white lilies. And white roses. Tiger lilies have a more assertive connotation. They symbolize energy, enthusiasm and joy. And that reminds me of you."

My cheeks grow warm. I've been enjoying my little side job and watching Genesis's bump grow. She's not in maternity clothes yet, but I think it will become necessary soon.

I shiver suddenly, remembering the bouquet I received.

"What do yellow tulips mean?"

"Happiness. At least that's what the Victorians believed. 'There's sunshine in your smile' is what they would say. There's all sorts of meanings to flowers. Don't get me started on roses. Yellow for friendship, red for passion…and make me shut up now." She makes me laugh, but I'm still chilled. I can't think who would send tulips to me. Genesis reaches for her clipboard with its thick sheaf of papers.

"What are my orders for the day?"

Genesis laughs.

"I need you to pick up three items. They're all in Terryville, so I think you can do all three, but if you can't, I've put them in their order of importance. I'll be at the job site, but again, if you need to get back for Bram, do it and I'll pick up things this evening."

I'll call Mom and ask her if she can be a little late to the bookstore. I don't like to make things hard for Genesis. Mom has employees.

I finish my cup of coffee while I look at the list and the map she's provided. I shouldn't have any trouble doing all three in three hours, which gives Mom plenty of time to get to the store.

"I should get going then."

"Something bothering you?"

"Someone keeps sending me flowers."

"How is that a bad thing?"

"Ben says he's not doing it."

She rubs her chin.

"That boy who thinks he's a girl…?"

"Jenae? Jerry? Maybe. He's not talking to me right now, so that's seems unlikely."

"I don't know about that. If he likes you, maybe he's got some conflicted feelings. My brother went through something similar…until he met his wife. Thank God he didn't cut anything off."

I snort.

"I really should get going or I won't be able to get these all done. Thanks for breakfast in your glorious flower garden. I'm going to miss you being a neighbor."

"You're doing great this summer. I will definitely try to rehire you next year."

Again, my cheeks get hot, and I forestall more embarrassment by heading toward the truck she allows me to use when I work for her.

I like the idea of being a tiger lily and suddenly, I like my name for the first time in my life.

Ben

I flip up a page and sigh. This is not going well and it's alternately making me feel like I'm a horrible human being or a faker. Pete will never read most of this, though I do hope I'll eventually find some words in all this ink that I can use to say "I'm sorry you feel guilty about your bad choices, but we're not friends anymore."

Am I sorry? Is he? While reading the letter, I do feel his grief, maybe made all the more poignant because he didn't even attempt to express it. Maybe, as Grandpa Jack would say, he's hit rock bottom and he's got no choice but to hang out there for a while.

Does that upset me? Do I feel compassion for his lot?

Not really. He got away with hurting Cheyenne and then he killed Alyse and made me watch. There's a tiny part of my soul that cares that he's in pain, but for the most part, I think he deserves it.

That probably makes me a bad person. I've been praying about that lately and so far, God has just let my thoughts bounce back at me like there's a wall between Him and me.

Why would there be? I'm not exercising 70 times 7, but surely God didn't mean I had to forgive someone who killed someone in front of me.

Yeah, I know.

One reason I know the God of the Bible exists is because He doesn't think like I do. He expects me to do things I don't want to do. If He were a figment of my imagination, He'd agree with me. Hence why I'm writing these snatches of letter.

I look up from my scrawling because Chuck sits down in the chair on the other side of the table.

"That scowl gets any deeper and your face is gonna crack."

Chuck started as a coworker and he's now sort of my supervisor, but he doesn't know how to do the whole separation from the workforce thing.

"Yeah, I guess I was kind of concentrating."

"You guess? It looked painful. Let me guess – your friend that killed that girl."

Chuck listened while I vented last summer before I started seeing Kevin. Somewhere in the last year and a few weeks, I stopped venting, but I guess other people still watch.

"He wrote me an amends letter." I sound far too perky for that admission. Chuck cocks his head like he's trying to figure me out.

"He whine?"

"No. And that's the problem. It was a heartfelt letter. I could tell he took his time with it. Cut right to the heart of the matter. Didn't make excuses. Thanked me for my friendship and says he's trying to accept we'll never be friends again. Offered to make amends in whatever form I'll accept them."

Chuck used to run with a biker gang and he still dresses like he'd like to. He wears his long hair tied back in a ponytail most days.

"Yeah, I can see where that would harsh your mellow. I assume you're writing him back. You know there are limits to the number of pages he can receive, right?"

"I'm not planning on mailing it." Chuck glances down at my notebook and chuckles.

"That's probably good. He doesn't need any more Debbie downer in the place that he's at right now."

I start to retort and then I remember – Chuck is one of the company's *diversity* hires. He spent a few years locked up somewhere and this was the only place that would hire him, despite the fact that he's a great worker. Temple hires the *legally challenged* for reasons I haven't been told – maybe just because someone has to. It's like when employers started hiring handicapped people. Billy's one of those hires too.

"Okay, tell me what you're thinking."

"Sing Sing is a dark depressing place and he's surrounded by guys who aren't just dangerous when they get a 5th in them. If he's writing amends letters, he's rising above his circumstances, but even then, he's got to feel like he's drowning. I did and I wasn't a burbite who'd never had to defend myself before. So much as you want to stomp on him and make him hurt some more, hold that feeling back because he really doesn't need that now. You want to send him a harsh letter in a year or so, okay. That'll be water off a duck's back by then. It might make him sad, but ultimately, he won't care. That's where I was when my ole lady cut me off. I was about two, two and a half in and I moped around for a few days, but compared to my surroundings, I just couldn't feel it. But if she'd sent me that letter in the first year…." He draws a languid finger across his throat.

I look down where I wrote some of my harsher feelings. Do I want Pete dead? Wow, it's hard to answer that.

"Is it really that bad?"

"Yeah. I know the stereotype – three hots and a cot, but a million bad things happen in there every day and most people go through a couple of years of depression before they get used to the place. And your friend sounds like he was already pretty self-destructive, so…. Maybe you don't really care what happens to him, but trust me, you'll care if he commits suicide right after getting your letter."

Well, that's true. It's entirely possible – given what I've written – that I hate Pete now, but I still care enough to not really want him dead because of something *I've* done.

"So, if you're not planning to mail it – what's it all about?"

"It's about working out my feelings about Pete."

He nods, scratches his beard.

"You know, he maybe wrote a letter like that to you too before he wrote the one he mailed."

"You write a lot of letters in prison?"

"I ain't an addict, Ben, I mean, sure, I got caught trafficking a lot of drugs, but I never used really. I did enjoy the experiments though." He grins then sobers. "That's why I had to send you to Billy to buy pot, because I don't do that anymore at all. But my cellie was a druggie – had been a druggie – and I watched him write a lot of letters and only mail about five, so…yeah...I'd bet your friend agonized over every word. Anyway – time to get back to work."

I look around to see the plant-filled greenhouse space that is Temple's lunchroom emptying out. Chuck stands. I close my notebook and follow him back toward the loading dock.

Lily

I stare at the message, unsure how I feel about it.

> **JENAE– I'm coming to see you. Can I come to your house.**

I don't really want a rival for Ben's affections. I kind of wish she or he or whatever would find another object of obsession or whatever they'd call it in a romance novel. On the other hand, I'd like us to end as friends.

> **LILY– Yeah, it's okay. When?**

> **JENAE– 20 mins.**

I stare at myself in the mirror. Normally, if Natalie or Melissa were coming by, I'd try to spruce up a little. I've been gardening all day, and my hair is up in a messy bun. I haven't quite got the hang of long hair and I know it doesn't look good. But I don't want Jenae – Jerry – thinking I wanted to look nice for her/him. God, a girl could go nuts thinking about such complicated relationships. I make sure my bangs aren't sticking straight up, but otherwise meet him/her as I am.

She's awkward at the front door with my dad, which is a good excuse for us to go upstairs. The room that would be Bram's room has become something like a den to replace the one he uses as a bedroom off the living room. I don't know what the rules are for a trans-girl in my room. Definitely his boy parts are not allowed. A hysterical thought drifts through my head that he, er, she might prefer it that way.

"Nice room. I guess your parents wouldn't want me in your room."

"We haven't discussed it. Sorry."

"My parents wouldn't want a girl in my room either." I'm hesitant about meeting her eye and when I do, I notice he hasn't shaved today.

"I went off the puberty blockers a while ago. I was gaining weight, had a migraine for a month. It wasn't what they advertised." I avert my eyes because he…she seems to be on the verge of tears. "I'm just tired of feeling like…nothing's right. And the counselor suggested it and I thought – yeah, go for it. Everybody was so supportive, but I still felt like crap except that night when we were at the concert."

Now I have to say something.

"It was fun…it was…until…." I can't say it.

"Until I made it weird."

Okay, so he's thought about it.

"Yeah. I'm sorry."

"It's fine. I came on too strong and you're not gay. But you're the first girl I ever felt this way about. Made me think. I have to think about it more. If I weren't trans, would you…?"

"I don't know. Maybe before, but right now…."

"Ben?"

"Yeah. I'm just—sorry, I just -- ."

"I get it. We'll stay friends. Maybe you'll change your mind when he goes off to college."

I laugh. I doubt I'll want to do that, but it's a good place to leave it.

"I quit that therapist, by the way. She didn't want to me stop taking the hormones. Do you know how hard it is to find a therapist who will explore if you're actually trans or just confused?"

I shake my head.

"But there's this guy – he's willing to risk his license. My parents are willing to pay cash, so…. I don't know yet. Maybe it's better that you're not up for dating me now. I'm too messed up to date anyone."

"You're a nice…person. You'll find somebody. After what happened with Peter, I thought I never would, but he was right next door, so…. Just take your time. Concentrate on you and don't make any rash decisions."

"Don't worry. I won't off myself." He sighs. "I was on the edge before the puberty blockers, sure dying was preferrable to living like how I felt, but then they made me feel even worse. And when I stopped them, I started to feel better, so…. I won't hurt myself. I promise."

He gives me the salute from *Hunger Games* and I laugh, but the mention of suicide chills me to the bone. Why do I attract self-destructive men? Peter…Jerry. I'm like an emotional-support animal for the neurotic.

"So, I enjoyed texting you and stuff, and I was so glad to hear from you, but this counselor says we need to just be friends, so maybe I won't text you every hour for a while."

"I enjoy texting you too. You shouldn't be a stranger. If Ben and I break up, I might have a different view of you."

"Yeah?" He smiles. He's a lot better looking than when he used to hang around trying to tease me at school. "Yeah! Thanks for that. I read somewhere that friends make the best partners."

"Could be. Ben was my friend all last summer."

"Yeah, but it was – well, it got all weird between you. You write back to Peter yet?"

"No. I should. But I'm still having trouble knowing what to write."

He nods, stirs, and stands up from the sofa.

"I should go. It's getting dark out."

"There's supposed to be a storm coming in." As I say it, one of the trees in the front yard bends in the wind as if in agreement.

He makes a face at the window.

"I rode my bike, so I should get going. You wouldn't happen to have a jacket I could borrow, would you?"

"Hmm, not that would fit your shoulders. But, wait. I have a sweater my grandmother sent. I think she bought it for the Russian circus and when they left town, she decided to give it to me."

He laughs.

"See, one reason I'm probably not a girl, I don't know where that reference comes from, but I suspect a Disney princess."

"*Anastacia.* Let me go get it for you."

I actually like this sweater for just kicking around. It's enormous and golden, but it's *comfortable*. When I hand it to him, he laughs again.

"Good thing I'm coming off the trans thing because no boy would be caught dead in this thing."

I laugh with him as he dons it. It really looks ridiculous. It always does on me and it's worse on a…guy. Wow, my head is so messed up by the whiplash.

I walk him to the door. He's looking at the sky with some trepidation, but he rides off on his bike like he thinks he'll beat the rain home.

I close the door feeling that I have somehow successfully helped a friend out with something major. I wasn't all the answer by a long shot, but I played my role even if I didn't know I was doing it. Ben's right about honesty. Maybe one reason lies came easily to Peter is that our whole culture today is built on lies. We tell a lot of them with the best of intentions. I could have lied to Jenae – Jerry – and said I'd think about dating him – her – but how does pretending someone is something they aren't help them? I'm glad he thought to come apologize. I have a good feeling about him.

There's no getting away from my past, though. My thoughts circle back to Peter and the concept of truth. Maybe there were truths we were supposed to tell Peter that we didn't because we were afraid he'd take it wrong. Are there still truths we should tell Peter?

Steeling my spine, I pick up the notebook I've been using to try and write Peter and I sit down on the window seat in my bedroom to try and write some truths.

Elephants

Peter
July

I think Joel's keeping secrets from me again and I really miss the eye contact, which is weird since you don't make eye contact with anyone in here. Well, Boudreaux and Luis, rarely with Seth and Declan. As my only connection with the outside world, I don't like that Joel isn't engaging and I'm scared he'll remember he's just doing this to be kind. We're talking about his kids and Audrey and his brother Nathan, who I remember because he interviewed me for my sentencing report, but there's an elephant in the room and I don't know what it is. I need to know.

"What's up?"

He pauses, glances at me, sighs.

"Yeah, too smart. I should know better."

"Whatever it is, just say it." I don't mean that. I'm terrified, but I also do absolutely mean it. I'm discovering an intense dislike of secrets now that I'm learning how to recognize the ones I keep.

"Some things have come up, so…this is not me not trusting you. This is me asking questions to eliminate you from the picture."

Now I'm intrigued instead of terrified.

"Okay. Is this to do with our earlier discussion about burner phones? I still don't have one, but I did learn how to get one."

Lots of people here have them. They coordinate drug shipments with them. His gaze flickers nervously. I shrug.

"Who would I call? Who would accept my call? You and Jack Anderson, Lucy. And you'd all be on me about breaking the rules, which I'm trying not to do. So why would I risk adding more time to my sentence for something that is no benefit for me?"

He's still not meeting my gaze, so I wait.

"Do you still have a thing for Lily Wexler?"

What a weird question.

"Yeah, no. I've got no choice but to move on. She pick up a stalker or something?"

Now he's really staring at me.

"Wow, that's insightful."

"Consider where I am, Joel. I've learned a lot of dark stuff. So, she okay?"

"I'm not authorized to tell you anything."

I start to laugh and then I "see" Lily's white face as I roared toward her and Ben. I blink, but it doesn't dissolve. I take a deep breath and let it out slowly. Joel's talking to me, but I can only hear the motor's roar.

"You okay?" I blink at Joel. He's concerned. I never saw him with Alyse, so I don't usually experience PTSD during our visits.

"This conversation is triggering me. I understand you can't talk about any of them with me. Thank you for believing me."

"I told them you weren't part of what's going on. But they still wanted me to ask."

"It's fine." Alyse hits the railing as the boat abruptly stops and pain explodes across my lower abdomen. This is my life and I have to live it. Of course, they suspect me. I made myself into the Big Bad Wolf.

"I brought photos, by the way." I push off the Alyse specter to enjoy this moment. Odd that I look forward to someone else's child being born, but it feels like hope for the future somehow.

"Great. Hard to believe she was pregnant that day at court."

"You didn't know?"

"I was pretty distracted that day. And self-centered."

"That's one of those times when being self-centered is totally understandable."

I don't know if I should tell him that Luis considers self-centeredness to be a grievous sin, so I change the subject.

"So how does it feel to be dad to a little girl?"

"Amazing. Jakey is a wonderful kid and I love being his father, but little girls – I'm a daddy."

That's not likely to be part of my life. I've given that some thought lately. If I get out of prison when I'm in my early 40s, would I want kids? To start with kids at my dad's age? Somehow, I think it's going to be hard to find a partner. I try to smile while he tells me a baby story, but I'm struggling with seeing the wreck over and over.

"I'm sorry. You're not doing okay right now, are you?"

"It's my life. I don't want to complain."

"It's not complaining to acknowledge that you're having a tough time."

"Yeah, but I'll use it to manipulate you, so it's better if I don't."

"You can't manipulate someone who is on to you."

Is that true? I'm now surrounded by people who recognize my manipulative ways, so I suppose it *is* true.

"I also brought you a book and an art set Lucy sent. She ran it by the administration first, but you know they'll hold that for a day or two."

I nod. It will be more like a week or two. Nothing goes smoothly here.

"So, what book?"

"*The Gulag Archipelago*."

"The Russian dude?"

"Solzhenitsyn, yeah." Last time we talked about how the book about the Soviet prison system was strangely hopeful. I've got nothing but time on my hands, so why not read a book?

"You're determined I get an education, yeah?"

"Nothing beats a classical reading list. I'm hoping you come out of this having gained something."

"It's giving me time to put things to rest. Hopefully, I'll get the depression out of the way before I can use it to manipulate people."

"You're mourning, Peter. Nobody should expect you to do that silently."

"They don't care, Joel."

"You mean your dad?" I nod. He sighs. "A part of his mourning is anger directed at you, which…." He doesn't want to say it, so I finish his sentence.

"Is part of the reason prison isn't such a bad place right now. If I were out there, I'd want to fix things, but I can't from here and that's, I hope, giving him some time to recover."

"You're not still angry about how he disowned you?" We've discussed this before. The disownment, much as it hurt, protected me from lawsuits. While the why is understandable, the how still stings.

I shrug. Maybe I'm not angry anymore. Maybe I'm resigned to my fate. I did a horrible thing, and I can't ever take it back. My life will always be rocky because of it. When I get out, I'll get a job and never bother Dad – Alan -- again. If the grandparents are still talking to me, I'll give them my change of address so he can find me if he ever changes his mind.

I feel tears pressing the back of my eyes. Yeah, it's easy to be strong when you're not required to provide proof of it.

"This conversation depressing you?"

"I'd be depressed anyway." I shrug. "It hurts that Ben and Lily believe I could be stalking her. It's like…we were friends for 12, 13 years and it's like he doesn't even know me. And, I thought I was accepting that, but now there's this ache in my chest and I just…."

I sigh and he nods.

"I wish there were a magic formula, Peter, but there isn't."

It's my turn to nod. I struggle with acceptance, but I'm getting there. Boudreaux says denial can sometimes protect us from becoming too depressed. *Take acceptance in small doses.* I take a deep breath and shake myself, trying to dispel the sadness that presages depression.

"So is Alia letting you guys sleep?"

"What do you know about that?"

"One of the guys here says babies don't let you sleep."

Cam is here in the visiting room cuddling with his toddler. Last month she wailed when her mother took her out of the room at the end of visiting.

"Audra asked if she could visit with the kids."

"Kids don't belong here, Joel. Don't confuse compassion with doing something that might harm your kids."

"You aren't toxic, Peter."

"I don't know about that right now, but this place is. Toxic. I might change my mind eventually, but right now…." I shrug. The guards are moving toward the doors. Joel sees it too.

"Okay, so we'll discuss the book next time."

"Yeah. Oh, um, my counselor recommended I get some guitar practice time."

"You doing that?"

"Still building calluses, but yeah. I'm getting to a point where I can see I'll be able to lose myself in the music soon."

"Anything that gets you out of your head, right?"

"Yeah. He says it'll be stress-relieving."

The guards give a 5-minute warning.

"I should go, get the sexual molestation out of the way."

He nods and we stand. We're not close enough to hug, but we shake hands. Others touching me has become odd. It never happens in here except for cavity searches.

"You hang in there. This is all temporary."

"Or not." I shrug. Life in here is very monotonous and utterly unpredictable. I'm not ready to see sunshine on the horizon and he doesn't push beyond the reminders.

I walk him to the forming line as Cam's toddler screams. We shake hands again and I move to the door where I'm required to go. Nobody else is there, but the guard gestures me through. I get ready to pull down my pants and bend over the table.

"Your lawyer is your friend?"

Demario is pulling on the gloves. I hate post-visitation. Not enough to tell Joel not to come.

"He's kind of a boy scout."

I pull down my pants and bend over. Demario is quick and efficient, and he doesn't loiter in my anus. This is my life now and I don't want to get used to it, but I am adapting to it.

July

Ben

Talking with Chuck got me thinking about the stress Pete must be under and all the tricks he might have learned from his fellow prisoners. I don't know how I feel about that, but when I look up at the hardware store and see Joel Barnes, Pete's attorney, I consider it's worth the effort to push him a little on the subject.

"Hey, Ben. How's it going?" I wonder what the odds are that two people who don't live in the same village in a huge town would run into each other at a hardware store in a third village. Maybe it's a God thing.

"It's going. Did you talk to Pete?"

"I did—and I called your dad – Pete doesn't have a burner. He seemed genuine on that topic. I see him enough that I can tell when he's not exactly telling the truth, so I believe him."

"Someone is sending her flowers and calling her. I don't want to believe that Pete's gone that far around the bend, but I'm not sure he wouldn't. He's already gone places I didn't expect."

"Yeah, that…. Look, there are way more likely people out here than Peter, who has no money to buy flowers."

"Yeah, right!"

"No, Ben. Alan disowned him and he's not accepting money from his grandparents. Jobs in there don't pay much. He doesn't have money."

Alan disowned him? Wow. I guess it makes sense, but I never saw that coming.

"Look, Ben, maybe – I think you should involve the police. My wife works for Grey Media, and she's been telling me about some disappearances along the Gold Coast. They think it might be a serial killer. They don't know how he targets his victims although there's a theory he reaches them through the internet. It might be a good idea to contact the police and figure out what they think."

A serial killer?! Thinking it could be Pete just irritated me, but – wow, some people think a lot darker than I do. Joel apparently does and – how dark do you have to be to be a serial killer?

"Is he okay?" I can't believe I'm asking, but here I go.

"I gave him zero information besides that Lily had picked up an admirer and he didn't push…much, so I'm going to return the favor and tell you that I'm not reporting on him. His life is about what you'd expect it to be and he's dealing with it as best he can."

I can't imagine Pete dealing with it at all. But it's been a year, and a lot of stuff has gone on in the interim. I should just leave it alone because I really don't want to know, and Joel really won't tell me.

"If you ever seriously want to know, Ben, there are waivers that allow him to see his victims through the glass, non-contact."

"I'm not afraid of him."

He shrugs as if to say 'maybe you should be'.

"It's just an offer. If you request, they'll ask him if he agrees and they'll allow a visit. Now, I gotta go or I'll run out of time for the day. It was nice to see you and I hope whatever is going on with this stalker is innocent, but like I said...."

He turns toward the cashier counter, and I get back to looking for the weed trimmer line Dad sent me here for.

Lily

It's great to get away from the house for something that isn't work or church and it's lovely that Genesis invited my friends to a garden tea in her lovely courtyard. While I usually enjoy the high thick stone wall that keeps the yard quiet, Melissa and Natalie are watching Wes try to teach Bram how to navigate a skateboard ramp in a wheelchair. Bram probably thought it was intriguing, but now he's clearly nervous. And Melissa and Natalie aren't making it any easier as they're whistling and clapping at every effort.

"Stop it!" I tell them. "Bram doesn't need any distractions."

"Your brother is cute." Tema walks away from the other two girls and comes to sit down at the table, smoothing her skirt to protect the back of her thighs from the cool metal. The sun is just coming around to the patio.

"*My* brother?"

"Yeah. I mean, ignore the wheelchair and he's cute. Too young for me, but still cute."

I hadn't thought about that, I guess. Bram's face is changing, becoming more mature. It's a little lopsided, like the rest of his body, but the right side of his face sort of follows the left side when he smiles now.

"I don't see it, but then it would probably be weird if I did."

"Yeah, I feel that way about my brother Andreas. He's cute, but it would be weird if I spent much time dwelling on it. I hope this is okay, that I tagged along. We just ran out of time."

"It's fine," Genesis says with a big smile, bearing a cozy-wrapped pot of tea out to the garden table. "The more the merrier."

She heads back into the house. I offered to help, and she told me no, so….

"Do you remember me from last year?"

"Sort of. We had Spanish together, right?"

"Yes. I always wanted to ask you over, but Alyse could be so jealous."

"That's what Jenae said."

"Jenae – you mean Jerry?"

"Yes. I'm still getting used to that."

"I'd never get used to it. I know it's wrong to be transphobic, but it's just weird."

"She asked me out."

"What?! And you said…."

"I'm not gay. Plus, I'm starting to date Ben, and I don't think I should date a lot of guys at once."

"No, that's adding complications to your life that you don't need."

She tucks some of her chocolate brown curls behind her ear. She's got these great bouncy curls that tumble across her shoulders and frame incredible eyes.

"Exactly. I wish he'd understand, but instead he sends me tulips."

I think it's Jenae. Ben has been really quiet on the subject lately, but I think it's Jenae.

Melissa and Natalie come over and start chattering with Tema, so I open my contacts and send off a text to Jenae, thanking her for the flowers.

Then it's time to enjoy the tea with scones and some conversation. Tema knows Melissa from an art class they took this summer.

"I'm not very good," she admits. "I enjoyed it though."

"I love your bright colors," Melissa says.

"I think I use those to overcompensate for my lack of talent but thank you."

"So where do you live?" I figure best to get her off a negative subject.

"Perryville. Just close enough to go to Port Mallory schools, but my parents don't have to pay the property taxes."

"Is it that bad?"

"Not in this neighborhood," Natalie says. "But yeah, Port Mallory is kind of pricey."

I know there are a lot of really expensive homes in Port Mallory. The home Peter grew up in comes to mind. But our house and the Andersons are more modest, more suburban. And the Wyngate Estate is all rentals these days. Now I'm going to have to ask my parents about taxes. They were pretty desperate when we were moving here. Did they buy more house than necessary?

My phone dinged a while ago, but I ignored it because the conversation is so good. Now I open it.

JENAE– You like the flowers? Maybe you'll stop being a bitch now.

Oh, my! Now I've irritated Jenae/Jerry and I still have no idea who is sending me flowers. I get creep vibes up and down my arms and I shiver in the warm summer sun.

Ben

I love evenings this time of year. We live at the end of the road where Alan Wyngate owns the land across from us and beyond the termination of the road. We don't have streetlights, so the evening is dark and warm, and the flowers fill the air with a mix of sweet and spicy scents.

The only thing that would be better than this is to have great company to share it with, but Lily's parents are out and she's watching Bram. I didn't even bother to ask her because I know she'd just feel badly that she couldn't come for a walk with me.

It's been years since I've been down the abandoned road that goes into the Wyngate property. Well, last summer I did walk as far as the tree fort Pete and I built when we were kids, but I've not gone any further in a half-decade. I think this is some sort of private preserve that even predates the family selling the land that makes up our subdivision. Pete and I used to play back here, and it never occurred to me to wonder where the road went. I think I was scared to go that deeply into the woods. We got as far as building the tree-fort, but we only ever went as far as the narrow bridge before me. It's covered in moss, and I think we were scared to cross it.

I've done one year of engineering school. I concentrated on getting my 101's out of the way, so I really have no special knowledge to inform me on the safety of this bridge. I'm on my belly directing my cell phone light into the shadows, noting the creek it crosses doesn't look deep, when I hear a giggle behind me. I nearly drop my phone into the water while trying to look over my shoulder.

"What are you doing?" Lily is staring at me like I've lost my mind.

"Trying to decide if the bridge will hold my weight."

She frowns and it's adorable. Then she laughs and holds out her hand.

"Here, let me hold your phone. You can look and have both hands to prevent falling into the stream."

I doubt that's going to work, but she slides off the verge to stand on a narrow strand of sand and directs the beams of both my phone and hers under the bridge. The stones that hold the bridge up don't seem to be failing and the beams that support the bridge look solid, if somewhat mossy, but I'm not absolutely sure about the wood decking.

"You coming with me?"

"Sure."

"Why are you here?"

"Wes came and said he'd stay with Bram while I go for a walk with you, and he said you went this way."

My little brother as a matchmaker? That's kind of hilarious and touching at the same time.

"So, I don't trust the decking, but there should be a ledge along the sides."

"Or we could walk on the railings."

I stare at the moss covering the railings for a long moment and then she giggles.

"You're teasing me?"

"I am." She directs her cell light to the ledge. "Well, I guess I don't want to live forever."

She holds onto the railing and carefully steps onto the mossy surface. I don't trust it, so I wait until she's about a quarter of the way across before adding my weight to the structure. The old wood feels spongy, and groans about halfway across, but I don't get dumped into the water. It feels like forever when I reach the safety of the other side.

"That was fun. What death-defying feat is next?" She's looking around at the woods.

"Ever see the Blair Witch Project movies?" I flash my cell flashlight around at the trees.

"Cool. I always wanted to star in a movie that isn't believable."

"Why are you being so rough on me?" I try to sound slightly melodramatic. I don't have the histrionic range Pete had, so I think I sound pretty silly. She grins at me.

"I'm kind of wondering why we're doing this after dark."

"I have no idea. Just wanted an adventure, I guess."

She nods, scanning the area again.

"What's here?"

"I don't know. Never been."

The road is basically a path. You could get a 4-wheeler down it. I occasionally feel the rounded shape of a cobblestone, but this road hasn't been maintained in a long time. Dad, who grew up in our house, doesn't remember it ever being an active road. I keep scanning ahead with my cell light. There is a Blair Witch Project-feel to all this. The trees are mostly second-growth, but there are some bigger trees. I don't see any buildings.

We keep walking. The path takes a significant downward turn, which makes sense somehow. The valley descends in a series of ledges and the creek runs along one.

"I mostly just wanted to get away from everyone."

"Sorry."

"Not like that. You were always welcome to join me. I just thought you couldn't. I wanted to get away from lights and sound."

"What do you think we'll find?"

"Buildings."

"We'll find buildings?"

"We have found buildings."

I direct my phone through the trees where I can see the edge of a building.

"Oooo, very Blair Witchy."

Sticking to the path doesn't take us to what looked like a shack, but as the path takes a turn, a lake opens to our right and there's enough moonlight to see several buildings along the path.

"Wow! I had no idea this was here."

The buildings look to have been recently repaired – maybe within a few years judging from the dried leaves built up on the porches. Our flashlight beams directed into windows show bare but nice interiors for two of the cottages. The third one looks like it's under renovation. The fourth one has a decent porch, but the windows are boarded up. The fifth is in rough shape, spongy porch floors and peeling paint. There might be more along this shore, but there's another bridge and it looks really dodgy, so we don't go further. It's hard to tell by cell phone light, but I think there are three other cottages.

"I wonder what this is all about."

"Peter never mentioned this?"

"Not to me. But his family does a lot of real estate stuff. He didn't pay a lot of attention."

"This is like a labor of love."

I stare at the cottage we're nearest to. She's right. Someone was working on these cottages and just stopped. Something tickles my memory, but I can't bring it to mind.

She clearly wants to solve the mystery.

"It's family property. Maybe someone started a project they didn't finish."

That makes sense.

"Pete would have loved a project like this. He really did most of the building of our fort."

"I didn't know he knew how to do carpentry."

"He didn't—not when we started. He pumped Dad and Grandpa Jack and then practiced on the fort." I find myself smiling at that unexpectedly pleasant memory.

"See, he wasn't always bad."

"Yeah. And maybe his letter ought to convince me that he didn't go bad at heart, but he did let alcohol lead him to some bad places."

She smiles at me, does this weird dance move that Alyse used to do – like she's boosting up the sky with her hands.

"What?"

"I'm celebrating your progress."

"Really? You better be careful, or I'll kiss that patronizing look off your face."

"I dare you!"

She spreads her arms in a "bring it" gesture and laughs as I move in. I wrap my arms around her waist, and she calms. I can feel her breath on my collar bone as I lean in to kiss her.

Lily

This is my first kiss from a man. I still remember the sweet kiss Peter gave me, but now, kissing Ben, I know he's an adult and Peter was still a boy. Wow, my toes curl and parts of my anatomy I didn't know exist last year responds. Ben kisses me until I'm breathless and when we break apart, we stand there in the circle of each other's arms, leaning our foreheads together.

"I've wanted to do that since you were dating Pete."

He lifts his head so he can see my face. Judging my reaction? Is he confessing?

"I feel wanted."

"You don't think I was wrong?"

"No. You didn't act on it when it would have hurt Peter. That was honorable. Does it upset you that I didn't heed your warnings about Peter?"

"No. I was actually used to that. Not the warning girls off him. Until Cheyenne I never really thought he was dangerous to anyone. There were rumors he was gay, which I doubted at the time, and I've since learned he definitely wasn't—isn't. Turns out he had ethics with women. But – yeah, off track. Pete always got the girls. Even when he didn't really know what to do with them. He was nearly a year younger than me. Girls were a mystery to him and yet girls acted like he was rolled in catnip."

An image of Peter covered in green bits and surrounded by cats pops into my head and I smile. It might be the first funny thought I've had about Peter in a year.

"So, when you ignored my warning, I figured it was just that."

"Maybe that was some of it, but I also needed to see it for myself, which I didn't until Trevor's party." I sigh, worried he'll take this wrong. "You expected me to just agree with you. Was it because I was younger?"

He might be frowning. It's getting darker as the half-moon is covered by gathering clouds.

"That might have been part of it. Somehow you grew up this winter."

I throw my shoulders back so my breasts strain against the fabric of my t-shirt. Somehow, I know he blushes.

"Not that way. You're wiser now."

I could argue that Peter forced that on me, but I find myself not wanting to talk about him.

"I'm glad you did that."

"What?"

"Kissed me. Can we do it again?"

"Yes, but on the other side of the bridge. There's that taste to the air. I think a thundershower is coming."

I look at the sky and he's right. The sky is darker than when we started and there is a taste – metallic, almost electric. We don't hurry back to the bridge, but we're going uphill so short of running, we can't really hurry. It seems to take longer to get to the bridge and when we do get to it, it's not the same bridge, but a shiny stretch of spread metal with cable railings. We pause, staring at it, suddenly feeling very Blair Witchy.

"I think we know how the builder crossed the stream, probably with a 4-wheeler. Come on!"

"Aren't you worried we're going to get lost?"

"Nope. See the light?"

He points out the clouds which glow with reflected light ahead of us and not behind us.

"Let's go."

The spread-metal bridge is much safer than the old stone bridge. I'm still a little nervous on this new path, but I'm trying to trust Ben. It turns out that the spread-metal bridge isn't that far downstream from the stone bridge.

"Why not rebuild the old bridge?"

"I don't know. Anyway…that was fun! Thanks for coming with me."

"No problem. I'd like to come back sometime in the light."

"Yeah, we should do that."

He catches my hand and slows us to a stroll.

"It's not raining yet, so let's just enjoy this."

As if the heavens heard him, the clouds part and a weak beam of moonlight casts the path in black-and-white light play. I stop walking and he pauses a second later, drawing me up beside him so I can stand in the circle of his arm as we watch the silver wood. There's a word that describes it so well. Sylvan. I never knew the true meaning of that word until this moment.

We kiss again, long, deep and sweet. And then he guides me back to the neighborhood and to my front door. He kisses me again. I go into the house alone. Mom and Dad must be home because Wes isn't here anymore. Bram is watching another nature video. Peter was so right about aphasiacs, enjoying it.

"Lily and Ben sitting in tree. K-I-S-I-N-G. Then comes love, then come wedding. Then comes baby in a carriage."

Bram's got the beat and most of the words and I smile large and hug him.

"Spose…to…tease."

"Yeah, but you said words, so I can't be mad."

"But kiss Ben?"

"Yes. I kissed Ben."

"Sitting in tree?"

"Not exactly. And there won't be babies anytime soon."

"When?"

Oh, my! Well, how to answer that?

"We just kissed, and babies take a long time. We're not even married."

He frowns.

"Um, what is…um, marred?"

"Married?" He nods. "Mom and Dad are married."

He tilts his head, considering something. He's not stupid. He's just disabled.

"You're – what called – kissing?"

It takes an imagination to piece together a communication with Bram, but I'm getting good at it.

"Dating. I don't know if we're dating yet, but I'll let you know when I know."

I know I've used too complicated language when he frowns but then he slowly nods. He figured it out. He smiles. I take it he's proud of figuring it out. He should be.

"Wes teach you that song?"

He laughs.

"It's a good tease." He smiles, but then yawns. "Do you need help to get to bed?"

"No. No got…uh, button."

He does usually need help with buttons. I step back so he can roll to his bedroom, which used to be a den or a family room before we moved in. I wonder if he'll ever be able to climb stairs. But, no, I won't be sad about Bram tonight. I will instead go to bed dreaming of kissing Ben.

Disappearances

Peter
July

Seth holds the letter under the lamp over his desk, scanning through it.

> *Dear Tilly. When I found out you and Dad – Alan – were married, I acted like a child. I don't have an excuse for that jerk move except that I was going through an emotional time. It's not an excuse. Maybe it's a piss-poor explanation. Anyway – I wish I could do it differently.*
>
> *The story of my life. Woulda, coulda, shoulda....*
>
> *Some people pointed out to me that you were kind of a mother to me, but you*

weren't. I never thought of you as a substitute for Laren. I think you were like an older friend and I'm sorry I destroyed that. I took you for granted and then it was too late.

So, no doubt, I owe you amends, and I hope you'll give me an opportunity to do that. I know this is kind of late in the process. You're not listed as one of my victims, but I know you are. I'm sorry that I treated you so cavalierly. You know what I'm talking about. You covered for me so many times. I shouldn't have put you in that position. I hope you'll let me show that I wouldn't do that now.

Peter

"You sure you want to refer to your parents by their first names?"

Seth is frowning at the letter in his hands.

"Yeah. She's not my mother." He's still staring at me. Tilly is not who he is talking about. "He disowned me, and she sends me cards designed to make me suicidal."

"You'd be suicidal even without that, you know?"

I sigh. The rash on my shoulder burns and I refrain from scratching because it'll only make it worse. The price of not feeling like killing myself is the side effects of the drugs that keep me a bit back from the abyss. A year and one month and I can, if I've been stable, request a medication holiday. Meanwhile, I fall asleep if I sit down unless my body feels like I'm being hit by electricity. I hate my life!

"You do you, man, but it's going to be hard to reconcile with them if you've stopped thinking of them as your parents."

Declan sits up from his bunk. He often takes a nap after his work assignment. I see his ear plugs are in his hand. He must have been listening to us.

"When parents…hate. I don't call my parents by names. My parents."

Declan and I understand one another. He asked me to help him with an art project. He's actually a better artist than I am, but I guess the subject is too personal for him. It's about his crime. Will engraving it into his skin make it easier to endure? I somehow doubt it. I suspect Luis would slap me silly if I tattooed myself.

"Just tell me what you think of what I wrote."

"It's a good letter. You didn't ask Luis?"

"He would tell me to concentrate on my letter to Alan."

"Hmmm, well, are you using it as a delay tactic?"

"I don't know. I just don't want them to get a divorce and her disappear from my life before I reach out to her."

"Why do you think she'd do that?"

Declan chuckles.

"Servants." Seth frowns. He usually *gets* Declan, but apparently this isn't part of his experience. "They come, go. Here, gone. And then you never see. Yeah?"

Declan looks to me for verification. I realize for the first time that we're probably from the same background, more or less. Less politics than my life, but maybe as much money that is no longer accessible.

"Yeah. She's my step-mother, but I didn't know that until she was already out of my life and so in my heart she's a dearly loved servant. And they aren't permanent, even though as a kid you think they are."

"But it became personal for her." Seth is really confused.

"The more I think about it, it's personal for most of them after a while. Yeah, they're paid to be there, but they still care. She clearly did. She went above and beyond. But I think she and my dad are divorcing, so… I just don't want to let her get away."

Seth nods, hands the paper back to me.

"It's a good letter. Mail it. But let Luis read it first and get back to writing the letter to your dad. And, kid, don't call him Alan. You're going to build a wall that will be hard to break down."

I take my letter and head back to the house. I pass through the midst of activity in the rec area and people who might wish me harm or want something from me. I'm aware, but I'm not afraid. I don't know what I'll do when trouble comes my way, but I feel sort of prepared for it these days. This is my life, and I don't know any way to live it other than just to get through it – head down, serving my own time, not asking any favors, not accepting any either. Maybe this is my life for another 24 years, so I just need to keep putting my feet one after the other and – ignore the smell of Jacobs's hooch. I wish I could put that scent out of my reach, but I can't. I put the letter away and lay down on my bunk, arm over my eyes, trying to breathe through my mouth, which only means I can taste it. I fall asleep and dream I've got a perfect glass with the exact right amount of bourbon, and I jerk awake to puke in the toilet. Yeah, I've not accepted my life, but maybe tomorrow will be different from today. That's why AA says one day at a time keeps us from getting ahead of ourselves. I'll get through today and keep saying no to what will poison me and then tomorrow, it'll be slightly better than today.

I hope.

July

Ben

It's a beautiful Saturday morning and a perfect view from the top of Laurel Ridge's West Side. Lily's improvement as a mountain biker is impressive. She still can't keep up with me, but I'm not unhappy with going slow so long as I'm with her.

She's covered in mud and laughing, her hazel eyes glowing with enthusiasm one moment and semi-terrified the next. When we reach the top, I call a halt and we dismount to eat a picnic breakfast of fruit, my mom's cinnamon scones, bacon, and coffee liberally laced with milk and cocoa.

She pulls her brown hair out of its ponytailer and smooths tendrils back from her face. It will be warm later today, but doing this so early in the day makes it so we're not sweating to death as we toil up the ridge. I offer her a cup of coffee from the thermos.

"Mmm, you do this well." I smile at her, not sure how to reply. "I'm a frou-frous coffee drinker."

"Ah, so I'm brewing mellow coffee?" She nods. "My roommate at Dartmouth Travis taught me how to do a good press."

"Travis was a good influence."

"He was. We enjoyed that year. He says his last year's roommate was annoying. Since I'll be going back in as a sophomore, he and I are applying to be roommates again. I was fortunate he was doing his sophomore summer so I could contact him easily."

"That's great! That's got to be a big weight off your mind."

"Sure." She's smiling, but I'm suddenly aware that we won't see each other much once I'm back at Dartmouth. I feel an odd feeling in my chest at that thought. It's similar to what I felt about going back to school last year. Kevin says anxiety is normal after the trauma I experienced. He assures me that if I work on it, it will pass. I'm hoping that happens soon.

"Something?" She's watching me over the rim of the cup.

"Do I have to share?"

Her forehead crinkles, but she's still smiling.

"I won't tie you down and tickle you if you don't, but – you know – secrets."

"They're dangerous, I know. But I'm not sure what I'm thinking, so it would be hard to share it."

She nods and shrugs. I guess she can live with mystery. I'm not ready to say I'm afraid we'll drift apart. Maybe she doesn't think the same way about me.

I sip some coffee and admire how neatly she eats scones. Then we head back to the Jeep, and she keeps up with me on the way down the mountain. I almost wish I didn't have to go to work, but I can't duck out at this late moment. Russell has a big cruise tonight.

We reach the Jeep and load our bikes. We're elbow-to-elbow and heat flushes through my body. We have an age-gap and having sex with her would be illegal. I'm a 20-year-old virgin, so it won't be difficult to tell myself no, but my body still wants me to say "yes". I briefly remember a Sunday school lesson about my old man fleshly nature.

She's blushing. It's not exercise flushing. She's experiencing the same thing I am…I think.

"We should get home," I tell her. "Wes stayed over at someone's house last night, so he might not be available for Bram this morning."

"Bram knew that."

"You sure?"

"I think he understands Wes better than he understands anyone. But I'm going to start stinking if I don't get a shower quickly."

"I think you smell healthy and real."

She gives me a lopsided smile, so I head toward her house. I still haven't moved out of Tilly's, and I need a shower too, but I've got clothes at my parents' house.

When we reach the house, I slow because there's a cop car sitting in front of her house.

"What could that mean?" Her voice quavers and I don't know how to answer, so I park, and we walk into her house together.

Lyle stands up from the sofa where he's talking with Mariskov. For just a second, I'm back to the day he interviewed me about Pete's wreck and it's like being stabbed in the gut.

"Lily, I hope you have a moment to talk with me. Do you remember me from last year? Detective Jordan Mariskov."

"Yes. What is it?"

"Do you know Jerald Helton?"

Lily

I love mountain biking, especially with Ben. It's hard work, but it feels like freedom when we're dropping off the slope. I've never felt so comfortable doing something so physical. He seems pleased with my progress, and I want him to be proud of me. I don't have the energy to do this all day, but I'm sad that he'll go to work for the afternoon and evening. I want to spend it with him.

I suppose I could ask to volunteer on the boat tonight. I'm about to suggest that when we pull into our block and see the cop car. I remember Detective Mariskov from last year. He says he has a few questions to ask me. Then he says a name I don't recognize for a moment.

"Jenae?" he offers.

"Oh, yeah! Yeah, I know her…him."

"Do you happen to know where he might be?"

"No. At home with his parents?"

"Jerry disappeared a week ago. His parents say he was coming here to visit you."

"Yeah. He dropped by. We talked for a few minutes and then he got on his bike and rode away."

"What time was this?"

"About 8."

"And you haven't heard from him since?"

"No. Uh…well, we texted a few days later. I thought he'd sent me some flowers, but he said he didn't. I – I guess I figured I'd hear from him, but I haven't. I got busy and didn't think to text her…him."

"I don't expect you to be politically correct with me." He smiles gently. I don't remember him being so gentle last year when he questioned me about the wreck. "Did you notice anything as he left? A car out of place or someone about who shouldn't have been there?"

I start to shake my head and then I see Ben's face white as a sheet.

"There's been a brown van hanging around. I've seen it a few times."

I search my memory for a snatch of something half-forgotten.

"Did you see it too?"

"Not here. I was working – maybe two weeks ago and I kept seeing this van – brown, like Ben said. I thought I was being paranoid, and it disappeared before I got back to Port Mallory."

Mariskov frowns and looks at his phone, typing something in.

"Can you describe this van? See the license plate by any chance?"

"It was a Ford, maybe Econoline. Sliding side door." Ben licks his lips. "Um, New York plates – Excelsior – Adirondacks -- first two letters were DJ, and the last number was maybe a 6 or an 8."

I'm seriously impressed and so is Mariskov. Ben shrugs.

"I thought the driver might be casing houses for burglary, so I paid attention, but I never got close enough to see the whole plate."

Mariskov nods, writes it down. Then sits there rubbing his chin. He doesn't smell like he smokes, but I think he used to. I've seen cigarette smokers do the same sort of gesture when pondering something.

"Lily, have you been getting weird phone calls, Facebook hits from people you don't know?"

I feel my mouth drop open as Ben and I exchange looks.

"Yeah. We thought it might be my ex-boyfriend."

"Peter Wyngate?" I nod. I never felt right about that, and Ben now looks a little guilty. "We can check. Inmates aren't allowed to have burner phones, but they do. Not all of them and he submitted to some scrutiny to be allowed to reach out to his victims. So that suggests he's not texting you. When did this all start?"

When did it? I think back and he gives me the moment that takes.

"The night of the riots. I was at the Barns Courtney concert, and I lost my purse and my phone. I got it replaced the next day, but then I started getting these texts, like someone was texting from my phone. I reported it to the carrier, but it continued. I've gotten some Facebook DMs that were strangers to me. I didn't respond and at Ben's suggestion, I blocked them recently. But I've also been receiving flowers."

Mariskov writes it down.

"Sorry to ask this, but what's your Facebook and email address? And I'll ask you for your passwords. Give me a while and then I'll let you know when you can change your passwords. But we need to try and track these messages." He sighs. "You need to know why I'm worried. There have been five disappearances in the last two years, all along the Gold Coast. A medium-colored van has been spotted. We've found two bodies, both exhibiting signs that suggest this is a serial killer."

The air squeezes out of my lungs.

"We don't know exactly how he's targeting his victims, but they all seem to have Internet involvement and the flowers are a thing as well. Did you notice what shop delivered these flowers?"

I look at Ben.

"Red and white striped shirt. It was weird. He delivered the flowers at the coffee shop."

"What? You saw him?"

"I don't – he was my age. I don't think…I don't know."

"Describe him."

"Twenty-ish. Brown hair – darker than mine. Um – maybe a little shorter than me. I was sitting down, so that's a guess. He was less muscular. Thinner."

"Grey eyes," I add. "But there was a Nikolides Florist's van across the street."

"I'll still check it out. Were the other flowers delivered by the same company."

I never saw the trucks. Dad brought me the first arrangement. Mom…no, it was Bram. Mom gave him a hard time about talking to people on the porch, but I could tell he was excited by the exchange.

"My dad isn't here to describe him, and my brother is speech-disabled, so…."

"Wait. You two keep talking. I'm going to see if Bram can draw a picture."

Ben leaves us in the living room.

"What was Jerry wearing the last time you saw him?"

I describe my sweater that I loaned Jerry.

"He was wearing skinny-fit jeans and a white t-shirt. And he seemed more…well, male."

"Interesting. But he didn't object to taking a girl's sweater?"

"Yeah. I don't know."

Mariskov asks me a bunch of other questions, and he seems about to run down when Ben returns with two drawings. Because Bram is brain-damaged, the left side of the drawing is indistinct, but it's not the same kid as at the coffee stand. Mariskov stares at the picture for a moment then takes a photograph of it. Then he stares at the drawing of the van – a basic floral van. Bram can't reproduce the name on the van, but it has a spray of flowers in the right place.

"Same company?"

"No. I don't know the company."

"I think that's Port Mallory Florist," Ben offers.

"Your brother wouldn't know?"

"He has aphasia which includes dyslexia. You've likely got everything he can produce. I'm surprised he could do even that. How'd you get him to do it?"

"It took a bit of explaining, but he's really a lot better than he's been in the past. And Wes is here, so that was convenient."

As if to prove his brother was telling the truth, Wes appears behind Ben. He's got a third picture in his hand.

"I tried to get him to draw the name, but he just got frustrated. But he did another drawing."

He hands the drawing over. It's a van sitting in the abandoned driveway up the street and there's someone behind the wheel.

Mariskov stares at it a long time.

"He's a good artist. And that shape is a Ford."

"Wow." I knew Bram could draw, but I didn't realize how well. Peter taught him. Back then Bram was confused by the visual field cut that's part of his disability, but he's improved a lot on his own.

"I'll run this by my team. Thank you for your time. We should talk to your parents now because I don't think you should stay here for a few days. You're apparently a target of a serial killer who knows where you live."

Ben

Lily's dad got back in time to talk to Detective Mariskov, and they agreed that she'd be safer somewhere different. Her dad drew me aside and reminded me that it is against the law for a 20-year-old to have sex with a 16-year-old. I was surprised he never brought it up when I started dating Lily, but I suppose parents think that way when the idea of sleeping near each other comes up. I promised him he didn't need to worry about my intentions. He seemed to believe me.

I stare at the number on my screen. Apparently, this Saturday is cursed. I consider not answering, but I can't quite do that. So, I answer Trevor's call.

"Hey."

"Hi, Ben." There's a long pause. "Been a while." He sounds…somber, and – is it too much to hope for...sober.

"Hi, Trevor. What's up?" There's a long pause and I think he might hang up, but then he speaks.

"I'm hoping I haven't ruined our friendship." Okay, so he wants something.

"I answered the phone, man, but if this is to ask for a ride, forget about it."

I'm done if that's what he's up to.

"Nope. I'm not trying to leave Briarcliff. I decided last week that I was definitely staying."

I smile.

"Good for you."

"Yeah? It will be. Still have moments where it feels like it's all a bad idea, but yeah, I decided."

"Good. You haven't ruined our friendship, but I don't think I can go through it again, so…."

"Yeah. I get it. Kind of clear when you told the cabbie to call the cops on me."

"Not sorry about that, man."

"No, I know. You couldn't go through it again. I don't think I can go through it again either."

Wow. It's not what I expected at all. But I roll with it.

"How are you feeling?" I don't want to ask him about the pain, but he was in a serious accident.

"Pain's there, but I'm learning it's mostly not real. Hopefully by the time I get out of here, I'll have a handle on it."

"What changed your mind?"

There's a long pause.

"Peter wrote me. It was months ago, but Dad gave it to me last week. I was really thinking of blowing this place. Yeah, I'd go to jail, but I didn't care. I'd get high and it would be okay. But then the letter was there. I don't know why I read it, but it was good. And the timing was just right. He begged me to get help. So, I decided to stay."

I don't know what to say. I knew about the letter, but Pete knows Trevor in a way I'll never understand.

"You weren't pissed off when you saw he'd written you?"

"Yeah. That's why I read it." That makes no sense, but I can imagine Pete making a decision like what Trevor's talking about. "But he's right. I'm going to die if I keep using. And, I know he's been through it and knows what I'm feeling. And he still asks me to give it up."

"What do you do with that?"

"Don't know yet. My anger just washed away and…I don't know. And I'm just taking it one day at a time."

I nod, and then grunt "Yeah." We sit in silence for a moment.

"So, are you allowed visitors yet?"

"Yeah. You got to turn out your pockets and stuff to come in."

"Makes sense for now." I wouldn't bring anything like that to Trevor, but I know he has friends who would. "So when?"

We exchange the information.

"I've got group, so I gotta go. Thanks for not hanging up on me."

"Did you really think I would?"

"After how you acted with Peter after the accident he had with Cheyenne? Yeah, I figured you might."

I don't breathe for a moment. That Trevor is pointing out my hypocrisy is painful.

"Anyway, they're calling group and I'm not supposed to be late. See you when you visit."

"Definitely."

We hang up and I turn to Lily who is staring out the window at the lilac forest, golden sunlight falling on her beautiful face.

Lily

Ben stepped out to ask Captain Russell if it was okay to bring me with him to work on *the Mimi*. The call is going on for way too long for a simple call. He seems to be having a pleasant conversation whatever it is. I'm feeling restless, but I don't know what I should do with myself. I sit down on the couch with my Bible and skim through the New Testament, finally turning Hebrews 13:6 "So we say with confidence, 'The Lord is my helper; I will not be afraid. What can mere mortals do to me?"

They can kill me and bury my body somewhere nobody can find.

But how often does that happen in anyone's life? And even if this creep finds me and kills me…yes, I'm confident that I will wake up in heaven. So, of what do I have to be afraid? Except dying in some horrible way. I shudder and yet feel my Savior is beside me.

It's been a while since Ben stepped outside. I get up to look out the window and I don't see him. My heartbeat increases. I hadn't thought he might be in danger by giving me shelter. My cheeks flush as Ben comes in the front door.

"Cap says you're more than welcome. We'll need to get going pretty soon. How you doing?"

"Okay." That's a lie and I'm sure he'll sense it. "That was a long phone call. Should I ask?"

"Trevor called, so I settled some things with him. He's doing okay. Sober. Getting healthy."

"Great." That sounds a little weak. "It really is. I'm glad for him. Glad for you."

"Yeah. It's good for him and I'm glad we're still friends. He…." He chews the inside of his lip. "He got a letter from Pete."

"Oh?! Well, I guess he and Trevor have a lot in common. Probably the right person to reach out to him."

He nods. I put on a jacket, knowing it might be cold out on the water.

"I still don't know how to forgive him."

"Trevor or Peter?"

"Pete."

I nod. We walk out to the Jeep, quiet, thinking. As we travel along the sun-dappled road, something occurs to me.

"I want to go to church tomorrow. You should come with me."

I expect him to argue with me, but he just keeps driving. I wonder what that means, but I don't want to push him if he's thinking about it.

Graduation

Peter
July

It's hot today and I'm trying to stay cool by standing in a narrow shadow near the weight stacks while Seth lifts way more than I'll ever be able to lift. I decided a few weeks ago that I don't really want to get big and muscle-bound. I want to be fit and toned. Everybody lifts here, so I do need to be ripped to project the undeserved reputation of being a killer. I don't need to look like Schwarzenegger in his prime, just like I could hurt someone at least as bad as I hurt Tyler.

I feel badly about that. I saw him a few days ago. He's over in A Block, so theoretically, we might never see each other, but I was in the infirmary trying to convince the PA that this rash all over my shoulders needs to be treated before the itching drives me crazy. Tyler was being brought in in a wheelchair and helped into bed. Although I never saw him before I bashed his head in, I knew it had to be him. He drools and all four limbs are affected. The PA saw the look in my eyes and dragged me into an office to berate me. Tyler tried to rape me, I didn't mean to hurt him, his permanent disability is therefore his own fault.

I've got so much anti-depressant in my system I doubt I can actually get suicidal. That admission made the PA laugh, but he also told Luis, so now they're all watching me again. I did manage to get Luis to tell me what's wrong with Tyler. It's a brain stem injury and although my attempt at self-protection caused the skull fracture that contributed to the aneurysm's bleeding, the bleed would probably have happened eventually anyway. Tyler was respirator-dependent for a month and required extensive rehabilitation to relearn to feed himself and talk. He's not likely to walk again.

Luis pointed out that thanks to what I did, other kids like me won't be hurt by Tyler in the future, but I still feel bad. I might be looking for an excuse to be depressed, but I also think ordinary people would feel bad about permanently paralyzing someone.

I'm deep in analyzing my feelings on this subject when I sense movement on my left. A shadow with a drawn-back arm looms on the wall behind the stacks. I turn to meet the threat and pin this kid to the weight machine by his throat. He reaches up to scrabble at my arm, inadvertently dropping his shiv in the process.

Seth swings clear of the weight bench.

"What the hell, kid?" I don't know him, so I have no choice but to call him "kid". He's turning red, so I ease him down slightly so he can stand on his tiptoes and pass some air. I don't want to kill anyone, but he did try to kill me. "Something for you to understand. Try this shit again and I will actually hurt you."

I hear the corrections officers coming up behind me and Seth speaking to them. The kid's coloring is returning to normal.

"You got this, right? You're going to stay away from me now. Right?"

He nods. I remove my hand and he starts to bend for the shiv. The COs mob him before I can bring up my knee into his face. CO Pool pushes me back from the main event. I get my hands up where he can see them.

"Stupid fish, yeah?"

"He came at me with that. Do you need to cuff me?"

"Not if you're willing to cooperate. Calvin, clear off. Let's not make it bigger than it needs to be."

Seth, whose last name is Calvin, casts me an apologetic look before I let Pool lead me away to a small room off the corridor that gives us access to the yard.

"Tell me what happened."

Okay, this is weird. Shouldn't he be taking me to the Disciplinary Office?

"I was just waiting my turn at the weights. I saw a shadow on the wall, and I reacted. You see his shiv?"

"I did. You didn't touch it?"

"No. I want to get out of here someday, not end up doing all day and all night. I have a right to defend myself, not a right to punish the guy."

Pool laughs and I remember that he was the abusive CO from the Disciplinary Office. Back then, he seemed abusive. Now he seems somewhat supportive. It occurs to me that everybody knows what happened to me when I was in Ad Seg and maybe they don't want to repeat it any more than I do.

"Good. You learned that lesson. You might get called as a witness against him. Will you testify?"

I sigh.

"And paint a target on my back?"

Pool nods.

"So, you're going in the report, but I'll also record that you'd rather not be involved. You might hear from the DO. Just be honest. Okay?"

I nod, seeing for the first time that Pool wears a single stud earring that is a cross. It comes back to me that Luis said Pool is what he calls a Type 5 CO. It's a theory he uses to define the world he lives in, and it makes sense. Type 1s are the COs who hang out in the command center – that odd collection of cells set off from the rest of the tier. You never see Type 1s on the tier. I don't know why I resent that, but Luis says they're lazy cowards, so maybe that's my reason too.

Type 2s want to be our "friend". There's a CO named Franklin who is one of those. He plays cards with some of the cons, and he's even given me a pass on the anal search. I hate the probe, but I don't want to be treated differently from anyone else. It's dangerous to stand out around here and my name, my height and my pretty face make me stand out enough already.

Type 3s are abusive assholes. I got a couple of bruised ribs a few weeks ago when I didn't move quickly enough for one of them. There was no other reason and also no physical chance to move as fast as he wanted me to, so he slammed his baton into my ribs.

Type 4s and Type 5s are so similar you might miss the distinction. They're both fair. They are sticklers for the rules. You get so much arbitrary treatment here that consistency is refreshing. Type 4s don't care if their application of the rules is good for the cons. Type 5s do. Luis honestly believes they hope to turn us out of here better than we arrived. They use the rules to achieve that objective. Since I want the same objective, I don't think Pool's an asshole. I don't trust him, but that's because we're on opposite sides of an uncrossable divide.

"So, I can go?" Never assume you can read a CO's mind.

"You can wait at the gate."

There's probably some rule that says I can't return to yard-out, so I don't argue. I just go wait at the gate because it's better than the alternative of going to the Disciplinary Office. There's not that much time left anyway. I pull up my jumpsuit and zip it to my collarbones since I'm not wearing a t-shirt right now. The sunlight felt good on my rash, but I don't want anyone getting any ideas. Seth looks relieved when he sees me waiting.

"You get a write-up?"

"No. Pool understood I was defending myself. Any idea why that kid tried to ventilate me?"

"How tall are you?"

"I don't—six-two." I know for sure I've grown a bit since I got here, which might say something about my stress levels now compared to my free life. That's a bizarre thought.

"You're tall and muscular. You've got a reputation coz of Tyler. But you're still new-ish. So, the fish are tempted to make their bones with you because they suspect they might live through the attempt on your life. And, you just added to the legend by not shanking that idiot. When he gets out of the hole, if he ain't crazy, he'll have some cred toward making his bones. They might send him up against you again, but probably not. Ask Pool in a few days what the sentence is." When I give him a skeptical look, he laughs. "Pool's a good guy." He fingers his left earlobe and I know I'm right about Corrections Officer Pool. He's a Type 5.

The gate buzzes and the group shuffles through. Seth doesn't stop me from going to my house alone, but I know he, Declan, or one of the other guys, will show up at my door in 10 minutes to make sure I'm not dragging myself down into darkness. Maybe it's the adrenaline from nearly being killed, but I don't feel depressed right now. I crack open *The Gulag Archipelago* and settle down to read about a situation that's worse than mine.

July

Ben

I went to church because Lily asked me to. Despite the fact that our parents are great friends who share a weekly Bible study with a third couple, her family attends another church than mine does. Mine are Presbyterians and they're a little stiff. Pam's dad retired last year from being their pastor and the new guy is supposedly less boring, but I haven't been to know that myself. When I took Lily to the coffee shop, I didn't go inside the church until it was during the benediction

I kind of thought I liked Lily's pastor but now he's poking me where I'm in pain already. I don't know how I can forgive Pete for what happened to Alyse. And now I'm being confronted by this guy about forgiveness.

"I bet Simon Peter thought Jesus was going to commend him for his generosity, but Jesus knew Simon Peter. Just like he knows us." Pastor Barrett looks across the audience. Does he look at me? It feels like he's staring at me. "What did Jesus mean by this? Seventy-times seven. There's a lot of theories about this. The Greek word is "heddomekontakis" which literally translates as "seventily seven." Most English Bibles multiply it. Seventy times seven. I wasn't a Bible school student because I was good at math, but I'm told that's 490. That's a big number. It would be hard to keep track if someone kept insulting me. I could keep track for a few dozen and then I'd start losing count. And maybe that's the point.

"Of course, the number seven is here and that represents completion and divine perfection through Scripture. We're supposed to forgive until we reach perfect perfection. Jesus is telling us to forgive to infinity and beyond.

"This phrase has other references. In the Old Testament a man of vengeance named Lamech said "I have killed a man for wounding me, a young man for injuring me. If Cain is avenged seven times, then Lamech seventy-seven times." Lamech had a big ego, and this was a hyperbolic way of expressing his desire for revenge. But Jesus had the opposite view.

"Four hundred ninety is the number of years that Israel violated God's command to honor a special Sabbath year before he allowed them to finally be conquered by Babylon for their sins. God endured 490 years of His chosen people's sins. Can we do less?

"Well, of course, we're humans. We're never going to be perfect. It is impossible for a finite human being to forgive to infinity, but Jesus still says for us to do it."

My mind drifts from the sermon into a sermon of its own. What Pete did was unforgiveable. Is my refusal to forgive also unforgiveable? Wow. I guess I need to answer that for myself. If Pete weren't repentant for what he'd done, maybe I wouldn't be so conflicted. It's easy to hate someone who says "I don't care. I did it and I don't think it matters." Pete's letters have been careful to say he's guilty and he knows it. He's not the problem here. I'm mad and I don't want to let it go and I can't really blame Pete for that since I haven't seen him in over a year.

How many times can I forgive him? How many times *have* I forgiven him? I doubt it's been more than a few hundred times. We really didn't fight much when we were kids. Both of us got mad at Trevor in fourth grade and I didn't talk to him until middle school. Then I discovered Pete had been talking to him for two years. Their fathers are best friends. They were stuck on a yacht together and Pete couldn't ignore him. The subject of our friendship with Trevor never came up until middle school, and Pete just let me hold my grudge until we were all together and then he let Trevor and me work it out without interference. He was actually a good friend.

But how do I forgive him for making me watch Alyse die?

They're singing the final song and I shake Pete's specter off so I can pay attention to the benediction. I'll decide what to do about my own sin later.

Lily

Ben's not saying so much as he takes me to lunch at the Speakeasy. I want to ask him what he's thinking, but something tells me he'll be more forthcoming if I give him time to mull it over. So, I try not to chatter and he's quiet as we take a table and consider the décor.

"You've never been here before?"

"No, but I know the story."

"There's a story?" Ben frowns. He doesn't know the story.

"The décor – it came from the island house."

"Really?" He stares around the room, eyes scanning over the tucked furniture, dark paneling, fake brick wall and Art Deco casings.

"That's the story anyway."

"You read this somewhere."

"In the *Port Mallory Messenger*."

"The shopper?"

"Yeah. I read it while I was waiting while Bram was in therapy."

"My goodness. You'll read anything, won't you?"

"Back of cereal boxes." We laugh together. Then we descend into silence.

"Um, it was a good sermon today." Ben sort of mutters like he's reluctant to talk about it.

"It was. Hard."

"For us, yeah. Timely."

We both nod.

"There was a lot to think about it. And I'm not ready to talk about it, so – can we talk about something else?"

The concept of seventy-times-seven and how that impacts our feelings about Peter has got to be a struggle for him. It's a struggle for me and he's more conflicted than I am.

"Of course, we can talk about something else." We sit staring into space. Fortunately, the waitress comes to take our order. That fills a few minutes. "Sorry, I just…." I giggle. "Hard to change the subject."

"Yeah. It's like if someone tells you not to think of green elephants. It's impossible not to do that." We chuckled together. "I'm just not sure how I feel about it and I need time to think."

I nod.

"My counselor would say I can forgive someone, but I don't have to forget what they did."

Ben sighs.

"My counselor would say the same." He rubs his jaw. "But…does that sort of forgiveness apply to Pete? And that's where I need you to give me some time to think."

Again, we stare into space.

"Let's not talk about green elephants then."

Ben's eyes shift back and forth, and he grins.

"Can't do it. They're green and enormous, long trunks."

"Big ears." We laugh together. "Skinny tails."

More laughter.

"Can we do this all the way through lunch?"

"Maybe. It's not so easy to not think of something you're not supposed to think about."

Silence descends again however.

"I'm worried about Jenae—Jerry."

"You should be. I mean, maybe he's just run off somewhere to sort out his—his issues. And maybe he's been kidnapped by a serial killer."

"I've been trying to pray for him and—it's hard."

"Is it? Because why?"

"Maybe because I don't know what I should pray for."

Ben plucks at his upper lip, deep in thought.

"What's that Bible verse – about the Spirit speaking in deep groans when we don't know what to pray for?"

"Romans 8. I read that a while ago. It's right before the verse about all things working together for the good of those who believe God because we're being molded to His purposes."

"There's your answer. Don't pray for something specific. Just pray for *him*."

I smile at him.

"That's brilliant."

Ben's mouth twists.

"It is. Too bad I didn't do that when Pete needed me to do it for him."

I take his hand and we sit there a while in silence, not trying to fix him, or excuse the past, but just sharing the moment. When the moment passes, I pray for Jenae. I hold an image in my head until our food comes and then we find a topic to discuss that doesn't make us sad. But one thing I noticed is that the image in my head was of *Jerry* as he was that night before he left, wearing that enormous sweater my grandmother gave me.

Ben

I gave Lily my bed here at Tilly's cottage. The couch is a little short for me, so I sit up with a notebook and try to write Pete about seventy-times-seven. I say try, but I don't succeed.

It's a great concept. Forgive as long as you need to, like God did the Israelites. But at some point, He stopped forgiving and gave them their just discipline. They were exiled to Babylon and spent 70 years in slavery because of 490 years of their own ungodly behaviors.

Nobody needs forgiveness 70 times 7 more than Pete does, but I can't apply that simple Biblical concept to my best friend. Former best friend. Not yet anyway. Maybe never. Pete chose to do what he did. He violated moral standards over and over. And then he killed Alyse. I'm not ready to forgive and I'm beginning to wonder if Pete is ready to accept forgiveness.

"I'm going to end this before I beg for forgiveness and other stuff I haven't earned." Although toward the end, I felt like I didn't know Pete at all, I probably knew Pete better than he knew himself. He was smarter than the average guy, but he lacked insight into himself. And yet sometimes, he'd back himself into brilliant insight without even realizing it.

His letter practically begs me not to forgive him too easily while also begging me to leave the door open for when he's ready. So, seventy times seven doesn't and can't apply to Pete because neither of us is ready to forgive him and I don't know if he's ever going to be ready for that time.

Which leaves me in an uncomfortable place where I can't forgive Pete for Pete's sake, but I need to forgive him for my own.

And so, I am still right where I was before.

Lily

The light from the living room woke me. I guess when this was Tilly's personal pad, she didn't think there was any reason to hang solid doors in the opening between the two rooms. She didn't even put curtains on the French doors.

I creep to the door to peek at Ben, who has his back to me. Although I can't read the title, I can tell he's really engrossed in whatever he's reading and whatever it is must reference the Bible that he has open on the coffee table.

I don't interrupt him. I tiptoe back to bed. If I close my eyes, I'll eventually sleep. Or not. My mind's eyes fill with scenes of Jerry cut into a million pieces. I sigh and stare at the ceiling. You can tell this house must have been built in the 1930s or so. It has real wood moldings along a board and batting ceiling. Tilly kept the decorations very simple – restful. She probably only spent a few days a month here, so it made sense that she wanted to keep the maintenance simple.

I wonder if Peter ever came here. Somehow, I don't feel like he did. He never let slip that she was his stepmother, and I can't reconcile that. I just can't imagine all the lies he kept. For Tilly, for his dad, for Alyse…maybe that's why lying to me and Ben seemed so reasonable for him. Lies were the foundation of his life.

The light turns off in the living room, plunging the bedroom from semi-darkness to near-blackness. It's a dark night and there are no yard lights. Apparently, Tilly didn't worry much about burglars. I roll onto my side and try to close my eyes, but I keep seeing Jerry chained in a basement. I sigh and roll over onto my other side. I yawn. I stare at the doors. My eyes grow heavy. A man-shape stands on the far side of the couch. My eyes snap open. There's nothing there. My eyes drag close. I feel my body sinking into the mattress. There was a Freddy Kruger movie where the main character got dragged into the mattress. I'm helpless to resist and the next thing I know, I hear birds and the sun sprays across the ceiling.

Confronting Myself

Peter
July

I put a finger under the verse I'm trying to understand. It's a big complicated topic and most people don't do it in a prison cell. Or maybe they do and I'm just weird.

"I tell you the solemn truth – the one who does not enter the sheepfold by the door, but climbs in some other way, is a thief and a robber. The one who enters by the door is the shepherd of the sheep. The doorkeeper opens the door for him, and the sheep hear his voice. He calls his own sheep by name and leads them out. When he has brought all his own sheep out, he goes ahead of them, and the sheep follow him because they recognize his voice. They will never follow a stranger but will run away from him because they do not recognize the stranger's voice."

I get why the people didn't understand what Jesus was saying. First, I don't know anything about sheep. I assume Jesus-time people did. Why would he use the metaphor if they didn't know about sheep? I doubt I'm going to find a book about sheep farming in the Sing Sing library, so I'm just going to have to accept what Jesus says about them. They only follow the sheep herder's voice and they run away from strangers. What do I know? But this guy grew up in sheep country.

So, I know from Luis that Christians are the sheep. If I were in the sheepfold, would I know God's voice? More and more, I read parts of the Bible and think "yeah, that's right." Is that hearing the sheepherder's voice? Not sure yet. So maybe I'm one of the people who still doesn't understand. Jesus is repeating this for me.

"I tell you the solemn truth, I am the door for the sheep. All who came before me were thieves and robbers, but the sheep did not listen to them. I am the door. If anyone enters through me, he will be saved, and will come in and go out, and find pasture."

I assume he meant the door to the sheepyard. So, he's the door and the herder. I want to ask Luis what it means, but he's with some suicidal guy in the infirmary. I'm trying to avoid the smell of hooch that somehow I know is ready for consumption.

"The thief comes only to steal and kill and destroy; I have come so that they may have life, and have it abundantly."

Life? I'm staring down 24 years of the grey walls of Sing Sing, and I'm struggling to remember why I don't want to sell my soul for a swallow of horrible booze. If Jesus could take that urge away, I'd follow him into outer space. The smell wafts toward me and I rub my nose, trying to dispel it. Are Jacobs and his cell mate the thieves? They're offering me five minutes of Shangri-La" for the degradation of my body and spirit. That sounds like a criminal act. Maybe thievery is something like that.

"I am the good shepherd. The good shepherd lays down his life for the sheep. The hired hand, who is not the shepherd and does not own sheep, sees the wolf coming and abandons the sheep and runs away. So, the wolf attacks the sheep and scatters them. Because he is a hired hand and is not concerned about the sheep, he runs away."

Who is he talking about here? I scan back to see who he is talking to. Maybe the Pharisees? Maybe this is over my head. But they run away. Is he talking about religious leaders in general? He seems to be. I can't even remember the minister's name at my dad's church. But Jesus is saying people like him runaway when Christians need them. But Jesus won't.

God, that smells awful. I burp as sweat prickles at my forehead.

"I am the good shepherd. I know my own and my own know me—just as the Father knows me and I know the Father—and I lay down my life for the sheep."

My mind's eye fills with a picture of Jesus hanging on the cross and my imagination paints an audience of sheep and wolves – the sheep crying and the wolves stalking them. My stomach turns ominously at the overwhelming smell of Jacobs' hooch. I burp again.

"I have other sheep that do not come from this sheepfold. I must bring them too, and they will listen to my voice, so that there will be one flock and one shepherd."

Okay, I'm skipping that because it's over my head. I'm already swimming in waters over my head, so I move on. I'll ask Luis about it later and he'll try to meet my ignorance.

"This is why the Father loves me—because I lay down my life, so that I may take it back again. No one takes it away from me, but I lay it down of my own free will. I have the authority to lay it down,

and I have the authority to take it back again. This commandment I received from my Father."

Jesus died for the sheep. Am I one of his sheep? A snippet of memory from the night I walked down the aisle at the camp rolls through my brain. Did I walk into the sheepfold that night? And if I did, was it because I heard the Shepherd's voice?

They must have put the lid back on the crock. I still feel like I swallowed something foul, but at least the smell is gone. I set the book on the edge of the desk and settle onto my back to stare at the underside of Luis' bunk and think about what I just read.

July

Ben

I pour coffee into the thick stoneware mugs that Tilly's stocked her cabinets with. Such a practical woman! Growing up, I'd rarely seen Tilly out of her "uniform" of blue. She was hiding in plain sight. Nobody questions the wallpaper. I feel like I know her better now even though I haven't talked directly to her in over a year.

"How did you sleep?"

Lily doesn't look like she slept well, but my back is stiff.

"The couch is a little short for me."

"If nothing gets solved today, I'll take the couch tonight."

"You won't. If this guy finds you, I want to be the first thing he encounters."

I see her accept the idea that she needs to be protected right now. She doesn't like it, but we know I'm much more able to do some harm to anyone who breaks in than she is.

My mom made scones which go great with the coffee and we're talking about what I read in the Louie Giglio book he finished last night. I look past her when a curiously underwhelming car pulls up in the driveway and Detective Mariskov gets out. I see it before she does, but she hears it and turns to look at the approaching car. She stands, hand on her chest, her face growing white. I stand up beside her. He's carrying a package in his right hand as he approaches the deck.

"We've found something, and I need you to identify it for us."

"How did you know we were here?" My Spidey senses are tingling.

"I've got a tracker on her phone."

He says it calmly as if it is the most normal thing in the world. He pulls another clear packet out of the darker packet.

"I'm sorry to do this, but it's part of the job."

The envelope contains something made of gold yarn. Lily gasps.

"Is this the sweater Jerry borrowed that night?"

"Yes. Oh, God! No! No! No!"

I don't know what I need to do for her, so I pull her into my chest. Mariskov slides the package back into its envelope.

"Thank you. It doesn't mean…maybe…we don't know…we didn't find a body. We think Jerry himself might have dropped it, so…."

He turns back to his car, leaving Lily and I to deal with our turmoil. Lily sits down on the porch steps and runs her hands through her hair.

"Maybe he's still alive. They didn't find a body and if he was able to shuck off the sweater…it's good news."

I nod. I don't know what to say. What she's saying is hopeful and I don't want to evoke the idea of false hope. I feel like an idiot praying for this guy I've never met, but I don't want to not pray. If anyone needs prayer, it's this guy Jerry, who has to be terrified…if he's still alive.

Lily

My parents are freaking out. Now that there's evidence that Jerry didn't just run off to join the rainbow coalition, they feel like they need to do more to protect me, but what can they do? There's a serial killer and maybe he grabbed Jerry because he was wearing my sweater. Clearly, I can't go anywhere alone, but I feel like I should be safe in the house, yet Dad's taking days off and Helen is hanging around to make sure I'm never alone.

The only good side is that I'm spending a lot of time with Ben because we all agree I'm safer in the woods with him than I am at the house. I can't go to work with him, so I'm staying home with Bram, but we're locking the doors and Wes is hanging out more.

I'm painting a battered sideboard that my mom got at a garage sale a couple of weeks ago—back when life was still normal. I really like the strong blue. The original idea was to sand the blue in strategic locations to allow the primer to show through, but I really like....

"See...him?" Bram rolls his chair through the doorway into the sunroom.

I look up and then in the direction he points. I scan the backyard. Dad is slowly rebuilding the fence taller, working one section at a time. Between the new taller section and the old lower section, you can see the wooded creek behind our place and then the neighbor's house on the other side of the creek. Standing in the trees, barely visible among the leaves, is a man-shaped figure. I spring up to pull the curtains to the sunroom. Wes comes running in to help me with that.

"We were playing videogames and he saw him. I made sure the doors were all locked at that end of the house."

I made sure of the same thing before I started painting, but I don't say that. I dial Detective Mariskov's phone number and get voice mail, while I peek through the curtain. The figure is gone, but I leave a voice mail anyway.

"What did you see?" Wes and Bram turn from the curtains.

"Man." Bram points again to where we saw the figure.

"A middle-aged man in grey pants and a black hoodie. You?"

"Just a figure."

I wrap up the paintbrush, certain I'm not going to be able to do any more today.

"Fence." Wes and I both turn to Bram, perplexed.

"What about the fence?"

His forehead creases. He awkwardly pantomimes hammering.

"Yeah. Dad does need to finish it." He nods. Is he really understanding me? I wish I knew.

"Bram, did you see his face?" Wes gestures toward the backyard, indicates his face.

Bram frowns, then shakes his head.

"Far." But he frowns and rolls over to the place he usually does his drawing. On the way, he stops to speak to Wes. "Um, up…look…car."

I have no idea what he's saying, but Wes reads Bram really well and shoots up the stairs to look out a window in the den and then in my bedroom. He comes running back down.

"There was a brown van driving away."

My heart starts beating very hard. It was really him! We came that close.

And then my phone rings. Detective Mariskov is returning my call.

Ben

It's a beautiful early evening and I wish I felt safe for us to go for a walk, but I don't. After Detective Mariskov worked with Wes and Bram on another sketch of the man in the woods, I drove all the way to Peter's former home before I headed to the cottage just to make sure nobody followed us. We're both on hyper-alert and Lily didn't really want to leave her family on their own, but she also knows they're safer without her there.

We're watching a chick flick – something with a male main character who plays music while the girl tries to decide between him and another guy. I'm trying to pay attention, but it really could use a few explosions.

My cell vibrates across the coffee table, and I reach for it while Lily pauses Netflix. Her mouth is tight, like she's trying not to throw up. The screen tells me this is Mariskov calling.

"Ben?"

"Yes. What's going on?"

"We have news for you. We've found Jerry."

I meet Lily's gaze and we both hold our breath.

Lily

I'm nervous as we get off the elevator.

There's a cop at his door, which feels weird as we walk down the long hospital corridor. Detective Mariskov said we'd be precleared, but my stomach flutters as my father speaks with the guard who speaks into the microphone strapped to his shoulder. He takes his time, but then says we can go in after he pats us down. It's my first experience with this and it's pretty degrading, especially when he asks a nurse to do it on his behalf. It feels like sexual assault to me.

Ben submits to the search even though he technically doesn't have to come in with us. Dad opts out.

"You two can go in and visit. I'll wait out here."

Ben waits for the cop to tell him he's done and then he smiles at me, and we continue forward into Jerry's room. He's only been here a couple of hours. The long slender woman who stands fussily beside his bed blinks at us in suspicion. Jerry sits against the pillows on the hospital bed, his face bruised, and his hands bandaged, his upper lip showing just the beginnings of a mustache. He looks exhausted but stirs as soon as he sees us.

"Mom, this is Lily, and I think her friend Ben."

A big smile breaks across his face as his gaze falls on me.

"Thank God, you're okay!" he says, his voice visibly deeper than I remember it. "Ben, right?"

"Yeah." They look awkward, like they think they should shake hands, but Jerry's are bandaged. "What happened?"

"Yeah." Jerry holds his hands up awkwardly. It must hurt to use them." He looks at his mother. "Can you leave us alone for a few minutes, Mom? I need to talk to them."

She looks like she might refuse, but then he nods his head to the door, and she gathers herself.

"Your father suggested I join him in the cafeteria. You'll wait until one of us gets back, won't you?"

"Of course," Ben agrees for the both of us.

"Thank you. I just don't want…." She simpers and flees the room.

"She hates hospitals. Fortunately, this won't be a long stay, I think." Jerry shifts his weight, pivoting on his elbows, wincing in pain. He glances down at his mitted hands. "So, this--I dug myself out of a window well with my bare hands. By that time, I'd decided he was going to kill me, so I didn't waste a moment to consider the costs. Torn fingernails, scraped knuckles, a dislocated finger." He laughs in such a male way. "Pretty sure that grows hair on your chest." Ben nods, but Jerry only has eyes for me. "But I was so worried about you, Lily."

"Why?"

"He thought I was you when he first grabbed me. But he didn't stay fooled for long. Then he beat me into unconsciousness. This is way more than what you can see." He points to his face.

"How'd you get away?" Ben asks what I can't.

"I don't think he knew I'm a boy. He was used to dealing with weak little girls. When he caught me digging myself out of the window well, he grabbed me and – I'd had enough. I turned the tables on him. Never felt so good to be a male since I was 10. Anyway, I left him in a heap on the floor of the basement and ran. I'm not going to be walking for a little while. Tore up my feet pretty good, sprained an ankle, cut one heel to the bone. But I got out to the highway and flagged down a car."

"And, him?" I feel a shiver run up my back.

"I don't know. I just needed to get out of there. If I could have bashed his head in with a rock or a shovel – but I just ran. There's still a cop at my door, so I'm guessing he's still out there." He pulls the blankets a little higher, like that gives him the creeps as much as it gives me. "That's why I was worried about you. He really wanted you. He was so upset when he found out he'd grabbed the wrong *girl.* I'm so glad you're safe."

"I'm so sorry you went through this because of me." Jerry frowns as if a thought has occurred to him. "How did you survive so long?"

"Well, he likes to play with his food, so he wanted me to play a role for him." His eyes grow large and shiny as he considers that. "I've been playing a role for a while now, so I gave him what he wanted. And, yeah." He shrugs, winces. "I don't want to talk about that."

Ben and I nod. He sighs.

"I just needed to see you to make sure you were okay."

"Of course."

His gaze shifts beyond us as Detective Mariskov enters the room and Jerry stares at him.

"Your directions to the house worked and then we were able to ping off Lily's old phone. They contained the threat and they've now taken him into custody. The threat is over, Lily. You can go back to your life. There will be a trial, of course, but you're safe. Both of you are safe. And the evidence is pretty strong."

Ben offers his hand to shake and Mariskov accepts. Jerry gives him a mittened wave in lieu of a shake. He's starting to look tired compared to when we came in, but we promised his mother we wouldn't leave before she came back. Fortunately, Mariskov asks us to leave.

"Jerry and I need to talk, and I want to do this before he's too wore out."

Ben nods.

"Jerry, I'm so glad you're okay – well, going to be okay. And I'm sorry--."

"No, you shouldn't be. I could – well, get the drop on him and that's something you couldn't have done. I'm glad to have been able to do that for you. And, Ben…thanks for taking care of her and – I get it, so you don't have to worry about…well, me."

Ben nods, seeming to smile genuinely.

We leave. My dad's not in the hallway.

"Detective Mariskov told him you'd be going soon so he said to meet him at the handicapped entrance around 4:30." The cop points toward the elevator at the far end of the hall.

Ben glances at his phone.

"Twenty minutes for a ten-minute trip."

We start in that direction. Because I've spent so much time at this hospital, I know my way around pretty well.

"Hey, thank you for coming with me."

"Wouldn't have missed it for the world. Was he always so butch?"

"No." Ben pushes the elevator button. "He really had me fooled for a bit. I thought he was a girl."

I shake my head, mocking myself lightly. Ben laughs as we get on the elevator, and I push the button for the floor and exit we want.

"I don't think he'll be doing that anymore. I think he sees the advantage of testosterone now."

"I read somewhere that most transgendered boys are homosexuals, really."

"I don't think so – in his case. He really wants to be with you. He just knows you're with me and I'm four years older and he knows he can't compete."

I feel sad for Jerry for a moment, but because I've been through so much, I think he's too young for me anyway.

"Thank you for making that clear." I turn around to catch the right door, which opens in front of us. I pause for a moment to look up and down the corridor to ensure we're headed in the right direction. It's kind of a maze at this point.

Ben gives me a crazy grin.

"Absolutely my pleasure!"

Eyes Not Used Yet

Peter
August

It's not ideal, doing artwork in a prison bunk, but it is what it is and I'm going to do it anyway. I started the broad outlines of the sketch out at one of the tables on the tier, but I couldn't finish because the bells rang. So, I'm sitting with my back against the wall, the photo Joel sent me held in the toes of my right foot as I add details to the sketch. Declan's right. It's got potential to be a really good rendering of Audrey holding Alia soon after she was born.

There's something about it that creates a longing in my heart. Alia is laying against Audrey's shoulder, her tiny fingers splayed against her mother's bare shoulder, her body hiding what I'm pretty certain is Audrey's bare breast. I try not to think about that part because it's been a while since I got to interact with breasts, and I've got years ahead before I can again. I'm focused on mother and child, not frustrating myself with what I can't have. Alia's large luminous eyes are open and staring at nothing and there's an expression in them – innocence – a sense that her eyes haven't been used yet and don't need to see all the ugliness in the world.

I'm not sure my skill as an artist is up to portraying what I feel, but I want to try. If this sketch doesn't work out, I'll try again. I've already got three drafts in my notebook. I think this one I'm doing will be the best. I've got all the time in the world to make this a beautiful work of art as a gift for a woman who I think is a wonderful mother, the wife of the man I owe so much to.

I should thank Helen Anderson for her attempted mothering of me. I don't know how to do that. I don't have photos of the Anderson family. I wonder what Jack would say if I asked for one.

It's enough that I'm doing this now. Maybe I just need to leave the Andersons alone and concentrate on what's before me. I will always want to go back and change the past, but what if isn't real. I've got to learn to live in reality.

So, I work the shape of Alia's fingers and consider what I'll do to render her eyes so innocent. Maybe pull the sketch in a little closer. And maybe not pencil, but pen and ink. I'll have to get all the details on the sketch first and then go over with ink. Sepia might work well. I can't use paint. I have to use what I have.

Somewhere down the tier someone is screaming about something and I'm trying to ignore it. I've learned screaming doesn't necessarily mean anything. It's still a stressful environment, but it's less stressful if you are aware, but not flustered by what's going on not directly involving me.

Luis reads a book in his bunk, and he doesn't interrupt me. We're learning how to share the space without always being in each other's pocket. Well, I'm learning. He's been doing this since the last century. And he's absolutely not paying attention to the screaming, so it must be okay.

Yeah, pull the sketch in closer. The beauty is in the details and a closer frame allows more detail. A bell tells me I'm running out of time, so I slide the photo and the sketch into my notebook and put them both on their spot on the shelf above the desk.

I lay down with a sigh. I have good nights occasionally now, but sleep is still scary. I close my eyes and see the blue hull filling my view. Before the vision follows me into sleep, I think about Alia's innocent gaze, and I slip down through the layers of consciousness and don't wake up the tier tonight.

August

Ben

My eyes burn as I watch Lily with her family. We spent hours at the police station this evening giving official statements and looking at mug shots. This guy had no record. Catching him was completely an accident. Jerry dropped the sweater when the guy grabbed him. Mariskov put a tracker for Lily's lost phone. Bram produced a sketch that Mariskov could use against DMV records. And they knew where Jerry had flagged down the car.

"We don't usually get that much actionable information in these cases. That's why it took two years to catch this guy."

I can't help thinking they played it too close to the vest. Who knew the Gold Coast had a serial killer? Only the cops. Would people have been able to aid in the effort if they'd known they should pay attention?

So, it's past midnight and I'm falling asleep sitting up, but I don't want to leave Lily and she is still talking to her mom and dad. Her brother Jemmy showed up this evening, flying in from Boston because she was being stalked by a serial killer. He comes out of Bram's bedroom and hugs his sister. They're a great family and I'm glad she has them, but it's been a really long day for me, and I've got a headache brewing.

I'm beyond grateful that she's safe now, but on the way home, she was talking about a couple of texts she got that don't seem to be from the weirdo. Or…they don't come from her old phone but from a number that just goes to voice mail. When we got here, I read them and they are a little weird, but just because they don't come from her old phone doesn't mean they didn't come from the serial killer, who we've decided not to invoke his name because he shouldn't exist.

I'm not sure how we're going to figure out who sent these texts. They seem friendly, but they also don't seem that strange. Maybe I'm just too tired to see what she's seeing.

Dad is yawning as he comes to me. Mom and Wes left a while ago, so I kind of expected him to decide its time for us to go home.

"You look exhausted. Are you ready to head out?"

"I shouldn't be worried about leaving her with her family, right?"

"You shouldn't, but you've been on edge for days, so it makes sense. But you have work in the morning, and you should have some sleep before you do that."

"It's still Monday, isn't it?"

"It's technically Tuesday."

"Yeah." I drag myself out of the sofa and go to Lily who smiles at me. I could live for years basking in that smile. "I'm exhausted. Are you okay if I go?"

"Yes. Thank you so much for…well, the past week. And keeping me safe. But you look ready to fall asleep on your feet and there's lots of people here in case anything happens. We can talk to Mariskov and see what that other number is."

"Okay." We hug. It occurs to me that this parting might seem strange to me because she's so much younger than I am. I'm ready to take a relationship further and she absolutely shouldn't be. I need to stow those thoughts, get some sleep and start again tomorrow. This isn't a freaking romance movie where the couple walks hand and hand into the sunset after the bad guy is dispatched.

I'll handle this better tomorrow in the warm light of day. Surely, I know that. But I need to get that sleep before I'll really be convinced of it."

"I'm fine," she assures me.

"We'll keep an eye on her," Lyle says.

So, there's no reason for me to be worried about her, but I am. With Dad waiting at the door, I can't really find an excuse to stay, but I really wish I could.

Lily

I can't sleep and I would normally sit on the window seat and read a book, but I need new curtains that cover the window completely because I don't want anyone to see me in the window ever again. I feel like one of those Amsterdam prostitutes standing in a window, my wares on display for the highest bidder. But I attracted a serial killer. Who knows how many nights he watched me from that abandoned driveway? And I didn't know, so I gave him what he wanted, and he soaked it all up until he almost reached out and destroyed me.

Ben has been great, and I don't know that anyone will ever be my hero the way he has been this week. More than pulling me away from the railing last year, what he did this week just went above and beyond. I don't know how to repay that. I think many guys would think I owed them sex, but Ben has been nothing but a gentleman.

The thing about living on this road is that we never get through-traffic. Back in Manchester cars sent lights flashing across my ceiling several times a night, but here that never happens. So, I stare at the ceiling and just sort of absorb the monotony. It doesn't make me fall asleep, which leaves me staring at the ceiling. I'm tempted to text Ben, but he's probably asleep. I roll over on my side, but it creeps me out to put my back to the door, so I roll to my other side.

My cell chirrups and blinks once. I'd normally sleep through that but I'm awake, so I reach for it.

UNKNOWN- Thinking of you.

It's that same number. I dial it back in a voice call, but the phone has already been turned off. I consider if 2 am is the right time to do this, but he did say I could call his work phone whenever I needed to. It's not an emergency, so I text Mariskov the number and explain that this is the fourth message and that whoever is texting me keeps powering off before I can call back.

There's no immediate answer so I return to staring at the ceiling, which somehow works to lull me to sleep this time, so I wake up to sun streaming in my window. I find a response saying he'll look into it, but it's probably not something to worry about since the text came in after the serial killer had been arrested. He's right, of course, but I can't let it go. I input the number into my laptop, but it's a burner cell. Now I don't know what to do.

Ben

I dragged myself to work this morning, having wrestled with my pillow half the night. It bothers me – those texts. Who could be reaching out to my girlfriend? And why is their phone turned off when they're not texting? By the time I got to work this morning, I was pretty well certain Pete has a burner phone.

Yeah, I know. Joel says he doesn't. Barnes seems to be a good guy who isn't easily bamboozled by his clients. I want to believe him. But I don't trust Pete and I can't think of anyone else who might be doing this. But how do I prove that?

I call Joel Barnes and leave a voice mail. He turns off his phone when he's in court, so I'm sure that's why his phone goes direct to voicemail. I get moving toward clocking out. Even though I'm exhausted, I want to see Lily. She's in the backyard tending the flower garden she planted this spring.

"Hey." She gets up off her knees and turns toward me. "I talked to Mariskov today."

"Oh?" I wonder what he wants.

"He says it will be a few days before he can give us a report on…that guy. I also asked him about the phone number that's been calling me."

Now I'm interested.

"And?"

"He ran a trace."

"They can do that with burner phones?"

"Apparently. He texted me last night at 2:00 am."

"Oh, my goodness."

"It freaked me out. But Mariskov says it can't be our guy. The tower it pings on is on the other side of Stoneybrook. He thinks it's probably just another kind of creep."

"The other side of Stoneybrook? So, it couldn't be Pete."

"I asked if there was a way and Mariskov doesn't think so. I guess really complex phones can make use of VPNs and ping off false towers. Jemmy was explaining it. But Mariskov says the type of cell phones they can get in Sing Sing aren't that complex. Jemmy's researching it and will let me know."

I put my arm around her shoulder.

"Then you and I should go to the Golden Shanghai for dinner."

"Aren't you tired?"

"I am and I definitely need a shower before we go, but yes, I need to spend the evening with you where I'm not feeling like your body guard."

Her eyes shine briefly and then she nods.

"Jemmy's here, so I know I can do that." She looks down at her dusty jeans. "And a shower—definitely."

"Wear that red dress from the concert night."

"Yeah?"

"Please. I liked it for the half a second I got to see it."

"Do you want your jacket back too?"

I laugh. As far as I'm concerned, she can keep the jacket, so I shrug and grin before leaving her alone to get ready. We agree we're leaving in an hour.

And an hour and a half later, we're sitting down at Golden Shanghai to order food. She's dressed in her red dress, and I picked a royal blue shirt and khakis. We've been on a few dates now, but this feels like something special.

"You feel better?"

"Oh, yeah! I hated feeling like I was being watched all the time. I don't think I'll ever hear a Barns Courtney song quite the same again."

"That is when it started, wasn't it?"

"I think so. How did he get my phone?"

"Probably picked it up out the gutter." I sigh. "At least nobody died this summer."

She looks at me over the menu.

"Really? This summer hasn't been bad…for me."

"Yeah?" I want to kiss her right here in front of God and everyone. "There've been good parts."

"I wouldn't have missed *us*."

"Me neither." There's a long uncomfortable silence. "I leave in two weeks." She lowers her gaze. "I don't want to…want to lose this…whatever we've started here." Her gaze comes back up to meet mine. "You know?"

Lily

I do know. I realize I've been scared to have this conversation. He's nearly four years older than me and I sensed he would move on at the end of the summer. He's going to Dartmouth and I'm finishing school and…. But he doesn't want that.

"What are you saying?"

He catches the upper corner of his lip between his teeth, considering his words.

"I don't know yet. I just know I intend to date you when I come back—unless you're dating someone else. Because I've never been with anyone who makes me feel like you do."

"Wow." I don't know what else to say.

"And I know things could change, but there's email and phone calls and I'll be home at Christmas and…. What do you think?"

"Yeah." He's giving me space to answer when the waitress comes for our order and so it's several minutes later when he repeats his question. What do I think? Think? Oh, boy!

"We could email and talk on the phone. Get to know each other better."

"Maybe…." He stares across the room, his forehead furrowed. "I don't think he's between us anymore, but maybe this winter…it'll give us time."

I nod. He reaches for my right hand with his left and draws us nearer, so we're sitting in the back of the booth, not on top of each other, but much closer than we started.

What do I know about relationships? This is my first one with a grownup. And Lord knows we've been through far too much for people our ages. But I know I want this…or think I do. And there's time to consider it…to grow closer or to decide to move on. And maybe that's all we need…for now.

Accepting the Unchangeable

Peter
August

Joel and I embrace briefly at the start of the visit and take our seats, my hands on top of the table. That's almost second nature now. Visible hands doesn't just work with the COs. Other prisoners trust you more if they can see your hands. *I* trust people more when I can see their hands.

"You feel – harder – more muscular."

"Been working out. Kind of relieves the boredom a bit. I heard the storm last week. Was it as good as it sounded?"

"Yeah, blew out the plastic in my addition. Fortunately, I got all the windows in already, so it was just the doors."

Most of his time not spent being a lawyer is spent adding onto his house. Not for the first time I wish I could help him with that. I have sketchy carpentry skills gained from building a tree fort with Ben when we were kids, but what do you give someone who sacrifices his time to make sure you aren't all alone in the world? I wish I could give what little I possess.

"How are your grandparents?"

"Good, from what I can tell. I guess they're still managing Dad's properties as well as their own, so they're kind of busy. Do you know about that? Dad?"

"Your grandparents occasionally call me about you and, since you're spending less time in the infirmary, I tell them not to worry. Lucy has said a few things about your father, but really, I don't know that much since he stepped down from the governor's office. You write him an amends letter?"

"I'm working on one – the second one. Didn't I tell you I wrote one in rehab?"

"Probably. I know you got a couple of responses from your reckless endangerments."

"And from Russell. He says I can look him up when I'm free to do so. Most of the recklesses want me to get better, do better, avoid them at all costs." I smile because they don't really matter to me. The only one with any real meaning was Hil, Trevor's stepbrother, who didn't write a response letter but said I could look him up once I'm on parole. Well, and there was one other. "Dr. Lundquist told me to volunteer at a cemetery."

"Groundskeeping? Sounds depressing."

"Brushing my teeth can be depressing."

"Is that a little better?"

"I think so. Plenty of side effects from the anti-depressants but getting up in the morning is easier."

He nods. I'm not lying. It is a little bit easier to get up in the mornings. My appetite is still dodgy, but I can swallow food. I still see Alyse everywhere, but I try not to allow it to derail me.

Joel figures out that we need to change the subject.

"Audra loved the drawing by the way. She's having it framed."

I feel my cheeks grow hot. Maybe that's a flare of momentary pride and not the bad kind. It's so rare these days that I do something I feel good about, but maybe I'm having more of those moments lately.

"So, I have to ask you an uncomfortable question." I stare at him, my pulse surprisingly not as fast as it normally gets when he opens with that.

"You don't have a burner cell?"

"I told you I don't. I know how to get one now, but I still don't want to add to my sentence or lose the few privileges I've earned." I can't expect him to trust me. I've been in legal trouble the whole time he's known me and even though I sometimes think of him as a friend, I know he's my lawyer. "What am I doing that's causing this?"

He considers the question a little longer than I like.

"I kind of became friends with the Andersons."

I am so jealous, but I guess I've learned some new tricks because I mean what I say even as it hurts.

"That's great. They're good people."

"Yeah." He gives me a sidelong analyzing stare. "You're not asking about Ben?"

I walk once round the abyss before I reply.

"He hasn't answered my letter so…. In 12 Step I'm learning I can't make people forgive me. I could be depressed all the time about that, or I could step back from the ledge and accept that he doesn't want to hear from me, and I can't do anything about that right now."

I shrug and try to push off miserable. It's a clingy bastard, but I keep trying.

"But it's easier if I don't talk about him."

Joel nods. Is what I'm reading in his brown eyes pride of my maturity? It's not something I'm used to seeing so I just set it aside for now. When I'm silent a bit, he speaks.

"So, Lily's picked up an admirer, someone kept sending her flowers. They caught the guy, but not all of the calls she got traced to the same burner cell."

He's asking me to confess, but I've got nothing for him.

"I told you before, thinking about Lily comes with baggage, so I try not to. And I don't have money to send flowers. I barely have money for toiletries."

He nods. Does he believe me? The default in my life is for nobody but Luis to really believe me and even he knows I lie to myself a lot.

"You know, you can ask me or your grandparents to put some cash on your commissary?"

"Yeah. But I need to be a grownup, much as I can be in this situation. And if they start putting cash on my books, someone will notice and the whole extortion thing will start again."

"How likely will that be to happen if *I* do it?"

"That's not the point. Or not the whole point." He's waiting and I don't know if I have the words. "I'm in this because I…." Wow! I know what I feel but it's so hard to put into words. "A lot of the guys in here have nothing and no one. Luis hasn't seen a family member in over a decade.

And despite of what I did, I still have Lucy and you—and kind of, Mike."

"He says he's not a letter writer."

"Yeah. And I love the pictures he sends. It's just—if I'm honest, a lot of the stories I hear, these guys relied on outside relatives a lot and a lot of them, especially in 12 Step, ask the question – well, if I hadn't drained her income, maybe she'd still visit me." He shifts in his seat. "So, I know that's not a problem for them and not really for you, but I can't. I need to be a grownup and grownups work their crappy 10-cent-an-hour job to pay for crème rinse."

"Or haircuts?"

I chuckle, running a hand over my head. I'm not a skin head, but my hair has never been so short. Curly hair is messy without the right products. I promise myself if the stress of this place doesn't make it fall out, I'll actually go curly when I get out. The guy who buzzed my hair offered to cut it so it would curl rather than frizz, but I'd had enough of it, and this is practical. It's not like I need to attract sexual attention right now. I definitely don't want to attract it.

"I'm sorry I keep asking about the burner."

"Nah, I kind of earned the mistrust." I gesture at the walls around us. "But I don't think I'd do that even if I were in a position to do it. I don't want to be a weirdo. You know, it could just be a high school guy with funds." It's something more than that and he knows it, but I'm not allowed to know, so I shift the topic. "I could have afforded some nice flowers when I was in high school."

"You never did?"

"Only for Alyse for a few times … and, yeah, I'm talking to the counselors about that relationship."

Boudreaux wasn't even surprised to hear about my mom. Neither was Luis.

"Good for you. You're not really talking about her, are you?"

I shrug. I really want to lie to him as well as myself.

"It's hard, so…not much…she's always…." *Growing cold in my arms.* I move because sometimes that vanquishes the vision before it fully forms. Sunset colors paint the walls of the visiting center, but I don't see Alyse yet. He must see we're getting too close to a trigger.

"So, Jacob and I built this giant Lego tower last week."

I shove Alyse into a space in the back of my mind so I can focus on this low-stress story about Joel's son. I hope the day will come when I can return fun personal stories with him. It's only another three years before I'm eligible for parole. While that feels like forever, it really isn't. I tell him about what I'm getting from the book he sent me last month. Nah, it's a deep book, so I probably don't need another book this month, but next—sure. I'm also reading a kind of mindless western about two guys running around in a Stutz Bearcat without any mention of how they're refilling the tank. That makes Joel laugh, so maybe I'm less depressed than I was last visit.

He wants to know if I can do an art project for him for his anniversary. And suddenly, for an instant, it feels like this is a real friendship and not just my lawyer feeling sorry for me. The warm feeling dissipates, but I have stopped looking gift-horses in the mouth, so I don't question it.

Sunlight streaks through the high windows. Unlike the ones on the tier, these windows get cleaned regularly. I know one of the crew who takes care of that. It's an administrative trick to make visitors feel better about their convicts' stay here in the Big House, but I don't care. The real sun pushes away the illusory sunset colors and for a moment I'm not depressed.

August

Ben

I have to get everything I take with me into my Jeep. Last time I overpacked and had to rent a small UHaul, but ended up not using a lot of what I took. That just made the small amount of space I have in my dorm room even smaller. I measured and I know how many boxes will fit, plus a couple of suitcases. Anything more has to stay because I haven't got room for it. I feel pretty good about that.

I don't need summer clothes, but I do need workout clothes which look a little like summer clothes. Last time I didn't take my Bible. This time I'm fitting it in even if it doesn't fit. I roll jeans and stuff socks in shoes and--.

"Hey." Lily stands in the open door of the garage, backlit by bright sunlight.

"Hey! What's up?"

"Um, Detective Mariskov came by."

I just got back from my last day of work at Temple, so I missed the visit. She sits down on the camp chair Wes recently vacated.

"Something up?"

"He showed me pictures, asked if I knew any of the missing girls, which I didn't, but I also saw a photo of the guy who did all this."

She doesn't like to say his name and I don't blame her.

"The night of the concert, a man offered me help to get out of there. And it was him."

I can't breathe for a moment. He came that close?

"You're sure?"

"Yeah. So now the question is did he fixate on me that night or had he been following me earlier?"

"How do we know?"

"Right. I don't remember ever seeing him before that night, but…. Detective Mariskov says he kept meticulous files on his victims for months before he moved on them. And he didn't have that with me. It's unclear if it started before the riot or after."

I set down the shirts I'm rolling and pull her into my chest. A shiver runs through her. It's been a rough year for her, and I don't think I can take any of that away from her. I almost want to stay behind, not go to school, because she needs me. I know I shouldn't, but I want to.

"I could have disappeared that night and nobody would have known I was one of his victims. And I thought he was just a nice man trying to rescue me from a bad situation. What is wrong with me that I didn't feel as endangered by him as I did by the crowds?"

I push her back enough so I can look in her face.

"Those crowds were dangerous, and nobody expected a serial killer to be hanging out in a mob."

"But…first I trusted Peter and then I almost trusted a serial killer--."

I literally shush her with an index finger.

"Pete was—probably still is--an extremely flawed human being, but he's not a serial killer. He was…how did you put it once…he's handsome and charming. And reckless and foolish and probably deeply sorry for what he's done. This is why he couldn't be a serial killer. He has a conscience. I think."

I do think, but it wouldn't take much to dislodge me from that position. It's sad that I can only see Pete's better qualities in comparison to a serial killer.

"There are more than a dozen young women missing and probably dead. This guy was extremely dangerous. There was a calculation surrounding him. I wouldn't be surprised if he went to the middle of that riot hoping he could catch some young woman unawares."

"That's not his previous behavior and suddenly he was following me. Why?"

"Sweety – okay, I can't think like a serial killer, but you're beautiful. There's something so incredibly attractive about you. So, yeah, it's…weird that he went after you in one sense. Can't blame you for wondering why you. But it makes sense to me. And it may be a part of your life…well, forever. That doesn't make you wrong. It's not a knock on you. It's good, actually. And the chances of something like this happening to you ever again are really low."

"Are you sure? I mean, shouldn't my life have gone back to normal after Peter?"

"It's that attractiveness that maybe attracted both of them. But it also attracted me. It's a neutral force. You just got unlucky this year. That doesn't mean there's anything wrong with you."

She's nodding, trying to wrap her mind around it.

"God—He was watching out for me. And I am so grateful for that care. But He didn't protect Jenae – Jerry."

"Which disrupted the Gold Coast's routine. Jerry's a hero. Did you see the news this morning?"

"I did. Wow. That Suki lady got herself a great exclusive."

"I'm just glad she's not still talking about Pete anymore."

Lily giggles.

"Me too. There does seem to be a circularity in all of this."

"Yeah. It's helping me to see Pete in a different light. Not ready to forgive or forget, but I'm closer than I was."

She sighs, looks around at my boxes.

"You're leaving."

"I am. Sorry I can't stick around, but I do have to get back to college."

"Yeah. I know. And we can talk all the time on the phone."

"Maybe you can come up to visit me. I don't know if I'll make it home for Thanksgiving, but I'll definitely be back for Christmas."

She nods.

"So, I have something for you. Just wait here and I'll be right back." I skip up to my room for the box on my desk and then hurry back to the garage where I present the box to Lily. It's really a pretty good-sized box and her eyes light up to see it.

Just what I wanted to see.

Lily

My phone buzzes just as I go into my room, and I answer it because it's Ben.

"Hey, silly. You just got on the ferry. Did you forget something?"

"You. I don't want to forget you."

I giggle. I don't know if this is love, but we're definitely infatuated. I smile at my beautiful bouquet of silk roses. They're red, yellow and white and in the middle of it is a bright orange tiger lily. How he knew is a mystery to me. So many people think about white lilies. How did he know I identify with the tiger lily?

"I'll be back for Christmas."

"I know. Really. I got over it. You need to live your life and I need to live mine. We can't just stop living. Besides, this is proof we can still reach out to talk to one another."

"Yeah. I might lose cell service any minute. What are you doing?"

"Looking at my bouquet. It's sitting on top of my dresser and the sun is flowing over it. It just seems --."

"Yeah. The sun is spilling through a window here and dividing into different beams. It's like God—He's smiling at us."

"Yeah. Yeah." The phone crackles. "I see that."

"I'm going to miss you and—love...."

The phone goes dead, and my heart goes into freefall. Wow, this is going to be hard. Ben has become such a fixture in my life. I sit for a while staring at my bouquet until the sun shifts and the aura fades. I need something else to do besides moon over Ben. I pull up Melissa's number.

We didn't talk for a while after the whole beach incident, but she called me and told me that she woke up in the bushes around dawn. We were both mad at Natalie for a while, but she apologized for getting drunk and promised to never do it again. Do I trust her when I shouldn't have trusted Peter? Well, for now, yes, but I'll not leave myself in her power again. I will drive myself next time.

"Hey! So glad to hear from you."

"Yeah. Are you taking Kashner's art class this semester?"

"I am. Natalie too."

"Good. Get the band back together." That's my dad's saying. These girls are not my bosom friends, but maybe they could be if we give it time.

"Yeah." I don't know if she understands the saying. Should I explain? "So, we're going to Jones Beach on Saturday. Have you been?"

"No." Peter called it the *poor man's Fire Island.* It's part of the same line of barrier islands. He described it as fun, so I'm willing to give it a try. "I want to check it out, but I need to make sure it's okay for my brother for that day. I'll let you know."

"Sure. We'd miss you if you couldn't come. We could pick another day."

"Let me call you back in a few minutes." I text Mom, Dad, and Wes. Before long, I can call Melissa back. "My dad is going to be available for Bram and his friend is coming over, so I have the whole day. What time do we want to meet?"

###

The End

A Word from Lela Markham

About 30 years ago, a friend was mugged in a park by two men he thought were friends. In his attempt to escape them, he got into his car and didn't take due care. When they tried to stop him, he hit the gas and struck them, resulting in one of them dying. Some of the scenes and attitudes referenced in this book come from his four years of incarceration in the Alaska prison system, but Peter is his own character and his thoughts come from him more than my friend. His rock-bottom is painful and as the ripples of his mistake echo out into the world, he is helpless to influence what others think of him.

While I think his story is important, his victims also have stories that matter and life goes on. Ben and Lily were always meant to be together. And while Peter certainly isn't ready for a happily-ever-after, they are. But they're young, so maybe happy for now is more apropos.

If you'd like to discuss it, feel free to drop me an email at lelamarkham@gmail.com or visit my Facebook page LelaMarkham7. You can come for the morality discussion and stay for the liberty conversations.

If you enjoyed this book, leave a review.

Watch for Book 5 “Empire of Dirt”

Behind the Scenes

631-555-2596
1527 Main Street
Port Mallory NY 11772

info@banburylaw.com
https://banburylaw.com

October 20, 2022

The Honorable Governor Alan Wyngate
138 Eagle Street
Albany, New York 12202

Governor Wyngate,

After a thorough investigation of the facts in your son's criminal prosecution, these are my recommendations.

A criminal defendant may not inherit anything from someone whose death they caused. Your daughter Alyse Wyngate was also party to the trust fund you set up for your offspring and therefore, Peter Wyngate may not inherit either portion of the trust fund.

Because you do not currently have other children, the trust fund presents a challenge and a prize for any of Peter's victims who might with to sue for damages. Given the number of victims, the judgments could exceed the half of the trust fund he is no longer eligible to receive, meaning he could be facing millions in fines, restitutions, and legal judgments upon his release from prison.

A straight-forward solution would be to liquidate the trust fund, allowed because there are no legal heirs at this time. You are, of course, entitled to do whatever you want with the contents of the fund. I recommend utilizing the funds to pay off Peter's debts. In the process, you may also wish to legally disown Peter to protect your own assets. So far, no lawsuits have been filed naming you, but that it likely only a matter of time. A proactive offer of settlements would be prudent at this time.

Respectfully,

CLWintp. Esq

Charles Winthrop, Esquire

Other Great
Breakwater Harbor Books

http://www.breakwaterharborbooks.com/

Check out my fine fellow authors at Breakwater Harbor Books

Fantasy, Science Fiction, Romance, Historical, Horror, Dark Paranormal, Crime Thriller, Women's Fiction, Psychological Fiction, Christian, Poetry, Wasabi Punk .....

Moscow, 2138. With the world only beginning to recover from the complete societal collapse of the late 21st Century, Zoya scrapes by prepping corpses for funerals and dreams of saving enough money to have a child. When her brother forces her to bring him a mysterious package, she witnesses his murder and finds herself on the run from ruthless mobsters. Frantically trying to stay alive and save her loved ones, Zoya opens the package and discovers two unusual data cards, one that allows her to fight back against the mafia and another which may hold the key to everlasting life.

www.breakwaterharborbooks.com

Other Lela Markham Books

Fantasy

Daermad Cycle

The Willow Branch

Mirklin Wood

Fount of Wraiths

Anthologies

Echoes of Liberty

Fire & Faith

Unbound

Encountering Jesus

Gateways

Fairytale Riot

Overmorrow

Romance

Worlds I Wish I'd Said

Apocalyptic

Transformation Project

Life As We Knew It

Objects In View

A Threatening Fragility

Day's End

Gathering In

Winter's Reckoning

A Death in Jericho

Worm Moon

Corralling Liberties

Satire

Hullaballoo on Main Street

Meet Lela Markham

Hi. I was raised in a house made of books in Alaska and told tales from the time I could talk. A teacher eventually made me write one of them down. I hated the exercise, but it was the spark that ignited a fire that has never gone out.

My daring husband, two fearless offspring and I live the adventure of a lifetime here on the Last Frontier where the midnight sun encourages wandering the wilderness and the long dark winters favor reading, writing and staring at the northern lights … hence the moniker Aurorawatcher.

It's all about the aurora watching!

www.ingramcontent.com/pod-product-compliance
Lightning Source LLC
LaVergne TN
LVHW010555100826
845148LV00014B/2721

* 9 7 9 8 9 8 7 5 0 1 8 4 9 *